Milan Kundera was born in 1929 in Czechoslovakia and since 1975 has been living in France.

375,–
new

MILAN KUNDERA
Immortality

TRANSLATED FROM THE CZECH
BY PETER KUSSI

faber and faber
LONDON · BOSTON

First published in 1991
by Faber and Faber Limited
3 Queen Square London WC1N 3AU
Open market paperback edition published 1992
This paperback edition
first published in 1992

Phototypeset by Input Typesetting Ltd, London
Printed by Mackays of Chatham plc, Chatham, Kent

A CIP record for this book
is available from the British Library

ISBN 0 571 14456 X

10 9

CONTENTS

PART ONE

The face

1

The woman might have been sixty or sixty-five. I was watching her from a deck-chair by the pool of my health club, on the top floor of a high-rise that provided a panoramic view of all Paris. I was waiting for Professor Avenarius whom I'd occasionally met here for a chat. But Professor Avenarius was late and I kept watching the woman; she was alone in the pool, standing waist-deep in the water, and she kept looking up at the young lifeguard in sweatpants who was teaching her to swim. He was giving her orders: she was to hold on to the edge of the pool and breathe deeply in and out. She proceeded to do this earnestly, seriously, and it was as if an old steam engine was wheezing from the depths of the water (that idyllic sound, now long forgotten, which to those who never knew it can be described in no better way than the wheezing of an old woman breathing in and out by the edge of a pool). I watched her in fascination. She captivated me by her touchingly comic manner (which the lifeguard also noticed, for the corner of his mouth twitched slightly). Then an acquaintance started talking to me and diverted my attention. When I was ready to observe her once again, the lesson was over. She walked around the pool towards the exit. She passed the lifeguard, and after she had gone some three or four steps beyond him she turned her head, smiled, and waved to him. At that instant I felt a pang in my heart! That smile and that gesture belonged to a twenty-year-old girl! Her arm rose with bewitching ease. It was as if she were playfully tossing a brightly coloured ball to her lover. That smile and that gesture had charm and elegance, while the face and the body no longer had any charm. It was the charm of a gesture drowning in the charmlessness of the body. But the

3

woman, though she must of course have realized that she was no longer beautiful, forgot that for the moment. There is a certain part of all of us that lives outside of time. Perhaps we become aware of our age only at exceptional moments and most of the time we are ageless. In any case, the instant she turned, smiled and waved to the young lifeguard (who couldn't control himself and burst out laughing), she was unaware of her age. The essence of her charm, independent of time, revealed itself for a second in that gesture and dazzled me. I was strangely moved. And then the word Agnes entered my mind. Agnes. I had never known a woman by that name.

woman. Though she must of course have realized that she was no
longer beautiful, forgot that for the moment. There is a certain
part of all of us that lives outside of time. Perhaps we become
aware of our age only at exceptional moments and most of the
time we are ageless.

2

I'm in bed, happily dozing. With the first stirrings of wakefulness,
around six in the morning, I reach for the small transistor radio
next to my pillow and press the button. An early-morning news
programme comes on, but I am hardly able to make out the
individual words and once again I fall asleep, so that the
announcer's sentences merge into my dreams. It is the most
beautiful part of sleep, the most delightful moment of the day:
thanks to the radio I can savour drowsing and waking, that
marvellous swinging between wakefulness and sleep which in
itself is enough to keep us from regretting our birth. Am I
dreaming, or am I really at the opera hearing two tenors in
knightly costumes singing about the weather? Why are they not
singing about love? Then I realize that they are announcers, they
stop singing and interrupt each other playfully: 'It's going to be
a hot, muggy day, with possible thunderstorms,' says the first,
and the second chimes in, flirtatiously: 'Really?' And the first voice
answers, equally flirtatiously: '*Mais oui*. Pardon me, Bernard. But
that's the way it is. We'll just have to put up with it.' Bernard
laughs loudly and says: 'We are being punished for our sins.'
And the first voice: 'Bernard, why should I have to suffer for your
sins?' At that point Bernard laughs even harder, in order to make
it clear to all listeners just what kind of sin is involved, and I
understand him: this is the one deep yearning of our lives: to let
everybody consider us great sinners! Let our vices be compared
to thunderstorms, tornadoes, hurricanes! When Frenchmen open
their umbrellas later in the day, let them remember Bernard's
ambiguous laugh with envy. I tune in to another station because
I feel sleep coming on again and I want to invite into my dream

5

some more interesting visions. On the neighbouring station a female voice announces that it is going to be a hot, muggy day, with possible thunderstorms, and I'm glad that we have so many radio stations in France and that at precisely the same time they all say the same thing about the same things. A harmonious combination of uniformity and freedom, what more could mankind ask? And so I turn the dial back to where a moment ago Bernard was boasting about his sins, but instead of him I hear another voice singing about some new Renault, so I turn the dial and hear a choir of women's voices celebrating a sale of furs, I turn back to Bernard's station, catch the last two measures of a hymn to the Renault followed immediately by the voice of Bernard himself. In a sing-song that imitates the fading melody he announces the publication of a new biography of Ernest Hemingway, the one hundred and twenty-seventh, yet this time a truly significant one because it discloses that throughout his entire life Hemingway never spoke one single word of truth. He exaggerated the number of wounds he had suffered in the First World War, and he pretended to be a great seducer even though it was proved that in August 1944 and then again from July 1959 onward he had been completely impotent. 'Oh really?' laughs the other voice and Bernard answers flirtatiously, '*Mais oui* . . .' and once again all of us find ourselves on the operatic stage, along with the impotent Hemingway, and then suddenly some very grave voice comes on to discuss the trial that has been engrossing France for several weeks: in the course of a completely minor operation a young woman died, due to carelessly administered anaesthetic. In this connection, an organization formed to protect people it called 'consumers' submitted a proposal that in future all surgical operations be filmed and the films filed away. Only in this way, maintains the Consumer Protection Association, is it possible to guarantee that any Frenchman or Frenchwoman who

6

dies on the operating table will be suitably avenged by the courts. Then I fall asleep again.

When I wake up, at almost half-past eight, I try to picture Agnes. She is lying, like myself, in a wide bed. The right side of the bed is empty. Who could her husband be? Clearly, somebody who leaves the house early on Saturday mornings. That's why she is alone, sweetly swinging between waking and sleeping.

Then she gets up. Facing her is a TV set, standing on one long, stork-like leg. She throws her nightgown over the tube, like a white, tassled theatre-curtain. She stands close to the bed and for the first time I see her naked: Agnes, the heroine of my novel. I can't take my eyes off this beautiful woman and as if sensing my gaze she hurries off to the adjoining room to get dressed.

Who is Agnes?

Just as Eve came from Adam's rib, just as Venus was born out of the waves, Agnes sprang from the gesture of that sixty-year-old woman at the pool who waved at the lifeguard and whose features are already fading from my memory. At the time, that gesture aroused in me immense, inexplicable nostalgia and this nostalgia gave birth to the woman I call Agnes.

But isn't a person, and to an even greater extent, a character in a novel, by definition a unique, inimitable being? How then is it possible that a gesture I saw performed by one person, a gesture that was connected to her, that characterized her, and was part of her individual charm, could at the same time be the essence of another person and my dreams of her? That's worth some thought:

If our planet has seen some eighty billion people it is difficult to suppose that every individual has had his or her own repertory of gestures. Arithmetically, it is simply impossible. Without the slightest doubt, there are far fewer gestures in the world than there are individuals. That finding leads us to a shocking conclusion: a gesture is more individual than an individual. We could put it in the form of an aphorism: many people, few gestures.

I said at the beginning, when I talked about the woman at the pool, that 'the essence of her charm, independent of time, revealed itself for a second in that gesture and dazzled me'. Yes, that's how I perceived it at the time, but I was wrong. The gesture revealed nothing of that woman's essence, one could rather say that the woman revealed to me the charm of a gesture. A gesture cannot be regarded as the expression of an individual, as his creation (because no individual is capable of creating a fully original gesture, belonging to nobody else), nor can it even be regarded as that person's instrument; on the contrary, it is gestures that use us as their instruments, as their bearers and incarnations.

Agnes, now fully dressed, went into the hall. There she stopped and listened. Vague sounds from the adjoining room made her realize that her daughter had just got up. As if to avoid meeting her, Agnes hurried out into the corridor. In the elevator she pressed the button for the lobby. Instead of going down, the elevator began to twitch like a person afflicted with Saint Vitus' dance. This was not the first time the elevator had startled her with its moods. On one occasion it began to go up when she wanted to go down, another time it refused to open and kept her prisoner for half an hour. She had the feeling that it wanted to reach some sort of understanding with her, to tell her something in its rough, mute, animal way. She complained several times to the concierge, but because the elevator behaved quite normally and decently towards the other tenants the concierge considered Agnes' quarrel with it her own private matter and paid no attention. This time Agnes had no other choice but to get out and take the stairs. The moment the stairway door closed behind her, the elevator regained its composure and followed her down.

Saturday was always the most tiring day for Agnes. Paul, her

8

husband, generally left before seven and had lunch out with one of his friends, while she used her free day to take care of a thousand chores more annoying than the duties of her job: she had to go to the post office and fret for half an hour in a queue, go shopping in the supermarket where she quarrelled with the saleswoman and wasted time waiting at the check-out, telephone the plumber and plead with him to be precisely on time so that she wouldn't have to wait the whole day for him. She tried to find a moment to squeeze in a bit of rest at the sauna, something she could not do during the week; in the late afternoon she would always find herself with a vacuum cleaner and duster, because the cleaning woman who came on Fridays was becoming more and more careless.

But this Saturday differed from other Saturdays: it was exactly five years since her father had died. A particular scene appeared before her eyes: her father is sitting hunched over a pile of torn photographs, and Agnes' sister is shouting at him: 'Why have you torn up Mother's pictures!' Agnes takes her father's part and the sisters quarrel, overtaken by a sudden hatred.

She got into her car, which was parked in front of the house.

Agnes, we know, just in such conversations she knew she badly at most, even about able to read that this alienated her some with her other woman. She turned her head in the door said thousand of classes young women within a few minutes the cue of seconds, her smile...

3

The elevator took her to the top floor of the high-rise, that housed the health club with its big swimming pool, jacuzzi, sauna, Turkish bath, and view of Paris. Rock music boomed from speakers in the locker room. Ten years ago, when she first started coming, the club had fewer members and it was quiet. Then, year by year, the club improved: more and more glass, more lights, more artificial flowers and cactuses, more speakers, more music, and also more and more people, further multiplied by the enormous mirrors which the management one day decided to spread across the walls of the gym.

She opened a locker and began to undress. Two women were chatting close by. One of them was complaining in a quiet, slow alto voice that her husband was in the habit of leaving everything lying on the floor: books, socks, newspapers, even matches and pipes. The other, in a soprano, spoke twice as fast; the French habit of raising the last syllable of a sentence an octave higher made the flow of her speech sound like the indignant cackling of a hen: 'I'm shocked to hear you say that! I'm disappointed in you! I'm really shocked! You've got to put your foot down! Don't let him get away with it! It's your house, after all! You've got to put your foot down! Don't let him walk all over you!' The other woman, as if torn between a friend whose authority she respected and a husband whom she loved, explained with melancholy: 'What can I do, that's how he is! And he's always been like that. Ever since I've known him, leaving things all over the place!' 'So then he's got to stop doing it! It's your house! You can't let him get away with it! You've got to make that crystal clear!' said the soprano voice.

Agnes never took part in such conversations; she never spoke badly of Paul, even though she sensed that this alienated her somewhat from other women. She turned her head in the direction of the alto: she was a young woman with light hair and the face of an angel.

'No, no! You know perfectly well you're in the right! You can't let him act like that!' continued the other woman and Agnes noticed that as she spoke she kept rapidly shaking her head from left to right and right to left, at the same time lifting her shoulders and eyebrows, as if expressing indignant astonishment that someone had refused to respect her friend's human rights. Agnes knew that gesture: her daughter, Brigitte, shook her head and lifted her brows in precisely the same way.

Agnes undressed, closed the locker and walked through the swing doors into a tiled hall, with showers on one side and a glass-enclosed sauna on the other. There, women sat squeezed together on long wooden benches. Some were wrapped in special plastic sheets that formed an airtight cover around their bodies (or certain parts of the body, most often the belly and behind), so that the skin would perspire all the more readily and the women would believe they would lose weight more quickly.

She climbed to the highest bench, where there was still some room. She leaned against the wall and closed her eyes. The noise of music did not reach this far, but the voices of the women, who chattered away at full blast, were just as loud. An unfamiliar young woman entered the sauna and the moment she walked through the door began to order everyone about; she made them all sit closer together, then she picked up a pitcher and poured water on the stones. With much hissing hot steam started to rise, making the woman sitting next to Agnes wince with pain and cover her face. The newcomer noticed it, declared, 'I like hot steam; it gives me that real sauna feeling,' squeezed herself between two naked bodies and at once began to talk about

11

yesterday's television talk show featuring a famous biologist who had just published his memoirs. 'He was terrific,' she said.

Another woman nodded in agreement: 'Oh yes! And how modest!'

The newcomer said: 'Modest? Didn't you realize how extremely proud that man was? But I like that kind of pride! I adore proud people!' She turned to Agnes: 'Did you find him modest?'

Agnes said that she hadn't seen the programme. As if interpreting this remark as veiled disagreement, the newcomer repeated very loudly, looking Agnes straight in the eye: 'I detest modesty! Modesty is hypocrisy!'

Agnes shrugged and the newcomer said: 'In a sauna I've got to feel real heat. I've got to work up a good sweat. But then I must have a cold shower. A cold shower! I adore that! Actually I like my showers cold even in the morning. I find hot showers disgusting.'

Soon she declared that the sauna was suffocating; after repeating once more how she hated modesty she got up and left.

As a little girl, Agnes used to go for walks with her father and once she asked him whether he believed in God. Father answered: 'I believe in the Creator's computer.' This answer was so peculiar that the child remembered it. The word computer was peculiar, and so was the word Creator, for Father would never say God but always Creator as if he wanted to limit God's significance to his engineering activity. The Creator's computer: but how could a person communicate with a computer? So she asked her father whether he ever prayed. He said: 'That would be like praying to Edison when a lightbulb burns out.'

Agnes thought to herself: the Creator loaded a detailed program into the computer and went away. That God created the world and then left it to a forsaken humanity trying to address him in an echoless void — this idea isn't new. Yet it is one thing to be abandoned by the God of our forefathers and another to be

12

abandoned by God the inventor of a cosmic computer. In his place, there is a program which is ceaselessly running in his absence, without anyone being able to change anything whatever. To load a program into the computer: this does not mean that the future has been planned down to the last detail, that everything is written 'up above'. For example, the program did not specify that in 1815 a battle would be fought near Waterloo and that the French would be defeated, but only that man is aggressive by nature, that he is condemned to wage war and that technical progress would make war more and more terrible. Everything else is without importance from the Creator's point of view and is only a play of permutations and combinations within a general program which is not a prophetic anticipation of the future but merely sets the limits of possibilities within which all power of decision has been left to chance.

That was the same with the project we call mankind. The computer did not plan an Agnes or a Paul, but only a prototype known as a human being, giving rise to a large number of specimens which are based on the original model and haven't any individual essence. Just like a Renault car. Its essence is deposited outside, in the archives of the central engineering office. Individual cars differ only in their serial numbers. The serial number of a human specimen is the face, that accidental and unrepeatable combination of features. It reflects neither character nor soul, nor what we call the self. The face is only the serial number of a specimen.

Agnes recalled the newcomer who had just declared that she hated hot showers. She came in order to inform all the women present that (1) she likes saunas to be hot (2) she adores pride (3) she can't bear modesty (4) she loves cold showers (5) she hates hot showers. With these five strokes she had drawn her self-portrait, with these five points she defined her self and presented that self to everyone. And she didn't present it modestly (she said, after all, that she hated modesty!), but belligerently. She used passionate verbs such as 'adore' and 'detest', as if she wished to proclaim her readiness to fight for every one of those five strokes, for every one of those five points.

Why all this passion? Agnes asked herself, and she thought: When we are thrust out into the world just as we are, we first have to identify with that particular throw of the dice, with that accident organized by the divine computer: to get over our surprise that precisely *this* (what we see facing us in the mirror) is our self. Without the faith that our face expresses our self, without that basic illusion, that arch-illusion, we cannot live or at least we cannot take life seriously. And it isn't enough for us to identify with our selves, it is necessary to do so *passionately*, to the point of life and death. Because only in this way can we regard ourselves not merely as a variant of a human prototype but as a being with its own irreplaceable essence. That's the reason why the newcomer needed not only to draw her self-portrait but also to make it clear to all that it embodied something unique and irreplaceable, something worth fighting or even dying for.

After spending a quarter of an hour in the heat of the sauna, Agnes rose and took a dip in a small pool filled with ice-cold water. Then she lay down to rest in the lounge, surrounded by other women who even here never stopped talking.

She wondered what kind of existence the computer had pro-grammed for life after death.

Two possibilities came to mind. If the computer's field of activity is limited to our planet, and if our fate depends on it alone, then we cannot count on anything after death except some permutation of what we have already experienced in life; we shall again encounter similar landscapes and beings. Shall we be alone or in a crowd? Alas, solitude is not very likely, there is so little of it in life, so what can we expect after death! After all, the dead far outnumber the living! At best, existence after death would resemble the interlude she was now experiencing while reclining in a deck-chair: from all sides she would hear the continuous babble of female voices. Eternity as the sound of endless babble: one could of course imagine worse things, but the idea of hearing women's voices for ever, continuously, without end, gave her sufficient incentive to cling furiously to life and to do everything in her power to keep death as far away as possible.

But there is a second possibility: beyond our planet's computer there may be others that are its superior. Then, indeed, existence will not need to resemble our past life and a person can die with a vague yet justified hope. And Agnes imagined a scene that had lately been often on her mind: a stranger comes to visit her. Likeable, cordial, he sits down in a chair facing her husband and herself and proceeds to converse with them. Under the magic of the peculiar kindliness radiating from the visitor, Paul is in a good mood, chatty, intimate, and fetches an album of family photographs. The guest turns the pages and is perplexed by some of the photos. For example, one of them shows Agnes and Brigitte standing under the Eiffel Tower, and the visitor asks: 'What is that?'

'That's Agnes, of course,' Paul replies. 'And this is our daughter, Brigitte!'

'I know that,' says the guest. 'I'm asking about this structure.'

Paul looks at him in surprise: 'Why, that's the Eiffel Tower!'

'Oh, that's the Eiffel Tower,' and he says it in the same tone of voice as if you had shown him a portrait of Grandpa and he had said: 'So that's your grandfather I've heard so much about. I am glad to see him at last.'

Paul is disconcerted, Agnes much less so. She knows who the man is. She knows why he came and what he was going to ask them about. That's why she is a bit nervous; she would like to be alone with him, without Paul, and she doesn't quite know how to arrange it.

4

Agnes' father had died five years ago. She had lost Mother a year
before that. Even then Father had already been ill and everyone
had expected his death. Mother, on the contrary, was still quite
well, full of life; she seemed destined for a contented, prolonged
widowhood, so Father was almost embarrassed when it was she,
not he, who suddenly died. As if he were afraid that people
would reproach him. People, meaning Mother's family. His own
relatives were scattered all over the world and except for a distant
cousin living in Germany, Agnes had never met any of them.
Mother's people, on the other hand, all lived in the same town:
sisters, brothers, cousins, and a lot of nephews and nieces.
Mother's father was a farmer from the mountains who had
sacrificed himself for his children; he had made it possible for all
of them to have a good education and to marry comfortably.

When Mother married Father, she was undoubtedly in love
with him, which is not surprising for he was a good-looking man
and at thirty already a university professor, a respected occupation
at that time. It pleased her to have such an enviable husband, but
she derived even greater pleasure from having been able to
bestow him as a gift upon her family, to which she was closely
tied by the traditions of country life. But because Agnes' father
was unsociable and taciturn (nobody knew whether it was because
of shyness or because his mind was on other things, and thus
whether his silence expressed modesty or lack of interest),
Mother's gift made the family embarrassed rather than happy.

As time passed and both grew older, Mother was drawn to her
family more and more; for one thing, while Father was eternally
locked up in his study she had a hunger for talking, so that she

spent long hours on the phone to sisters, brothers, cousins, and nieces, and took an increasing interest in their problems. When she thought about it now, it seemed to Agnes that Mother's life was a circle: she had stepped out of her milieu, courageously coped with an entirely different world and then began to return: she lived with her husband and two daughters in a garden villa and several times a year (at Christmas, birthdays) invited all her relatives to great family celebrations; she imagined that after Father's death (which had been expected for so long that everyone regarded him indulgently as a person whose officially scheduled period of stay had expired) her sister and niece would move in to join her.

But then Mother died, and Father remained. When Agnes and her sister Laura came to visit him two weeks after the funeral, they found him sitting at the table with a pile of torn photographs. Laura picked them up and then began to shout: 'Why have you torn up Mother's pictures?'

Agnes, too, leaned over the table to examine the debris: no, they weren't exclusively photos of Mother, the majority were actually of him alone, only a few showed the two of them together or Mother alone. Confronted by his daughters, Father kept silent and offered no explanation. Agnes hissed at her sister: 'Stop shouting at Dad!' but Laura kept on shouting. Father rose to his feet, went into the next room and the sisters quarrelled as never before. The next day Laura left for Paris and Agnes stayed behind. It was only then that Father told her he had found a small apartment in town and planned to sell the villa. That was another surprise. Everyone considered Father an ineffectual person who had handed over the reins of practical life to Mother. They all thought that he couldn't live without Mother, not only because he was incapable of taking care of anything himself but also because he didn't even know what he wanted, having long ago ceded her his own will. But when he decided to move out, suddenly, without the least hesitation, a few days after Mother's death, Agnes understood that he was putting into effect something he had been planning for a long time, and, therefore, that he knew perfectly well what he wanted. This was all the more intriguing since he could have had no idea that he would survive Mother and therefore must have regarded the small apartment in town as a dream rather than a realistic project. He had lived with Mother in their villa, he had strolled with her in the garden, had hosted her sisters and cousins, had pretended to listen to their conversations, and all the time his mind was elsewhere, in a bachelor apartment; after Mother's death he merely moved to the place where he had long been living in spirit.

It was then that he first appeared to Agnes as a mystery. Why had he torn up the photos? Why had he been dreaming for so long about a bachelor apartment? And why had he not honoured Mother's wish to have her sister and niece move into the villa? After all, that would have been more practical: they would surely have taken better care of him in his illness than some nurse who would have to be hired sooner or later. When she asked the reason for his move, he gave her a very simple answer: 'What would a single person do with himself in such a large house?' She couldn't very well suggest that he take in Mother's sister and her daughter, for it was quite clear that he didn't want to do that. And so it occurred to her that Father, too, was returning full circle to his beginnings. Mother: from family through marriage back to family. He: from solitude through marriage back to solitude.

It was several years before Mother's death that he first became seriously ill. At that time Agnes took two weeks off work to be with him. But she did not succeed in having him all to herself, because Mother did not leave them alone for a single moment. Once, two of Father's colleagues from the university came to visit him. They asked him a lot of questions, but Mother answered them. Agnes lost her patience: 'Please, Mother, let Father speak for himself!' Mother was offended: 'Can't you see that he is sick!' Towards the end of those two weeks his condition improved slightly, and finally Agnes twice managed to go out alone with him for a walk. But the third time Mother went along with them again.

A year after Mother's death his illness took a sharp turn for the worse. Agnes went to see him, stayed with him for three days, and on the morning of the fourth day he died. It was only during those last three days that she succeeded in being with him as she had always dreamed. She had told herself that they were fond of each other but could never really get to know one another because they had never had an opportunity to be alone. The only time they even came close was between her eighth and twelfth years, when Mother had to devote herself to little Laura. During that time they often took long walks together in the countryside and he answered many of her questions. It was then that he spoke of the Creator's computer and of many other things. All that she remembered of those conversations were simple statements, like fragments of valuable pottery which now as an adult she tried to put back together.

His death ended the pair's sweet three-day solitude. The funeral was attended by all Mother's relatives. But because Mother herself was not there, there was nobody to arrange a wake and everyone quickly dispersed. Besides, the fact that Father had sold the house and had moved into a bachelor apartment was taken by relatives as a gesture of rejection. Now they thought only of the wealth awaiting both daughters, for the villa must have fetched a high price. They learned from the notary, however, that Father had left everything to the society of mathematicians he had helped to found. And so he became even more of a stranger to them than he had been when he was alive. It was as if through his will he had wanted to tell them to kindly forget him.

Shortly after his death Agnes noticed that her bank balance had

19

grown by a sizeable amount. She now understood everything. Her seemingly impractical Father had actually acted very cleverly. Ten years earlier when his life was first threatened, she had come to visit him for two weeks, and he had persuaded her to open a Swiss bank account. Shortly before his death he had transferred practically all his money to this account and the little that was left he had bequeathed to the mathematicians. If he had left everything to Agnes in his will, he would have needlessly hurt the other daughter; if he had discreetly transferred all his money to her account and failed to earmark a symbolic sum for the mathematicians, everyone would have been burning with curiosity to know what had happened to his money.

At first she told herself that she must share the inheritance with her sister. Agnes was eight years older and could never rid herself of a sense of responsibility. But in the end she did not tell her sister anything. Not out of greed, but because she did not want to betray her father. By means of his gift he had clearly wished to tell her something, to express something, to offer some advice he was unable to give her in the course of his life, and this she was now to guard as a secret that concerned only the two of them.

She parked, got out of the car and set out towards the avenue. She was tired and hungry and because it's dreary to eat alone in a restaurant, she decided to have a snack in the first bistro she saw. There was a time when this neighbourhood had many pleasant Breton restaurants where it was possible to eat inexpensively and pleasantly on crêpes or galettes washed down with apple cider. One day, however, all these places disappeared and were replaced by modern establishments selling what is sadly known as *fast food*. She overcame her distaste and headed for one of them. Through the window she saw people sitting at tables, hunched over greasy paper plates. Her eye came to rest on a girl with a very pale complexion, and bright red lips. She had just finished her lunch, pushed aside her empty cup of Coca-Cola, leaned her head back and stuck her index finger deep into her mouth; she kept twisting it inside for a long time, staring at the ceiling. The man at the next table slouched in his chair, his glance fixed on the street and his mouth wide open. It was a yawn without beginning or end, a yawn as endless as a Wagner melody: at times his mouth began to close but never entirely; it just kept opening wide again and again, while his eyes, fixed on the street, kept opening and closing counter to the rhythm of his mouth. Actually, several other people were also yawning, showing teeth, fillings, crowns, dentures, and not one of them covered his mouth with his hand. A child in a pink dress skipped along among the tables, holding a teddy-bear by its leg, and it too had its mouth wide open, though it seemed to be calling rather than yawning. Now and again the child would bump one of the guests with the teddy-bear. The tables stood close together, and it was obvious even through the glass that along with the food the guests must also be swallowing the smell of their neighbours' perspiration. A wave of ugliness, visual, olfactory, and gustatory (she vividly imagined the taste of a greasy hamburger suffused by sweetish water) hit her in the face with such force that she turned away, determined to find some other place to satisfy her hunger.

The pavement was so crowded that it was difficult to walk. The tall shapes of two fair, yellow-haired Northerners were clearing a way through the crowd ahead of her: a man and a woman, looming head and shoulder over the throng of Frenchmen and Arabs. They both had a pink knapsack on their backs and a child strapped in front. In a moment she lost sight of the couple and instead saw in front of her a woman dressed in baggy trousers barely reaching the knees, as was the fashion that year. The outfit seemed to make her behind even heavier and closer to the ground. Her bare, pale calves resembled a pair of rustic pitchers decorated by varicose veins entwined like a ball of tiny blue snakes. Agnes said to herself: that woman could have found a dozen outfits that would have covered her bluish veins and made her behind less monstrous. Why hadn't she done so? Not only have people stopped trying to be attractive when they are out among other people, but they are no longer even trying not to look ugly!

She said to herself: when once the onslaught of ugliness became completely unbearable, she would go to a florist and buy a forget-me-not, a single forget-me-not, a slender stalk with miniature blue flowers. She would go out into the street holding the flower before her eyes, staring at it tenaciously so as to see only that single beautiful blue point, to see it as the last thing she wanted to preserve for herself from a world she had ceased to love. She would walk like that through the streets of Paris, she would soon become a familiar sight, children would run after her, laugh at her, throw things at her and all Paris would call her: *the crazy woman with the forget-me-not* . . .

22

She continued on her way: her right ear was assaulted by a tide of music, the rhythmic thumping of percussion instruments surging from shops, beauty parlours, restaurants; her left ear picked up the sounds of the road: the composite hum of cars, the grinding rattle of a bus pulling away from a stop. Then the sharp sound of a motorcycle cut through her. She couldn't help but try to find the source of this physical pain: a girl in jeans, with long black hair blowing behind her, sat on a small motorcycle as rigidly as if she were sitting behind a typewriter; the silencer had been removed and the bike made a terrible noise.

Agnes recalled the young woman who had entered the sauna a few hours earlier and, in order to introduce her self, and to force it upon others, had announced the moment she walked through the door that she hated hot showers and modesty. Agnes was certain that it was exactly the same impulse that led the black-haired girl to remove the silencer from her motorcycle. It wasn't the machine that made the noise, it was the self of the black-haired girl; in order to be heard, in order to penetrate the consciousness of others, she attached the noisy exhaust of the engine to her soul. Agnes watched the flowing hair of that blaring soul and she realized that she yearned intensely for the girl's death. If at that moment a bus had run her over, leaving her lying in a bloody pool on the road, Agnes would have felt neither horror nor sorrow, but only satisfaction.

Suddenly frightened by her hatred she said to herself: the world is at some sort of border; if it is crossed everything will turn to madness: people will walk the streets holding forget-me-nots or kill one another on sight. And it will take very little for the glass to overflow, perhaps just one drop: perhaps just one car too many, or one person, or one decibel. There is a certain quantitative border that must not be crossed, yet no one stands guard over it and perhaps no one even realizes that it exists.

She kept walking. The pavement was becoming more and more

23

crowded and nobody bothered to move out of her way, so she stepped off the kerb and continued to make her way between the edge of the pavement and the oncoming traffic. She had been used to doing this for a long time: people didn't get out of her way. She was aware of it, she felt it to be her misfortune and often tried to overcome it: she tried to gather courage, to walk bravely ahead, to stick to her path and force the oncoming person to give way, but she never succeeded. In this everyday, banal test of power she was always the loser. Once, a child of about seven had walked straight at her; Agnes tried not to swerve from her path, but in the end she had no choice if she didn't wish to collide with the child.

A memory came to her mind: when she was about ten years old, she went with both her parents for a walk in the mountains. As they strolled down a broad forest path, they came upon two village boys standing with their arms and legs spread wide; one of them held a stick sideways, as if to bar their way: 'This is a private road! You must pay a toll!' he shouted and lightly touched Father's chest with his stick.

It was probably just a childish prank and all that was needed was to push the boys aside. Or it was their way of begging and Father only needed to pull a coin out of his pocket. But Father turned aside and chose to continue along a different path. In truth, it really made very little difference since they were strolling aimlessly and didn't care where they were going, but nevertheless Mother was angry with Father and couldn't keep from remarking· 'He even gives in to a couple of twelve-year-olds!' Agnes, too, was somewhat disappointed by Father's behaviour.

A new assault of noise interrupted the recollection: some men wearing safety helmets were pounding the asphalt with pneumatic drills. Into this racket, from somewhere overhead, as if from heaven, came a piano rendition of a Bach fugue. Someone on a top floor had evidently opened a window and turned up the volume all the way, so that Bach's severe beauty sounded a warning to a world that had gone awry. However, Bach's fugue was no match for the pneumatic drills and cars; on the contrary, cars and drills appropriated Bach as part of their own fugue, so that Agnes had to cover her ears with her hands and continued to walk like that down the street.

At that moment a passer-by coming in the opposite direction gave her an angry glance and tapped his forehead, which in the international language of gestures says that you are crazy, scatty or weak in the head. Agnes caught that glance, that hatred, and was seized by a furious anger. She stopped. She wanted to throw herself at that person. She wanted to strike him. But she couldn't, the crowd was already pushing him along and somebody bumped into her, because on the pavement it was impossible to stop for more than three seconds.

She had to keep walking, but she couldn't stop thinking of him: both of them were caught up in the same noise and yet he found it necessary to make her understand that she had no reason and perhaps not even any right to cover her ears. That man was censuring her for the trespass of her gesture. It was equality itself which reprimanded her for refusing to undergo what everyone must undergo. It was equality itself which forbade her to disagree with the world in which all of us live.

The longing to kill that man was not just a fleeting reaction. Even after the immediate excitement had passed, that longing remained, though it was joined by her surprise that she was capable of such hatred. The image of a person tapping his forehead floated in her innards like a fish full of poison, slowly decaying and impossible to spew out.

The memory of Father came back to her. Ever since she had seen him retreat from those twelve-year-old boys she often imagined him in this situation: he is on a sinking ship; there are only a few lifeboats and there isn't room for everyone; there is a furious stampede on deck. At first Father rushes along with the others, but when he sees how they all push and shove, ready to trample each other under foot, and a wild-eyed woman strikes him with her fist because he is in her way, he suddenly stops and steps aside. And in the end he merely watches the overloaded lifeboats as they are slowly lowered amid shouts and curses, towards the raging waves.

What name to give this attitude? Cowardice? No. Cowards are afraid of dying and will fight to survive. Nobility? Undoubtedly, if he had acted out of regard for his fellows. But Agnes did not believe this was his motive. What was it then? She couldn't say. Only one thing seemed certain: on a sinking ship where it was necessary to fight in order to board a lifeboat, Father would have been condemned in advance.

Yes, that much was certain. The question that arises is this: had Father hated the people on the ship, just as she now hates the motorcyclist and the man who mocked her because she covered her ears? No, Agnes cannot imagine that Father was capable of hatred. Hate traps us by binding us too tightly to our adversary. This is the obscenity of war: the intimacy of mutually shed blood, the lascivious proximity of two soldiers who, eye to eye, bayonet each other. Agnes was sure: it was precisely this kind of intimacy that her father found repugnant. The mêlée on the ship filled him with such disgust that he preferred to drown. The physical contact with people who struck and trampled and killed one another seemed far worse to him than a solitary death in the purity of the waters.

The memory of Father began to deliver her from the hatred that had possessed her. Little by little, the poisonous image of a man tapping his forehead disappeared and in its place a phrase came into her mind: I cannot hate them because nothing binds me to them; I have nothing in common with them.

26

6

Agnes owes the fact that she isn't German to Hitler's defeat in the war. For the first time in history, the defeated were not allowed a scrap of glory: not even the painful glory of the shipwrecked. The victor was not satisfied with mere victory but decided to judge the defeated and judge the entire nation, so that at that time it was not at all easy to speak German or to be German.

Agnes' forebears on her mother's side were farmers living in the borderland between the German and French parts of Switzerland. Thus, even though from an administrative viewpoint they were French Swiss, they spoke both languages equally well. Father's parents were Germans living in Hungary. As a young man Father studied in Paris, where he learned to speak passable French; after his marriage, however, German naturally became the couple's common language. It was only after the war that Mother recalled the official language of her parents, and Agnes was sent to a French lycée. Father was permitted only a single Germanic pleasure: to recite to his elder daughter, in the original, Goethe's poetry.

This is the most famous German poem ever written, one which all German children must learn by heart:

> On all hilltops
> There is peace,
> In all treetops
> You will hear
> Hardly a breath.
> Birds in the woods are silent.
> Just wait, soon

You too will rest.

The idea of the poem is simple: in the woods everything is asleep, and you will sleep too. The purpose of the poetry is not to dazzle us with an astonishing thought, but to make one moment of existence unforgettable and worthy of unbearable nostalgia.

In a literal translation the poem loses everything. You will recognize how beautiful it is only when you read it in German:

> Über allen Gipfeln
> ist Ruh,
> in allen Wipfeln
> spürest du
> kaum einen Hauch.
> Die Vögel schweigen im Walde.
> Warte nur, balde
> ruhest du auch.

Every line has a different number of syllables, there is an alternation of trochees, iambs, dactyls, the sixth line is oddly longer than the others, and even though the poem consists of two couplets, the first grammatical sentence ends asymmetrically in the fifth line, which creates a melody that had never existed before, in any poem, as magnificent as it is ordinary.

Agnes' Father learned it while still in Hungary, where he attended German public schools, and the first time Agnes heard it from him she was the same age he had been then. They recited it in the course of their strolls together, exaggerating all the accents and trying to march to the rhythm of the poem. In view of the irregularity of the metre this was not at all simple, and they succeeded only when they got to the last two lines: War-te nur – bal-de – ru-hest du – auch! They always shouted the last word so loudly that it could be heard for miles around: auch!

The last time Father recited the little poem to her was two or three days before his death. At first she thought that he was trying to return to his mother tongue and his childhood; then she noticed that he was gazing into her eyes in an eloquent, intimate way and it occurred to her that he wanted to remind her of their happy strolls of long ago; then at last she realized that the poem speaks of death: he wanted to tell her that he was dying and that he knew it. It had never occurred to her before that those innocent lines, so good for schoolchildren, might have this meaning. Father was lying in bed, his forehead damp with fever, and she grasped his hand; trying to master her tears, she whispered along with him: *Warte nur, balde ruhest du auch*. Soon you too will rest. And she recognized the voice of Father's approaching death: it was the calm of silent birds in the treetops.

After his death, calm did indeed begin to reign. That calm was in her soul and it was beautiful; let me repeat: it was the calm of silent birds in the treetops. And as time went on, Father's last message sounded more and more distinctly in that silence, like a hunter's horn sounding from the depths of a forest. What did he wish to tell her with his gift? To be free. To live as she wished to live, to go where she wished to go. He himself had never dared to do so. That is why he had given his daughter all the means she needed to dare.

From the moment she got married Agnes lost all the pleasures of solitude: at work she spent eight hours a day in one room with two colleagues; then she returned home, to a four-room apartment. Not a single one of the rooms was hers: there was a large living room, a bedroom for the parents, a room for Brigitte and Paul's small study. When she complained, Paul suggested that she consider the living room her own room and he promised her (with undoubted sincerity) that neither he nor Brigitte would disturb her there. But how could she feel at home in a room with a dining table and eight chairs used only for dinner guests?

It is probably clear by now why that morning she felt so happy in the bed that Paul had just left a moment ago, and why she passed so quietly through the hall so as not to attract Brigitte's attention. She even welcomed the capricious elevator, because it permitted her a few moments of solitude. She looked forward to the drive, too, because in the car nobody talked to her and nobody looked at her. Yes, the most important thing was that nobody looked at her. Solitude: a sweet absence of looks. Once, both of her colleagues were off sick and she worked for two weeks all alone in the office. She was surprised to notice that she was far less tired at the end of the day. Since then she knew that looks were like weights that pressed her down to the ground, or like kisses that sucked her strength; that looks were needles which etched the wrinkles in her face.

In the morning, as she was waking up, she heard a news broadcast about a young woman who in the course of a completely minor operation died because of carelessly administered anaesthetic. Three doctors had been brought to trial and a consumer-protection organization had proposed that in future all operations should be filmed and the film permanently filed. Everyone applauded this proposal! Every day, we are stabbed by thousands of looks, but this is not enough: in the end one single stare will be instituted which will not leave us for a moment, will follow us in the street, in the woods, at the doctor's on the operating table, in bed; pictures of our life, down to the last detail, will be filed away to be used at any time, in court proceedings or in the interest of public curiosity.

These thoughts reawakened in her a longing for Switzerland. Actually, she had been going there two or three times a year ever since Father's death. Paul and Brigitte spoke with indulgent smiles of her hygienic-sentimental needs: she goes there to sweep leaves off Father's grave and to breathe fresh air by the wide-open window of a Swiss hotel. But they were wrong: even though she had no lover there, Switzerland was the one deep and systematic act of betrayal she committed against them. Switzerland: the song of birds in the treetops. She dreamed about staying there some day and never coming back. Several times she went so far as to look at Swiss apartments for sale or for rent, and even drafted a letter in her mind in which she announced to her daughter and husband that although she still loved them she had decided to live alone, without them. She begged them, however, to let her hear from them from time to time, because she wanted to be sure that nothing bad had happened to them. This was the most difficult thing to express and to explain: that she needed to know how they were, even though at the same time she had no desire whatever to see them or to be with them.

Of course, these were only dreams. How could a sensible woman leave a happy marriage? All the same, a seductive voice from afar kept breaking into her conjugal peace: it was the voice of solitude. She closed her eyes and listened to the sound of a hunting horn coming from the depths of distant forests. There were paths in those forests, her father stood on one of them, smiling and inviting her to join him.

7

Agnes sat in an armchair, waiting for Paul. Ahead of them was dinner of the kind the French call 'diner en ville'. Because she hadn't eaten all day she felt tired and so to relax she thumbed through a thick magazine. She did not have the strength to read the text but merely looked at the photographs, which were all in colour, page after page. In the middle of the magazine there was a report of a catastrophe that had occurred in the course of an air show. A burning plane had crashed into a crowd of onlookers. The photographs were large, each one a full-page spread. They showed terrified people fleeing in all directions, charred clothing, burnt skin, flames rising from bodies; Agnes could not help staring at the pictures, and she thought of the wild joy of the photographer who had been bored watching the banal spectacle and suddenly saw that luck was falling his way from the sky in the shape of a burning aeroplane!

She turned a few pages and saw nude people on a beach, and in big letters the headline: *These pictures won't be included in a Buckingham Palace album!* and a short text ending with the sentence: '. . . a photographer was there, and once again the Princess finds herself centre stage, thanks to her dangerous liaisons.' A photographer was there. A photographer is everywhere. A photographer hidden in the shrubbery. A photographer disguised as a lame beggar. The eye is everywhere. The lens is everywhere.

Agnes recalled that once as a child, she was dazzled by the thought that God sees her and that he was seeing her all the time. That was perhaps the first time that she experienced the pleasure, the strange delight that people feel when they are being watched,

watched against their will, watched in intimate moments, violated by the looks to which they are exposed. Her mother, who was a believer, told her 'God sees you', and this is how she wanted to teach her to stop lying, biting her nails and picking her nose, but something else happened: precisely at those times when she was indulging in her bad habits, or during physically intimate moments, Agnes imagined God and performed for his benefit.

She thought of the Queen's sister and told herself that nowadays God's eye has been replaced by a camera. The eye of one has been replaced by the eyes of all. Life has changed into one vast *partouze* in which everyone takes part. Everyone can see an English princess celebrating her birthday in the nude on a subtropical beach. The camera is seemingly interested only in famous people, but it is enough for a jet to crash near you, your shirt goes up in flames and in an instant you too have become famous and are included in the universal *partouze*, which has nothing to do with delight but merely serves solemn notice to all that they have nowhere to hide and that everyone is at the mercy of everyone else.

Once Agnes had a date with a man and just as she was kissing him in the lobby of a big hotel, a bearded fellow appeared unexpectedly before her, in jeans and leather jacket, with five pouches hanging round his neck and across his shoulders. He hunched down and squinted through his camera. She began to wave her arm in front of her face, but the man laughed, jabbered something in bad English, and kept on jumping backwards like a flea while clicking the shutter. It was a meaningless episode: some sort of congress was taking place in the hotel and a photographer had been hired so that the scholars who had assembled from all parts of the world would be able to buy souvenir pictures of themselves. But Agnes could not bear the idea that somewhere there remained a document testifying to her acquaintance with the man she had met there; she returned to the hotel the next day, bought up all her photos (showing her at the man's side, with one arm extended across her face), and tried to secure the negatives, too; but those had been filed away by the picture agency, and were already unobtainable. Even though she wasn't in any real danger, she could not rid herself of anxiety because one second of her life, instead of dissolving into nothingness like all the other seconds of life, would remain torn out of the course of time and some stupid coincidence would make it come back to haunt her like the badly buried dead.

She picked up another magazine, more devoted to politics and culture. It contained no catastrophes or nude beaches with princesses; instead, it was full of faces, nothing but faces. Even in the back, where there were reviews of books, each article featured a photograph of the author under review. Many of the writers were unknown, and their photos could be considered useful information, but how to justify five photographs of the President of the Republic, whose chin and nose everyone knows by heart? Even the editorial had a small picture of the author over the text, evidently in the same spot every week. Articles about astronomy were illustrated by the enlarged smiles of astronomers and even the advertisements – for typewriters, furniture, carrots – contained faces, lots and lots of faces. She looked through the magazine again, from first page to last. She counted ninety-two photographs showing nothing but a face; forty-one photographs of a face plus a figure; ninety faces in twenty-three group photographs and only eleven photographs in which people played a secondary role or were totally absent. Altogether, the magazine contained two hundred and twenty-three faces.

Then Paul came home and Agnes told him about her numbers.

'Yes,' he agreed. 'The more indifferent people are to politics, to the interests of others, the more obsessed they become with their own faces. The individualism of our time.'

'Individualism? What does it have to do with individualism,

34

when a camera takes your picture in a moment of agony? On the contrary, it means that an individual no longer belongs to himself but becomes the property of others. You know, I remember my childhood: in those days if you wanted to take somebody's picture you asked for permission. Even when I was a child, adults would ask me: little girl, may we take your picture? And then one day they stopped asking. The right of the camera was elevated above all other rights and that changed everything, absolutely everything.'

She opened the magazine again and said: 'If you put the pictures of two different faces side by side, your eye is struck by everything that makes one different from the other. But if you have two hundred and twenty-three faces side by side, you suddenly realize that it's all just one face in many variations and that no such thing as an individual ever existed.'

'Agnes,' said Paul, and his voice had suddenly become serious. 'Your face does not resemble any other.'

Agnes failed to notice the serious tone of Paul's voice and smiled.

'Don't smile. I really mean it. If you love somebody you love his face and then it becomes totally different from everyone else's.'

'Yes, you know me by my face, you know me as a face and you never knew me any other way. Therefore it could never occur to you that my face is not my self.'

Paul answered with the patient concern of an old doctor: 'Why do you think your face is not you? Who is behind your face?'

'Just imagine living in a world without mirrors. You'd dream about your face and imagine it as an outer reflection of what is inside you. And then, when you reached forty, someone would put a mirror before you for the first time in your life. Imagine your fright! You'd see the face of a stranger. And you'd know quite clearly what you are unable to grasp: your face is not you.'

'Agnes,' said Paul, and he rose from his armchair. He stood

close to her. In his eyes she saw love and in his features, his mother. He looked like her, just as his mother probably looked like her father who in turn also looked like somebody. When Agnes saw Paul's mother for the first time, she found her likeness to him painfully unpleasant. Later on, when Paul and Agnes made love, some sort of spite reminded her of this likeness and there were moments when it seemed to her as if an old woman were lying on top, her face distorted with lust. But Paul had forgotten long ago that his face bore an imprint of his mother and he was convinced that it was his and no one else's.

'We got our names, too, merely by accident,' she continued. 'We don't know when our name came into being or how some distant ancestor acquired it. We don't understand our name at all, we don't know its history and yet we bear it with exalted fidelity, we merge with it, we like it, we are ridiculously proud of it as if we had thought it up ourselves in a moment of brilliant inspiration. A face is like a name. It must have happened some time towards the end of my childhood: I kept looking in the mirror for such a long time that I finally believed that what I was seeing was my self. My recollection of this period is very vague, but I know that the discovery of the self must have been intoxicating. Yet there comes a time when you stand in front of a mirror and ask yourself: this is my self? And why? Why did I want to identify with *this*? What do I care about this face? And at that moment everything starts to crumble. Everything starts to crumble.'

'What starts to crumble? What's the matter with you, Agnes? What's the matter with you lately?'

She glanced at him, then lowered her head. He looks incorrigibly like his mother. Besides, he looks like her more and more. He looks more and more like the old woman his mother had been.

He took her in his arms and lifted her up. She looked at him and he noticed only now that her eyes were full of tears.

He pressed her to him. She understood that he loved her and

this suddenly filled her with sadness. She felt sad that he loved her so much, and she felt like crying.

'We should be getting dressed, we'll have to leave soon,' he said. She slipped out of his arms, and ran off to the bathroom.

8

I write about Agnes, I try to imagine her, I let her sit on a bench in the sauna, walk around Paris, leaf through a magazine, talk with her husband, but the thing that started it all, the gesture of a woman waving to a lifeguard by the side of a pool, it must seem as if I had forgotten that. Does Agnes any longer wave to anyone in this manner? No. Strange as it seems, I believe that she has not done so for many years. Long ago, when she was very young, yes, in those days she used to wave like that.

At that time she was still living in a Swiss town surrounded by mountain-tops silhouetted in the distance. She was sixteen and went to the movies with a schoolfriend. The instant the lights went out he took her hand. Soon their palms became sticky but the boy did not dare let go of the hand he had so daringly grasped, for that would have meant admitting that he was perspiring and ashamed of it. And so they sat, with clammy hands, for an hour and a half and let go only when the lights came back on.

He tried to prolong the date, leading her down the streets of the old part of town and then uphill to the courtyard of an old cloister, teeming with tourists. He obviously had thought out everything in advance, because he led her quite briskly to a deserted passage, under the rather trite pretence that he wanted to show her a certain painting. They reached the end of the passage, but instead of a picture there was only a dark brown door, marked with the letters WC. The boy had not noticed the sign and stopped. She knew perfectly well that he was not very interested in paintings and that he was only looking for a secluded place where he could kiss her. Poor boy, he had found nothing better than a dirty corner next to a lavatory! She burst out laughing, and to make it clear that she wasn't laughing at him she pointed out the sign. He laughed, too, but he was seized by hopelessness. It was impossible to hug and kiss her with those letters in the background (all the more, since this was to be their first, and thus an unforgettable, kiss), and so he had no choice but to turn back with a bitter sense of capitulation.

They walked silently and Agnes was angry: why didn't he simply kiss her in the middle of the street? why did he have to lead her instead down an obscure passage to a lavatory where generations of old and ugly and smelly monks had been relieving themselves? His embarrassment flattered her, because it was a sign of his bewildered love, but it irritated her even more, because it testified to his immaturity; going with a boy the same age seemed like lowering oneself: she was only interested in older boys. But perhaps because she thus was secretly rejecting him and yet knew at the same time that he was in love with her, a sense of justice prompted her to help him in his amorous efforts, to support him, to rid him of childish embarrassment. She resolved that if he couldn't find the necessary courage, she would.

He was walking her home and she planned that the moment they reached the gate of her house she would throw her arms around him and kiss him, which would no doubt make him stand stock still, completely flabbergasted. But at the last moment she lost the desire to do so, because his face was not merely sad but forbidding, even hostile. And so they merely shook hands and she walked off down the garden path to her door. She sensed that the boy remained standing motionless, gazing after her. She felt sorry for him once more; she felt for him the compassion of an older sister and at that point she did something quite unpremeditated: as she kept on walking she turned her head back towards him, smiled and lifted her right arm in the air, easily, flowingly, as if she were tossing a brightly coloured ball.

That instant when Agnes suddenly, without preparation, lifted her arm in a flowing, easy motion was miraculous. How was it possible that in a single fraction of a second, and for the very first time, she discovered a motion of the arm and body so perfect and polished that it resembled a finished work of art?

In those days a woman of about forty used to come to see Father. She was the departmental secretary, and she would bring papers for him to sign and take other papers back with her. Even though these visits had no special significance, they were accompanied by a mysterious tension (Mother would always turn silent), arousing Agnes' curiosity. Whenever the secretary was leaving, Agnes ran to the window to watch her inconspicuously. Once, as she was heading towards the gate (thus walking in a direction opposite to that which Agnes was to take somewhat later, followed by the gaze of her unfortunate schoolfriend), the secretary turned, smiled, and lifted her arm in the air in an unexpected gesture, easy and flowing. It was an unforgettable moment: the sandy path sparkled in the rays of the sun like a golden stream and on both sides of the gate jasmine bushes were blooming. It was as if the upward gesture wished to show this golden piece of earth the direction of flight, while the white jasmine bushes were already beginning to turn into wings. Father was not visible, but the woman's gesture indicated that he was standing in the doorway of the villa, gazing after her.

That gesture was so unexpected and beautiful that it remained in Agnes' memory like the imprint of a lightning bolt; it invited her into the depths of space and time and awakened in the sixteen-year-old girl a vague and immense longing. At the moment when she suddenly needed to say something important to her school friend and had no words for it, that gesture came to life and said on her behalf what she herself was unable to say.

I don't know how long she kept using it (or, more precisely, how long it kept using her), but surely up to the day when she noticed her sister, younger by eight years, tossing up her arm while saying good-bye to a girlfriend. When she saw her gesture performed by a sister who had been admiring and imitating her from earliest childhood, she felt a certain unease: the adult gesture did not fit an eleven-year-old child. But more important, she realized that the gesture was available to all and thus did not really belong to her: when she waved her arm, she was actually committing theft or forgery. From that time on she began to avoid that gesture (it is not easy to break the habit of gestures which have become used to us) and she developed a distrust of gestures altogether. She tried to limit herself to the most important ones (to nod 'yes' or shake her head 'no', to point at an object her companion had failed to see), to use only gestures that did not pretend to be her original expression. And so it came to be that the bewitching gesture of Father's secretary walking down the golden path (which bewitched me when I saw the woman in the swimsuit take leave of the lifeguard) had completely gone to sleep in her.

And then one day it awoke. It happened before Mother's death, when she was staying two weeks in the villa with her sick Father. As she was saying good-bye to him on the last day, she knew that they wouldn't see each other again for a long time. Mother wasn't at home and Father wanted to see her to her car which was parked in the street. She forbade him to accompany her beyond the door, and walked alone over the golden sand past the flower-beds to the gate. She had a lump in her throat and an enormous yearning to say something beautiful to Father, something that could not be expressed by words, and so without quite knowing how it happened she suddenly turned her head and with a smile tossed her arm in the air, easily, flowingly, as if to tell him they still had a long life ahead of them and would still see each other many more times. An instant later she recalled the forty-year-old woman, who twenty-five years earlier had stood in the same place and had waved at Father in the same way. That upset and confused her.

It was as if two distant times had suddenly met in a single second, and two different women in a single gesture. The thought passed through her head that those two women might have been the only ones he had ever loved.

9

In the salon where they were all sitting after dinner over glasses of brandy and half-finished cups of coffee, the first courageous guest rose to his feet and bowed with a smile to the lady of the house. The others decided to take it as a signal and along with Paul and Agnes jumped out of their armchairs and hurried to their cars. Paul drove; Agnes sat next to him and absorbed the incessant movement of traffic, the blinking of the lights, the pointless agitation of a metropolitan night. And she once again had the strong, peculiar feeling that was coming over her more and more often: the feeling that she had nothing in common with those two-legged creatures with a head on their shoulders and a mouth in their face. There was a time when she was interested in their politics, their science, their inventions, when she considered herself a small part of their great adventure, until one day the feeling was born in her that she did not belong among them. That feeling was strange, she resisted it, she knew that it was absurd as well as amoral, but in the end she told herself that she could not command her feelings: she was no longer able to torment herself with thoughts of their wars nor to enjoy their celebrations, because she was filled with the conviction that none of it was her concern.

Did it mean that she was cold-hearted? No, it had nothing to do with the heart. Anyway, nobody handed out as much money to beggars as she. She could never ignore them as she passed them on the street, and they, as if they sensed it, turned to her, picking her out at once from a throng of a hundred other pedestrians as the one who saw and heard them. – Yes, it is true, but I must add the following: even her hand-outs to beggars were

43

based on *negation*: she gave them money not because beggars, too, belonged to mankind but because they did not belong to it, because they were excluded from it, and probably, like her, felt no solidarity with mankind.

Non-solidarity with mankind: that was her attitude. Only one thing could wrench her out of it: concrete love towards a concrete person. If she truly loved someone, she could not be indifferent to the fate of other people because her beloved would be dependent on that fate, he would be part of it, and she could no longer feel that mankind's torments, its wars and holidays, were none of her concern.

She was frightened by that last thought. Was it true that she didn't love anyone? And what about Paul?

She thought of the moment a few hours earlier, before they had left for dinner, when he had taken her in his arms. Yes, something was going on inside her: recently she was pursued by the idea that her love for Paul was merely a matter of will: merely the will to love him; merely the will to have a happy marriage. If she eased up on this will for just a moment, love would fly away like a bird released from its cage.

It is one o'clock at night: Agnes and Paul are undressing. If they were asked to describe their partner's motions at such times, they would be embarrassed. For a long time now they haven't been looking at each other. Disconnected, their instrument of memory fails to record anything of those common night-time moments that precede lying down in the marital bed.

The marital bed: the altar of marriage; and when one says altar, one implies sacrifice. Here one of them sacrifices for the other: both have trouble falling asleep and their partner's noisy breathing wakes them; so they wriggle towards the edge of the bed leaving a broad space down the middle; they pretend to be sound asleep in the hope of making sleep easier for their partner, who will then be able to turn from side to side without disturbing the other.

Unfortunately, the partner does not make use of this opportunity because he, too (and for the same reason), pretends to be asleep and fears to budge.

Not being able to fall asleep and not allowing oneself to move: the marital bed.

Agnes is stretched out on her back and images keep passing through her head: that strange, kindly man is visiting them again, the one who knows all about them and yet has not heard of the Eiffel Tower. She would give anything to be able to talk with him in private, but he deliberately chose a time when both of them were at home. In vain Agnes tried to think of a ruse to get Paul out of the house. The three of them are sitting round a low table with three cups of coffee and Paul is trying to entertain the visitor. Agnes is only waiting for the guest to start speaking about his reason for coming. Actually, she knows the reason. But only she knows, Paul doesn't. At last the visitor interrupts Paul's conversation and comes to the point: 'You, I believe, have guessed where I'm from.'

'Yes,' says Agnes. She knows that the guest has come from another, distant planet, one with an important status in the universe. And she quickly adds, with a shy smile: 'Is life better over there?'

The visitor only shrugs: 'Agnes, surely you know where you are living.'

Agnes says: 'Perhaps death must exist. But was there no other way to arrange things? Is it really necessary for a person to leave a body behind, a body that must be buried in the ground or thrown into a fire? It's all so horrible!'

'That's well known all over, that the Earth is horrible,' says the visitor.

'And another thing,' says Agnes. 'Perhaps you'll consider this question silly: those who live in your place, do they have faces?'

'No. Faces exist nowhere else but here.'

45

'So then those who love over there, how do they differ from one another?'

'They're all their own creations. Everybody, so to speak, thinks himself up. But it's hard to talk about it. You cannot grasp it. You will, some day. I came to tell you that in the next life you won't return to Earth.'

Of course, Agnes knew in advance what the visitor would say to them, and she was hardly surprised. But Paul is amazed. He looks at the visitor, looks at Agnes and she has no choice but to say: 'And Paul?'

'Paul won't stay here either,' says the visitor. 'I've come to tell you that. We always tell people we have selected. I only want to ask you one question: do you want to stay together in your next life, or never meet again?'

Agnes knew the question was coming. That was the reason she wanted to be alone with the visitor. She knew that in Paul's presence she would be incapable of saying: 'I no longer want to be with him.' She could not say it in front of him nor he in front of her, even though it is probable that he too would prefer to try living the next life differently, without Agnes. Yet saying aloud to each other's face, 'We don't want to remain together in the next life,' would amount to saying 'no love ever existed between us and no love exists between us now'. And that's precisely what is so impossible to say aloud, for their entire life together (already over twenty years of life together), has been based on the illusion of love, an illusion which both of them has been anxiously guarding and nurturing. And so whenever she imagined this scene, she knew that when it came to the visitor's question she would capitulate and declare against her wishes, against her desire: 'Yes. Of course. I want us to be together in the next life.'

But today for the first time she was certain that even in Paul's presence she would find the courage to say what she wanted, what she really wanted, in the depth of her soul; she was certain

46

that she would find this courage even at the price of ruining everything between them. Next to her she heard the sound of loud breathing. Paul had really fallen asleep. As if she were putting the same reel of film back in the projector, she ran through the whole scene once again: she is speaking to the visitor, Paul is watching them with astonishment, and the guest is saying: 'In your next life, do you want to stay together or never meet again?'

(It is strange: even though he has all the necessary information about them, terrestrial psychology is incomprehensible to him, the concept of love unfamiliar, so he cannot guess what a difficult situation he would create by his sincere, practical and well-intended question.)

Agnes gathers all her inner strength and answers in a firm voice: 'We prefer never to meet again.'

These words are like the click of a door shutting on the illusion of love.

PART TWO
Immortality

1

The thirteenth of September 1811. It is the third week the young newly-wed, Bettina née Brentano, has been staying with her husband the poet Achim von Arnim at Goethe's in Weimar. Bettina is twenty-six, Arnim thirty, Goethe's wife Christiane forty-nine; Goethe is sixty-two and no longer has a single tooth in his head. Arnim loves his young wife, Christiane loves her old gentleman and Bettina, even after her marriage, continues her flirtation with Goethe. This particular morning Goethe has stayed at home and Christiane accompanies the young couple to an art exhibition (arranged by a family friend, Councillor Mayer), containing some paintings Goethe had praised. Madame Christiane does not understand art but she remembers what Goethe said about the paintings and she can comfortably pass off his opinions as her own. Arnim hears Christiane's authoritative voice and notices the glasses on Bettina's nose. Every time Bettina, rabbit-like, wrinkles up her nose, those glasses bob up and down. Arnim knows the signs: Bettina is irritated to the point of fury. As if sensing an approaching storm, he slips discreetly into the next room.

The moment he's gone, Bettina interrupts Christiane: no, she doesn't agree at all! those pictures are really impossible!

Christiane, too, is irritated, for two reasons: first of all, this young patrician, in spite of being married and pregnant, dares to flirt with her husband, and on top of that she contradicts his opinions. What in the world does she want? To lead the parade of Goethe's fans and at the same time to lead the parade of his detractors? Christiane is incensed by each of these ideas, but even more by the fact that one logically cancels out the other. So she

51

announces in a very loud voice that it is impossible to consider such outstanding paintings impossible.

Whereupon Bettina reacts: it is not only possible to declare them impossible, but it is necessary to add that the pictures are ridiculous! yes, they are ridiculous, and she brings up a series of arguments to support this contention.

Christiane listens and finds that she doesn't in the least understand what the young woman is trying to tell her. The more excited Bettina gets, the more she uses words she has learned from young university graduates of her acquaintance, and Christiane knows she is using them precisely because Christiane will not understand them. She is watching Bettina's glasses bobbing up and down on her nose and it seems to her that her unintelligible language and her glasses are one and the same. Indeed, it is remarkable that Bettina is wearing glasses at all! After all, everyone knows that Goethe has condemned the wearing of glasses in public as a breach of good taste and an eccentricity! So if Bettina, in spite of that, wears glasses in Weimar it is because she wants to show, brazenly and defiantly, that she is part of the young generation, precisely the one which is distinguished by Romanticism and glasses. And we know what people are trying to say by their proud and ostentatious identification with the younger generation: that they will still be alive when their elders (in Bettina's case, Christiane and Goethe) have long been ludicrously pushing up the daisies.

Bettina keeps on talking; she is getting more and more excited, and Christiane's hand suddenly flies out in the direction of her face. At the last moment she realizes that it isn't proper to slap a guest. She pulls back so her hand merely skims Bettina's forehead. Bettina's glasses fall to the ground and shatter. Throughout the gallery people turn and stare in embarrassment; poor Arnim rushes in from the next room and because he can't think of anything better he squats down and starts to collect the pieces, as if he wanted to glue them back together.

Everyone waits tensely for hours to hear Goethe's verdict. Whose side will he take, once he hears the whole story?

Goethe takes Christiane's side and forbids the young couple to enter his house ever again.

When a wine-glass breaks, it signifies good luck. When a mirror breaks, you can expect seven years of misfortune. And when a pair of glasses breaks? That means war. Bettina declares in all the salons of Weimar: 'That fat sausage went crazy and bit me!' The remark passes from mouth to mouth and Weimar is bursting with laughter. That immortal remark, that immortal laughter still resounds down to our own time.

2

Immortality. Goethe was not afraid of the word. In his book *From My Life*, with its famous sub-title *Poetry and Truth, Dichtung und Wahrheit*, he writes about the curtain in the new Dresden theatre which he eagerly scrutinized when he first saw it at the age of nineteen. In the background it showed (I am quoting Goethe) 'Der Tempel des Ruhmes', the Temple of Fame, surrounded by the great dramatists of all time. In the centre, without paying them any attention, 'a man in a light cloak was striding directly towards the Temple; he was shown from the back, and there was nothing remarkable about him. It was supposed to be Shakespeare; without predecessors, unconcerned about paragons of the past, he walked alone straight towards immortality.'

Of course, the immortality that Goethe talks about has nothing in common with religious faith in an immortal soul. What is involved is the different, quite earthly immortality of those who after their death remain in the memory of posterity. Everyone can achieve immortality to a smaller or greater degree, of shorter or longer duration, and this idea already starts occupying people's minds in early youth. They used to say about the mayor of a certain Moravian village, which I often visited on boyhood outings, that he had an open coffin at home and that in happy moments when he felt well satisfied with himself, he would lie down in it and visualize his funeral. These were the most beautiful moments of his life, these reveries in the coffin: he dwelt on his immortality.

Naturally, when it comes to immortality people are not equal. We have to distinguish between so-called *minor immortality*, the memory of a person in the minds of those who knew him (the kind of immortality the village mayor longed for), and *great immortality*, which means the memory of a person in the minds of people who never knew him personally. There are certain paths in life which from the very beginning place a person face to face with such great immortality, uncertain, it is true, even improbable, yet undeniably possible: they are the paths of artists and statesmen.

Of all the European statesmen of our time, the one who has most occupied himself with the thought of immortality has probably been François Mitterrand: I remember the unforgettable ceremony which followed his election as President in 1981. The square in front of the Pantheon was filled with an enthusiastic crowd and he was withdrawing from it: he was walking alone up the broad stairway (exactly as Shakespeare walked to the Temple of Fame on the curtain described by Goethe), holding the stems of three roses. Then he disappeared from the people's sight and remained alone among the tombs of sixty-four illustrious corpses, followed in his thoughtful solitude only by the eyes of the camera, the film crew and several million Frenchmen, watching their television screens, from which thundered Beethoven's Ninth. He placed the roses one by one on three chosen tombs. He was a surveyor, planting the three roses like three markers into the immense building-site of eternity, to stake out a triangle in the centre of which was to be erected the palace of his immortality.

Valéry Giscard d'Estaing, who was President before him, invited a sanitation worker to breakfast in the Elysée Palace. That was the gesture of a sentimental bourgeois who longed for the love of common people and wanted them to believe that he was one of them. Mitterrand was not so naïve as to want to resemble sanitation workers (no president can fulfil such a dream!); he wanted to resemble the dead, which was much wiser, for death and immortality are an indissoluble pair of lovers, and the person whose face merges in our mind with the faces of the dead is already immortal while still alive.

I was always fond of the American President Jimmy Carter, but I felt something approaching real love when I saw him on the television screen, jogging with a group of fellow workers, trainers and bodyguards; his forehead suddenly began to sweat, his face became distorted with pain, fellow joggers rushed to his side clutching and supporting him: it was a minor heart attack. Jogging was supposed to be an occasion for showing the nation the President's eternal youth. That's why cameramen had been invited, and it was not their fault that instead of an athlete bursting with health they had to show an ageing man with bad luck.

A man longs to be immortal, and one day the camera will show us a mouth contorted into a pathetic grimace – the only thing we will remember about him, the only thing which will remain as a parabola of his entire life. He will enter a kind of immortality which we may call *ridiculous*. Tycho Brahe was a great astronomer, but all we remember about him today is that in the course of a festive dinner at the emperor's court he was ashamed to go to the lavatory, so his bladder burst and he departed among the ridiculous immortals as a martyr to shame and urine. He departed among them just like Christiane Goethe, turned for ever into a crazy sausage that bites. No novelist is dearer to me than Robert Musil. He died one morning while lifting weights. When I lift them myself, I keep anxiously checking my pulse and I am afraid of dropping dead, for to die with a weight in my hand like my revered author would make me an epigone so unbelievable, frenetic and fanatical as immediately to assure me of ridiculous immortality.

3

Let us imagine that, in the time of Emperor Rudolf, cameras (such as those that immortalized Jimmy Carter) already existed and that they filmed the feast at the emperor's court during which Tycho Brahe writhed in his chair, turned pale, crossed and uncrossed his legs, and stared at the ceiling with glazed eyes. If on top of everything he had been aware that he was being watched by several million spectators, his torments would have been even greater and the laughter echoing in the corridors of his immortality would sound even louder. People would surely demand that the film about the famous astronomer who was ashamed to urinate be broadcast every New Year's Eve, when everybody feels like laughing and there is seldom anything to laugh about.

This notion arouses in me a question: has the character of immortality changed in the epoch of cameras? I can answer that without hesitation: essentially, no; for the photographic lens had existed long before it was invented; it existed as its own non-materialized essence. Even when no lens was aimed at them, people already behaved as if they were being photographed. No crowd of photographers ever scampered around Goethe, but the shadows of photographers projecting from the depths of the future did scamper around him. This happened, for example, in the course of his famous audience with Napoleon. The Emperor, then at the peak of his career, gathered in a conference at Erfurt all the European rulers who were to endorse the division of power between himself and the Emperor of the Russians.

Napoleon was a true Frenchman in that he was not satisfied with sending hundreds of thousands to their death but wanted in addition to be admired by writers. He asked his cultural adviser to name the most significant intellectual figures of contemporary Germany and he learned that the foremost was a certain Mr Goethe. Goethe! Napoleon tapped his forehead. The author of *The Sorrows of Young Werther*! During his Egyptian campaign he found out that all his officers were immersed in that book. Because he knew the book himself, he got terribly angry. He berated the officers for reading such sentimental drivel and forbade them ever to lay their hands on another novel. Any novel! Let them read history books, that's far more useful! On the present occasion, however, satisfied that he knew who Goethe was, he decided to invite him. Indeed, he was quite happy to do so, because his adviser informed him that Goethe was famous above all as an author of plays. In contrast to novels, Napoleon appreciated the theatre. It reminded him of battles. And because he himself was one of the greatest authors of battles as well as their unsurpassed director, he was convinced in his heart of hearts that he was also the greatest tragic poet of all time, greater than Sophocles, greater than Shakespeare.

The cultural adviser was a competent man, yet he often got things mixed up. True, Goethe was greatly interested in the theatre, but his fame had less to do with that. In the mind of Napoleon's adviser, Goethe had apparently merged with Friedrich Schiller. Since Schiller was closely associated with Goethe, it was after all not too big a mistake to unite the two friends into one poet; it may even be possible that the adviser had acted quite deliberately, led by the laudable didactic intention of synthesizing German classicism for Napoleon's benefit into the single figure of Friedrich Johann Goethschill.

When Goethe (without any inkling that he was Goethschill) received the invitation, he knew that he had to accept. He was exactly one year short of sixty. Death was approaching and with death also immortality (for as I said, death and immortality form an inseparable pair more perfect than Marx and Engels, Romeo and Juliet, Laurel and Hardy), and Goethe had to consider that he was being invited to an audience with an immortal. Even though he was at that time deeply involved with *The Theory of Colours*, which he regarded as the high point of all his work, he abandoned his desk and left for Erfurt, where, on October 2, 1808, an unforgettable meeting between the immortal commander and the immortal poet took place.

4

Surrounded by the restless shadows of photographers, Goethe climbs the broad staircase. He is accompanied by Napoleon's aide, who leads him up another staircase and down a series of corridors into a large salon. At the far end, Napoleon is sitting at a round table eating his breakfast. All around bustling men in uniform hand him various reports, to which he gives brief answers as he munches. Only after a few minutes have passed does the aide dare to indicate Goethe, who is standing motionless at a distance. Napoleon glances at him and slides his right hand under his jacket, so that his palm touches the bottom left rib. (In the past, he used to do this because he suffered from stomach pains, but later he developed a liking for the gesture and automatically sought recourse to it when he saw himself surrounded by photographers.) He quickly swallows a morsel (it is not good to be photographed when the face is distorted by chewing, because newspapers maliciously publish just such photographs!), and says loudly, for everyone to hear: '*Voilà un homme!*' 'There is a man!'

That is precisely the kind of pronouncement nowadays called a 'sound-bite'. Politicians make long speeches in which they keep shamelessly repeating the same thing, knowing that it makes no difference whether they repeat themselves or not since the general public will never get to learn more than the few words journalists cite from the speeches. In order to facilitate the journalists' work and to manipulate the approach a little politicians insert into their ever more identical speeches one or two concise, witty phrases which they have never used before, and this in itself is so unexpected and astounding that the phrases immediately become famous. The whole art of politics these days lies not in running the *polis* (which runs itself by the logic of its own dark and uncontrollable mechanism), but in thinking up 'sound-bites' by which the politician is seen and understood, measured in opinion polls and elected or rejected in elections. Goethe is not yet familiar with the term 'sound-bite' but, as we know, things exist in their essence even before they are materially realized and named. Goethe recognizes that the words Napoleon has just said were an outstanding 'sound-bite' destined to prove very useful to both of them. He is pleased and takes a step closer to Napoleon's table.

You can say what you like about the immortality of poets, but military commanders are even more immortal, so it is quite fitting that it is Napoleon who poses questions to Goethe, rather than the other way round. 'How old are you?' he asks. 'Sixty,' Goethe answers. 'For that age you look fine,' says Napoleon with approbation (he is twenty years younger) and Goethe is flattered. When he was fifty he was terribly fat and had a double chin, and this didn't bother him very much. But as his years increased the thought of death recurred more and more frequently and he began to realize that he might enter immortality with a hideous paunch. He therefore decided to lose weight and soon became a slender man, no longer handsome but at least capable of evoking memories of his former good looks.

'Are you married?' Napoleon asks, full of sincerity. 'Yes,' answers Goethe with a slight bow. 'Any children?' 'One son.' At that moment a general leans towards Napoleon and announces an important piece of information. Napoleon becomes thoughtful. He pulls his hand out from under his waistcoat, picks up a scrap of meat with his fork, puts it in his mouth (the scene is no longer being photographed) and answers with his mouth full. It's a while before he remembers Goethe. Full of sincerity he puts the question: 'Are you married?' 'Yes,' answers Goethe with a slight bow. 'Any children?' 'One son,' Goethe answers. 'And tell me about Karl Augustus,' Napoleon suddenly fires off the name of Goethe's ruler, prince of the Weimar state, and from his tone it is obvious that he doesn't like the man.

Goethe cannot speak ill of his lord, yet neither can he argue with an immortal, so he merely says with diplomatic evasiveness that Karl August has done a great deal for art and science. This reference to art and science gives the immortal commander an opportunity to stop chewing, get up from the table, stick his arm under his waistcoat, take a few steps towards the poet and launch into a speech about the theatre. At that moment the invisible crowd of photographers comes to life, cameras begin to click and the commander, who has taken the poet aside for an intimate conversation, has to raise his voice so that everyone in the hall can hear him. He suggests to Goethe that he write a play about the Erfurt conference, which is about to guarantee at last an era of peace and happiness for humanity. 'The theatre,' he says very loudly, 'should become the school of the people!' (Already the second beautiful 'sound-bite' for tomorrow's newspapers.) 'And it would be an excellent idea,' he adds in a softer voice, 'if you dedicated this play to the Emperor Alexander!' (This, indeed, was the man the Erfurt conference was about! This was the man Napoleon needed to win over!) And then he goes on to give Goethschill a short lecture on literature; in the course of it he is interrupted by reports from aides and loses the thread of his thought. In order to find it he repeats twice more, out of context and without conviction, the words 'theatre – school of the people', and then (yes! finally! He has found the thread!) he mentions Voltaire's *The Death of Caesar*. According to Napoleon, this is an example of the way a dramatic poet missed an opportunity to become a teacher of the people. He should have shown in this play how that great commander worked for the well-being of humanity and how only the destined short span of his life prevented him from fulfilling his aims. The last words sound melancholy and the commander looks the poet in the eye: 'Behold, a great theme for you!'

But then he is interrupted again. High-ranking officers enter the hall, Napoleon pulls his arm out from under his waistcoat, sits down at the table, picks up a piece of meat with his fork and chews, listening to reports. The shades of photographers disappear from the hall. Goethe looks around. He examines the pictures on the walls. Then he approaches the aide who brought him here and asks him whether he is to consider the audience over. The aide nods, a fork delivers a piece of meat to Napoleon's mouth and Goethe departs.

5

Bettina was the daughter of Maximiliana La Roche, a woman with whom Goethe was in love when he was twenty-three. If we don't count a few chaste kisses, it was a non-physical kind of love, purely sentimental, and it left no consequences, if only because Maximiliana's mother promptly married her daughter off to the wealthy Italian merchant Brentano. When he saw that the young poet planned to continue flirting with his wife, Brentano threw him out of his house and forbade him ever to appear there again. Maximiliana then gave birth to twelve children (that Italian stud fathered twenty in his lifetime!), and she christened one of them Elisabeth; that was Bettina.

Bettina was attracted to Goethe from her earliest youth. For one thing, because in the eyes of all Germany he was striding towards the Temple of Fame, for another because she learned of the love he had once borne for her mother. She began to immerse herself passionately in that distant love, all the more bewitching for its distance (My God, it took place thirteen years before she was born!), and the feeling slowly grew in her that she had some sort of secret right to the great poet, because in the metaphoric sense of the word (and who should take metaphors seriously if not a poet?) she considered herself his daughter.

It is a well-known fact that men have an unfortunate tendency to avoid paternal duties, to fall delinquent in alimony payments and to ignore their children. They refuse to grasp that a child is the very essence of love. Yes, the essence of every love is a child and it makes no difference at all whether it has ever actually been conceived or born. In the algebra of love a child is the symbol of the magical sum of two beings. Even if a man loves a woman without so much as touching her he must reckon with the possibility that his love may engender an issue and emerge into the world even thirteen years after the last meeting of the lovers. This is more or less what Bettina had been telling herself before she finally gathered enough courage to come to Weimar and call on Goethe. It was in the spring of 1807. She was twenty-two years old (about the same age as Goethe when he courted her mother), but she still felt like a child. That feeling mysteriously protected her, as if childhood were her shield.

To carry the shield of childhood in front of her: that was her life-long ruse. A ruse, and yet also something natural, for already as a child she had become used to playing at being a child. She was always a little in love with her elder brother, the poet Clemens Brentano, and she greatly enjoyed sitting on his lap. Even then (she was fourteen) she knew how to savour the triple ambiguity of being at the same time a child, a sister and a desirable woman. Is it possible to push a child off one's lap? Not even Goethe would be able to do so.

In 1807, on the day of their first meeting, she sat herself on his lap, if we can trust her own description: first she sat on the couch, facing Goethe; he talked in a conventionally mournful tone of voice about the Duchess Amelia, who had died a few days earlier. Bettina said that she knew nothing about it. 'How is that possible?' Goethe said with surprise. 'Aren't you interested in the life of Weimar?' Bettina said: 'I am interested in nothing but you.' Goethe smiled and said the following fateful words to the young woman: 'You are a charming child.' As soon as she heard the word 'child', she lost all shyness. She announced that she was uncomfortable on the couch and jumped to her feet. 'Sit down where you feel comfortable,' said Goethe and Bettina sat on his lap and hugged him. She felt so good snuggled up against him that soon she fell asleep.

It's hard to say whether things really happened like that or whether Bettina made it up, but if she did then so much the better: she is revealing to us how she wants us to see her, and she describes her method of approaching men: in a child-like way she was impudently sincere (declaring that she didn't care about the death of the Duchess, and that she was uncomfortable on the couch on which dozens of visitors had been grateful to sit); in a child-like way she jumped on his lap and hugged him; and to top it all off: in a child-like way she fell asleep there!

Nothing is more useful than to adopt the status of a child: A child can do whatever it likes, for it is innocent and inexperienced; it need not observe the rules of social behaviour for it has not yet entered a world ruled by form; it may show its feelings, whether they are appropriate or not. People who refused to see the child in Bettina used to say that she was crack-brained (once, while dancing with joy, she fell and knocked her head against the corner of a table), badly brought up (in society she would sit on the floor rather than in a chair), and, especially, catastrophically unnatural. On the other hand, those willing to see her as an eternal child were bewitched by her natural spontaneity.

Goethe was moved by the child. She reminded him of his own youth, and he gave Bettina a beautiful ring as a present. That evening, he noted tersely in his diary: *Mamsel Brentano*.

6

How many times did they actually meet, those famous lovers Goethe and Bettina? She came to visit him again later that year, in the autumn of 1807, and stayed in Weimar for ten days. Then she didn't see him again until three years later: she came for three days to the Bohemian spa of Teplitz, without realizing that Goethe was also there for a cure in the healing waters. And a year later came that fateful two-week Weimar visit at the end of which Christiane knocked off her glasses.

And how many times had they actually been alone together, face to face? Three, four times, hardly more. The less they saw of each other the more they wrote, or more precisely: the more she wrote to him. She wrote him fifty-two lengthy letters, in which she addressed him with the familiar 'du' and spoke of nothing but love. Except for this avalanche of words, however, nothing else actually happened, and we can only ask ourselves why their love story became so famous.

This is the answer: it became famous because from the very beginning it concerned nothing else but love.

Goethe soon began to sense that. He got his first disturbing inkling when Bettina revealed that already long before her first visit to Weimar she had become close friends with his aged mother, who also lived in Frankfurt. Bettina kept asking questions about her son, and the old lady, pleased and flattered, would spend all day recounting dozens of recollections. Bettina thought that her friendship with his mother would open Goethe's house to her, as well as his heart. That calculation proved not quite correct. His mother's adoring love struck Goethe as somewhat comical (he never even bothered to pay her a visit from Weimar) and he sniffed danger in the alliance of an extravagant girl and a naïve mother.

I imagine he must have experienced mixed feelings when Bettina repeated to him the stories she had heard from the old lady. At first he was of course flattered by the interest shown in him by a young woman. Her stories awoke many slumbering memories that pleased him. But soon he also found among them some anecdotes that could not possibly have happened, or that made him seem so ridiculous that they should not have happened. Moreover, coming from Bettina's lips his childhood and youth took on a certain colouration and meaning that made him uncomfortable. Not because Bettina might wish to use these childhood memories against him, but rather because a person (any person, not just Goethe) finds it distasteful to hear his life recounted with a different interpretation from his own. Goethe thus found himself threatened: the girl, who associated with young intellectuals of the Romantic movement (for whom Goethe hadn't the least sympathy), seemed dangerously ambitious and took it for granted (with an aplomb bordering on shamelessness) that she would be a writer. One day she actually said it outright: she wanted to write a book based on his mother's recollections. A book about him, about Goethe! He recognized at once that behind the expressions of love lurked the menacing aggressiveness of the pen, and that put him on his guard.

But just because he was constantly on his guard with her, he did everything he could to avoid being unpleasant. He couldn't afford to turn her into an enemy, she was too dangerous; he preferred to keep her under constant, kind control. But he knew at the same time that even kindliness must not be overdone, because the slightest gesture that she could interpret as an expression of loving favour (and she was ready to interpret his every sneeze as a declaration of love) would make her even more daring.

Once she wrote to him: 'Don't burn my letters, don't tear them up; that might hurt you, for the love I express in them is tied to you firmly, truly, vitally. But don't show them to anyone. Keep them hidden, like a secret beauty.' First he smiled condescendingly at the self-assurance with which Bettina considered her letters to be like a beauty, but then he was struck by the sentence: 'But don't show them to anyone.' Why did she say that to him? Did he have the slightest desire to show them to anyone? By that imperative *don't show!* Bettina betrayed her secret desire *to show*. He could not doubt that the letters he wrote to her from time to time would eventually have other readers as well, and he knew that he was in the position of an accused being warned by the court: anything you say from now on may be used against you.

He therefore tried to chart a careful middle way between kindliness and restraint: his replies to her ecstatic letters were at the same time friendly and restrained, and for a long time he countered her familiar 'du' with the formal 'Sie'. When they found themselves together in the same town, he was kindly in a fatherly way, invited her to his house, but he tried to make sure they would always be in the presence of other people.

What, then, was at stake between them?

In 1809, Bettina wrote to him: 'I have a strong will to love you for eternity.' Read carefully this apparently banal sentence. More important than the word 'love' are the words 'eternity' and 'will'.

I won't keep you in suspense any longer. What was at stake between them was not love. It was immortality.

7

In 1810, in the course of those three days when the two of them accidentally found themselves together in Teplitz, she admitted to him that she would soon marry the poet Achim von Arnim. She probably made the announcement with some embarrassment, for she was not sure whether Goethe would take her marriage as a betrayal of the love she had been so ecstatically proclaiming. She didn't know enough about men to guess the quiet joy the news would bring to Goethe.

Right after Bettina's departure he wrote a letter to Christiane in Weimar, with this cheerful sentence: '*Mit Arnim ists wohl gewiss.*' 'With Arnim it's quite certain.' In the same letter he rejoices that Bettina was on this occasion 'really prettier and nicer than before' and we can guess why she seemed so to him: he was sure that the existence of a husband would from now on shield him from the extravagances that had prevented him from appreciating her charms in a relaxed and good-humoured frame of mind.

In order to understand this situation, we mustn't forget one important consideration: from his earliest youth Goethe had been a womanizer, and so by the time he had met Bettina he had been a womanizer for forty years continuously; during this time there had developed inside him a mechanism of seductive reactions and gestures which could be activated by the slightest impulse. Until now he had kept it in check with Bettina, with enormous difficulty. But when he realized that 'with Arnim it's quite certain' he told himself with relief that his caution was no longer necessary.

She came to his room that evening, once again with the air of a child. She told him some anecdote or other in a delightfully naughty way and while he remained seated in his armchair she sat down facing him on the floor. Being in a good mood ('with Arnim it's quite certain!'), he leaned towards her and patted her cheek the way we pat a child. At that moment the child fell silent and lifted to him eyes full of womanly longing and insistence. He clasped her hands and lifted her from the floor. Don't forget the scene: he was seated, she stood facing him and in the window the sun was setting. She was gazing into his eyes, he was gazing into hers, the mechanism of seduction was set in motion and he did not resist it. In a voice somewhat lower than usual, and continuing to gaze into her eyes, he asked her to bare her bosom. She didn't say anything, she didn't do anything; she blushed. He got up from the chair and unbuttoned the front of her dress. She kept gazing into his eyes and the red of the sunset merged with the blush that ran down her skin to the very pit of her stomach. He placed his hand on her breast: 'Has anyone ever touched your breast?' he asked her. 'No,' she answered. 'It seems so strange, when you touch me,' and all the time she kept gazing into his eyes. Without removing his hand from her breast, he too kept gazing into her eyes, savouring long and avidly in their depths the shame of a girl whose breast no one had ever touched before.

This is approximately how Bettina herself recorded the scene, which probably had no sequel and remained in the midst of their story, more rhetorical than erotic, the sole exquisite jewel of sexual arousal.

8

After their parting, the traces of that magic moment stayed with them for a long time. In the letters that followed their meeting, Goethe called her *Allerliebste*, dearest of all. Yet this did not make him forget what was at stake, and in the very next letter he informed her that he was beginning to write his memoirs, *Poetry and Truth*, and that he needed her help: his mother was no longer among the living and nobody else was capable of summoning up his youth. Bettina had spent much time in her presence: let her write up what the old lady had told her and send it to him!

Didn't he know that Bettina herself hoped to publish a book of recollections dealing with Goethe's childhood? That she was actually negotiating with a publisher? Of course he knew about it! I would bet that he asked her for this service not because he needed it but only to prevent her from publishing anything about him herself. Disarmed by the magic of their last meeting as well as by the fear that her marriage to Arnim might estrange Goethe from her, she obeyed. He succeeded in rendering her harmless the way a time bomb is rendered harmless.

And then, in September 1811, she arrived in Weimar; she arrived with her young husband, and she was pregnant. Nothing is so pleasant as meeting a woman we once feared and who, disarmed, is no longer threatening. Yet even though she was pregnant, even though married, even though lacking any possibility of writing a book about him, Bettina did not feel disarmed and had no intention of giving up her battle. Understand me well: not a battle for love; a battle for immortality.

It can readily be assumed that Goethe, in view of his situation in life, thought about immortality. But is it possible that Bettina, an unknown young woman, also thought about it, and at such an early age? Yes, of course. One starts thinking about immortality in childhood. Furthermore, Bettina belonged to the generation of the Romantics who were dazzled by death from the moment they first saw the light of day. Novalis didn't live to see thirty and yet in spite of his youth nothing inspired him as much as death, death the sorceress, death transmuted into the alcohol of poetry. They all lived in transcendence, they surpassed themselves, stretched their arms far out into the distance, to the end of their lives and far beyond their lives, to the outer reaches of non-being. And as I have already said, wherever there is death there is also immortality, her companion, and the Romantics addressed death as familiarly as Bettina addressed Goethe.

Those years between 1807 and 1811 were the most beautiful time of her life. In 1810 she went to Vienna and called, unannounced, on Beethoven. She suddenly became acquainted with the two most immortal Germans, the handsome poet as well as the ugly composer, and she flirted with both. That double immortality intoxicated her. Goethe was already elderly (in those days a sixty-year-old was considered an old man), exquisitely ripe for death, while Beethoven, even though he was only forty, was actually five years closer to death than Goethe. So Bettina stood between them like a gentle angel between two giant black tombstones. It was so beautiful that she did not in the least mind Goethe's almost toothless mouth. On the contrary, the older he got the more attractive he became, because the closer he was to death the closer he was to immortality. Only a dead Goethe would be able to grasp her firmly by the hand and lead her to the Temple of Fame. The closer he was to death, the less willing she was to give him up.

That's why, in that fateful September of 1811, though married and pregnant, she played the child with even greater abandon than ever before, talked in a loud voice, sat on the floor, sat on the table, on the edge of the dresser, on the chandelier, climbed trees, walked as if dancing, sang when everyone else was engaged in weighty conversation, made sententious pronouncements when everyone else wanted to sing, and tried as hard as she could to be alone with Goethe. But she managed to accomplish this only once during that entire two-week period. According to her account, it happened more or less this way:

It was evening, and they sat by the window of his room. She started talking about the soul and then about the stars. At that moment Goethe looked out of the window and pointed out a big star to Bettina. But Bettina was near-sighted and didn't see anything. Goethe handed her a telescope: 'We're lucky! That's Jupiter! This autumn it shows up beautifully!' Bettina, however, wanted to talk about the stars of lovers, not the stars of astronomers, and so when she put the telescope to her eye she deliberately failed to see anything and declared that the telescope wasn't strong enough for her. Goethe patiently went off to fetch a telescope with stronger lenses. He forced her to look through it again, and again she insisted that she couldn't see a thing. This gave Goethe an opportunity to discuss Jupiter, Mars, other planets, the sun and the Milky Way. He talked for a long time and when he finished she excused herself and without any urging, of her own free will, went off to bed. A few days later she declared at the art exhibition that all the pictures on exhibit were impossible, and Christiane knocked her glasses to the floor.

9

Bettina experienced the day of the broken glasses, the thirteenth of September, as a great defeat. At first she reacted to it belligerently, announcing all over Weimar that she had been bitten by a crazy sausage, but she soon realized that her indignation would cause her never to see Goethe again, which would change her great love for an immortal into a slight episode destined to be forgotten. That's why she made kind-hearted Arnim write a letter to Goethe in which he attempted to apologize for her. But the letter remained unanswered. The young couple left Weimar, and then stopped there once again in January 1812. Goethe refused to see them. In 1816 Christiane died, and shortly afterwards Bettina wrote Goethe a long letter filled with apology. There was no response from Goethe. In 1821, in other words ten years after their last meeting, she again visited Weimar and announced her presence to Goethe, who was receiving guests that night and could not very well prevent her from entering his house. However, he didn't say a single word to her. In December of the same year she wrote to him once again, without receiving any answer.

In 1823 the town council of Frankfurt decided to put up a monument to Goethe, and commissioned a sculptor by the name of Rauch to execute the work. When she saw a model of it, Bettina didn't like it; she realized immediately that fate was offering an opportunity that she mustn't waste. Even though she had no drawing skill, she set to work that very night and produced her own sketch for the sculpture: Goethe was seated in the position of a classical hero; he held a lyre in his hand, a girl representing Psyche stood between his knees; his hair resembled flames. She sent the drawing to Goethe and something quite surprising happened: a tear appeared in Goethe's eye! And so after thirteen years (it was July 1824, he was seventy-five and she thirty-nine years old) he received her at his house, and even though he was very stiff he nevertheless indicated that everything was forgiven and that the time of scornful silence was behind them.

It seems to me that in this phase of the story the two protagonists arrived at a coolly clear-headed understanding of the situation: both knew what the other was about, and each knew that the other knew it. By her drawing Bettina characterized for the first time in an unambiguous way what the game had been all about from the beginning: immortality. Bettina did not pronounce this word, she merely touched upon it silently, the way we touch a string and set it into long, silent vibration. Goethe heard. At first he was only foolishly flattered but gradually (after wiping away a tear) he began to grasp the real (and less flattering) significance of Bettina's message: she was letting him know that the old game was continuing; that she had not surrendered; that she was the one to sew the ceremonial shroud in which he would be exhibited to posterity; and that nothing he could do would stop her, least of all his stubborn silence. He reminded himself of something he had known for a long time: Bettina was dangerous; and it was therefore better to keep her under benign surveillance.

Bettina knew that Goethe knew. This is evident from their next meeting, in the autumn of that year; she describes him in a letter sent to his niece: soon after receiving her, writes Bettina, 'Goethe began to quarrel with me, but then he again caressed me with words so as to regain my favour.'

How could we fail to understand him! He felt with brutal urgency that she was getting on his nerves and he was angry with himself for having interrupted that glorious thirteen-year silence. He began to quarrel with her as if he wanted to rebuke her at one stroke for everything he had ever held against her. But he quickly pulled himself up short: why the sincerity? why tell her what he was thinking? The important thing, after all, was to stick to his resolution: neutralize her; pacify her; keep her under surveillance.

At least six times during their conversation, Bettina recounts, Goethe left the room under various pretences and secretly drank some wine, which she detected on his breath. At last she laughingly asked him why he was drinking on the sly, and he took offence.

Bettina's behaviour is more interesting to me than Goethe's tippling: she did not act like you or me, for we would have merely watched Goethe with amusement, keeping discreetly and politely silent. To say to him what others would never dare ('I smell alcohol on your breath! Why are you drinking? And why secretly?'), that was her way of stripping him of some of his intimacy, of coming into closer touch with him. This kind of aggressive indiscretion, to which in the name of childhood Bettina had always claimed a right, suddenly reminded Goethe of the Bettina he had thirteen years ago decided never to see again. He silently rose to his feet, and picked up a lamp as a signal that the visit had come to an end and that he was about to lead his visitor down the dark hallway to the door.

At that moment, continues Bettina in her letter, in order to prevent him from leaving the room, she knelt down on the threshold and said: 'I want to see whether I am able to stop you and whether you are a spirit of good or a spirit of evil, like Faust's rat; I kiss and bless this threshold, which is crossed every day by the greatest of spirits and my greatest friend.'

And what did Goethe do? I again quote Bettina word for word. He supposedly said: 'I will not tread on you nor on your love, in order to pass; your love is too dear to me; as far as your spirit is concerned, I will slip by it' (and he indeed carefully by-passed her kneeling body), 'because you are too wily and it's better to stay on good terms with you!'

The sentence which Bettina put in his mouth sums up, it seems

77

to me, everything that Goethe had been silently saying to her in the course of their meeting: I know, Bettina, that your drawing of the monument was a brilliant ruse. In my wretched senility I allowed myself to be moved by the sight of my hair turned to flames (alas, my pitiful, thinning hair!), but I soon understood that what you wanted to show me was not a drawing but a pistol that you are holding, aiming far into my immortality. No, I didn't know how to disarm you. That's why I don't want war. I want peace. But no more than peace. I will pass by you carefully, and I won't touch you, I won't embrace or kiss you. First, I have no desire for it and second, I know that anything I may do will be turned by you into ammunition for your pistol.

10

Two years later Bettina returned to Weimar; she saw Goethe almost every day (he was seventy-seven at the time) and towards the end of her stay she committed one of her charming bits of effrontery, when she tried to gain an entrée to the court of Karl August. Then something unexpected happened: Goethe exploded. 'That annoying gad-fly (*diese leidige Bremse*),' he wrote to the Archduke, 'passed on to me by my mother, has been extremely troublesome for years. Once again she is returning to the old tricks which suited her when she was young; she talks of nightingales and chirps like a canary. With your Highness' permission, I will forbid her, like a stern uncle, to cause any further annoyance from now on. Otherwise your Highness will never be safe from her fawning.'

Six years later she again appeared in Weimar, but Goethe did not receive her. The comparison to an annoying gad-fly remained his last word on the whole story.

Strange. At the time he received the sketch for the monument, he resolved to keep peace with her. Even though he was allergic to her very presence, he tried to do everything possible (even at the cost of smelling of alcohol) to spend an entire evening with her 'on good terms'. Why was he now willing to let all that exertion go up in smoke? He had been so careful not to depart for immortality with a rumpled shirt, so why did he suddenly write that terrible sentence about the annoying gad-fly, for which people will still reproach him a hundred or three hundred years from now, when *Faust* or *The Sorrows of Young Werther* will have been forgotten?

It is necessary to understand the dial of life:

Up to a certain moment our death seems too distant for us to occupy ourselves with it. It is unseen and invisible. That is the first, happy period of life.

But then we suddenly begin to see our death ahead of us and we can no longer keep ourselves from thinking about it. It is with us. And because immortality sticks to death as tightly as Laurel to Hardy, we can say that our immortality is with us, too. And the moment we know it is with us we feverishly begin to look after it. We have a smoking jacket made for it, we buy a new tie for it, worried that others might select the clothes and tie, and select badly. This is the moment when Goethe decides to write his memoirs, his famous *Poetry and Truth*, when he summons the devoted Eckermann (strange coincidence of dates: that same year, 1823, Bettina sent him her sketch for the monument), and lets him write *Conversations with Goethe*, that beautiful portrait produced under the benevolent control of the one portrayed.

This second period of life, when a person cannot tear his eyes away from death, is followed by still another period, the shortest and most mysterious, about which little is known and little is said. Strength is ebbing, and a person is seized by disarming fatigue. Fatigue: a silent bridge leading from the shore of life to the shore of death. At that stage death is so close that looking at it has already become boring. It is again unseen and invisible, in the way objects are when they become too intimately familiar. A weary man looks out of the window, sees the tops of trees and silently recites their names: chestnut, poplar, maple. And those names are as beautiful as being itself. The poplar is tall and looks like an athlete raising his arm to the sky. Or it looks like a flame that has soared into the air and petrified. Poplar, oh poplar. Immortality is a ridiculous illusion, an empty word, a butterfly-net chasing the wind, if we compare it to the beauty of the poplar that the weary man watches through the window. Immortality no longer interests the weary old man at all.

And what does a weary old man watching a poplar do when a woman suddenly appears and wants to sit on the table, kneel on the threshold and deliver sophisticated pronouncements? With a sense of inexpressible joy and a sudden surge of vitality he calls her an annoying gad-fly.

I am thinking of the moment when Goethe penned the words 'annoying gad-fly'. I am thinking of the pleasure he experienced and I imagine him suddenly coming to a realization: in his whole life he had never acted as he wished to act. He considered himself the administrator of his immortality, and that responsibility tied him down and turned him stiff and prim. He was afraid of all eccentricity even though it also strongly attracted him, and when he committed some eccentricity he subsequently tried to trim it down so as to keep it within the bounds of that sunny equanimity which he sometimes identified with beauty. The words 'annoying gad-fly' did not fit into his work, nor into his life, nor into his immortality. Those words were pure freedom. They could only have been written by someone who already found himself in the third stage of life, when a person ceases to minister to his immortality and no longer considers it a serious matter. Not everyone reaches this furthest limit, but whoever does reach it knows that there, and only there, can true freedom be found.

These thoughts passed through Goethe's mind, but he forgot them at once for he was old and weary and his memory was bad.

11

Let us recall: she first came to him in the guise of a child. Twenty-five years later, in March 1832, when she heard that Goethe was seriously ill, she sent her own child to him at once: her eighteen-year-old son Sigmund. On his mother's instructions, the shy boy stayed in Weimar six days with no inkling of what it was all about. But Goethe knew: she was sending him her ambassador, who was to let him know by his mere presence that death was impatiently waiting behind the door and that Bettina was about to take Goethe's immortality into her own hands.

Then death did indeed walk through the door, Goethe struggled for a week, by March 22 lay dying and a few days later Bettina wrote to Goethe's executor, Chancellor von Müller: 'Goethe's death certainly made an indelible impression on me, but not a sorrowful impression. I cannot express the precise truth in words, but it seems to me I come closest to it when I say that it was an impression of glory.'

Let us note carefully Bettina's emendation: not sorrow, but glory.

Shortly thereafter she requested the same Chancellor von Müller to send her all the letters she had ever written to Goethe. When she read them she was disappointed: her whole story with Goethe seemed a mere sketch, perhaps a sketch for a masterpiece but a sketch all the same, and a very imperfect one at that. It was necessary to set to work. For three years she kept correcting, rewriting, adding. Dissatisfied as she was with her own letters, those from Goethe pleased her even less. When now she reread them she was offended by their brevity, their reserve, and even, at times, their impertinence. At times he wrote to her as if he took her child-like mask literally, as if he were bestowing mildly indulgent lessons on a schoolgirl. That's why now she had to change their tone: where he called her 'my dear friend' she put 'my dear heart', she toned down reprimands with flattering postscripts and added sentences that acknowledged Bettina's power over the fascinated poet as his inspiring Muse.

Of course, she rewrote her own letters even more radically. No, she didn't alter the tone, the tone was just right. But she altered, for example, their dates (to erase the long pauses in their correspondence, which might deny the constancy of their passion), she discarded many unsuitable passages (for example the one in which she begged Goethe not to show her letters to anyone), she added other passages, dramatized various situations, expanded to a greater depth her views on politics, art, and especially on music and Beethoven.

She finished the book in 1835 and published it under the title *Goethes Briefwechsel mit einem Kinde*, Goethe's correspondence with a child. Nobody questioned the authenticity of the correspondence until 1920, when the original letters were discovered and published.

Alas, why didn't she burn them in time?

Imagine yourself in her place: it isn't easy to burn intimate documents that are dear to you; it would be like admitting to yourself that you won't be here much longer, that tomorrow you may die; and so you put off the act of destruction from day to day, and then one day it's too late.

Man reckons with immortality, and forgets to reckon with death.

12

Now, perhaps, when the end of our century provides us with the proper perspective, we can allow ourselves to say: Goethe is a figure placed precisely in the centre of European history. Goethe: the great centre. Not the centre in the sense of a timid point that carefully avoids extremes, no, a firm centre that holds both extremes in a remarkable balance which Europe will never know again. As a young man Goethe studied alchemy, and later became one of the first modern scientists. Goethe was the greatest German of all, and at the same time an anti-patriotic and a European. Goethe was a cosmopolitan, and yet throughout his life he hardly ever stirred out of his province, his little Weimar. Goethe was a man of nature, yet also a man of history. In love, he was a libertine as well as a romantic. And something else:

Let's recall Agnes in the elevator that shook as if seized by Saint Vitus' dance. Even though she was a cybernetics expert, she didn't have any idea what was going on in the head of that machine which was as strange and impenetrable to her as the mechanism of the various objects with which she daily came into contact, from the small computer next to her phone, to the dishwasher.

In contrast, Goethe lived during that brief span of history when the level of technology already gave life a certain measure of comfort but when an educated person could still understand all the devices he used. Goethe knew how and with what materials his house had been constructed, he knew why his oil lamp gave off light, he knew the principle of the telescope with which he and Bettina looked at Jupiter; and while he himself could not perform surgery, he was present at several operations and when he was sick he could converse with the doctor in the vocabulary of an expert. The world of technical objects was completely open and intelligible to him. This was Goethe's great moment at the centre of European history, a moment that brings on a pang of nostalgic regret in the heart of someone trapped in a jerking, dancing elevator.

Beethoven's work begins where Goethe's centre ends. It is located in the moment when the world starts gradually losing its transparency, darkens, becomes more and more incomprehensible, rushes into the unknown, while man, betrayed by the world, escapes into his self, into his nostalgia, his dreams, his revolt, and lets himself be deafened by the voices inside him so that he no longer hears the voices outside. That cry from inside sounded to Goethe like an unbearable noise. Goethe hated noise. That's a well-known fact. He couldn't even bear the barking of a dog in a distant garden. It is said that he disliked music. That's an error. What he disliked was the orchestra. He liked Bach because Bach still conceived of music as a transparent combination of independent voices, each of which could be distinguished. But in Beethoven's symphonies the voices of individual instruments dissolve in an amalgam of clamour and lament. Goethe couldn't bear the roar of an orchestra just as he couldn't bear the loud laments of the soul. Bettina's friends among the younger generation saw the divine Goethe stop up his ears and look at them with distaste. This they couldn't forgive him and they attacked him as an enemy of the soul, of revolt and of feeling.

Bettina was the sister of the poet Brentano, wife of the poet Arnim and she venerated Beethoven. She belonged to the Romantic generation and yet she was a friend of Goethe. Nobody else could claim such a position: she was like a queen ruling over two kingdoms.

Her book was a magnificent tribute to Goethe. All her letters were but a single *song* of love to him. Yes, but because everyone knew about the glasses that Mrs Goethe had knocked to the ground and about Goethe's infamous betrayal of the loving child in favour of the crazy sausage, that book is at the same time (and to a much greater extent) a *lesson* in love given to the dead poet, who on coming face to face with great emotion behaved like a cowardly philistine and sacrificed passion to the miserable tranquillity of marriage. Bettina's book was at the same time a homage and a thrashing.

13

The year Goethe died Bettina wrote a letter to her friend, Count Hermann von Pückler-Muskau, describing an incident that had occurred one summer, twenty years earlier. She said she had had the story straight from Beethoven. In 1812 (ten months after the black days of the broken glasses) Beethoven visited the Teplitz spa for a few days, and there he met Goethe for the first time. One day he went out for a walk with him. They were walking down an avenue when suddenly they came upon the Empress with her family and entourage. As soon as Goethe saw them, he stopped listening to what Beethoven was saying, stepped to the side of the road and took off his hat. Beethoven, on the other hand, pulled his hat even further over his forehead, frowned so that his thick eyebrows shot out another two inches, and kept on walking without slowing his pace. And so it was up to the courtiers to stop, stand aside and make their greeting. It was only after he had passed them that he turned, and waited for Goethe. And he told him just what he thought of his servile, lackey-like behaviour. He bawled him out as if he were a snot-nosed schoolboy.

Did this scene actually take place? Did Beethoven make it up? From beginning to end? Or did he only add some colour? Or did Bettina add some colour? Or did she make it up from beginning to end? Nobody will ever know. But one thing is certain: when she wrote her letter to Pückler-Muskau, she realized that the anecdote was priceless. Only this story was capable of revealing the true significance of her love with Goethe. But how to make it known? 'Do you like the story?' she asked Hermann von Pückler-Muskau. '*Kannst du sie brauchen?* Can you use it?' The Count did not intend to use it and so Bettina considered the possibility of publishing her correspondence with him; but then something much better occurred to her: in 1839 she published in the journal *Athenäum* a letter in which the same story is told by Beethoven himself! The original of this letter, dated 1812, has never been found. All that remains is a copy in Bettina's hand-writing. It contains several details (such as the precise date) which show that Beethoven never wrote it, or at least that Beethoven hadn't written it the way Bettina copied it. But whether the letter is a forgery or a semi-forgery, the anecdote enchanted everyone and became famous. And everything suddenly became clear: it was no accident that Goethe gave preference to a sausage over a great love: while Beethoven was a rebel striding forward with his hat pulled down over his forehead and his hands behind his back, Goethe was a servant humbly bowing by the side of the road.

14

Bettina studied music, she even wrote a few compositions, and so had some basis for understanding what was new and beautiful about Beethoven's music. Nevertheless, I ask this question: was it Beethoven's music that captivated her, its notes, or was it rather what the music *represented*, in other words, its vague affinity to the ideas and attitudes that Bettina shared with her generation? Does love for art really exist and has it ever existed? Is it not a delusion? When Lenin proclaimed that he loved Beethoven's *Appassionata* above all else, what was it that he really loved? What did he hear? Music? Or a majestic noise which reminded him of the solemn stirrings in his soul, a longing for blood, brotherhood, executions, justice and the absolute? Did he derive joy from the tones, or from the musings stimulated by those tones, which had nothing to do with art or with beauty? Let's return to Bettina: was she attracted to Beethoven the musician or Beethoven the great anti-Goethe? Did she love his music with the quiet love that draws us to a magical metaphor or to the harmony of two colours on a painting? Or was it rather the kind of aggressive passion that makes us join political parties? Be that as it may (and we will never know the actual truth), Bettina sent into the world the image of Beethoven striding forward with his hat pulled down over his forehead and this image has kept on marching down the centuries.

In 1927, a hundred years after Beethoven's death, the famous German journal *Die literarische Welt* asked the most notable contemporary composers what Beethoven meant to them. The editors had no inkling what a posthumous execution this would turn out to be for the man with the hat pulled over his forehead. Auric, a member of the Paris Six, stated in the name of his whole generation: they were so indifferent to Beethoven that he wasn't even worth criticizing. Could he possibly be rediscovered one day and re-evaluated, as was the case with Bach a hundred years ago? Out of the question. Ridiculous! Janáček, too, confirmed that he had never been thrilled by Beethoven's work. And Ravel summed it up: he didn't like Beethoven because his fame was based not on his music, which is obviously imperfect, but on the literary legend built around his life.

Literary legend. In our case, it is based on two hats: one is pulled over the forehead with the giant eyebrows; the other is in the hand of a deeply bowing man. Magicians like to work with hats. They let objects disappear in them or they make flocks of pigeons fly from them to the ceiling. Bettina released from Goethe's hat the ugly birds of his servility, and from Beethoven's hat she caused to disappear (surely unwittingly), his music. She prepared for Goethe what was given to Tycho Brahe and what will be given to Jimmy Carter: ridiculous immortality. But ridiculous immortality lies in ambush for everyone; to Ravel, a Beethoven with his hat over his eyebrows was more ridiculous than the deeply bowing Goethe.

It thus follows that even though it is possible to design, manipulate and orchestrate one's immortality in advance, it never comes to pass the way it has been intended. Beethoven's hat became immortal. The plan succeeded. But what the significance of the immortal hat would turn out to be, that could not be determined in advance.

15

'You know, Johann,' said Hemingway, 'they keep bringing up accusations against me, too. Instead of reading my books they're writing books about me. They say that I didn't love my wives. That I didn't pay enough attention to my son. That I punched a critic on the nose. That I lied. That I wasn't sincere. That I was conceited. That I was macho. That I claimed I had received two hundred and thirty war wounds whereas actually it was only two hundred and ten. That I abused myself. That I disobeyed my mother.'

'That's immortality,' said Goethe. 'Immortality means eternal trial.'

'If it's eternal trial, there ought to be a decent judge. Not a narrow-minded schoolteacher with a rod in her hand.'

'A rod in the hand of a narrow-minded teacher, that's what eternal trial is about. What else did you expect, Ernest?'

'I didn't expect anything. I had hoped that after death I would at last be able to live in peace.'

'You did everything you could to become immortal.'

'Nonsense. I wrote books. That's all.'

'Yes, precisely!' laughed Goethe.

'I have no objection to my books being immortal. I wrote them in such a way that nobody could delete a single word. To resist every kind of adversity. But I myself, as a human being, as Ernest Hemingway, I don't give a damn about immortality!'

'I understand you very well, Ernest. But you should have been more careful while you were still alive. Now it's too late.'

'More careful? Are you referring to my boastfulness? I admit that when I was young I loved to blow my own trumpet. I loved to show off in front of people. I enjoyed the anecdotes that were told about me. But believe me, I wasn't such a monster as to do it on account of immortality! When I realized one day that this was the point of it all, I panicked. From that time on I must have told people a thousand times to leave my life alone. But the more I pleaded the worse it got. I moved to Cuba to get out of their sight. When I won the Nobel Prize I refused to go to Stockholm. Believe me, I didn't give a damn about immortality, and now I'll tell you something else: when I realized one day that it was holding me in its clutches, it terrified me more than death itself. A man can take his own life. But he cannot take his own immortality. As soon as immortality has you aboard, you can't get off, and even if you shoot yourself you'll stay on deck along with your suicide and that's horrible, Johann, that's horrible. I was lying dead on the deck and I saw my four wives squatting around me, writing down everything they knew, and standing behind them was my son and he was scribbling too, and that old dame Gertrude Stein was there writing away and all my friends were there blabbing out all the indiscretions and slanders they had ever heard about me, and behind them a hundred journalists with microphones jostled each other and an army of university professors all over America were busy classifying, analysing, and shovelling everything into articles and books.'

16

Hemingway was trembling and Goethe clutched his arm: 'Calm down, Ernest! Calm down, my friend. I understand you. What you've just been telling me reminds me of my dream. It was my last dream, after that I had no more or else they were confused and I could no longer distinguish them from reality. Imagine a small puppet theatre. I am behind the scenes, I control the puppets and recite the text. It is a performance of *Faust*. My *Faust*. Did you know that *Faust* is at its most beautiful when performed as a puppet play? That's why I was so happy that no actors were present and I alone recited the lines, which on that day sounded more beautiful than ever before. And then I suddenly glanced at the seats and saw that the theatre was empty. That puzzled me. Where was the audience? Was my *Faust* so boring that everyone had gone home? Was I not even worth booing? Bewildered, I turned round and I was aghast: I expected them out front, and instead they were at the back of the stage, gazing at me with wide-open, inquisitive eyes. As soon as my glance met theirs, they began to applaud. And I realized that my *Faust* didn't interest them at all and that the show they wished to see was not the puppets I was leading around the stage, but me myself! Not *Faust*, but Goethe! And then I was overcome by a sense of horror very similar to what you described a moment ago. I felt they wanted me to say something, but I couldn't. My throat felt locked tight, I put down the puppets and left them lying on the brightly lit stage that nobody was watching. I tried to maintain a dignified composure, I walked silently to the coat-rack where my hat was hanging, I put it on my head and without a glance at all those curiosity-seekers I left the theatre and went home. I tried to look neither to the right nor the left and especially not behind me, because I knew they were following. I unlocked the heavy front door and slammed it behind me. I found an oil lamp and lit it. I lifted it with my shaking arm and went to my study, hoping that my rock collection would help me forget this unpleasant episode. But before I had time to put the lamp down on the table, I happened to glance at the window. Their faces were pressed against the glass. Then I realized that I would never get rid of them, never, never, never. I realized that the lamp was lighting up my face, I saw it by those wide-open eyes that were scrutinizing me. I put out the lamp and yet I knew that I shouldn't have done so; now they realized that I was trying to hide from them, that I was afraid of them and this was sure to incite them all the more. But by now my fear was stronger than my reason and I ran off into the bedroom, pulled the covers off the bed, threw them over my head, stood in the corner of the room, and pressed myself against the wall . . .'

17

Hemingway and Goethe are receding down the roads of the other world and you ask me what was the point of bringing the two together. After all, they don't belong together at all, they have nothing in common! So what? With whom do you think Goethe would like to pass his time in the other world? With Herder? With Hölderlin? With Bettina? With Eckermann? Just think of Agnes. Think of her terror when she imagined that she might have to hear once again the hum of women's voices that she hears every Saturday in the sauna! She does not wish to spend her afterlife with Paul or with Brigitte. Why should Goethe long for Herder? I can tell you, though it's practically blasphemy, that he didn't even long for Schiller. He would never have admitted this to himself while he was alive, because it would make for a sad summing up not to have had a single great friend in one's lifetime. Schiller was undoubtedly the person dearest to him. But the word 'dearest' only means that he was dearer to him than all others, who frankly speaking were not so very dear to him at all. They were his contemporaries, he hadn't chosen them. He hadn't even chosen Schiller. When he realized one day that he'd have them around him all his life, he felt a pang of anxiety. There was nothing to be done, he had to come to terms with it. But was there any reason for being with them after death?

It was therefore only out of my most sincere love for him that I dreamed up someone at his side who interested him very much (in case you have forgotten, let me remind you that Goethe was fascinated by America throughout his life!), someone who wasn't like the band of pale-faced Romantics that came to dominate Germany towards the end of his life.

'You know, Johann,' said Hemingway, 'it's a stroke of luck that I can be with you. You make everybody tremble with respect, and so all my wives as well as old Gertrude Stein are giving me a wide berth.' Then he burst out laughing: 'Unless of course it is on account of that unbelievable scarecrow get-up of yours!'

In order to make Hemingway's remark intelligible, I have to explain that immortals on their walks in the other world can choose to look the way they did at any time in their lives. And Goethe chose the private look of his last years; nobody except those closest to him knew him in that guise: because his eyes were sensitive to light he wore a green eye-shade attached to his forehead by a piece of string; he had slippers on his feet; and a heavy, stripey wool scarf was tied round his neck because he was afraid of catching cold.

The remark about his unbelievable scarecrow get-up made Goethe laugh happily, as if Hemingway had just said some words of great praise. He leaned close to him and said softly: 'I put on this get-up mainly because of Bettina. Wherever she goes, she talks of her great love for me. So I want people to witness the object of that love. Whenever she sees me, she runs for her life. And I know she stamps her feet in fury because I parade around this way: toothless, bald and with this ridiculous gadget over my eyes.'

PART THREE

Fighting

The sisters

The radio station I listen to is state-owned, so it is free of advertising, and news programmes alternate with the latest hit songs. The next station on the dial is privately owned, there is advertising instead of music but the ads resemble the latest hits to such an extent that I never know what station I am listening to, and as I doze off again and again I know it even less. In my drowsy state I learn that since the war two million people have been killed on the roads of Europe; in France alone, highway accidents have caused on average ten thousand deaths and three hundred thousand injuries per year, a whole army of the legless, handless, earless, eyeless. Deputy Bertrand Bertrand (a name as beautiful as a lullaby), incensed by these terrible statistics, did something remarkable, but at that point I fell asleep and learned the story only half an hour later, when the same news item was repeated: Deputy Bertrand Bertrand, a name as beautiful as a lullaby, proposed in Parliament that beer advertising should be banned. This caused a great uproar in the National Assembly; many deputies opposed the idea, supported by representatives of the radio and TV who would lose money as a result. Then came the voice of Bertrand Bertrand himself: he talked of the fight against death, the fight for life. During his short speech the word 'fight' was repeated at least five times, and this immediately reminded me of my native land, of Prague, of banners, posters, the fight for peace, the fight for happiness, the fight for justice, the fight for the future, the fight for peace; a fight for peace which ends up with the destruction of everybody by everybody, the Czech people wisely add. But now I am asleep again (every time somebody pronounces the name Bertrand Bertrand I fall into a deep slumber) and when I wake up I hear some comments about gardening, so I quickly turn the dial to the next station. I hear a report about Deputy Bertrand Bertrand and about the proposed ban on beer advertising. Slowly I begin to grasp the logical connections: people are killed on highways as if they were on a battlefield, but it is impossible to ban cars because they are the pride of modern man; a certain percentage of accidents is caused by drunken drivers but wine cannot be banned for it is the time-honoured glory of France; a certain percentage of drunkenness is caused by beer, but beer, too, cannot be banned because it would violate all the international free-trade agreements; a certain percentage of people who drink beer are motivated to drink by advertising and here is the enemy's Achilles' heel, here is the point where the brave Deputy decided to strike! Long live Bertrand Bertrand, I tell myself, but because that name affects me like a lullaby, I fall asleep at once until I am awakened by a seductive, velvet voice, yes it is Bernard the announcer, and as if all the news concerned nothing but highway accidents he reports the following: last night a girl sat down on a highway, with her back to the oncoming traffic. Three cars, one after the other, managed to swerve aside at the last moment and ended up in the ditch, all smashed up, with a number of dead and injured. The suicidal girl herself, when she realized her lack of success, slipped from the scene and only the mutually consistent testimony of the injured bore witness to her existence. That report strikes me as so horrible that I cannot go back to sleep. There is nothing to do but get up, have some breakfast and sit down at my writing desk. But for a long while I simply couldn't concentrate, I saw that girl sitting on the dark highway, hunched down, her forehead pressed to her knees, and I heard the screams rising from the ditch. I had to force myself to get rid of this image in order to be able to continue with my novel, which if you remember began with my waiting at the swimming pool for Professor Avenarius and seeing an unknown woman wave to the lifeguard. We saw that gesture again when Agnes was standing in front of her house saying good-bye to her shy schoolfriend. Agnes continued to use that gesture whenever a boy took her home after a date and walked her to the garden gate. Her little sister Laura would hide behind a bush and wait for Agnes to return home; she wanted to see the kiss and to watch her sister walk to the front door. She waited for the moment when Agnes turned round and lifted her arm in the air. This movement conjured up a misty idea of love which Laura knew nothing about but which would always remain connected in her mind with the image of her attractive, gentle sister.

When Agnes caught Laura borrowing her gesture in order to wave to her friends, it upset her and, as we know, ever since then she took leave of her lovers soberly and without outward display. In this short history of a gesture we can recognize the mechanism determining the relationship of the two sisters: the younger one imitated the elder, reached out her arm towards her, but at the last moment Agnes would always escape.

After she left the lycée Agnes moved to Paris to study at the university. Laura reproached her sister for having left their beloved countryside, but after graduation she, too, went to Paris to study. Agnes took up mathematics. After she had received her degree everyone predicted a great scholarly career for her, but instead of continuing her research she married Paul and took a well-paid yet commonplace job without any prospects of glory. Laura regretted that and when she herself entered the Paris Conservatoire she determined to make up for her sister's lack of success and become glorious in her stead.

One day Agnes introduced her to Paul. At the very first sight of him Laura heard an invisible someone saying to her: 'There is a man! A real man. The only man. No other exists.' Who was that invisible person? Was it perhaps Agnes herself? Yes. It was she,

101

pointing out the way to her sister and yet at the same time claiming that way for herself.

Agnes and Paul were kind to Laura and took such good care of her that she felt as much at home in Paris as she had in her home town. Yet the happy sense of staying within the family embrace was darkened by the melancholy knowledge that the only man she could ever have loved was at the same time the only man she must never try to win. When she spent time with the couple, moods of happiness alternated with bouts of sorrow. She would grow silent, gaze into space, and Agnes would take her by the hand and say: 'What's the matter, Laura? What's the matter, my little sister?' Sometimes, in the same situation and moved by a similar motive Paul, too, took her by the hand and all three would happily plunge into a voluptuous hot bath fed with many streams of feeling: sisterly and amorous, compassionate and sensual.

Then she married. Agnes' daughter Brigitte was ten years old when Laura decided to give her a present of a small cousin. She begged her husband to make her pregnant, which was readily accomplished but ended in grief: Laura had a miscarriage and the doctors told her that she could never have a child without undergoing serious surgery.

Dark glasses

Agnes grew fond of dark glasses while she was still at the lycée. It wasn't really because they protected her eyes against the sun, but because wearing them made her feel pretty and mysterious. Dark glasses became her hobby: just as some men have a cupboardful of ties, just as some women buy dozens of rings, Agnes had a collection of dark glasses.

In Laura's life, dark glasses came to play an important role after her miscarriage. She wore them almost constantly and apologized to friends: 'Excuse the glasses but I've been doing a lot of crying and I can't show my face to people without them.' From that time on dark glasses became her badge of sorrow. She put them on not to hide her weeping but to let people know that she wept. The glasses became a substitute for tears and in contrast to real tears had the advantage that they didn't sting the eyelids, didn't make them red or swollen, and actually looked becoming.

Laura's fondness for dark glasses was once again, as so many times before, inspired by her sister. But the story of the glasses also shows that the relationship of the sisters cannot be reduced to the mere statement that the younger imitated the elder. Yes, she imitated, but at the same time she corrected: she gave dark glasses a deeper significance, a more weighty significance, so that the dark glasses of Agnes had to blush before those of Laura for their frivolity. Every time Laura appeared with them on, it meant that she was suffering, and Agnes had the feeling that out of tact and modesty she ought to take her own glasses off.

There is still something else that is revealed by the story of the dark glasses: Agnes appears as the one favoured by fate, and Laura as the one unloved by fate. Both sisters came to believe that face-to-face with fortune they were not equal, and Agnes probably bore this even harder than Laura. 'I have a dear sister who loves me and has had nothing but bad luck in life,' she would say. That's why she was so happy to welcome Laura to Paris; that's why she introduced her to Paul and begged him to befriend her; that's why she took it upon herself to find her a pleasant apartment, and to invite her to her own house whenever she suspected that Laura was unhappy. But no matter what Agnes did, she remained the one unjustly favoured by fate and Laura remained the one fortune ignored.

Laura had a great talent for music; she was an excellent pianist, yet at the Conservatoire she took it into her head to study singing. 'When I play the piano I sit facing a foreign, unfriendly object. The music doesn't belong to me, it belongs to that black instrument facing me. But when I sing, my own body changes into a piano and I turn into music.' It wasn't her fault that she had a voice so weak it ruined everything: she failed to become a soloist and all that remained of her musical career for the rest of her life was participation in an amateur choir that she attended twice a week for rehearsals and joined a few times a year for concerts.

After six years her marriage ended in ruin, too, in spite of all the goodwill she had poured into it. It is true that her very wealthy husband had to leave her a beautiful apartment and to pay her a large amount of alimony, so she was able to set up a stylish fur shop which she ran with a talent for business that surprised everyone; however, this pedestrian, all too materialistic success was not capable of rectifying the wrong that had been done to her on a higher, spiritual and emotional plane.

Laura, the divorcee, went through many men, she had the reputation of being a passionate lover and pretended that these loves were a cross she carried through life. 'I have known many men,' she would often say, in such a melancholy and pathetic way that it sounded like a complaint against fate.

'I envy you,' Agnes would answer, and Laura would put on her dark glasses as a badge of sorrow.

The admiration Laura felt in her distant childhood whenever she watched Agnes saying good-bye to a boy at the garden gate had never left her, and when she finally came to realize that her sister was not going to have a dazzling scholarly career she could not hide her disappointment.

'How can you criticize me?' Agnes defended herself. 'You are selling fur coats instead of singing opera, and I, instead of attending international conferences, have a pleasantly meaningless job in a computer company.'

'Yes, but I did everything possible to become a singer. You left the scholarly life of your own free will. I was defeated. You gave up.'

'And why must I have a career?'

'Agnes! We only have one life! You have to fill it! After all, we want to leave something behind!'

Agnes was surprised. 'Leave something behind?' she said with sceptical astonishment.

Laura reacted in a voice of almost pained disagreement: 'Agnes, you're being negative!'

This was a reproach that Laura often addressed to her sister, but only silently. She said it aloud only two or three times. The last time was after her mother's death, when she saw her father sitting at the table tearing up photographs. What her father was doing seemed totally unacceptable to her: he was destroying a piece of life, a piece of shared life, his and her mother's; he was tearing up pictures, tearing up memories that were not only his but belonged to the whole family, especially the daughters; he was doing something he had no right to do. She started shouting at him and Agnes came to her father's defence. When they were alone, the two sisters quarrelled for the first time in their life, passionately and cruelly. 'You're being negative! You're being negative!' Laura shouted at Agnes. Then she put on her dark glasses and left, sobbing and infuriated.

The body

When they were already quite old, the famous painter Salvador Dali and his wife Gala had a pet rabbit, who lived with them, followed them around everywhere, and of whom they were very fond. Once, they were about to embark on a long trip and they debated long into the night what to do with the rabbit. It would have been difficult to take him along and equally difficult to entrust him to somebody else, because the rabbit was uneasy with strangers. The next day Gala prepared lunch and Dali enjoyed the excellent food until he realized he was eating rabbit meat. He got up from the table and ran to the bathroom, where he vomited up his beloved pet, the faithful friend of his waning days. Gala, on the other hand, was happy that the one she loved had passed into her guts, caressing them and becoming the body of his mistress. For her there existed no more perfect fulfilment of love than eating the beloved. Compared to this merging of bodies the sexual act seemed to her no more than ludicrous tickling.

Laura was like Gala. Agnes was like Dali. She was fond of many people, men and women, but if because of some bizarre agreement it had been stipulated as a precondition of friendship that she would have to take care of their noses and wipe them regularly, she would have preferred to live without friends. Laura, who was aware of her sister's queasiness, berated her: 'What does it mean when somebody attracts you? How can you exclude the body from such a feeling? Does a person whose body you erase still remain a person?'

Yes, Laura was like Gala: perfectly identified with her body, in which she felt at home as in a well-furnished house. And the body was more than what is visible in a mirror; the most valuable part was inside. That's why references to the body's organs and functions became a favourite part of her vocabulary. If she wanted to express that her lover had driven her to desperation the night before, she would say: 'The moment he left I had to throw up.' Even though she often talked of vomiting, Agnes wasn't sure whether her sister had ever actually done so. Vomiting was not Laura's truth but her poetry: a metaphor, a lyrical image of pain and disgust.

Once, when the sisters went shopping at a lingerie shop, Agnes saw Laura gently stroking a brassière that the saleswoman was showing her. That was one of those moments when Agnes realized the difference between her sister and herself: for Agnes, the brassière belonged in the category of objects designed to correct some bodily defect, such as a bandage, a prosthetic device, glasses, or the collar people wear after injuries to the neck. A brassière is supposed to support something that due to faulty design is heavier than it should be and therefore must be shored up, perhaps like the balcony of a poorly constructed building that must be provided with pillars and supports to keep it from collapsing. In other words: a brassière reveals the *technical* nature of the female body.

Agnes envied Paul for being able to live without constant awareness of his body. He inhaled, exhaled, his lungs worked like a big automatic bellows and that's how he perceived his body: he gladly forgot it. Nor did he ever talk about his physical problems; this did not stem from modesty but rather from some vain longing for elegance, since disease was an imperfection of which he was ashamed. He suffered for many years from stomach ulcers, but Agnes didn't find out about it until the day an ambulance rushed him to the hospital after a terrible attack that seized him as soon as he had concluded a dramatic defence plea in the courtroom. This vanity of his was certainly ridiculous, but Agnes found it rather touching and almost envied Paul for it.

Agnes told herself that even though Paul was probably exceptionally vain, his attitude revealed the difference between the male and female lot in life: a woman spends much more time on discussions of her physical problems; she was not fated to forget about her body in a carefree way. It starts with the shock of the first bleeding; the body is suddenly present and she stands facing it like a poor mechanic ordered to keep a small factory running: to change tampons every month, to swallow pills, snap the brassière in place, get ready for production. Agnes looked upon old men with envy: it seemed to her that they aged differently: her father's body slowly changed into its shadow, it dematerialized, it remained in the world merely as a carelessly incarnated soul. In contrast, the more useless a woman's body becomes, the more it is a body: heavy and burdensome; it resembles an old factory destined for demolition, which the woman's self must watch to the very end, like a caretaker.

What was capable of changing Agnes' relation to the body? Only a moment of excitement. Excitement: fleeting redemption of the body.

But even in this Laura would not agree. A moment of redemption? Why only a moment? For Laura the body was sexual from the beginning, *a priori*, constantly and completely, by its very essence. To love someone meant for her: to bring him one's body, to give him one's body, just as it was, with everything, inside and out, even with its own time, which is slowly, sweetly, corroding it.

For Agnes the body was not sexual. It only became so in exceptional moments, when an instant of excitement illuminated it with an unreal, artificial light and made it desirable and beautiful. And perhaps it was precisely because of that, though nobody knew this about Agnes, that she was obsessed by physical love and clung to it, for without it there would be no emergency exit from the misery of the body and everything would be lost. When she made love, she always kept her eyes open and if she was near a mirror she would watch herself: at that moment her body seemed to be bathed in light.

But watching one's own body bathed in light is a treacherous game. Once, when Agnes was with her lover, she detected in the course of love-making certain defects of her body which she hadn't noticed at the time of their last meeting (she would meet her lover only once or twice a year, in a big, anonymous Paris hotel) and she was unable to tear her eyes away: she didn't see her lover, she didn't see the intertwined bodies, she only saw old age which was beginning to gnaw at her. Excitement quickly vanished from the room and she closed her eyes and quickened the movements of love-making as if trying to prevent her partner from reading her mind: she decided then and there that this would be their last meeting. She felt weak and longed for her marital bed, where the bedside lamp always remained off; she longed for her marital bed as a refuge, as a quiet haven of darkness.

Addition and subtraction

In our world, where there are more and more faces, more and more alike, it is difficult for an individual to reinforce the originality of the self and to become convinced of its inimitable uniqueness. There are two methods for cultivating the uniqueness of the self: the method of *addition* and the method of *subtraction*. Agnes subtracts from her self everything that is exterior and borrowed, in order to come closer to her sheer essence (even with the risk that zero lurks at the bottom of the subtraction). Laura's method is precisely the opposite: in order to make her self ever more visible, perceivable, seizable, sizeable, she keeps adding to it more and more attributes and she attempts to identify herself with them (with the risk that the essence of the self may be buried by the additional attributes).

Let's take her cat as an example. After her divorce, Laura remained alone in a large apartment and felt lonely. She longed for a pet to share her solitude. First she thought of a dog, but soon realized that a dog needed the kind of care she would be unable to provide. And so she got a cat. It was a big Siamese cat, beautiful and wicked. As she lived with the cat and regaled her friends with stories about it, the animal that she had picked more or less by accident, without any special conviction (after all, her first choice was a dog!), took on an ever growing significance: she began to lavish praise on her pet and forced everyone to admire it. She saw in the cat a superb independence, pride, freedom of action and constancy of charm (so different from human charm, which is always spoiled by moments of clumsiness and unattractiveness); in the cat, she saw her paradigm; in the cat, she saw herself.

It is not at all important whether Laura's nature resembled that of a cat or not, the important thing is that she made the cat part of her coat of arms and that the cat (love for the cat, apologias for the cat) became one of the attributes of her self. From the beginning, many of her lovers were irritated by this egocentric and evil animal, which would spit and scratch for no apparent reason, and so the cat became an acid test of Laura's power; as if she wanted to tell everyone: you can have me, but the way I really am, and that includes the cat. The cat became the image of her soul, and a lover had to accept her soul if he wished to have her body.

The method of addition is quite charming if it involves adding to the self such things as a cat, a dog, roast pork, love of the sea or of cold showers. But the matter becomes less idyllic if a person decides to add love for communism, for the homeland, for Mussolini, for Roman Catholicism or atheism, for fascism or anti-fascism. In both cases the method remains exactly the same: a person stubbornly defending the superiority of cats over other animals is doing basically the same thing as one who maintains that Mussolini was the sole saviour of Italy: he is proud of this attribute of the self and he tries to make this attribute (a cat or Mussolini) acknowledged and loved by everyone.

Here is that strange paradox to which all people cultivating the self by way of the addition method are subject: they use addition in order to create a unique, inimitable self, yet because they automatically become propagandists for the added attributes, they are actually doing everything in their power to make as many others as possible similar to themselves; as a result, their uniqueness (so painfully gained) quickly begins to disappear.

We may ask ourselves why a person who loves a cat (or Mussolini) is not satisfied to keep his love to himself, and wants to force it on others. Let us seek the answer by recalling the young woman in the sauna, who belligerently asserted that she loved cold showers. She thereby managed to differentiate herself at once from one half of the human race, namely the half that prefers hot showers. Unfortunately, that other half now resembled her all the more. Alas, how sad! Many people, few ideas, so how are we to differentiate ourselves from each other? The young woman knew only one way of overcoming the disadvantage of her similarity to that enormous throng devoted to cold showers: she had to proclaim her credo 'I adore cold showers!' as soon as she appeared in the door of the sauna and to proclaim it with such fervour as to make the millions of other women who also enjoy cold showers seem like pale imitations of herself. Let me put it another way: a mere (simple and innocent) love for showers can become an attribute of the self only on condition that we let the world know we are ready to fight for it.

The one who chooses as an attribute of the self a love for Mussolini becomes a political warrior, while the partisan of cats, music or antique furniture bestows gifts on his surroundings.

Imagine that you have a friend who loves Schumann and hates Schubert, while you madly love Schubert and Schumann bores you to tears. What kind of record would you give your friend as a birthday gift? The Schumann he loves, or the Schubert you adore? Schubert, of course. If you gave him a record of Schumann you'd have the unpleasant feeling that such a gift would not be sincere and would be more like a bribe calculated to flatter your friend. After all, when you give someone a present, you want to do so out of love, you want to give your friend a piece of yourself, a piece of your heart! And so you give him Schubert's 'Unfinished', and the moment you leave he'll spit on it, put on a rubber glove, gingerly pick up the record with two fingers and throw it in the bin.

In the course of several years Laura presented her sister and brother-in-law with a set of plates and dishes, a tea-service, a fruit-basket, a lamp, a rocking-chair, about five ashtrays, a tablecloth, but above all a piano which two husky men hauled in one day as a surprise and asked where to put it. Laura beamed: 'I wanted to give you something that will force you to think of me even when I'm not with you.'

After the divorce Laura spent all her free time at her sister's. She devoted herself to Brigitte as if she were her own daughter, and when she bought her sister the piano it was mainly because she wanted to teach her niece how to play. Brigitte, however, hated the piano. Agnes was afraid that this might hurt Laura's feelings and she therefore pleaded with her daughter to use her willpower and try to display some enthusiasm for those black and white keys. Brigitte objected: 'Am I supposed to learn to play just to please her?' And so the whole affair ended badly, and after a few months the piano was reduced to a mere show-object, or rather a nuisance-object; to a sad reminder of a failure; to a big white body (yes, the piano was white!) that nobody wanted.

To tell the truth, Agnes liked neither the tea-service nor the rocking-chair nor the piano. Not that those gifts were in bad taste, but they all had something eccentric about them that wasn't in keeping with Agnes' character or her interests. She therefore responded with sincere joy but also with selfish relief (after the piano had already been standing in her apartment, untouched, for six years) when Laura became involved with Bernard, Paul's young friend. She sensed that someone happily in love would have better things to do than shower gifts on a sister or try to educate a niece.

Older woman, younger man

'That's wonderful news,' said Paul when Laura told him of her latest love, and he invited both sisters out to dinner. He was enormously happy that two people he liked so much loved each other, and he ordered two bottles of an exceptionally expensive wine.

'You'll come in contact with one of the most important families in France,' he said to Laura. 'Do you have any idea who Bernard's father is?'

Laura said: 'Of course! He's a Deputy!'

Paul said: 'You don't know a thing. Deputy Bertrand Bertrand is the son of Deputy Arthur Bertrand. Arthur was very proud of his family's name and wanted his son to make it even more famous. He pondered what name to select for him and then he hit on the brilliant idea of christening him Bertrand. Nobody would be able to overlook or forget such a double name! Just pronouncing Bertrand Bertrand makes it sound like an ovation, like a call to fame: Bertrand! Bertrand! Bertrand! Bertrand! Bertrand! Bertrand!'

With these words Paul lifted his glass, as if he were hailing a beloved leader and drinking a toast to him. And then he really took a sip: 'That's excellent wine,' he said, and continued: 'All of us are mysteriously affected by our names, and Bertrand Bertrand, who kept hearing it intoned several times a day, lived his life as if oppressed by the imaginary fame of those four melodious syllables. When he failed his final school exams, he took it much worse than his other schoolfriends. It was as if the double name automatically doubled his sense of responsibility. Thanks to his exceptional modesty he was capable of bearing the shame that fell upon him; but he was unable to come to terms with the shame that fell upon his name. At the age of twenty, he swore in the name of his name that he would consecrate his whole life to the fight for good. He soon learned, however, that it wasn't so easy to distinguish what is good from what is evil. For example, his father voted with the majority of Parliament to ratify the Munich agreement. He wanted to save the peace, because peace is undeniably good. But then it was pointed out that the Munich agreement opened the door to war, which is undeniably evil. The son wanted to avoid his father's mistakes and therefore clung only to the most basic certainties. He never expressed his opinion about Palestinians, Israelis, the October revolution, Fidel Castro or even about terrorists, because he knew there existed a border beyond which murder is no longer murder but heroism, and that he would never be able to recognize just where that border lay. So he spoke all the more passionately against Hitler, Nazism, gas chambers, and in a certain sense he regretted Hitler's disappearance in the ruins of his bunker, because ever since then good and evil have become unbearably relative. That's why he tried to concentrate on the good in its most direct form, undistorted by politics. His slogan was: "life is good". And so the struggle against abortion, against euthanasia and against suicide became the purpose of his life.'

Laura protested, laughing: 'You make him sound like a fool!'

'You see?' Paul said to Agnes. 'Laura is already taking her lover's side. That's very praiseworthy, just like this wine, for the choice of which you ought to applaud me! In a recent programme against euthanasia Bertrand Bertrand had himself filmed at the bedside of a patient who couldn't move, whose tongue had been amputated, who was blind and suffered constant pain. The camera showed Bertrand leaning over the bed and speaking to the patient of hope for the future. Just as he said the word "hope" for the third time, the patient suddenly became excited and started

116

to make a horrible, animal sound, the sound of a bull, a horse, an elephant or all three together; Bertrand Bertrand was frightened: he was unable to continue talking; he tried with the greatest of effort to keep a smile on his face, and the camera kept on filming that petrified smile of a terror-stricken, trembling Deputy and next to him, in the same frame, the face of the screaming patient. But I don't want to talk about that. I only wanted to say that he ruined things for his son when he chose his name. First he wanted him to have the same name as he himself, but then he realized it would be grotesque to have two Bertrand Bertrands in the world because people would wonder whether these are two persons or four. Yet he didn't want to give up the joy of hearing in his son's name an echo of his own, and so he got the idea of calling him Bernard. The trouble is that Bernard Bertrand does not sound like an ovation or a call to fame, but like a slip of the tongue, or even more like a phonetic exercise for actors or radio announcers, to train them to speak faster and more distinctly. As I said, our names mysteriously influence us and even in his crib Bernard was already predestined by his name to speak on the airwaves.'

Paul was mouthing all this nonsense only because he didn't dare say the main thing on his mind: the fact that Laura was eight years older than Bernard thrilled him! For Paul had some wonderful memories of a woman fifteen years older than himself, whom he knew intimately when he was about twenty-five. He wanted to talk about it, he wanted to explain to Laura that every man's life ought to include a love-affair with an older woman, and that this provided men with some of their most beautiful memories. 'An older woman is a jewel in the life of a man,' he felt like proclaiming, lifting his glass high. But he kept himself from making this rash gesture and contented himself with quiet memories of his former lover, who used to give him the key to her apartment so that he could go there whenever he wanted and do whatever he wanted; this was very convenient at that time, for he was angry with his father and longed to be away from home as much as possible. She never claimed a right to his evenings; when he was free he spent them with her, when he was not free he didn't have to explain anything to her. She never urged him to take her out, and when they were seen together in society she behaved like a loving aunt doting on her handsome nephew. When he got married she sent him a lavish wedding present which always remained a mystery to Agnes.

But it would have hardly been possible to say to Laura: I am happy that my friend loves an older, experienced woman who will treat him as a loving aunt treats a handsome nephew. Besides, before he had a chance to say anything Laura herself spoke up:

'The most wonderful thing about it is that he makes me feel ten years younger. Thanks to him I crossed out ten or fifteen bad years and I feel as if I had just returned to Paris from Switzerland and met him.'

This admission made it impossible for Paul to reminisce aloud about the jewel of his life and so he reminisced silently, sipped his wine and stopped taking in what Laura was saying. It was only a while later, in order to rejoin the conversation, that he asked: 'What did Bernard tell you about his father?'

'Nothing,' Laura said. 'I can assure you that his father is not a subject of our conversations. I understand he comes from an important family. But you know what I think about important families.'

'Aren't you curious?'

'No,' Laura laughed merrily.

'You should be. Bertrand Bertrand is Bernard Bertrand's biggest problem.'

'I doubt it,' said Laura, convinced that Bernard's biggest problem was now Laura herself.

'Do you know that old Bertrand was planning a political career for Bernard?' asked Paul.

'No,' Laura said, shrugging her shoulders.

'In that family a political career is inherited like a mansion. Bertrand Bertrand counted on his son some day running for Parliament in his place. But Bernard was twenty years old when he heard the following sentence on a news programme: "The plane crash over the Atlantic claimed one hundred and thirty-nine lives, including seven children and four journalists." We have long become used to the idea that in such reports children tend to be singled out as a special, exceptionally valuable type of humanity. But on this occasion the announcer included journalists among them, and Bernard suddenly saw the light: he saw that in our time politicians cut a ridiculous figure, and he decided to become a journalist. By coincidence, I happened to be teaching a seminar at the law school he attended. There the betrayal of his political career and the betrayal of his father were completed. Perhaps Bernard has already told you about it!'

'Yes,' said Laura. 'He worships you!'

At that point a black man entered with a basket of flowers. Laura waved at him. The man showed his beautiful white teeth and Laura picked a bunch of five half-faded carnations from his basket. She handed them to Paul: 'All my happiness I owe to you!'

Paul reached in the basket and pulled out another bunch of carnations: 'You are the one we are celebrating, not me!' and he handed the flowers to Laura.

'Yes, today we are celebrating Laura,' said Agnes and she took a third bunch of carnations from the basket.

Laura's eyes were moist. She said: 'I feel so good, I feel so good with you,' and rose to her feet. She pressed both bouquets to her breast, standing next to the black man who bore himself like a king. All black men resemble kings: this one looked like Othello before he'd grown jealous of Desdemona, while Laura looked like Desdemona in love with her king. Paul knew what would happen

119

next. When Laura was drunk she would always start singing. The yearning to sing came from deep inside her body and rose into her throat with such intensity that several men at adjoining tables turned to look at her with surprise.

'Laura,' Paul whispered, 'they won't appreciate your Mahler in this restaurant!'

Laura held a bouquet against each breast as if she were standing on stage. Under her fingertips she felt her breasts, whose glands seemed to be filled with musical notes. But for her, Paul's wish was always a command. She obeyed him and only sighed: 'I have an enormous urge to do something . . .'

At that moment, the black man, led by the delicate instinct of kings, took the last two bunches of crumpled carnations from the bottom of the basket and with a noble gesture handed them to her. Laura said to Agnes: 'Agnes, my dear Agnes, without you I'd never have come to Paris, without you I wouldn't have met Paul, without Paul I wouldn't have met Bernard,' and she placed all four bouquets before Agnes on the table.

The Eleventh Commandment

At one time journalistic fame was symbolized by the great name of Ernest Hemingway. His whole work, his concise, matter-of-fact style was rooted in the dispatches he sent to the Kansas City newspapers as a young man. In those days, being a journalist meant getting closer to reality than anyone else, exploring all its hidden crannies, getting one's hands grimy with it. Hemingway was proud that his books were so close to the earth and yet so high in the heaven of art.

But when Bernard pronounces the word 'journalist' to himself (and in France nowadays that word also includes radio and TV editors and even press photographers), he is not thinking of Hemingway, and the literary form in which he longs to excel is not reportage. Rather, he dreams of publishing editorials in some influential weekly that would make his father's colleagues tremble. Or interviews. Anyway, who is the most memorable journalist of recent times? Not Hemingway, who wrote of his experiences in the trenches, not Orwell, who spent a year of his life with the Parisian poor, not Egon Erwin Kisch, the expert on Prague prostitutes, but Oriana Fallaci, who in the years 1969 to 1972 published in the Italian journal *Europeo* a series of interviews with the most famous politicians of the time. Those interviews were more than mere conversations; they were duels. Before the powerful politicians realized that they were fighting under unequal conditions – for she was allowed to ask questions but they were not – they were already rolling on the floor of the ring, KO'ed.

Those duels were a sign of the times; the situation had changed. Journalists realized that posing questions was not merely a practical working method for the reporter modestly gathering information with notebook and pencil in hand; it was a means of exerting power. The journalist is not merely the one who asks questions but the one who has a sacred right to ask, to ask anyone about anything. But don't we all have that right? And is a question not a bridge of understanding reaching out from one human being to another? Perhaps. I will therefore make my statement more precise: the power of the journalist is not based on his right to ask but on his right *to demand an answer*.

Please note carefully that Moses did not include among God's Ten Commandments: 'Thou shalt not lie!' That's no accident! Because the one who says, 'Don't lie!' has first to say, 'Answer!' and God did not give anyone the right to demand an answer from others. 'Don't lie!' 'Tell the truth!' are words which we must never say to another person in so far as we consider him our equal. Perhaps only God has that right, but He has no reason to resort to it since He knows everything and does not need our answers.

The inequality between one who gives orders and one who must obey is not as radical as that between one who has a right to demand an answer and one who has the duty to answer. That is why the right to demand answers has, since time immemorial, only been accorded in exceptional circumstances. For example, to a judge inquiring into a crime. In our century, fascist and communist states have appropriated this right, not only in exceptional circumstances but permanently. The citizens of these countries have known that at any time there might come a moment when they would be called on to answer: what they did yesterday; what they think deep in their hearts; what they talk about when they get together with A and if they have an intimate relationship with B. It was precisely this sanctified imperative, 'Tell the truth!', this Eleventh Commandment, whose force they were unable to withstand, that turned them into a throng of infantilized wretches. Occasionally, of course, some C could be found who would steadfastly refuse to reveal what he and A had talked about, and as an act of rebellion (it was often the only possible way of rebelling), he would lie instead of telling the truth. But the police were aware of this and secretly installed listening devices in his apartment. The police did not do so from any disreputable motives, but only to arrive at the truth which the liar C was concealing. They merely insisted on their right to demand an answer.

In democratic countries anyone can thumb his nose at a policeman who dares to ask what he talked about with A or whether he has intimate contact with B. Nevertheless, even here the authority of the Eleventh Commandment is in full force. After all, people do need some Commandment to rule over them in our century, when God's Ten have been virtually forgotten! The whole moral structure of our time rests on the Eleventh Commandment; and the journalist came to realize that thanks to a mysterious provision of history he is to become its administrator, gaining a power undreamed of by a Hemingway or an Orwell.

This phenomenon became unmistakably clear when the American journalists Carl Bernstein and Bob Woodward uncovered the sordid dealings of President Nixon during his election campaign, forcing the planet's most powerful man to lie in public, then to admit publicly that he had lied, and finally to leave the White House with bowed head. We all applauded because justice had been done. Paul applauded all the more because he regarded this episode as a sign of a great historic transition, a milestone, an unforgettable moment, a changing of the guard; a new power had appeared, the only one capable of toppling the former professional power-brokers, the politicians. Toppling them from their throne not by means of arms or intrigues, but by the mere force of questioning.

'Tell the truth,' says the journalist and of course we may ask just what the word 'truth' means to the administrator of the

Eleventh Commandment. To prevent misunderstanding we stress that it is not a question of God's truth, for which Jan Hus died at the stake, nor a question of the truth of science and free thought, for which they burned Giordano Bruno. The truth elicited by the Eleventh Commandment is not connected with religion or philosophy, it is truth of the lowest ontological storey, a purely positivist factual truth: what did C do yesterday? what is he really thinking deep in his heart? what does he talk about when he gets together with A? and does he have intimate contact with B? Nevertheless, even though it is on the lowest ontological storey, it is the truth of our time and contains the same explosive force as did the truth of Hus or Giordano Bruno. 'Did you have intimate contact with B?' asks the journalist. C lies and insists that he doesn't know B. But the journalist laughs up his sleeve, for the photographer on his newspaper has already secretly snapped B naked in the arms of C and it is entirely up to him when the scandalous photos will be made public, along with quotes from C, the cowardly liar impudently denying that he ever knew B.

The election campaign is on, the politician jumps from plane to helicopter, from helicopter to car, exerts himself, perspires, bolts his lunch on the run, shouts into microphones, makes two-hour speeches, but in the end it will depend on Bernstein or Woodward which of the fifty thousand sentences that he uttered will be released to the newspapers or quoted on the radio. That's why the politician would prefer to address the radio or TV audience directly, but this can only be accomplished through the mediation of an Oriana Fallaci, who sets the media rules and asks the questions. The politician will want to exploit the moment when he is finally seen by the entire nation, and to say everything that's on his mind, but Woodward will ask him only about things that aren't on the politician's mind at all and that he has no desire to talk about. He will thus find himself in the classic situation of a schoolboy called to the blackboard, and will try to use the old schoolboy trick: he will pretend to be answering the question, but in reality will use material he has specially prepared at home for the broadcast. This trick may have worked on his teachers, but it does not work on Bernstein, who keeps reminding him mercilessly: 'You haven't answered my question!'

Who would want to be a politician these days? Who would want to spend his whole life being tested at the blackboard? Certainly not the son of Deputy Bertrand Bertrand.

Imagology

The politician is dependent on the journalist. But on whom are the journalists dependent? On those who pay them. And those who pay them are the advertising agencies that buy space from newspapers and time from radio and TV stations. At first glance it may seem that the agencies would unhesitatingly approach all the high-circulation newspapers capable of increasing the sale of their products. But that's a naïve view of the matter. Sales of products are less important than we think. Just look at the communist countries: the millions of pictures of Lenin displayed everywhere you go certainly do not stimulate love for Lenin. The advertising agencies of the Communist Party (the so-called agit-prop departments) have long forgotten the practical goal of their activity (to make the communist system better liked) and have become an end in themselves: they have created their own language, their formulas, their aesthetics (the heads of these agencies once had absolute power over art in their countries), their idea of the right life-style which they cultivate, disseminate and force upon their unfortunate peoples.

Are you objecting that advertising and propaganda cannot be compared, because one serves commerce and the other ideology? You understand nothing. Some one hundred years ago in Russia, persecuted Marxists began to gather secretly in small circles in order to study Marx's manifesto; they simplified the contents of this simple ideology in order to disseminate it to other circles, whose members, simplifying further and further this simplification of the simple, kept passing it on and on, so that when Marxism became known and powerful on the whole planet all that was left of it was a collection of six or seven slogans, so poorly linked that it can hardly be called an ideology. And precisely because the remnants of Marx no longer form any *logical* system of *ideas*, but only a series of suggestive images and slogans (a smiling worker with a hammer, black, white and yellow men fraternally holding hands, the dove of peace rising to the sky, and so on and so on), we can rightfully talk of a gradual, general, planetary transformation of ideology into imagology.

Imagology! Who first thought up this remarkable neologism? Paul or I? It doesn't matter. What matters is that this word finally lets us put under one roof something that goes by so many names: advertising agencies; political campaign managers; designers who devise the shape of everything from cars to gym equipment; fashion stylists; barbers; show-business stars dictating the norms of physical beauty that all branches of imagology obey.

Of course, imagologues existed long before they created the powerful institutions we know today. Even Hitler had his personal imagologue, who used to stand in front of him and patiently demonstrate the gestures to be made during speeches so as to fascinate the crowds. But if that imagologue, in an interview with the press, had amused the Germans by describing Hitler as incapable of moving his hands, he would not have survived his indiscretion by more than a few hours. Nowadays, however, the imagologue not only does not try to hide his activity, but often even speaks for his politician clients, explains to the public what he taught them to do or not to do, how he told them to behave, what formula they are likely to use and what tie they are likely to wear. We needn't be surprised by this self-confidence: in the last few decades, imagology has gained a historic victory over ideology.

All ideologies have been defeated: in the end their dogmas were unmasked as illusions and people stopped taking them seriously. For example, communists used to believe that in the course of capitalist development the proletariat would gradually grow poorer and poorer, but when it finally became clear that all over Europe workers were driving to work in their own cars, they felt like shouting that reality was deceiving them. Reality was stronger than ideology. And it is in this sense that imagology surpassed it: imagology is stronger than reality, which has anyway long ceased to be what it was for my grandmother, who lived in a Moravian village and still knew everything through her own experience: how bread is baked, how a house is built, how a pig is slaughtered and the meat smoked, what quilts are made of, what the priest and the schoolteacher think about the world; she met the whole village every day and knew how many murders were committed in the country over the last ten years; she had, so to speak, personal control over reality, and nobody could fool her by maintaining that Moravian agriculture was thriving when people at home had nothing to eat. My Paris neighbour spends his time in an office, where he sits for eight hours facing an office colleague, then he sits in his car and drives home, turns on the TV and when the announcer informs him that in the latest public opinion poll the majority of Frenchmen voted their country the safest in Europe (I recently read such a report), he is overjoyed and opens a bottle of champagne without ever learning that three thefts and two murders were committed on his street that very day.

Public opinion polls are the critical instrument of imagology's power, because they enable imagology to live in absolute harmony with the people. The imagologue bombards people with questions: how is the French economy prospering? is there racism in France? is racism good or bad? who is the greatest writer of all time? is Hungary in Europe or in Polynesia? which world politician is the sexiest? And since for contemporary man reality is a continent visited less and less often and besides, justifiably disliked, the findings of polls have become a kind of higher reality, or to put it differently: they have become the truth. Public opinion polls are a parliament in permanent session, whose function it is to create truth, the most democratic truth that has ever existed. Because it will never be at variance with the parliament of truth, the power of imagologues will always live in truth and although I know that everything human is mortal, I cannot imagine anything that could break this power.

I want to add to this comparison of ideology and imagology: ideology was like a set of enormous wheels at the back of the stage, turning and setting in motion wars, revolutions, reforms. The wheels of imagology turn without having any effect upon history. Ideologies fought with one another and each of them was capable of filling a whole epoch with its thinking. Imagology organizes peaceful alternation of its systems in lively seasonal rhythms. In Paul's words: ideology belonged to history, while the reign of imagology begins where history ends.

The word *change*, so dear to our Europe, has been given a new meaning: it no longer means *a new stage of coherent development* (as it was understood by Vico, Hegel or Marx), but a *shift from one side to another*, from front to back, from the back to the left, from the left to the front (as understood by designers dreaming up the fashion for the next season). Imagologues decided that in Agnes' health club all the walls should be covered by enormous mirrors; this was not done because gymnasts needed to observe themselves while exercising, but because on the roulette wheel of imagology mirrors had landed on a lucky number. If at the time I was writing these pages everyone decided that Martin Heidegger was to be considered a bungler and a bastard, it was not because his thought had been surpassed by other philosophers, but because on the roulette wheel of imagology, this time he had landed on an unlucky number, an anti-ideal. Imagologues create systems of ideals and anti-ideals, systems of short duration which are quickly replaced by other systems but which influence our behaviour, our political opinions and aesthetic tastes, the colour of carpets and the selection of books just as in the past we have been ruled by the systems of ideologues.

After these remarks I can return to the beginning of the discussion. The politician is dependent on the journalist. On whom are the journalists dependent? On imagologues. The imagologue is a person of conviction and principle: he demands of the journalist that his newspaper (or TV channel, radio station) reflect the imagological system of a given moment. And this is what imagologues check from time to time when they are trying to decide which newspaper to support. One day they turned their attention to the radio station where Bernard worked as a commentator and where every Saturday Paul broadcast his brief feature 'Rights and the Law'. They promised to obtain many advertising contracts for the station as well as launching a poster campaign all over France; but they insisted on certain conditions, to which the programme director, known as the Bear, was forced to submit: he gradually began to shorten the commentaries, so that the listeners would not be bored by long discussions; he allowed the commentators' five-minute monologues to be interrupted by the questions of another broadcaster, in order to give the impression of conversation; he added many more musical interludes, frequently even inserting background music under the words; and he advised everyone talking into a microphone to put on a relaxed, youthful, carefree air, an air that fills my morning dreams with bliss and turns weather reports into comic operas. Because he considered it important that his subordinates should continue to see him as a powerful Bear, he tried as hard as he could to safeguard the jobs of all his fellow workers. He surrendered on only one point. The imagologues found 'Rights and the Law' so obviously boring that they merely showed their excessively white teeth and refused to discuss it. The Bear promised to cancel the feature and then he became ashamed of his surrender. He was all the more ashamed because Paul was his friend.

The brilliant ally of his own gravediggers

The programme director was called the Bear because that was the only possible name for him: he was stocky, slow, and though he was good-natured everyone knew that his huge paw could pack quite a blow when he got angry. The imagologues who had the temerity to instruct him how to do his work all but drained the last drops of his bearish goodness. He sat in the studio cafeteria, surrounded by a few colleagues, and said: 'Those ad-agency swindlers are like Martians. They don't behave like normal people. When they say the most unpleasant things to your face, they have a gleam in their eyes. Their vocabulary is limited to fewer than fifty words, and their sentences mustn't contain more than four words each. Their speech is a combination of three technical terms I don't understand and of one or two breath-takingly banal ideas. These people aren't ashamed of being themselves and haven't the slightest inferiority complex. And that is precisely the proof of their power.'

At this point Paul appeared in the cafeteria. When they saw him, everyone became embarrassed, all the more so because Paul seemed to be in an excellent mood. He picked up a cup of coffee and joined the others at the table.

The Bear felt uneasy in Paul's presence. He was ashamed of having thrown him to the wolves and of not having the courage now to tell him to his face. He was seized by a new wave of hatred for the imagologues, and said: 'I'd be willing, when it comes to it, to give in to those cretins and change the weather reports into a dialogue between clowns, the trouble is that right after that Bernard might talk of a plane crash in which a hundred passengers died. I may be willing to sacrifice my life to amuse my fellow Frenchmen, but news reports are no laughing matter.'

They all looked as if they agreed, except for Paul. He laughed the laugh of a joyous provocateur, and said: 'My dear Bear! The imagologues are right! You confuse news with school teaching!'

The Bear recalled that while Paul's commentaries were sometimes quite witty, they were generally too complex and also full of unusual words that the whole staff would afterwards secretly look up in the dictionary. But he didn't feel like mentioning this now, and said with great dignity: 'I always had a high opinion of journalism and I don't want to lose it.'

Paul said: 'Listening to a news broadcast is like smoking a cigarette and crushing the butt in the ashtray.'

'That's just what I find so hard to accept,' said the Bear.

'But you are an inveterate smoker! So why do you mind that news reports are like cigarettes?' Paul laughed. 'Cigarettes are bad for your health, whereas the news does you no harm and is even a pleasant diversion before the start of a long day.'

'The war between Iran and Iraq is diverting?' asked the Bear and his compassion for Paul was slowly becoming mixed with irritation. 'Today's disasters, that railway accident, you find them amusing?'

'You make a common error, namely considering death a tragedy,' said Paul, and it was evident that he had got up that day in excellent form.

'I must admit,' the Bear said in an icy voice, 'that I have indeed always considered death a tragedy.'

'And you were wrong,' said Paul. 'A railway accident is horrible for somebody who was on the train or who had a son there. But in news reports death means exactly the same thing as in the novels of Agatha Christie, who incidentally was the greatest magician of all time because she knew how to turn murder into amusement, and not just one murder but dozens of murders, hundreds of murders, an assembly-line of murders performed for our pleasure in the extermination camp of her novels. Auschwitz is forgotten, but from the crematorium of Agatha's novels the smoke is forever rising into the sky and only a very naïve person could maintain that it is the smoke of tragedy.'

The Bear remembered that it was precisely with this kind of paradox that Paul had long been influencing his colleagues in the newsroom. And so it was that when the staff came under the critical scrutiny of the imagologues they were of little help to their chief, the Bear, for deep in their hearts they all considered his attitude *passé*. The Bear was ashamed of having submitted in the end, yet he knew he had no other choice. Such forced compromises with the spirit of the times, though quite banal, are actually inevitable unless we are ready to ask everyone who doesn't like our century to join in a general strike. In Paul's case, however, it was impossible to speak of a forced compromise. He was eager to put his wit and his intellect at the service of his century quite voluntarily, and, to the Bear's taste, much too fervently. That's why he answered in a voice still icier: 'I, too, read Agatha Christie! When I am tired, when I feel like turning into a child for a while. But if all our lives turn into child's play, then one day the world will die to the sound of childish prattle and laughter.'

Paul said: 'I'd prefer to die to the sound of childish laughter than to the sound of Chopin's *Funeral March*. And let me tell you this: all the evil in the world is in that *Funeral March*, which is a glorification of death. If there were fewer funeral marches there might perhaps be fewer deaths. Understand what I'm trying to say: respect for tragedy is much more dangerous than the thoughtlessness of childish prattle. Do you realize what is the eternal precondition of tragedy? The existence of ideals which are considered more valuable than human life. And what is the precondition of wars? The same thing. They drive you to your death because presumably there is something greater than your life. War can only exist in a world of tragedy; from the beginning of history man has known only a tragic world and has not been capable of stepping out of it. The age of tragedy can be ended only by the revolt of frivolity. Nowadays, people no longer know Beethoven's Ninth from concerts but from four lines of the *Hymn to Joy* which they hear every day in the ad for Bella perfume. That doesn't shock me. Tragedy will be driven from the world like a ludicrous old actress clutching her heart and declaiming in a hoarse voice. Frivolity is a radical diet for weight-reduction. Things will lose ninety per cent of their meaning and will become light. In such a weightless environment fanaticism will disappear. War will become impossible.'

'I am glad that you have finally found a way to eliminate war,' said the Bear.

'Can you imagine today's French youth rushing fervently to fight for their country? My dear Bear, in Europe war has become unthinkable. Not politically. Anthropologically unthinkable. European people are no longer capable of waging war.'

Don't tell me that two men who deeply disagree with each other can still like each other; that's a fairy tale. Perhaps they would like each other if they kept their opinions to themselves or if they only discussed them in a joking way and thus played down their significance (this, indeed, was the way Paul and the Bear had always spoken to each other until now). But once a quarrel breaks out, it's too late. Not because they believe so firmly in the opinions they defend, but because they can't stand not to be right. Look at those two. After all, their dispute won't change anything, it will lead to no decision, it will not influence the course of events in the slightest, it is quite sterile and unnecessary, confined to the cafeteria and its stale air, soon gone when the cleaning lady opens the windows. And yet, observe the rapt attention of the small audience round the table! Everyone is quiet, listening intently, they even forget to sip their coffee. The two rivals now care only about one thing: which of them will be recognized by the opinion of this small audience as the possessor of the truth, for to be proved wrong means for each of them the same thing as losing his honour. Or losing a piece of his own self. The opinion they advocate is itself not all that important to them. But because once they have made this opinion an attribute of their self, attacking it is like stabbing a part of their body.

Somewhere in the depths of his soul the Bear felt satisfaction that Paul would no longer be presenting his sophisticated commentaries; his voice, full of bearish pride, was getting ever quieter and icier. Paul, on the other hand, kept talking louder and louder, and his ideas were getting more and more exaggerated and provocative. He said: 'High culture is nothing but a child of that European perversion called history, the obsession we have with going forward, with considering the sequence of generations a relay race in which everyone surpasses his predecessor, only to be surpassed by his successor. Without this relay race called history there would be no European art and what characterizes it: a longing for originality, a longing for change. Robespierre, Napoleon, Beethoven, Stalin, Picasso, they're all runners in the relay race, they all belong in the same stadium.'

'Beethoven and Stalin belong together?' asked the Bear with icy irony.

'Of course, no matter how much that may shock you. War and culture, those are the two poles of Europe, her heaven and hell, her glory and shame, and they cannot be separated from one another. When one comes to an end, the other will end also and one cannot end without the other. The fact that no war has broken out in Europe for fifty years is connected in some mysterious way with the fact that for fifty years no new Picasso has appeared either.'

'Let me tell you something, Paul,' the Bear said in a slow voice, as if he were lifting his heavy paw for a shattering blow: 'If high culture is coming to an end, it is also the end of you and your paradoxical ideas, because paradox as such belongs to high culture and not to childish prattle. You remind me of the young men who supported the Nazis or communists not out of cowardice or out of opportunism but out of an excess of intelligence. For nothing requires a greater effort of thought than arguments to justify the rule of non-thought. I experienced it with my own eyes and ears after the war, when intellectuals and artists rushed like a herd of cattle into the Communist Party, which soon proceeded to liquidate them systematically and with great pleasure. You are doing the same. You are the brilliant ally of your own grave-diggers.'

A compleat ass

Bernard's familiar voice sounded from the transistor radio lying by their heads; he was conversing with an actor whose film was about to have its première. The actor raised his voice and woke them from their light sleep:

'I came to speak to you about films and not about my son.'

'Don't worry, we'll get to films, too,' Bernard's voice was saying. 'But first there are some questions about recent events. I've heard it said that you yourself played a role in your son's affair.'

'When you invited me to come here, you explicitly stated that you wanted to talk to me about films. So let's discuss films and not my private life.'

'You are a public figure and I'm asking you about things that interest the public. I'm only doing my job as a journalist.'

'I am ready to answer your questions dealing with films.'

'As you wish. But our listeners will wonder why you refused to answer.'

Agnes got out of bed. A quarter of an hour after she left for work Paul got up, too, dressed and went downstairs to collect his mail. One letter was from the Bear. He used many sentences, mixing excuses with a bitter humour, to inform Paul of what we already know: that the station no longer required his services.

He re-read the letter four times. Then with a wave of his arm he brushed it aside and left for the office. But he couldn't get anything done, couldn't keep his mind on anything except the letter. Was it such a blow to him? From a practical viewpoint, not at all. But it hurt all the same. He spent his whole life trying to get away from the company of lawyers: he was happy to be able to conduct a seminar at the university and he was happy to do radio broadcasts. Not that he didn't enjoy the practice of law; on the contrary, he was fond of his clients, he tried to understand their crime and to give it a meaning. 'I am not a lawyer, I am the poet of the defence!' he would say jokingly; he deliberately took the side of people finding themselves outside the law, and he considered himself (not without considerable vanity) a traitor, a fifth columnist, a humanist guerrilla fighter in a world of inhuman laws accumulated in thick tomes which he would take in his hands with the distaste of a blasé expert. He put great emphasis on remaining in touch with people outside the courthouse, with students, literary personalities and journalists, so as to preserve the certainty (not merely the illusion) of belonging among them. He clung to them, and now found it painful that the Bear's letter was driving him back to the office and the courtroom.

But something else wounded him, too. When the previous day the Bear had called him the ally of his own gravediggers, he considered it just an elegant taunt without any concrete basis. The word 'gravediggers' did not suggest anything to him. At that point he had known nothing about his gravediggers. But today, after receiving the Bear's letter, it suddenly became clear that gravediggers do exist, that they had him targeted, and were waiting for him.

He suddenly realized, too, that people saw him differently from how he saw himself or from how he thought he was seen by others. He was the only one among all his colleagues at the station who was forced to leave, even though (and he had no doubt about it) the Bear had defended him as well as he could. What was it about him that bothered the advertising men? For that matter, it would be naïve of him to think that it was only they who found him unacceptable. Others must have found him unacceptable, too. Without his realizing it in the slightest, something must have happened to his image. Something must have happened and he didn't know what it was, and he'd never know. Because that's how things are, and this goes for everyone: we will never find out why we irritate people, what bothers people about us, what they like about us, what they find ridiculous; for us our own image is our greatest mystery.

Paul knew that he would not be able to think of anything else all day and so he picked up the phone and invited Bernard to a restaurant for lunch.

They sat down facing each other and Paul was bursting to bring up the letter from the Bear, but because he had been well brought up he said first of all: 'I listened to you this morning. You cornered that actor as if he were a rabbit.'

'I know,' said Bernard. 'Maybe I overdid it. But I was in an awful mood. Yesterday I had a visit I'll never forget. A stranger came to see me, a man taller than me by a head, with an enormous belly. He introduced himself, smiled in an alarmingly affable manner and told me: "I have the honour of presenting you with this diploma." Then he handed me a big cardboard tube and insisted that I open it in his presence. It contained a diploma. In colour. In beautiful script. I read: "Bernard Bertrand is hereby declared a Compleat Ass." '

'What?' Paul burst out laughing, but he controlled himself as soon as he saw that Bernard's serious features didn't betray the slightest hint of amusement.

'Yes,' Bernard repeated in a mournful voice: 'I was declared a compleat ass.'

'By whom? Was there the name of an organization?'

'No. There was only an illegible signature.'

Bernard described the whole incident a few more times and then added: 'At first I couldn't believe my eyes. I had the feeling I was the victim of an attack, I wanted to shout and to call the police. But then I realized there was absolutely nothing I could do. The fellow smiled and reached out his hand: "Allow me to

140

congratulate you,'' he smiled, and I was so confused that I shook his hand.'

'You shook his hand? You really thanked him?' said Paul, trying hard to keep from laughing.

'When I realized that I couldn't have the man arrested, I wanted to show my self-control and I behaved as if everything happening were quite normal and had not touched me in the least.'

'That's unavoidable,' said Paul. 'When a person is declared an ass, he begins to act like an ass.'

'Unfortunately, that is so.'

'And you have no idea who this man was? He introduced himself, after all!'

'I was so flustered that I forgot the name right away.'

Paul couldn't help laughing again.

'Yes, I know, you'll say it was all a joke, and of course you're right, it was a joke,' said Bernard, 'but I can't help it. I've been thinking about it ever since, and I can't think about anything else.'

Paul stopped laughing, because he realized that Bernard was speaking the truth: he had undoubtedly thought of nothing else since yesterday. How would Paul react if he were to receive such a diploma? The same way as Bernard. If you're declared a compleat ass, it means that at least one person sees you as an ass and wants you to know it. That in itself is very unpleasant. And it is quite possible that it's not a question of just one person but that the diploma represents the initiative of dozens of people. And it is also possible that those people are preparing something else, perhaps sending a release to the newspaper, and in tomorrow's *Le Monde*, in the section devoted to funerals, weddings and honours, there may be an announcement that Bernard has been declared a compleat ass.

Then Bernard confided (and Paul didn't know whether to laugh or to cry over him) that the same day the anonymous man had given him the diploma he had proceeded to show it to everybody he met. He didn't want to remain alone in his shame, so he tried to involve others in it and so he explained to everybody that the attack was not meant only for him personally: 'If it had been designated only for me, they would have brought it to my house, to my home address. But they brought it to the station! It is an attack on me as a journalist! An attack on us all!'

Paul cut the meat on his plate, sipped his wine and said to himself: here sit two friends; one has been called a compleat ass, the other the brilliant ally of his gravediggers. He realized (while his sympathy for his younger friend grew even more poignant), that in his heart he would never again think of him as Bernard but only as compleat ass and nothing else, not because of malice but because nobody is capable of resisting such a beautiful name; nor would any of those to whom Bernard, in his unwise haste, showed the diploma ever think of him as anything else.

And it also occurred to him how decent it was of the Bear to call him the brilliant ally of his gravediggers only during their table-talk. If he had inscribed this title on a diploma, things would be a lot worse. And so Bernard's grief almost made him forget his own troubles and when Bernard said: 'Anyway, you too have had an unpleasant experience,' Paul merely waved it aside: 'It's just an episode,' and Bernard agreed: 'I thought right away that it couldn't really hurt you. You can do a thousand other things, and a lot better ones to boot!'

When Bernard walked with him to the car, Paul said with sadness: 'The Bear is wrong and the imagologues are right. A person is nothing but his image. Philosophers can tell us that it doesn't matter what the world thinks of us, that nothing matters but what we really are. But philosophers don't understand anything. As long as we live with other people, we are only what other people consider us to be. Thinking about how others see us and trying to make our image as attractive as possible is considered a kind of dissembling or cheating. But does there exist another kind of direct contract between my self and their selves except through the mediation of the eyes? Can we possibly imagine love, without anxiously following our image in the mind of the beloved? When we are no longer interested in how we are seen by the person we love, it means we no longer love.'

'That's true,' Bernard said mournfully.

'It's naïve to believe that our image is only an illusion that conceals our selves, as the one true essence independent of the eyes of the world. The imagologues have revealed with cynical radicalism that the reverse is true: our self is a mere illusion, ungraspable, indescribable, misty, while the only reality, all too easily graspable and describable, is our image in the eyes of others. And the worst thing about it is that you are not its master. First you try to paint it yourself, then you want at least to influence and control it, but in vain: a single malicious phrase is enough to change you for ever into a depressingly simple caricature.'

They stopped at the car and Paul glanced at Bernard's face, even more anxious and pale. Not long ago he had had the best of intentions to cheer up his friend and now he saw that his words had only wounded him. He regretted it: he had allowed himself to launch into his reflections only because he was thinking too much about himself, about his own situation, rather than about Bernard. But now it couldn't be helped.

They took leave of each other and Bernard said, with a hesitancy that Paul found moving: 'Only, I beg you, don't mention it to Laura. Don't even mention it to Agnes.'

Paul firmly shook his friend's hand: 'Trust me.'

He returned to the office and started to work. His meeting with Bernard had had a peculiarly soothing effect, and he felt a lot better than he had earlier in the day. Towards evening he went home. He told Agnes about the letter and immediately stressed that the whole thing meant nothing to him. He tried to say it with a laugh, but Agnes noticed that between the words and the laughter Paul was coughing. She knew that cough. He knew how to control himself whenever something unpleasant happened to him, but he was betrayed by that short, embarrassed cough, of which he was unaware.

'They needed to make the broadcast more amusing and youthful,' said Agnes. Her words were meant ironically, directed against those who had cancelled Paul's programme. Then she stroked his hair. But she shouldn't have done all that. In her eyes, Paul saw his own image: the image of a humiliated man, who people have decided is no longer young or amusing.

The cat

Each of us longs to transgress erotic conventions, erotic taboos, to enter with rapture into the kingdom of the Forbidden. And each of us has so little courage . . . Loving an older woman or a younger man can be recommended as the easiest, most readily available means of tasting the Forbidden. For the first time in her life, Laura had a man younger than herself, for the first time Bernard had a woman older than himself, and both of them experienced it as an exciting mutual sin.

When Laura told Paul some time ago that when she was by Bernard's side she felt ten years younger, it was the truth: she was filled with a wave of new energy. But that didn't make her feel younger than him! On the contrary, she savoured with a previously unknown pleasure having a younger lover who considered himself weaker than she and was nervous because he believed that his experienced lover would compare him with his predecessors. Eroticism is like a dance: one always leads the other. For the first time in her life, Laura was leading a man and this was just as intoxicating to her as being led was to Bernard.

An older woman gives a younger man, above all, the assurance that their love is far removed from the traps of marriage, because surely nobody could seriously expect that a young man, with the prospect of a successful life stretching far into the distance, would marry a woman older by eight years. In that respect, Bernard regarded Laura very much as Paul regarded the lady he came to exalt as the jewel of his life: he supposed that his lover had reckoned on the necessity of one day voluntarily ceding her place to a younger woman whom Bernard would be able to introduce to his parents without embarrassment. His faith in her maternal wisdom even allowed him to dream that she would serve as a witness at his wedding and completely conceal from his bride that she had once been (and perhaps would continue to be – why not?) his lover.

Their relationship continued happily for two years. Then Bernard was declared a compleat ass and became taciturn. Laura knew nothing about the diploma (Paul had kept his word) and because she was not accustomed to ask him about his work, she knew nothing about any of the other difficulties he had encountered at the radio station (misfortunes, as is well known, seldom come in single spies), and so she interpreted his silence as a sign that he no longer loved her. She noticed on several occasions that he wasn't listening to her and she was certain that at these moments his mind must have been on some other woman. Alas, in love it takes so little to make a person desperate!

One day when he came to see her, he was once again plunged in dark thoughts. She went to the next room to change and he remained in the living room alone with the Siamese cat. He wasn't especially fond of the cat but he knew that it meant a great deal to Laura. He sat down in an armchair, pondered his dark thoughts and mechanically stretched out his hand to the animal in the belief that it was his duty to stroke it. But the cat spat and bit his hand. The bite immediately became linked to the chain of misfortunes which had been following and humiliating him all week, so a violent fit of fury seized hold of him, he leaped out of the armchair and took a swipe at the cat. The cat streaked into a corner and arched its back, hissing horribly.

He turned round and saw Laura. She was standing in the doorway and it was obvious that she had been watching the whole scene. She said: 'No, no, you mustn't punish her. She was completely in the right.'

He looked at her, surprised. The cat's bite hurt and he expected his lover, if not to take his part against the animal, at the very

146

least to show an elementary sense of justice. He had a strong desire to walk over to the cat and give it such an enormous kick that it would splatter against the living room ceiling. It was only with the greatest effort that he managed to control himself.

Laura added, emphasizing each word: 'She demands that whoever strokes her really concentrates on it. I, too, resent it when someone is with me but his mind is somewhere else.'

When she had watched Bernard stroke the cat and seen the cat's hostile reaction to his detached absent-mindedness, she had felt a strong sense of solidarity with the animal: for the past several weeks Bernard had been treating her the same way: he would stroke her and think about something else; he would pretend he was with her but she knew very well he wasn't listening to what she was saying.

The cat biting Bernard made her feel as if her other, symbolic, mystical self, which is how she thought of the animal, was trying to encourage her, to show her what to do, to serve as an example. There are times when it is necessary to show one's claws, she told herself, and she decided that in the course of the intimate supper they were about to have at the restaurant, she would finally find the courage for a decisive act.

I will jump ahead and say it outright: it is hard to imagine anything more foolish than her decision. The action she planned was completely contrary to all her interests. For I must stress that during those two years of their relationship, Bernard had been completely happy with her, perhaps happier than Laura herself could possibly imagine. She represented an escape from the kind of life which from childhood on had been prepared for him by his father, the euphonious Bertrand Bertrand. At last he could live freely, according to his desires, with a secret place where none of his family would be able to intrude, a place where he could live quite differently: he adored Laura's bohemian way of life, her piano which she played now and again, the concerts to which she

147

took him, her moods and her eccentricities. With her, he found himself far from the rich, boring people of his father's circle. Their happiness, of course, depended on one condition: they had to remain unmarried. If they ever became man and wife everything would change at once: their union would suddenly be accessible to all kinds of meddling by his family; their love would lose not only its charm but its very meaning. And Laura would lose all the power she had had over Bernard.

How then was it possible that she could come to such a silly decision, contrary to all her interests? Did she know her man so poorly? Did she understand him so little?

Yes, no matter how strange it may seem, she didn't know him and didn't understand him. She was even proud that nothing about Bernard interested her but his love. She never asked about his father. She knew nothing about his family. Whenever he tried to talk about it she was conspicuously bored, and declared that rather than wasting time on such things she preferred to devote herself to Bernard himself. Still stranger, even in the dark weeks following the diploma incident, when he became taciturn and apologized for having so many worries, she would always say: 'Yes, I know what it's like to have worries,' but she never asked him the simplest of all imaginable questions: 'What kind of worries? Just exactly what is going on? Tell me what's bothering you!'

Strange: she was up to her ears in love with him and yet she had no interest in him. I could even say: she was up to her ears in love with him and *precisely for that reason* she had no interest in him. If we were to take her to task for her lack of interest and accuse her of not knowing her beloved, she wouldn't understand us. For Laura was ignorant of what it means *to know* somebody. In that respect she was like a virgin who thinks that she will have a baby if she kisses her boyfriend often enough! Recently she had been thinking about Bernard almost constantly. She thought of his body, his face, she had the feeling that she was always with him, that she was permeated by him. She was therefore certain that she knew him by heart and that nobody had ever known him as well as she. The emotion of love gives all of us a misleading illusion of knowing the other.

After this explanation, perhaps we can now believe that she told him over dessert (I might point out, as an excuse, that they had drunk a bottle of wine and two brandies, but I am certain she would have said it even if she had been quite sober): 'Bernard, marry me!'

The gesture of protest against a violation of human rights

Brigitte left her German lesson firmly determined to end her study of the language. First of all, she herself found no use for Goethe's tongue (the lessons had been forced on her by her mother), and in addition she felt deeply at odds with German. The language irritated her with its lack of logic. Today it really made her angry: the preposition *ohne* (without) takes the accusative case, the preposition *mit* (with) takes the dative. Why? After all, the two prepositions signify the positive and negative aspect of *the same* relationship, and so they should be linked to the same case. She raised the objection with her teacher, a young German, who became embarrassed and immediately felt guilty. He was a likeable, sensitive man who found it painful to belong to a nation once ruled by Hitler. Ready to blame his country for every possible fault, he believed at once that there was no acceptable reason why the prepositions *mit* and *ohne* should be linked to two different cases.

'It isn't logical, I know, but through the centuries this became the established usage,' he said, as if begging the young French-woman to take pity on a language cursed by history.

'I am glad that you admit it. It isn't logical. But a language *must* be logical,' Brigitte said.

The young German agreed: 'Unfortunately, we lack a Descartes. That's an unforgivable gap in our history. German lacks a tradition of reason and clarity, it's full of metaphysical mist and Wagnerian music and we all know who was the greatest admirer of Wagner: Hitler!'

Brigitte was interested in neither Wagner nor Hitler, and

pursued her own line of thought: 'A language which is not logical can be learned by a child, because a child doesn't think. But it cannot be learned by an adult. That's why as far as I am concerned, German is not a world language.'

'You are absolutely right,' said the German, and he added softly: 'Now you see the absurdity of the German desire for world domination.'

Well satisfied with herself, Brigitte got into her car and drove to Fauchon's to buy a bottle of wine. She wanted to park but found it impossible: rows of cars parked bumper to bumper lined the pavements for a radius of half a mile; after circling round and round for fifteen minutes, she was overcome by indignant astonishment at the total lack of space; she drove the car on to the pavement, got out and set out for the store. She was still quite far away when she noticed that something peculiar was going on. As she came closer she understood what was happening:

Fauchon, the famous food store, where everything was ten times more expensive than anywhere else with the result that it was patronized only by people who get more pleasure out of paying than out of eating, was overrun by about a hundred poorly dressed, unemployed people. They had surrounded the store and were milling inside. It was a strange protest: the unemployed did not come to break anything or to threaten anyone or to shout slogans; they just wanted to embarrass the rich, and by their mere presence to spoil their appetite for wine and caviar. And indeed, the sales staff as well as the shoppers smiled uneasily and it had become impossible to transact any business.

Brigitte pushed her way inside. She did not find the unemployed unpleasant nor did she have anything at all against the ladies in fur coats. She asked in a loud voice for a bottle of Bordeaux. Her determination surprised the sales woman who suddenly realized that the presence of the peaceable unemployed should not prevent her from serving this young customer. Brigitte paid for her bottle and returned to the car, where two policemen were waiting and asked her to pay a parking fine.

She started to abuse them and when they maintained that the car was illegally parked and was blocking the pavement, she pointed to the rows of cars squeezed tightly one behind the other: 'Can you tell me where I was supposed to park? If people are permitted to buy cars, they should also be guaranteed a place to put them, right? You must be logical!' she shouted at them.

I tell this story only for the sake of this detail: at the moment when she was shouting at the policemen, Brigitte recalled the unemployed demonstrators in Fauchon's and felt a strong surge of sympathy for them: she felt united with them in a common fight. That gave her courage and she raised her voice; the policemen (hesitant, just like the women in fur coats under the gaze of the unemployed) kept repeating in an unconvincing and foolish manner words such as forbidden, prohibited, discipline, order, and in the end let her off without a fine.

In the course of the dispute Brigitte kept rapidly shaking her head from left to right and right to left, at the same time lifting her shoulders and eyebrows. When she related the episode at home to her father, she kept making the same movements. We have encountered this gesture before: it expresses indignant astonishment at the fact that someone wants to deny us our most self-evident rights. Let us therefore call this *the gesture of protest against a violation of human rights*.

The concept of human rights goes back some two hundred years, but it reached its greatest glory in the second half of the 1970s. Alexander Solzhenitsyn had just been exiled from his country and his striking figure, adorned with a beard and hand-cuffs, hypnotized Western intellectuals sick with a longing for the great destiny that had been denied them. It was only thanks to him that they started to believe, after a fifty-year delay, that in communist Russia there were concentration camps; even progressive people were now ready to admit that imprisoning someone for his opinions was not just. And they found an excellent justification for their new attitude: Russian communists violated human rights, in spite of the fact that these rights had been gloriously proclaimed by the French Revolution itself!

And so, thanks to Solzhenitsyn, human rights once again found their place in the vocabulary of our times; I don't know a single politician who doesn't mention ten times a day 'the fight for human rights' or 'violations of human rights'. But because people in the West are not threatened by concentration camps and are free to say and write what they want, the more the fight for human rights gains in popularity the more it loses any concrete content, becoming a kind of universal stance of everyone towards everything, a kind of energy that turns all human desires into rights. The world has become man's right and everything in it has become a right: the desire for love the right to love, the desire for rest the right to rest, the desire for friendship the right to friendship, the desire to exceed the speed limit the right to exceed the speed limit, the desire for happiness the right to happiness, the desire to publish a book the right to publish a book, the desire to shout in the street in the middle of the night the right to shout in the street. The unemployed have the right to occupy an expensive food store, the women in fur coats have the right to buy caviar, Brigitte has the right to park on the pavement and everybody, the unemployed, the women in fur coats as well as Brigitte, belongs to the same army of fighters for human rights.

Paul sat in his armchair facing Brigitte, and lovingly watched her head, which was vigorously shaking to and fro in a quick tempo. He knew that his daughter liked him and that was more important to him than being liked by Agnes. His daughter's admiring eyes gave him something that Agnes was unable to give: they proved to him that he had not become estranged from youth, that he still belonged among the young. Hardly two hours had passed since Agnes, moved by his embarrassed coughing, had stroked his hair. How much dearer to him than that degrading caress were the motions of his daughter's head! Her presence energized him like a generator from which he drew strength.

To be absolutely modern

Ah, my dear Paul! He wanted to provoke and torment the Bear and put an X after history, after Beethoven and Picasso . . . He merges in my mind with the figure of Jaromil from a novel that I finished exactly twenty years ago, which, in a forthcoming chapter of this book, I shall leave for Professor Avenarius to find in a bistro on the Boulevard Montparnasse.

We are in Prague, the year is 1948, and eighteen-year-old Jaromil is madly in love with modern poetry, with Breton, Eluard, Desnos, Nazval, and following their example becomes a votary of Rimbaud's dictum from *A Season in Hell*: 'It is necessary to be absolutely modern.' However, what turned out to be absolutely modern in the Prague of 1948 was the socialist revolution, which promptly and brutally rejected the modern art Jaromil loved madly. And then my hero, along with some of his friends (just as madly in love with modern art) sarcastically renounced everything he loved (truly loved, with all his heart), because he did not wish to betray the great commandment 'to be absolutely modern'. His renunciation was full of the rage and passion of a virginal youth who longs to break into adulthood through some brutal act. Seeing him stubbornly renouncing everything dearest to him, everything he had lived for and would have loved to go on living for, seeing him renouncing Cubism and Surrealism, Picasso and Dali, Breton and Rimbaud, renouncing them in the name of Lenin and the Red Army (who at that moment formed the pinnacle of any imaginable modernity), his friends were dismayed; at first they felt amazement, then revulsion and finally something close to horror. The sight of his virginal youth ready to adapt to whatever proclaimed itself as modern, and to adapt not through cowardice (for the sake of personal gain or career), but courageously, as one painfully sacrificing what he loved, yes, this sight revealed a horror (a portent of the horror to come, the horror of persecution and imprisonment). It is possible that some of those watching him at the time thought to themselves: 'Jaromil is the ally of his gravediggers.'

Of course, Paul and Jaromil are not at all alike. The only link between them is their passionate conviction that 'it is necessary to be absolutely modern'. 'Absolutely modern' is a concept that has no fixed, clearly defined content. Rimbaud, in 1872, hardly imagined these words to mean millions of busts of Lenin and Stalin, and still less did he imagine promotional films, colour photos in magazines or the manic faces of rock singers. But that matters very little, because to be *absolutely* modern means: never to question the content of modernity and to serve it as one serves the absolute, that is, without hesitation.

Paul knew as well as Jaromil that modernity is different tomorrow from what it is today and that for the sake of the *eternal imperative* of modernity one has to be ready to betray its *changeable content*, to betray Rimbaud's verse for the sake of his credo. In 1968, using terminology still more radical than that used by Jaromil in 1948 in Prague, Paris students rejected the world as it is, the world of superficiality, comfort, business, advertising, stupid mass culture drumming its melodramas into people's heads, the world of conventions, the world of Fathers. During that period Paul spent several nights on the barricades and spoke with the same decisive voice as had Jaromil twenty years earlier; he refused to be swayed by anything, and supported by the strong arm of the student revolt he strode out of his father's world so that at the age of thirty or thirty-five he would at last become an adult.

But time passed, his daughter grew up and she felt very comfortable in the world as it is, in the world of television, rock, publicity, mass culture and its melodramas, the world of singers, cars, fashions, fancy food stores, and elegant industrialists turning into TV stars. Paul was capable of stubbornly defending his opinions against judges, policemen, commissioners and statesmen, but he was unable to defend them against his daughter, who sat in his lap and was in no hurry to leave her father's world and become an adult. On the contrary, she wanted to stay at home as long as possible with her tolerant daddy, who allowed her (with an almost tender indulgence) to spend Saturday nights shut away in her room with her boyfriend.

What does it mean to be absolutely modern when a person is no longer young and his daughter is quite different from the way he used to be in his youth? Paul easily found an answer: to be absolutely modern means in such a case to identify absolutely with one's daughter.

I imagine Paul, sitting at supper with Agnes and Brigitte. Brigitte is sitting sideways, eating, and watching TV. All three are silent because the volume is turned up. Paul's head is still ringing with the Bear's unhappy remark that he is the ally of his own gravediggers. He is jolted out of his thoughts by his daughter's laughter: in a TV commercial, a naked baby, hardly a year old, gets up from its pot, dragging behind it a strip of white toilet-paper like a gorgeous bridal veil. At that moment Paul remembers that he recently found out to his surprise that Brigitte had never read a single poem by Rimbaud. In view of how much he had loved Rimbaud at her age, he could rightfully regard her as his gravedigger.

It is rather melancholy for Paul to see his daughter laughing heartily at the nonsense on television and to know that she has never read his beloved poet. But then Paul asks himself: why did he actually love Rimbaud so much? how did he get to feel that way? did it start by his being enchanted with the poetry? No. In those days Rimbaud coalesced his thoughts into a single

157

revolutionary amalgam with Trotsky, Breton, the Surrealists, Mao, and Castro. The first thing of Rimbaud's that struck him was his slogan, mouthed by everybody: *changer la vie*. (As if such a banal formula required a poetic genius . . .) Yes, it's true that it was then he read Rimbaud's verse, learned some of it by heart and was fond of it. But he never read all of his poems and was fond only of those his friends talked about, while they in turn talked about them only because they had been recommended by their friends. Rimbaud was therefore not his aesthetic love, and perhaps he had never had an aesthetic love. He enrolled with Rimbaud, the way a person enrols under a flag, with a political party, or with a football team. What then did Rimbaud's poems really give Paul? Only the sense of pride that he belonged among those who loved Rimbaud's poetry.

His mind kept returning to his recent discussion with the Bear: yes, he had exaggerated, he had allowed himself to be carried away by paradox, he had provoked the Bear and everyone else, but after all, wasn't everything he'd said the truth? Isn't what the Bear so respectfully calls 'culture' only a self-delusion of ours, something undoubtedly beautiful and valuable but actually with less meaning for us than we are ready to admit?

A few days ago he had exposed Brigitte to the same ideas that had shocked the Bear, and he had tried to use the same words. He had wanted to see how she would react. Not only was she not the least bit offended by his provocative formulations, but she was willing to go a lot further. This was very important to Paul, because he had doted on his daughter more and more in recent years, and whenever he was puzzled about something he sought her opinion. At first he did so for educational reasons, to make her think about important matters, but soon the roles imperceptibly reversed themselves: he no longer resembled a teacher stimulating a shy pupil with his questions, but an uncertain man come to consult a clairvoyant.

We do not demand of a clairvoyant that she be wise (Paul did not have an exaggerated estimation of his daughter's talents or education), but that she be linked by invisible connections with some reservoir of wisdom existing outside her. When he heard Brigitte expound her views, he did not ascribe them to her personal originality but to the great collective wisdom of youth that spoke through her mouth, and he therefore accepted them with ever greater confidence.

Agnes rose from the table, collected the dishes and carried them to the kitchen, Brigitte turned round to face the television and Paul remained at the table, abandoned. He thought of the party game which his parents used to play: ten people would walk in a circle round ten chairs, and at a given signal all of them had to sit down. Every chair had an inscription. And now, the one left for him was inscribed: *the brilliant ally of his gravediggers*. And he knows that the game is over and that he will remain in that chair for ever.

What was to be done? Nothing. Anyhow, why shouldn't a person be the ally of his gravediggers? Should he challenge them to a fight? With the result that the gravediggers would spit on his coffin?

He heard Brigitte's laughter again and at that moment a new definition occurred to him, the most paradoxical, the most radical of all. He liked it so much that he almost forgot his sorrow. This was the new definition: to be absolutely modern means to be the ally of one's gravediggers.

To be a victim of one's fame

Telling Bernard: 'Marry me!' would have been a blunder in any case, but doing so after he had been declared a compleat ass was a blunder as big as Mont Blanc. For we must take into account something that at first may seem hard to believe, but which is necessary to understand Bernard: other than a childhood bout with scarlet fever he had never known any illness; other than the death of his father's hunting dog he had never encountered death; and other than a few bad marks in school he had never known failure; he lived in the unquestioned conviction that he had been blessed with good fortune and that everybody had only the most favourable opinion of him. Being declared an ass was the first big shock of his life.

It occurred in the midst of a strange series of coincidences. At about the same time, the imagologues were launching a campaign on behalf of his radio station and huge posters of the editorial team were appearing all over France: they were pictured in white shirts with rolled-up sleeves, standing against a sky-blue background, and their mouths were open: they were laughing. At first, he walked the streets of Paris filled with pride. But after a week or two of immaculate fame the paunchy giant had paid him a call and with a smile had handed him a cardboard tube containing the diploma. If this had happened before his huge photograph was exposed to the whole world, he might have taken it somewhat better. But the fame of the photograph lent the shame of the diploma a certain resonance: it was multiplied.

It would be one thing if *Le Monde* were to publish an announcement that someone named Bernard Bertrand had been declared a compleat ass; but if such an announcement concerned someone whose picture was on every street corner, it would be an entirely different matter. Fame adds a hundred-fold echo to everything that happens to us. And it is uncomfortable to walk the world with an echo. Bernard soon realized his vulnerability and told himself that fame was exactly what he had never cared for in the least. Certainly, he wanted success, but success and fame are two quite different things. Fame means that you are known by many people whom you yourself do not know and who make a claim upon you, want to know all about you and act as if they owned you. Actors, singers, politicians evidently feel a kind of delight in being able to give themselves to others in this way. But this was a delight for which Bernard had no desire. When he recently interviewed the actor whose son was mixed up in some painful affair, he enjoyed noticing how fame had become the actor's Achilles' heel, a weakness, a tail that Bernard could tug, twist, tie into knots. Bernard had always longed to be the one who asked questions, not the one who has to answer. Fame belongs to the one who answers, not the one who asks. The face of the answerer is lit up by a spot-light, whereas the questioner is filmed from behind. Nixon is in the limelight, not Woodward. Bernard never longed for the fame of the one in the bright lights but for the power of the one in the shadow. He longed for the strength of the hunter who kills the tiger, not for the fame of the tiger admired by those about to use him as a bedside rug.

But fame does not belong only to the famous. Everyone lives for a moment of brief fame and experiences the same feeling as a Greta Garbo, a Nixon or a skinned tiger. Bernard's open mouth laughed from the walls of Paris, and he felt as if he were being pilloried: he was seen, studied and judged by everybody. When Laura told him, 'Bernard, marry me!' he imagined her standing in the stocks by his side. And then he suddenly saw her (this had never happened to him before!) old, disagreeably extravagant and mildly ridiculous.

161

This was all the more foolish because he had never needed her as much as now. The love of an older woman still remained for him the most beneficial of all possible loves, providing only that this love were even more secret and the woman even wiser and more discreet. If instead of making the foolish proposal of marriage, Laura had decided to use their love to build an enchanted, fairy-tale castle tucked away from the social bustle, she would have been sure of keeping Bernard. But when she saw his huge photograph on every corner and linked it with his changed behaviour, his silent face and his absent-mindedness she decided without much reflection that success had brought him some new woman who was constantly on his mind. And because Laura refused to give up without a fight, she took the offensive.

Now you can understand why Bernard began to retreat. When one side attacks, the other must retreat, that is the law. Retreat, as is generally known, is the most difficult of military manoeuvres. Bernard undertook it with the precision of a mathematician: he had been used to spending up to four nights a week with Laura, now he limited his visits to two; he had been used to spending all his weekends with her, now he limited them to one in two, and he planned still other limitations for the future. He thought of himself as the pilot of a space-ship who is re-entering the atmosphere and must sharply reduce his speed. He put on the brakes, carefully but resolutely, while his attractive motherly friend faded before his eyes, gradually replaced by a woman constantly quarrelling with him, losing her wisdom and maturity, and brimming with unpleasant activity.

One day, the Bear told him: 'I met your fiancée.'

Bernard blushed with shame.

The Bear continued: 'She mentioned some sort of disagreement between the two of you. She is a likeable woman. Be nicer to her.'

Bernard grew pale with fury. He knew that the Bear had a big mouth and that by now everybody in broadcasting knew all about his lover. He thought of an affair with an older woman as a charming and almost daring perversion, but now he was sure that his colleagues would see his choice as nothing but proof of his assininity.

'Why do you go and complain about me to strangers?'

'What strangers?'

'The Bear.'

'I thought he was your friend.'

'Even if he was, why do you discuss our private life with him?'

She said sadly: 'I don't hide my love for you. Or am I forbidden to talk about it? Are you by any chance ashamed of me?'

Bernard kept silent. Yes, he was ashamed of her. He was ashamed of her, even though she made him happy. But she made him happy only at those times when he forgot that he was ashamed of her.

Fighting

Laura was highly distressed when she felt the space-ship of love slowing down in flight.

'What's the matter with you!'

'Nothing is the matter with me.'

'You've changed.'

'I simply need to be alone.'

'Is anything the matter with you?'

'I have a lot of worries.'

'If something is worrying you, you shouldn't be alone. When people have worries they should share them with each other.'

On Friday he left for his house in the country without asking her to come along. She followed him there on Saturday, uninvited. She knew that she shouldn't have done this, but she had long been in the habit of doing what she shouldn't and was actually proud of it, because this was precisely why men admired her and Bernard more than all the others. If she didn't like a concert or a play, she would get up in protest in the middle of the performance and walk out with an ostentatious fuss that would have the audience buzzing with disapproval. One day when Bernard sent the daughter of the concierge to her shop to deliver a letter she had been anxiously waiting for, Laura reached in a drawer, pulled out a fur hat worth at least two thousand francs, and as a token of her joy handed it to the sixteen-year-old girl. Another time she went with him on a two-day holiday to a rented sea-side villa and because she felt like punishing him for something or other, she spent the whole day playing with the twelve-year-old son of a local fisherman as if she had completely forgotten her lover's presence. Oddly enough, even though he felt hurt, he came to see her behaviour as an example of bewitching spontaneity ('that boy made me forget the whole world!'), combined with something disarmingly feminine (wasn't she maternally moved by a child?), and all his anger instantly vanished when the next day she proceeded to devote herself not to the fisherman's son but to him. Her capricious notions thrived happily in his loving, admiring eyes, one could even say that they flowered like roses; as for her, she saw her inappropriate behaviour and rash words as marks of her personality, as the charm of her self, and she was happy.

As soon as Bernard began to pull away from her, her extravagant behaviour did not alter but quickly lost both its happy character and its naturalness. The day she decided to follow him uninvited, she knew she wouldn't arouse any admiration, and she entered his house with a sense of anxiety that caused the brashness of her action, a brashness formerly innocent and even attractive, to become aggressive and forced. She was aware of that and she resented him for having deprived her of the delight she had felt in her own self, a pleasure that was now shown to have been quite fragile, rootless and entirely dependent on him, on his love and admiration. Yet something urged her all the more to continue acting eccentrically and foolishly and to provoke him into spitefulness; she felt like causing an explosion in the secret, vague hope that after the storm the clouds would disappear and everything would be as before.

'Here I am. I hope you're pleased,' she said with a laugh.

'Yes, I'm pleased. But I came here to work.'

'I won't bother you while you're working. I don't want anything from you. I just want to be with you. Have I ever bothered you during your work?'

He didn't answer.

'After all, we've often gone to the country together and you've prepared your broadcasts there. Have I ever bothered you?'

He didn't answer.

'Have I bothered you?'

There was no helping it. He had to answer: 'No.'

'So how is it that I'm bothering you now?'

'You're not bothering me.'

'Don't lie to me! Act like a man and at least have the courage to tell me straight out that you're angry with me for coming on my own. I can't stand cowardly men. I'd rather you told me to pack up this minute and go away. So tell me!'

He was at a loss. He shrugged.

'Why are you so cowardly?'

He shrugged again.

'Stop shrugging your shoulders!'

He felt like shrugging a third time, but controlled himself.

'Explain to me what's the matter with you.'

'Nothing's the matter.'

'You've changed.'

He raised his voice. 'Laura, I have a lot of worries!'

She also raised her voice. 'I have worries, too!'

He realized that he was behaving foolishly, like a child pestered by his mother, and he hated her for it. He didn't know what to do. He knew how to be pleasant to women, amusing, perhaps even seductive, but he didn't know how to be unkind, nobody had taught him that, on the contrary, everybody had drummed into his head that he must never be unkind to them. How is a man to act towards a woman who comes to his house uninvited? In what university do they teach that sort of thing?

He stopped answering her and went into the next room. He lay down on the couch and picked up the first book he saw lying near by. It was a paperback detective novel. He lay down on his back, held the book at arm's length and pretended to read. A minute or two went by and she followed him. She sat down in an armchair facing him. She looked at the colour illustration on the book cover and said: 'How can you read such things?'

166

He glanced at her with surprise.

'I'm looking at the cover,' she said.

He still failed to understand.

'How can you shove such a tasteless cover in my face? If you really insist on reading this book in my presence, at least you could do me a favour and tear the cover off.'

Without a word, Bernard tore off the cover, handed it to her and continued reading.

Laura felt like screaming. She told herself that she should now get up, leave and never see him again. Or gently push aside the book he was holding in his hand and spit in his face. But she lacked the courage for either of these things. Instead, she threw herself at him (the book fell out of his hand and dropped to the floor), kissed him furiously and began feeling him all over.

Bernard did not have the slightest desire to make love. But though he dared to refuse to talk to her, he was unable to refuse her erotic challenge. In that regard he was like every man in the world. What man would dare tell a woman who touched him seductively between the legs: 'Take your hands off!' And so the man who a moment ago tore off a book cover with sovereign disdain and handed it to his humbled lover, now reacted obediently to her touches, and kissed her while taking off his trousers.

However, she did not feel like making love, either. What propelled her towards him was desperation at not knowing what to do and the need to do something. Her passionate, impatient movements expressed her blind desire for the deed, her silent desire for the word. When they started to make love, she tried to make their embrace wilder than ever before, an immense conflagration. But how could this be achieved in the course of silent sex? (Their love-making was always silent, with the exception of a few lyrical, breathlessly whispered words.) Yes, how? through the violence of movements? the loudness of sighs? frequent changes of position? She knew of no other methods and

167

so she now used all three. Mainly, she kept changing the position of her body, by herself, on her own initiative; now she was on all fours, now she squatted down on him with her legs apart, and she kept inventing new, extremely demanding positions, which they had never used before.

Bernard interpreted her surprising physical performance as a challenge to which he could not help but respond. He felt in himself the first anxiety of a young boy afraid that others might question his erotic talents and erotic maturity. That anxiety gave back to Laura the power that she had recently been losing and upon which their relationship had initially been founded: the power of a woman older than her partner. Once again, he had the unpleasant impression that Laura was more experienced than he, that she knew what he did not, that she could compare him with others and judge him. So he performed all the required motions with exceptional zeal, and on the slightest hint that she was about to change her position he reacted with agility and discipline, like a soldier performing a military drill. The unexpectedly demanding mobility of their love-making kept him occupied to such an extent that he had no chance to decide whether or not he was excited or whether he was experiencing anything that could be called pleasure.

She didn't think about pleasure or excitement, either. She told herself silently: I won't let you go, I won't let you drive me away, I will fight for you. And her sex, moving up and down, turned into a machine of war which she set in motion and controlled. She told herself that it was her last weapon, the only one left to her, but an almighty one. As if it were an *ostinato* providing the bass accompaniment to a musical composition, she kept silently repeating to the rhythm of her motion: *I will fight, I will fight, I will fight*, and she was sure that she would win.

Just open any dictionary. To fight means to set one's will against the will of another, with the aim of defeating the opponent, to bring him to his knees, possibly to kill him. 'Life is a battle' is a proposition which must at first have expressed melancholy and resignation. But our century of optimism and massacres has succeeded in making this terrible sentence sound like a joyous refrain. You will say that to fight against somebody may be terrible, but to fight for something is noble and beautiful. Yes, it is beautiful to strive for happiness (or love, or justice, and so on), but if you are in the habit of designating your striving with the word 'fight', it means that your noble striving conceals the longing to knock someone to the ground. The fight *for* is always connected with the fight *against* and the preposition 'for' is always forgotten in the course of the fight in favour of the preposition 'against'.

Laura's sex kept moving powerfully up and down. Laura was fighting. She was making love and fighting. Fighting for Bernard. But against whom? Against the one whom she kept pressing to her body and then pushing away in order to force him to take some new physical position. These exhausting gymnastics on the couch and on the carpet, with both of them bathed in perspiration, both of them out of breath, resembled in pantomime a merciless fight in which she attacked and he defended himself, she gave orders and he obeyed.

Professor Avenarius

Professor Avenarius walked down the Avenue du Maine, passed the Montparnasse railway station and, not being in any hurry, decided to look around the Lafayette department store. In the ladies' clothing department, plastic mannequins dressed in the latest fashions watched him from all sides. Avenarius liked their company. He was especially attracted to these immobile women frozen in crazy gestures, whose wide-open mouths did not express laughter (their lips were not spread wide), but astonishment. Professor Avenarius imagined that these petrified women had just seen his splendidly erect member; this was not only enormous but differed from other members by the horned devil's head at its tip. As well as those who expressed admiring terror there were other mannequins whose mouths were not open but merely puckered up, small red circles with a tiny opening in the middle, ready at any moment to stick out their tongue and treat Professor Avenarius to a sensual kiss. And then there was a third group, whose lips traced dreamy smiles on their waxy faces. Their half-closed eyes clearly showed that they were savouring the quiet, prolonged enjoyment of intercourse.

The wonderful sexuality which these mannequins transmitted like waves of atomic radiation found no response; tired, grey, bored, irritated and totally asexual people passed by the display. Only Professor Avenarius strolled happily along, feeling like the director of a gigantic orgy.

But all beautiful things must come to an end: Professor Avenarius left the department store and descended a stairway to the underground maze of the Metro, in order to avoid the stream of cars on the boulevard above. He walked this way often, and nothing he saw surprised him. In the underground passage was the usual cast of characters. Two vagrants, *clochards*, were stumbling along, one of whom, holding a bottle of red wine, would from time to time lazily turn to passers-by and with a disarming smile ask for a further contribution. A young man, cradling his face in the palms of his hands, sat leaning against the wall; a chalk message in front of him stated that he had just been released from prison, could not find a job, and was hungry. Standing next to the wall opposite the ex-prisoner was a weary musician; on one side lay a hat with a few shiny coins, and on the other a brass trumpet.

All this was quite normal, but one thing was unusual and caught Professor Avenarius' attention. Right between the ex-prisoner and the two drunken *clochards* stood an attractive woman, hardly forty years old; she was not standing by the wall but in the middle of the subway and she held a red collection-box in her hand; with a dazzling smile of seductive femininity she was offering it to the passers-by; attached to the box was a sign: *Help the lepers!* The elegance of her clothing was in sharp contrast to her surroundings, and her enthusiasm lit up the gloom of the subway like a lantern. Her presence clearly annoyed the beggars who regularly spent their working hours here, and the trumpet standing at the musician's feet was undoubtedly a sign of his capitulation in the face of unfair competition.

When the woman's eyes met someone's gaze, she said so softly that the passer-by read her lips rather than heard her voice: 'Lepers!' Professor Avenarius, too, wished to read the words on her lips, but when the woman saw him she said only 'Le . . .' and did not finish '. . . pers', because she recognized him. Avenarius recognized her, too, and was at a complete loss to understand what she was doing there. He climbed the stairs and found himself on the other side of the boulevard.

He saw that he had wasted his time trying to avoid the stream of cars, because the traffic had been halted: from the direction of La Coupole crowds of people were flowing toward the Rue de Rennes. They were all dark-skinned. Professor Avenarius assumed they were young Arabs protesting against racism. Unconcerned, he walked a bit farther and opened the door of a café; the manager called out to him: 'Mr Kundera stopped by here. He said he would be late, so he asked that you excuse him. He left this book for you, to give you something to do in the meantime,' and he handed him an inexpensive paperback copy of my novel *Life Is Elsewhere*.

Avenarius stuck the book in his pocket without paying the slightest attention to it, because at that moment he remembered the woman with the red collection-box and he longed to see her again.

'I'll be back in a moment,' he said and went out. From the slogans over the heads of the demonstrators he finally realized that they were not Arabs but Turks and that they were not protesting against French racism but against the Bulgarization of the Turkish minority in Bulgaria. The demonstrators kept raising their fists, but in a somewhat dejected manner, for the Parisians' limitless indifference was driving them to the edge of despair. But now they saw the splendid, war-like pot-belly of a man marching along the edge of the pavement in the same direction as themselves, raising his fist and shouting: '*A bas les Russes! A bas les Bulgares!* Down with the Russians! Down with the Bulgarians!' so that new energy surged into them and their voices once again rang out across the boulevard.

At the top of the stairs which he had climbed a few moments ago he saw two ugly women distributing leaflets. He wanted to learn more about the Turkish cause; 'Are you Turks?' he asked one of them. 'Good Lord, no!' she exclaimed, as if he had accused her of something terrible. 'We have nothing to do with this demonstration! We are here to protest against racism!' Professor

172

Avenarius took a leaflet from each of the women and his glance happened to meet the smile of a young man nonchalantly leaning against the Metro ballustrade. Joyously provocative he, too, handed him a leaflet.

'This is against what?' Avenarius asked.

'It's for the freedom of the Kanakas in New Caledonia.'

Professor Avenarius descended into the Metro with three leaflets in his pocket; from afar he was already able to observe that the atmosphere in the subway had changed; the air of boredom had disappeared, something was going on: he heard the clarion call of a trumpet, the clapping of hands, laughter. And then he saw; the youthful woman was still there, but now she was surrounded by the two *clochards*: one held her free hand, the other gently supported the arm clasped around the collection-box. The one who held her arm was stretching out the musician's hat towards the passers-by, shouting: '*Pour les lépreux!* For the lepers! *Pour l'Afrique!*' and the trumpeter stood next to him, blowing his trumpet, blowing, blowing, yes, blowing his heart out and an amused crowd of people gathered around them, smiled, threw coins and banknotes into the *clochard*'s hat while he kept thanking them: '*Merci! Ah, que la France est généreuse!* Without France the lepers would croak like animals! *Ah, que la France est généreuse!*'

The woman didn't know what to do; now and again she tried to break free but when she heard the applause of the onlookers she took a couple of dance steps backwards and forwards. Once the *clochard* tried to turn her towards him and to dance with her cheek-to-cheek. She was struck by the smell of alcohol on his breath and she began to struggle free, her face full of anxiety and fear.

The young ex-prisoner suddenly rose to his feet and began waving his arms, as if he wanted to warn the two *clochards* about something. Two policemen were approaching. When Professor

Avenarius noticed them, he too began to dance. His splendid pot-belly shook from side to side, he made circular dancing movements with his arms bent at the elbow, and he smiled all round emanating an indescribable mood of peace and lightheartedness. As the policemen passed by, he smiled at the woman with the collection-box as if he were somehow connected with her and he clapped to the rhythm of the trumpet and his own steps. The policemen turned their heads listlessly and continued their patrol.

Buoyed up by his success, Avenarius danced with even greater verve, twirled around with unexpected agility, skipped backwards and forwards, and kicked his legs in the air, while his hands imitated the gesture of a can-can dancer lifting up her skirt. That inspired the *clochard* who was supporting the woman; he bent down and picked up the hem of her skirt with his fingers. She wanted to defend herself but she could not take her eyes off the portly man who was smiling encouragement; when she tried to return his smile, the *clochard* lifted her skirt waist high: this revealed her bare legs and green panties (an excellent match for the pink skirt). Again she wanted to defend herself, but she was powerless: she was holding the collection-box in one hand (nobody bothered any longer to drop a single coin into it, but she held it as tightly as if it contained all her honour, the meaning of her life, perhaps her very soul), while her other hand was immobilized by the *clochard*'s grip. If they had tied both her hands and begun to violate her, she couldn't have felt any worse. The *clochard* was lifting the hem of her skirt, shouting: 'For the lepers! For Africa!' while tears of humiliation ran down her face. But she tried to conceal her humiliation (an acknowledged humiliation is a double humiliation) and so she tried to smile as if everything was happening with her approval and for the good of Africa, and she voluntarily lifted up her leg, pretty though somewhat short.

Then she suddenly got a whiff of the *clochard*'s terrible stench, the stench of his breath as well as his clothing which, worn day and night for many years, had grown into his skin (if he were injured in an accident, a whole staff of surgeons would have to spend an hour scraping it off his body before they could put him on the operating table); at that point she couldn't hold out any longer; she wrenched herself loose from his grasp and pressing the collection-box to her bosom she ran to Professor Avenarius. He opened his arms and embraced her. She clung to his body, trembling and sobbing. He quickly managed to calm her down, took her by the hand and led her out of the Metro.

The body

'Laura, you look too thin,' Agnes said in a worried voice. She and her sister were dining in a restaurant.

'I have no appetite. I vomit everything up,' said Laura, and she took a drink of the mineral water she had ordered instead of the usual wine. 'It's awfully strong,' she said.

'The mineral water?'

'I need to dilute it.'

'Laura . . .' Agnes was about to chide her sister, but instead she said: 'You mustn't brood on things so much.'

'Everything is lost, Agnes.'

'What has actually changed between the two of you?'

'Everything. And yet we make love like never before. Like mad.'

'So what has changed, if you make love like mad?'

'Those are the only times when I'm sure he's with me. But the moment the love-making ends his mind is somewhere else. Even if we make love a hundred times more madly, it's all over. Because making love isn't the main thing. It's not a question of making love. It's a question of his thinking of me. I have had lots of men and today none of them knows anything about me nor I about them, and I ask myself why I bothered to live all those years when I didn't leave any trace of myself with anyone. What's left of my life? Nothing, Agnes, nothing! But these last two years I have really been happy because I knew that Bernard was thinking of me, that I was present in his head, that I was alive in him. Because for me that's the only real life: to live in the thoughts of another. Otherwise I am the living dead.'

'And when you're home by yourself listening to your records,

176

your Mahler, isn't that enough to give you a kind of small basic happiness worth living for?'

'Agnes, I'm sure you realize that's a foolish thing to say. Mahler means nothing to me, absolutely nothing, when I'm alone. I enjoy Mahler only when I'm with Bernard or when I know that he's thinking of me. When I'm not with him, I don't even have the strength to make my bed. I don't even feel like washing or changing my underwear.'

'Laura! Bernard is not the only man in the world!'

'He is!' said Laura. 'Why do you want me to lie to myself? Bernard is my last chance. I am not twenty or thirty. Beyond Bernard there is nothing but desert.'

She took a drink of mineral water and said: 'It's awfully strong.' She called to the waiter to bring her plain water.

'In a month he is leaving for a two-week stay on Martinique,' she continued. 'We were there together twice. But this time he told me in advance that he was going without me. After he said that I couldn't eat for two days. But I know what I'll do.'

The waiter brought a carafe of water; before his amazed eyes Laura poured some of it into her glass of mineral water and then she repeated: 'Yes, I know what I'll do.'

She fell silent, as if inviting her sister to ask a question. Agnes understood, and deliberately refrained from asking. But when the silence lasted too long, she capitulated: 'What are you thinking of doing?'

Laura answered that in recent weeks she had visited five doctors, complained of insomnia, and asked each of them to prescribe barbiturates for her.

From the time that Laura began to add hints of suicide to her usual complaints, Agnes felt increasingly depressed and fatigued. She tried many times to talk her sister out of her intention by means of both logical and emotional arguments; she emphasized the love she felt for her ('Surely you would never do something

177

like that *to me!*'), but it had no effect: Laura continued to speak of suicide as if she hadn't heard Agnes at all.

'I'll leave for Martinique a week ahead of him,' she continued. 'I have the key. The house is empty. I'll do it in such a way that he finds me there. So he'll never be able to forget me.'

Agnes knew that Laura was capable of doing foolish things and she was frightened when Laura said 'I'll do it in such a way that he finds me there': she imagined Laura's motionless body in the middle of the tropical villa's living room and the fact that this image was entirely realistic, conceivable, and quite in keeping with Laura, terrified her.

To Laura, loving somebody meant delivering to him one's body as a gift; delivering it the way she had a white piano delivered to her sister; putting it in the middle of the house: here I am, here are my one hundred and twenty-five pounds, my flesh, my bones, they are for you and I will leave them with you. She regarded such a gift as an erotic gesture, because for her the body was sexual not only during exceptional moments of excitement, but as I said earlier, it was sexual from the very start, *a priori*, continuously and in its entirety, with its surface and insides, asleep or wide-awake or dead.

For Agnes, the erotic was limited to a second of excitement, in the course of which the body becomes desirable and beautiful. Only this second justified and redeemed the body; as soon as this artificial illumination faded, the body became once again a dirty machine which she was forced to maintain. That's why Agnes would never have been able to say, 'I'll do it in such a way that he finds me there.' She would have been horrified by the idea that the one she loved would see her a mere body stripped of sex and enchantment, with a spastic grimace on her face and lying in a position she would no longer be able to control. She would be ashamed. Shame would prevent her from voluntarily becoming a corpse.

But Agnes knew that Laura was different: leaving her body stretched out dead in her lover's living room was quite consistent with her relationship to her body and her manner of love. That's why Agnes grew frightened. She leaned over the table and grasped her sister by the hand.

'I'm sure you understand me,' Laura was saying in a soft voice. 'You have Paul. The best man you could possibly wish for. I have Bernard. If Bernard left me, I'd have nothing, and I'd never have anyone else. And you know that I won't be satisfied with just a little. I won't watch the misery of my life. I have too high a conception of life. Either life gives me everything, or I'll quit. I'm sure you understand me. You're my sister.'

There was a moment of silence, during which Agnes groped for an answer. She was tired. The same dialogue was repeated week after week, confirming again and again the uselessness of anything that Agnes found to say. Suddenly, quite improbable words broke into this moment of fatigue and powerlessness.

'Once again, old Bertrand Bertrand was thundering in Parliament against the escalating suicide-rate. The house on Martinique is his property. Just imagine the pleasure I'm going to give him,' said Laura, laughing.

Even though the laughter was nervous and forced, it came to Agnes' aid like an unexpected ally. She began laughing herself and the laughter quickly lost its original artificiality and all at once became real laughter, the laughter of relief, both sisters' eyes were full of tears, they felt that they loved each other and that Laura would not take her own life. They began chatting about this and that, still holding hands and their words were those of sisterly love behind which was a glimpse of a villa in a Swiss garden and the gesture of an arm lifted in the air as though throwing a brightly coloured ball, like an invitation to a journey, like a promise hinting at an undreamt-of future, a promise that may not have been fulfilled but remained with them as a beautiful echo.

179

When the moment of giddiness passed, Agnes said: 'Laura, you mustn't do anything foolish. Nobody is worth suffering over. Think of me, and of my love for you.'

And Laura said: 'But I have an urge to do something. I must do something!'

'Something? What sort of something?'

Laura looked deep in her sister's eyes and shrugged her shoulders, as if to admit that for the time being a clear meaning of the word 'something' still eluded her. And then she tilted her head slightly, covered her face with a vague, rather melancholy smile, placed her finger-tips between her breasts and, pronouncing the word 'something' once again, she threw her hands forward.

Agnes was reassured: the expression 'something' didn't suggest anything concrete to her, but Laura's gesture left no doubt: that 'something' aimed to soar to beautiful heights and had nothing in common with a dead body lying down below, on the ground, on the floor of a tropical living room.

A few days later Laura visited the France-Africa society, whose chairman was Bernard's father, and volunteered to collect street-corner contributions for lepers.

The gesture of longing for immortality

Bettina's first love was her brother Clemens, who was to become a great Romantic poet, then, as we know, she was in love with Goethe, she adored Beethoven, she loved her husband Achim von Arnim, who was also a great poet, then she went mad for Count Hermann von Pückler-Muskau, who was not a great poet but wrote books (it was to him, incidentally, that *A Child's Correspondence with Goethe* was dedicated), and then, when she was already fifty, she harboured maternal-erotic feelings towards two young men, Philippe Nathusius and Julius Döring, who didn't write books but exchanged letters with her (parts of them were also published by her), she admired Karl Marx, whom she forced to accompany her on a long evening stroll while visiting his fiancée Jenny (Marx didn't feel like going, preferring to be with Jenny not Bettina; but not even a man capable of turning the whole world upside down was able to resist a woman who had been on familiar terms with Goethe), she had a weakness for Franz Liszt, but only fleetingly because it upset her that Liszt had only his own glory in mind, she tried passionately to help the mentally ill painter Karl Blechen (for whose wife she had the same contempt as she had once felt for Frau Goethe), she initiated a correspondence with Karl Alexander, heir to the throne of Saxony and Weimar, she wrote a book for the Prussian king Friedrich Wilhelm, *The King's Book*, in which she explained a king's duties toward his subjects, followed by *The Book of the Poor*, in which she showed the terrible misery of the poor, then she again turned to the king with a request to free Wilhelm Schleefel, who had been accused of taking part in a communist plot, followed by another plea to the king on behalf of Ludwig Mieroslawski, one of the leaders of the Polish revolution, who was awaiting execution in a Prussian jail. She had never personally met the last man she worshipped: Sandor Petofi, the Hungarian poet who died at the age of twenty-six as a soldier in the 1848 uprising. She thus not only introduced the world to a great poet (she called him *Sonnengott*, Sun God), but along with him she also called attention to his homeland, of which Europe had been virtually ignorant. If we recall that the Hungarian intellectuals who in 1956 rebelled against the Russian Empire and inspired the first great anti-Stalinist revolution called themselves 'the Petofi circle' after this poet, you will realize that through her loves Bettina is present throughout the long march of European history, reaching from the eighteenth century all the way to the middle of our own. Brave, stubborn Bettina: the nymph of history, the priestess of history. And I am justified in calling her priestess, because for Bettina history meant (all her friends used this metaphor) 'an incarnation of God'.

There were times when her friends reproached her for not thinking enough about her family or her financial circumstances, for sacrificing herself unduly for others, without reckoning the cost.

'I'm not interested in what you're telling me! I am not a bookkeeper! Here, this is what I am!' And she placed both hands on her chest in such a way that the two middle fingers touched the precise midpoint between her breasts. Then she gently inclined her head, put a smile on her face and threw her hands energetically and yet gracefully upwards. During this movement the knuckles of her hands touched and only at the end did her arms move apart and her palms turn forward.

No, you are not mistaken. This is the same gesture that Laura made in the previous chapter when she announced that she wanted to do 'something'. Let's review the situation:

When Agnes said, 'Laura, you mustn't do anything foolish.

Nobody is worth suffering over. Think of me, and of my love for you,' Laura answered, 'But I have an urge to do something. I must do something!'

When she said that, she had a vague idea of going to bed with another man. She had often thought of this already and it didn't contradict her longing for suicide. They were two extreme and quite legitimate reactions of a humiliated woman. Her vague dreaming about infidelity was rudely interrupted by Agnes' unfortunate attempt to make everything clear:

'Something? What sort of something?'

Laura realized that it would have been ridiculous to admit a longing for infidelity right after having talked of suicide. That's why she became flustered and only repeated the word 'something'. And because Agnes' gaze demanded a more concrete answer, she tried to give that vague word some meaning, if only by a gesture: she put her hands to her breast and threw them forward.

How did this gesture occur to her? It's hard to say. She had never used it before. An unknown someone prompted her to do it, the way a prompter prods an actor who has forgotten his lines. Even though the gesture did not express anything concrete, nevertheless it suggested that doing 'something' meant to sacrifice oneself, to give oneself to the world, to send one's soul soaring towards the blue horizon like a white dove.

The idea of standing in the Metro with a collection-box would have seemed totally foreign to her just a moment before and evidently would never have occurred to her had she not put her hands to her breast and thrown her arms forward. It was as if that gesture had its own will: it led her and she merely followed.

The gestures of Laura and Bettina are identical and there is certainly some connection between Laura's desire to help distant blacks and Bettina's attempt to save a condemned Pole. Nevertheless, the comparison doesn't seem convincing. I cannot imagine

Bettina von Arnim standing in the Metro with a collection-box and begging! Bettina was not interested in charitable acts! Bettina was not one of those rich women who organize collections for the poor because they have nothing better to do. She was nasty to her servants, forcing her husband von Arnim to chide her ('Servants are also human beings, and you mustn't drive them like machines!' he reminded her in one of his letters). What impelled her to help others was not a passion for good deeds but a longing to enter into direct, personal contact with God, whom she believed incarnate in history. All her love-affairs with famous men (and other kinds of men did not interest her!) were nothing but a trampoline upon which she threw her entire body in order to be tossed upward to the heights where the God incarnate in history dwells.

Yes, all that is true. But careful! Laura, too, was not one of the kind-hearted ladies on the boards of charitable organizations. She was not in the habit of giving money to beggars. She passed them by, and though they were only a few feet away she did not see them. She suffered from the defect of spiritual farsightedness. Africans who were thousands of miles away from her and from whose bodies one piece of flesh after another was dropping off were closer to her. They were located precisely at that point beyond the horizon to which the gesture of her arms dispatched her aching soul.

All the same, there is certainly a difference between a condemned Pole and sick Africans! What, to Bettina, was an intervention in history, was to Laura merely a charitable deed. But that was not Laura's fault. World history, with its revolutions, Utopias, hopes and despair had vanished from Europe, leaving only nostalgia behind. That is why the French have made charitable actions international. They were not led (like the Americans, for example) by Christian love for one's neighbours, but by a longing for lost history, a longing to call it back and to be present in it if only in the form of a red collection-box for blacks.

Let us call the gesture of Bettina and Laura *the gesture of longing for immortality*. Bettina, who aspires to grand immortality, wishes to say: I refuse to die with this day and its cares, I wish to transcend myself, to be a part of history, because history is eternal memory. Laura, though she only aspires to small immortality, wants the same: to transcend herself and the unhappy moment in which she lives to do 'something' to make everyone who had known her remember her.

Ambiguity

From earliest childhood, Brigitte liked to sit on her father's knee, but I believe that by the time she reached eighteen she liked sitting there even more. Agnes was not disturbed by this: Brigitte would often climb into bed with both parents (especially late in the evening, when they all watched TV) and there was greater physical intimacy between the three of them than had been the case between Agnes and her parents. All the same, the ambiguity of the scene did not escape her: an adult young woman with big breasts and a big behind sitting in the lap of an attractive man still in the prime of life, touching his shoulders and cheeks with those aggressive breasts and calling him 'Daddy'.

Once, Agnes held a lively party at her house, to which she had also invited her sister. When everybody was in a very good mood, Brigitte sat on her father's lap and Laura said: 'I want to do that, too!' Brigitte moved over to one knee, and so both of them ended up sitting on Paul's lap.

This situation reminds us once again of Bettina, because it was she more than anyone else who raised lap-sitting to a classical model of erotic ambiguity. I said that she crossed the entire erotic battlefield of her life under the protection of the shield of childhood. She carried this shield into her fifties, then exchanged it for the shield of motherhood and in turn let young men sit on her lap. And again it was a marvellously ambiguous situation: a mother must never be suspected of sexual interest in her son, and for that very reason the position of a young man sitting (even though in a metaphoric sense) on the lap of a mature woman is full of erotic significance which is all the more forceful for being vague.

I take the liberty of maintaining that without the art of ambiguity there is no real eroticism and the stronger the ambiguity, the more powerful the excitement. Who cannot recall from childhood the wonderful game of doctor! A little girl lies down on the ground and a little boy takes off her clothes under the pretence that he is her doctor. The girl is obedient, because it is not a curious little boy who examines her but a serious gentleman concerned about her health. The erotic content of this situation is enormous as well as mysterious, and the hearts of both are thumping. They are thumping all the harder because the boy mustn't stop being the doctor even for a moment and as he pulls off the girl's panties he speaks to her in very formal language.

The recollection of this blessed moment of childhood brings back an even more charming memory: a young Czech woman returned in 1969 to a provincial Czech town after a sojourn in Paris. She had left for France in 1967 to study and when she came back two years later she found her country occupied by a Russian army; people seemed frightened, and yearning to find themselves somewhere else. In the course of those two years of study, the young Czech woman had been attending seminars compulsory for anyone desiring to be intellectually *au courant*, in which she learned that during infancy, even before the Oedipal stage, we all go through a period which a famous psychoanalyst called *the mirror stage*, meaning that before we become aware of our parents' bodies we become aware of our own. The young Czech woman decided that it was this stage that many of her fellow country-women had skipped in their development. Glowing with the glamour of Paris and its famous seminars, she gathered around herself a circle of young women. She expounded a theory which none of them understood and introduced practical exercises which were as simple as the theory was complex: they all undressed completely and looked at themselves in a big mirror, then they all carefully examined each other and finally they held up small pocket mirrors to each other so that they could see parts of their own bodies they hadn't been able to see before. The instructor did not fail even for a moment to treat the group to her theoretical commentaries, whose fascinating incomprehensibility transported everyone far away from the Russian occupation, far from their provincial cares, as well as giving them a certain undefined and undefinable excitement about which they were loth to talk. It is probable that in addition to having been a student of the great Lacan, the group's leader was also a Lesbian, but I don't think that the group contained many confirmed Lesbians. And I admit that of all those women, I dream most of all of that totally innocent girl for whom during those seances nothing in the world existed except the dark words of Lacan, poorly translated into Czech. Ah, the scholarly meetings of naked women in a house in a provincial Czech town, the streets of which were patrolled by Russian soldiers – how much more exciting than orgies in which everyone tries to do what is required, what is already agreed, and what has only one poor meaning, and no other! But let us quickly leave the small Czech town and return to Paul's knees: Laura is sitting on one, and for the sake of experiment let's imagine the other knee occupied not by Brigitte but by her mother:

Laura is savouring the pleasant feeling that her behind is touching the man for whom she has been secretly longing; that feeling is all the more titillating because she is sitting on his lap not as a lover but as a sister-in-law, with the wife's full consent. Laura is the addict of ambiguity.

Agnes finds nothing provocative in the situation, but she cannot silence the comical sentence that keeps circling through her mind: 'Paul has one female buttock on each knee! Paul has one female buttock on each knee!' Agnes is the clear-minded observer of ambiguity.

And Paul? He is noisily joking, raising first one knee, then the other, to keep the two sisters from doubting even for a moment that he is a kind and fun-loving uncle always willing to indulge in horseplay for his little niece's benefit. Paul is the simpleton of ambiguity.

At the height of her amorous suffering Laura would often ask him for advice, and they would meet in various cafés. Let us note that not one word was ever spoken of suicide. Laura had begged her sister not to mention her morbid ideas to anyone and she herself had mentioned nothing of them to Paul. So the fine tissue of beautiful sorrow remained unharmed by too brutal an image of death; they would sit facing each other and now and again they touched each other. Paul would squeeze her hand or pat her on the shoulder as we do to someone whose self-confidence and strength we wish to bolster, because Laura loved Bernard and loving people deserve help.

I am tempted to say that at these moments Paul looked into her eyes, but that would not be accurate since during that period Laura again began to wear dark glasses; Paul knew that she did so in order to keep him from seeing her tear-stained eyes. The dark glasses suddenly took on many meanings: they gave Laura an air of severe elegance and unapproachability; at the same time, however, they pointed at something very physical and sensual: an eye full of tears, an eye that had suddenly become an opening into the body, one of those nine beautiful gates into a woman's body of which Apollinaire sings in his famous poem, a moist opening covered by a fig-leaf of dark glasses. On several occasions, the image of tears behind the glasses was so intense and the imagined tears so ardent that they turned into steam which surrounded them both and deprived them of judgement and sight.

Paul noticed the steam. But did he understand its significance? I don't think so. Imagine this situation: a little girl approaches a little boy. She starts taking off her clothes and says: 'Doctor, you have to examine me.' And the little boy says: 'My dear littie girl! I am no doctor!'

This is exactly how Paul behaved.

The clairvoyant

In his discussion with the Bear, Paul tried to act like the brilliant champion of frivolity, and yet with the pair of sisters on his knees he was anything but frivolous. How is this possible? Here is the explanation: he saw frivolity as a beneficent enema with which he would treat culture, public life, art, politics; an enema for Goethe and Napoleon. But beware: it was not the right prescription for Laura and Bernard! Paul's deep distrust of a Beethoven or Rimbaud was redeemed by his immeasurable faith in love.

The concept of love was linked in his mind with the image of the sea, that stormiest of all elements. When he and Agnes went on vacation, he used to leave the hotel window wide open at night, so that the sound of the pounding surf penetrated their love-making and they could merge with this great voice. He loved his wife and was happy with her; and yet in the depths of his soul there was a whisper of timid disappointment that their love never expressed itself in a more dramatic manner. He almost envied Laura for the obstacles that stood in her way, because only obstacles, Paul thought, were capable of turning love into a love story. He felt a bond of sympathetic solidarity with his sister-in-law, and her amorous troubles tormented him as if they were his own.

One day Laura telephoned to tell him that Bernard had left for a few days' vacation at the family villa on Martinique, and that she was ready to follow him there against his will. If she found him there with another woman, so be it. At least everything would be clear.

He tried to talk her out of this decision, to save her from unnecessary conflicts. But the discussion became interminable:

191

she kept repeating the same arguments over and over, and Paul had already made peace with the thought that in the end he would say to her, no matter how unwillingly: 'If you're really so sure that your decision is right, then don't hesitate, go!' But just as he was about to say this, Laura said: 'There is only one thing that could persuade me to drop this trip: if you were to forbid me from going.'

She was thus quite clearly pointing out to Paul what he was to do in order to keep her from going, and yet at the same time to enable her to preserve, before herself and before him, the dignity of a woman determined to see her desperation and her struggle to the very end. Let's recall that when Laura first set eyes on Paul, she heard in her mind precisely the same words that Napoleon once said about Goethe: 'There is a man!' If Paul had really been a man, he would have decisively forbidden her to go on the trip. But alas, he was not a man but a man of principle: he had long ago dropped the word 'forbid' from his vocabulary, and he was proud of it. He bristled: 'You know that I never forbid anyone anything.'

Laura insisted: 'I *want* you to forbid me things and to give me orders. You know that nobody has that right except you. I'll do whatever you tell me.'

Paul was perplexed: he had already been explaining to her for an hour that she shouldn't go after Bernard, and for an hour she kept arguing with him. 'Why, if she hadn't been persuaded by his arguments, did she want to obey his order?' He fell silent.

'Are you afraid?' she asked.

'Of what?'

'Of forcing your will upon me.'

'If I couldn't convince you, I have no right to order you.'

'That's what I meant: you're afraid.'

'I wanted to convince you through reason.'

She laughed: 'You're hiding behind reason, because you're afraid of forcing your will on me. You're scared of me!'

Her laughter threw him into still deeper perplexity, and so he said, just to end the conversation: 'I'll think about it.'

Later, he asked Agnes for her opinion.

She said: 'She mustn't follow him. That would be a terrible mistake. If you see her, do everything you can to talk her out of it!'

Agnes' opinion did not mean very much, however, for Paul's chief adviser was Brigitte.

After he explained her aunt's situation to her, Brigitte reacted immediately: 'Why shouldn't she go there? People should always do what they feel like doing.'

'But just imagine,' Paul objected, 'if she finds Bernard's lover there! That would mean an enormous scandal!'

'Did he tell her by any chance that he would be there with another woman?'

'No.'

'Then he should have told her. If he didn't, he's a coward and there's no sense in coddling him. What can Laura lose? Nothing.'

We can ask why Brigitte gave Paul this particular answer and not another. Out of solidarity with Laura? No. Laura often behaved as if she were Paul's daughter and Brigitte found this ridiculous and unpleasant. She didn't have the slightest desire for solidarity with her aunt; she was only concerned about one thing: pleasing her father. She sensed that Paul turned to her as he would to a clairvoyant and she wished to strengthen her magical authority. Guessing correctly that her mother was opposed to Laura's trip, Brigitte decided to take precisely the opposite attitude, to let the voice of youth seduce her father with a gesture of rash daring.

She shook her head with short horizontal motions, lifting her shoulders and eyebrows and Paul again had that marvellous feeling that his daughter was a generator charging him with energy. Perhaps he would have been happier if Agnes had pursued him everywhere he went, rushing to catch planes to search distant islands for his lovers. All his life he had wished that his beloved would be capable, for his sake, of beating her head against the wall, screaming in despair or jumping for joy all over the room. He told himself that Laura and Brigitte were on the side of daring and madness and that without a kernel of madness life would not be worth living. Let Laura follow the voice of her heart! Why should all our actions be tossed in the frying pan of reason like a crêpe?

Nevertheless, he still objected: 'Just remember that Laura is a sensitive woman. Such a trip could cause her a lot of pain.'

'If I were in her place, I would go and nobody in the world could stop me,' Brigitte concluded the conversation.

Then Laura telephoned. To avoid a long discussion, he said as soon as he heard her voice: 'I've thought the whole thing over and I want to tell you that you should do exactly what you feel like doing. If something is drawing you there, then go!'

'I had already decided not to go. You had such doubts about my trip. But since you approve it, I'll fly out tomorrow.'

Paul felt as if he'd been drenched by a cold shower. He realized that without his express encouragement Laura would not fly to Martinique. But he was not capable of saying anything; the conversation was finished. Tomorrow a plane would jet her across the Atlantic and Paul knew that he was personally responsible for this trip, a trip that in the depths of his soul he, like Agnes, considered totally nonsensical.

Suicide

Two days had passed since she boarded the plane. At six in the morning the telephone rang. It was Laura. She announced to her sister and brother-in-law that on Martinique it was exactly midnight. Her voice was unnaturally cheerful, which made Agnes conclude at once that things were turning out badly.

She was not mistaken: when Bernard saw Laura walking down the palm-lined avenue leading to the villa in which he lived, he went white with anger and said to her severely: 'I asked you not to come here.' She began to say something in explanation, but without another word he threw a few of his things into a suitcase, got into the car and drove off. She remained alone and wandered around the house; in one of the cupboards she discovered her red swimsuit which she had left there during a previous stay.

'No one was waiting for me. Only this swimsuit,' she said and passed from laughter to tears. Sobbing, she continued: 'It was disgusting, what he did. I threw up. And then I decided to stay. Everything will come to an end in this villa. When Bernard comes back he will find me here in this swimsuit.'

Laura's voice echoed through the room; both of them heard it, but they had only one receiver and passed it back and forth.

'For heaven's sake,' said Agnes, 'calm down, just calm down. Try to be cool and sensible.'

Now Laura was laughing once again: 'Just imagine, before the trip I got hold of twenty tubes of barbiturates, and I left them all in Paris. That's how nervous I was.'

'Oh, that's good, that's good,' said Agnes, and indeed she felt somewhat relieved.

'But I found a gun in one of the drawers,' Laura continued, and again she laughed. 'Bernard is obviously afraid for his life! He is afraid he'll be waylaid by some blacks! I see it as a sign!'

'What sort of sign?'

'That he left the gun for me!'

'You're crazy! He did no such thing! He didn't even know that you were coming!'

'Of course he didn't leave it intentionally. But he bought a gun that no one but me would ever use. Therefore he left it for me.'

Agnes again felt a sense of desperate powerlessness. She said: 'Please, put the gun back where it was.'

'I don't know how to handle it. But Paul . . . you hear me, Paul?'

Paul took the receiver: 'Yes.'

'Paul, I am so glad to hear your voice.'

'So am I, Laura, but I beg you . . .'

'I know, Paul, but I can't go on any more . . .' and she began to sob.

There was a moment of silence.

Then Laura said: 'That gun is lying in front of me. I can't take my eyes off it.'

'So put it back where it was,' said Paul.

'Paul, you were in the army, weren't you?'

'Yes.'

'You were an officer?'

'A lieutenant.'

'That means you know how to shoot a gun?'

Paul hesitated. But he had to say: 'Yes.'

'How does one know that a gun is loaded?'

'If it goes off, it's loaded.'

'If I press the trigger will it go off?'

'It might.'

'What do you mean: it might?'

'If the safety catch is off, the gun will fire.'

'And how do you know the catch is off?'

'Come on now, you're not going to explain to her how to kill herself!' shouted Agnes and she tore the receiver from Paul's hand.

Laura continued: 'I only want to know how to handle it. After all, that's something I should know, how one handles a gun. What does it mean when the catch is off? How do you turn it off?'

'That's enough,' said Agnes. 'Not another word about guns. Put it back where it was. We've had enough of this joking.'

Laura's voice suddenly became quite different, serious: 'Agnes! I am not joking!' and once again she started to cry.

The conversation was endless, Agnes and Paul kept repeating the same sentences, they assured Laura of their love, they begged her to stay with them, not to leave them, until she finally promised to return the gun to the drawer and go to sleep.

When they put down the receiver they were so exhausted that for quite some time they were unable to say a single word.

Agnes said at last: 'Why is she doing this! Why is she doing this!'

And Paul said: 'It's my fault. I sent her there.'

'She would have gone in any case.'

Paul shook his head. 'No. She was ready to stay. I did the stupidest thing of my life.'

Agnes did not want Paul to suffer from a sense of guilt. Not out of compassion for him, but rather out of jealousy: she didn't want him to feel so responsible for Laura, to be so tied to her in his thoughts. That's why she said: 'How can you be so sure that she actually found a gun?'

At first, Paul had no idea what she meant: 'What are you trying to say?'

'That there may not be any gun there at all.'

'Agnes! She is not putting on an act! That's obvious!'

197

Agnes tried to formulate her suspicion more carefully: 'It's possible there is a gun in the house. But it is also possible that she took some barbiturates along and deliberately brought up the gun in order to confuse us. And you cannot also rule out the possibility that she has neither barbiturates nor a gun and only wants to torment us.'

'Agnes,' said Paul, 'you're being cruel to her.'

Paul's reproach again put her on her guard: without his realizing it, Laura had become more important to him than she was; he had been thinking about her, occupying himself with her, worrying about her, he had been moved by her and Agnes was suddenly forced to think that Paul was comparing her to Laura and that she was emerging from the comparison as the one with less feeling.

She defended herself: 'I am not cruel. I only want to warn you that Laura will do anything to attract attention. That's natural, because she is suffering. Everyone has a tendency to laugh at her unfortunate love affair and to shrug their shoulders. Once she has a gun in her hand, no one can laugh any more.'

'And supposing her longing for attention leads her to take her own life? Isn't that possible?'

'It is possible,' Agnes admitted, and once again there followed a long, anxious silence.

Then Agnes said: 'I can imagine a person longing to take his life. Not being able to bear pain any longer. And the meanness of people. Wanting to get out of their sight, and vanish. Everyone has the right to kill himself. That's his freedom. I have nothing against suicide as a way of vanishing.'

She felt like stopping, but violent disapproval of her sister's behaviour made her go on: 'But that's not the case with her. She doesn't want *to vanish*. She is thinking of suicide because she sees it as a way *to stay*. To stay with him. To stay with us. To engrave herself for ever on all our memories. To force her body into our lives. To crush us.'

'You're being unjust,' said Paul. 'She's suffering.'

'I know,' said Agnes, and she broke into tears. She imagined her sister dead and everything she had just said seemed petty and base and unforgivable.

'And what if she merely wanted to lull us with her promises?' she said and began to dial the number of the villa on Martinique; the phone kept ringing and ringing, and their foreheads began to sweat again; they knew that they would never be able to hang up and would listen endlessly to the ringing that signified Laura's death. At last they head her voice; it sounded almost unfriendly. They asked where she'd been. 'In the next room.' Both of them spoke into the receiver. They spoke of their anxiety, of their need to hear her voice once more to be reassured. They repeated how much they loved her and how impatiently they were looking forward to her return.

The next morning they were both late for work and thought all day of nothing but her. In the evening they called her again, the conversation again lasted an hour and they again assured her how much they loved her and how eagerly they longed to see her again.

A few days later she rang the doorbell. Paul was at home alone. She was standing in the doorway, and she was wearing dark glasses. She fell into his arms. They went into the living room, sat down in armchairs facing each other, but she was so nervous that she got up after a little while and began pacing the room. She talked feverishly. Then he, too, rose from the chair and he too paced the room and talked.

Paul spoke with contempt about his former student, protégé and friend. That could of course be explained by a desire to make Laura's break-up easier. But he was himself surprised that he meant everything he said, seriously and sincerely: Bernard is a spoiled child of rich parents; an arrogant, conceited person.

Laura was leaning against the fireplace, gazing at Paul. And Paul noticed all of a sudden that she was no longer wearing dark glasses. She held them in her hand and gazed at him, her eyes swollen and moist. He realized that for quite a while she hadn't been listening to what he was saying.

He fell silent. The room became filled with a stillness, which made him through some sort of mysterious power move closer to her. She said: 'Paul, why didn't we two meet sooner? Before all the others . . .'

Those words spread out between them like a mist. Paul stepped into that mist and reached out his hand like someone who can't see and gropes his way; his hand touched Laura. Laura sighed and let Paul's hand stay touching her skin. Then she stepped aside and put her glasses back. That gesture made the mist lift and they were once again facing each other as brother-in-law and sister-in-law.

A while later Agnes returned from work and walked into the room.

Dark glasses

When she first saw her sister after her return from Martinique, rather than hugging her as one would a shipwrecked sailor who has just escaped death, Agnes remained surprisingly cool. She didn't see her sister, she saw only the dark glasses, that tragic mask which would dictate the tone of the next scene. Ignoring the mask, she said: 'Laura, you've lost a lot of weight.' It was only then that she stepped closer and lightly kissed her on both cheeks, as acquaintances always do in France.

If we consider that these were the first words spoken after those dramatic days, we must admit they were ill-chosen. They were not related to life, or death, or love, but to digestion. That in itself would not have been so bad, since Laura was fond of talking about her body and considered it a metaphor for her feelings. What was much worse was the fact that the sentence was not spoken with concern or with a melancholy admiration of the suffering that caused weight loss, but with an evident weary distaste.

There is no doubt that Laura accurately caught the tone of her sister's voice and realized its significance. But she, too, pretended that she didn't guess what the other was thinking, and said in a voice full of pain: 'Yes. I lost fifteen pounds.'

Agnes felt like saying: 'Enough! Enough! This has gone on far too long! Stop it!' but she controlled herself and said nothing.

Laura lifted her arm: 'Look at this, can this be my arm, this stick . . . I can't wear a single skirt. They all slip down to my knees. And my nose keeps bleeding . . .' As if to demonstrate the truth of what she had just said she tipped her head back and blew loudly through her nose.

Agnes watched the thin body with uncontrolled distaste and this idea occurred to her: what happened to those fifteen pounds that Laura lost? Did they disperse into the blue like used-up energy? Or did they follow her excrement into the sewer? What happened to the fifteen pounds of Laura's irreplaceable body?

In the meantime Laura took off her dark glasses and put them down on the mantelpiece of the fireplace she was leaning against. She turned her swollen eyelids towards her sister, as she had turned them a moment earlier towards Paul.

When she took off her glasses, it was like stripping her face bare. As if she were undressing. But not in the way a woman undresses before a lover; rather in the way she undresses before a doctor, relinquishing all responsibility for her body.

Agnes was unable to dismiss the words that buzzed in her head, and said aloud: 'Enough! Enough! We're all at the end of our tether. You'll break up with Bernard just as millions of women have already broken up with millions of men, without threatening to commit suicide.'

We might think that after weeks of endless conversation during which Agnes kept assuring her of her sisterly love, Laura must have been surprised by this outburst, but oddly enough she was not surprised; Laura reacted to Agnes' words as if she had been expecting them for a long time. She said with utter calm: 'Let me tell you what I think: you don't know what love is all about, you never did and you never will. Love was never your strong point.'

Laura knew just where her sister was most vulnerable, and Agnes was worried; she realized that Laura was saying these things now only because Paul was listening. It suddenly became clear to her that it was no longer a question of Bernard: that entire suicidal drama had nothing to do with him; most probably he would never find out about it; that drama was intended only for Paul and for Agnes. And it occurred to her, too, that when someone begins to fight, a force is let loose which does not stop at the first objective and that beyond Laura's first target, which was Bernard, there were others also.

It was no longer possible to avoid a fight. Agnes said: 'If you lost fifteen pounds because of him, that's material proof of a love which cannot be denied. Still, there is something I don't understand. When I love someone, I want only good things to happen to him. When I hate someone, I wish bad things on him. And in recent months you've been tormenting Bernard and us as well. What does that have to do with love? Nothing.'

Now, let's imagine the living room as a stage: to the far right there is a fireplace; opposite, a bookcase on the edge of the stage. In the background, the centre of the stage is taken up by a couch, a coffee table and two armchairs. Paul is standing in the middle of the room, Laura is by the fireplace keeping her eyes fixed upon Agnes, who is standing only a few steps away. Laura's swollen eyes are accusing her sister of cruelty, insensitivity and cold-heartedness. While Agnes was speaking, Laura kept retreating backwards to the middle of the room towards Paul, as if trying to express by this movement her astonished alarm at her sister's unfair attack.

When she came within a step or two of Paul, she stopped and repeated: 'You don't know what love is all about.'

Agnes stepped forward and took up her sister's former position at the fireplace. She said: 'I understand love perfectly well. In love the most important thing is the other person, the one we love. That's what it's all about, and nothing else. And I ask myself: what does love mean to a person who is capable of seeing nothing but herself. In other words, what does love mean to an absolutely egocentric woman.'

'To ask what love means makes no sense, my dear sister,' said Laura. 'Love is something you've either experienced or you haven't. Love is love, that's all you can say about it. It's a pair of wings beating in my heart and driving me to do things that seem unwise to you. And that's precisely what you have never experienced. You said I was incapable of seeing anybody but myself. But I see you, and I see right through you. When you kept assuring me of your love during these last few weeks, I knew perfectly well that coming out of your mouth that word has no meaning. It was just a trick. An argument to mollify me. To keep me from disturbing your tranquillity. I know you, sister, you've been living your whole life on the other side of love. Totally on the other side. Beyond the border of love.'

Both women talked of love, while snapping hatefully at each other. And the man who was with them despaired. He wanted to say something to ease the unbearable tension: 'We're all tired, the three of us. Excited. We need to get away somewhere and forget all about Bernard.'

But Bernard had long been forgotten and all that Paul's intervention accomplished was that the sisters' verbal contest was replaced by a silence without an ounce of kindness, without any reconciling memory, without the slightest hint of family solidarity.

Let's not lose sight of the scene as a whole: to the right, leaning against the fireplace, stood Agnes; in the middle of the room, facing her sister, stood Laura, with Paul two steps to the left. And now Paul shrugged in despair at his inability to prevent the senseless hatred that had broken out between the two women he loved. As if wishing to show his protest by getting as far away from them as possible, he turned and stepped towards the bookcase. He leaned back against it, turned his head to the window and tried not to see them.

Agnes saw the dark glasses lying on the mantelpiece and absent-mindedly picked them up. She glanced at them with hatred, as if she were holding in her hand a pair of her sister's dark tears. She found everything that came from her sister's body distasteful, and those big glass tears seemed to her like one of its excretions.

Laura looked at Agnes and saw her glasses in her sister's hands. She suddenly felt a need for them. She felt a need for a shield, a veil that would cover her face from her sister's hatred. Yet she couldn't make herself take the three or four steps needed to reach her sister-enemy and take the glasses out of her hands. She was scared of her. And so she savoured, with a kind of masochistic passion, the vulnerable nakedness of her face, marked with the traces of her suffering. She knew perfectly well that Agnes couldn't bear Laura's body, her speeches about her body and about the fifteen pounds she had lost, she knew it by feeling and intuition, and perhaps it was precisely for this reason, out of spite, that she now wanted to be as much of a body as possible, an abandoned, discarded body. She wanted to place that body in the middle of their living room and leave it there. To let it lie there, heavy and motionless. And if they didn't want it there, to force them to pick up that body, her body, to force one of them to take it, one by the arms, the other by the feet, carry it outside and drop it behind the house the way people secretly dispose of useless old mattresses late at night.

Agnes stood by the fireplace, holding the dark glasses in her hand. Laura was in the middle of the living room, moving away from her sister with small backward steps. Then she took one last step backward and the back of her body pressed against Paul, hard, very hard, for behind Paul was the bookcase and he has no room to get out of the way. Laura straightened her arms and pressed both palms firmly against Paul's thighs. She leaned back her head, too, so that it touched Paul's chest.

Agnes is on one side of the room, holding Laura's dark glasses; facing her on the other side, like a pair of statues, Laura is standing pressed against Paul. Both of them are motionless, as if made of stone. Nobody says a word. After a few moments, Agnes moves her index finger away from her thumb. The dark glasses, symbol of her sister's sorrow, those metamorphosed tears, drop to the tiled floor in front of the fireplace, and break.

PART FOUR

Homo sentimentalis

1

When Goethe faced eternal judgement, countless accusations and testimonies relating to the case of Bettina were brought up against him. Not to bore the reader with many insignificant matters, I will limit myself to three depositions which seem to be of primary importance.

First: the testimony of Rainer Maria Rilke, the greatest German poet since Goethe.

Second: the testimony of Romain Rolland, who in the 1920s and 1930s was the most widely read novelist from the Urals to the Atlantic, and who in addition enjoyed a great reputation as a progressive, anti-fascist, humanist, pacifist and friend of revolution.

Third: the testimony of the poet Paul Eluard, the brilliant member of what used to be called the avant-garde, a singer of love, or to use his own words, a singer of *'l'amour-poésie'*, love-poetry, for he considered these two concepts to merge into one (as we can see in one of his most beautiful collections of verse, *L'Amour la poésie*).

As a witness called before eternal judgement, Rilke uses exactly the same words he had written in his most famous prose work, published in 1910, *The Notebooks of Malte Laurids Brigge*, in which he addressed Bettina by means of this long apostrophe:

'How is it possible that everyone does not still speak of your love? What has happened since then that was more remarkable? What is it that occupies people? You yourself knew the worth of your love; you spoke about it to your greatest poet, so that he should make it human; for it was still but a natural element. But he, in writing to you, dissuaded people from it. They have all read his answers and believe them, because the poet is more comprehensible to them than nature. But perhaps some day it will become clear that here was the limit of his greatness. That lover was bestowed upon him (*auferlegt*) and he was unequal to her (*er hat sie nicht bestanden* – i.e., he failed to pass the test Bettina represented). What does it signify that he could not reciprocate (*erwidern*)? Such love needs reciprocity, it contains within itself both the challenge (*Lockruf*) and the response; it answers its own prayer. But he should have humbled himself in all his dignity before this love and written what she dictated, with both hands, kneeling, like John on Patmos. There was no choice for him before this voice which "fulfilled the angels' ministry" (*die das Amt der Engel verrichtete*); which had come to enfold him and carry him off into eternity. Here was a chariot for his fiery ascension. Here was a dark myth for his death, which he left unfulfilled.'

3

The testimony of Romain Rolland dealt with the relationship between Goethe, Beethoven and Bettina. The novelist explained it in detail in his book *Goethe and Beethoven*, published in Paris in 1930. Even though he expressed his viewpoint in terms of fine distinctions, he made no secret of the fact that his strongest sympathies were with Bettina: he explained events in approximately the same terms as she. He did not begrudge Goethe his greatness, but he regretted his political and aesthetic cautiousness, so unbecoming to genius. And Christiane? Alas, better pass her over in silence, she was '*nullité d'esprit*', a spiritual zero.

I must emphasize again that this viewpoint was expressed with delicacy and a sense of proportion. Epigones are always more radical than their inspirers. For example, I am reading a very thorough French biography of Beethoven published in the 1960s. There the author speaks directly of Goethe's 'cowardice', his 'servility', his 'senile fear of everything new in literature and aesthetics', etc. etc. Bettina, on the other hand, is endowed with 'clairvoyance and prophetic ability, which almost give her the stature of a genius'. And Christiane, as usual, is no more than a poor '*volumineuse épouse*', a corpulent wife.

4

Though Rilke and Rolland took Bettina's part, they speak of Goethe with respect. Paul Eluard, in his *Les Sentiers et les Routes de la Poésie* (let's be fair to him, it was written in 1949, during the worst stage of his career when he was an enthusiastic admirer of Stalin), as a true Saint Just of love-poetry, chose much harsher words:

'In his diary, Goethe mentions his first meeting with Bettina Brentano with only the words: "Mamsel Brentano". The distinguished poet, author of *Werther*, gave domestic peace precedence over the active deliriums of passion (*délires actifs de la passion*). And nothing of Bettina's imagination, nothing of her talents was to disturb his Olympian dream. If Goethe had let himself be swept away by passion perhaps his song might have descended to earth but we should have loved him no less, for in those circumstances he probably would not have chosen his role of courtesan and would not have poisoned his people by trying to convince them that injustice was preferable to disorder.'

5

'That lover was bestowed upon him', wrote Rilke, and we may wonder: what does this passive construction mean? In other words: *who* bestowed her upon him?

A similar question occurs to us when we read this sentence from Bettina's letter to Goethe, dated June 15, 1807: 'I needn't be afraid to abandon myself to this feeling, for it wasn't I who planted it in my heart.'

Who planted it there? Goethe? Surely that is not what Bettina wished to say. The one who planted it in her heart was somebody above both Goethe and herself; if not God, then at least one of those angels invoked by Rilke in the passage quoted.

At this point we can come to Goethe's defence: if somebody (God or angel) planted a feeling in Bettina's heart, it was natural for Bettina to obey that feeling: it was a feeling in *her* heart, it was *her* feeling. But it seems that nobody planted such a feeling in Goethe's heart. Bettina was 'bestowed upon him'. Assigned as a task. *Auferlegt*. Then how can Rilke blame Goethe for resisting a task that was assigned to him against his wishes and, so to speak, without any warning whatever? Why should he fall on his knees and write 'with both hands' what a voice from on high was dictating to him?

Obviously, we are not going to find a rational answer and must content ourselves with a comparison: let us think of Simon, fishing in the Sea of Galilee. Jesus approaches him and asks him to abandon his nets and follow him. And Simon replies: 'Leave me alone. I prefer my nets and my fish.' Such a Simon would immediately become a comic figure, a Falstaff of the New Testament, just as in Rilke's eyes Goethe had become a Falstaff of love.

Rilke says of Bettina's love that 'it needs no reciprocity, it contains within itself both the challenge and the response; it answers its own prayer.' A love that is planted in people's hearts by an angelic gardener needs no object, no response, no – as Bettina used to say – *Gegenliebe* (requited love). The beloved (Goethe, for instance) is neither the cause nor the object of love.

At the time she corresponded with Goethe, Bettina also wrote love letters to Arnim. In one of them she said: 'True love (*die wahre Liebe*) is incapable of infidelity.' Such a love, unconcerned about reciprocity (*die Liebe ohne Gegenliebe*) 'looks for the beloved in every transformation'.

If love had been planted in Bettina not by an angelic gardener but by Goethe or Arnim, love would grow in her heart for Goethe or Arnim, an inimitable, uninterchangeable love, destined for him who planted it, for him who is beloved and therefore a non-transformable, non-transferable love. Such a love can be defined as a *relation*: a privileged relation between two people.

But what Bettina calls *wahre Liebe* (true love), is not love-relation but *love-emotion*: a fire lit by a divine hand in a human soul, a torch in whose light the lover 'looks for the beloved in every metamorphosis'. Such a love (love-emotion) knows nothing of infidelity, for even when the object changes the love itself remains perpetually the same flame lit by the same divine hand.

At this point in our examination we begin to grasp why Bettina put so few questions to Goethe in her voluminous correspondence. My God, just imagine being able to correspond with Goethe! Think of all the things you'd want to ask him about! About his books. About the books of his contemporaries. About poetry. About prose. About paintings. About Germany. About Europe. About science and technology. You'd flood him with questions until he'd be forced to express his views with the utmost precision. You'd press him into saying what he hadn't said before.

But Bettina does not exchange opinions with Goethe. Nor does she discuss art with him. With one exception: she writes to him about music. But it is she who does the instructing! Goethe evidently is of a different opinion. Why is it that Bettina does not question him about the reasons for his disagreement? If she had known how to question him, Goethe's answers would have given us the first critique of musical Romanticism *avant la lettre*!

Alas, we'll find nothing of the kind in that voluminous correspondence, we'll find precious little about Goethe, simply because Bettina was far less interested in Goethe than we suspect; the cause and object of her love was not Goethe, but love.

7

Europe has the reputation of a civilization based on reason. But one can say equally well that it is a civilization of sentiment; it created a human type whom I call sentimental man: *homo sentimentalis*.

The Jewish religion imposes a law on its believers. This law wants to be accessible to reason (the Talmud is nothing but the perpetual rational analysis of God's commandments) and does not require any mysterious sense of the supernatural, no special enthusiasm or mystic flame in the soul. The criterion of good and evil is objective: it is a matter of understanding the written law and obeying it.

Christianity turned this criterion inside out: love God, and do as you wish! said Saint Augustine. The criterion of good and evil was placed in the individual soul and became subjective. If a soul is filled with love, everything is in order: that man is good and everything he does is good.

Bettina thinks like Saint Augustine, when she writes to Arnim: 'I found a beautiful saying: true love is always right, even when it is in the wrong. But Luther says in one of his letters: true love is often in the wrong. I don't find that as good as my dictum. Elsewhere, however, Luther says: love precedes everything, even sacrifice, even prayer. From this I deduce that love is the highest virtue. Love makes us unaware of the earthly and fills us with the heavenly; thus love frees us of guilt (*macht unschuldig*).'

In the conviction that loves make us innocent lies the originality of European law and its theory of guilt, which takes into consideration the feelings of the accused: if you kill someone for money in cold blood you have no excuse; if you kill him because he insulted you, your anger will be an extenuating circumstance and you'll get a lighter sentence; if you kill him out of unhappy love or jealousy, the jury will sympathize with you, and Paul, as your defence lawyer, will request that the murder victim be accorded the severest possible punishment.

8

Homo sentimentalis cannot be defined as a man with feelings (for we all have feelings), but as a man who has raised feelings to a category of value. As soon as feelings are seen as a value, everyone wants to feel; and because we all like to pride ourselves on our values, we have a tendency to show off our feelings.

The transformation of feelings into a value had already occurred in Europe some time around the twelfth century: the troubadours who sang with such great passion to their beloved, the unattainable princess, seemed so admirable and beautiful to all who heard them that everyone wished to follow their example by falling prey to some wild upheaval of the heart.

No one revealed *homo sentimentalis* as lucidly as Cervantes. Don Quixote decides to love a certain lady named Dulcinea, in spite of the fact that he hardly knows her (this comes as no surprise, because we know that when it's a question of *wahre Liebe*, true love, the beloved hardly matters). In chapter twenty-five of Book One, he leaves with Sancho for the remote mountains, where he wishes to demonstrate to him the greatness of his passion. But how to show someone else that your soul is on fire? Especially to someone as dull and naïve as Sancho? And so when they find themselves on a mountain path, Don Quixote strips off all his clothes except for his shirt, and to demonstrate to his servant the immensity of his passion he proceeds to turn somersaults. Each time he is upside down, his shirt slides down to his shoulders and Sancho gets a glimpse of his sex. The sight of the knight's small, virginal member is so comically sad, so heart-rending, that Sancho, in spite of his callous heart, cannot bear to look at it any longer, mounts Rosinante and gallops off.

When Father died, Agnes had to arrange the funeral ceremony. She wanted the ceremony to be free of any speeches and to consist only of the Adagio from Mahler's Tenth Symphony, one of her father's favourite pieces of music. But this music is extremely sad, and Agnes was afraid that she might not be able to hold back her tears during the ceremony. It seemed unbearable to her to cry in front of everyone; she therefore put the Adagio on the record-player and listened to it. Once, twice, three times. The music reminded her of Father and she wept. But after the Adagio had resounded through the room eight, nine times, the power of the music faded; and after she had heard the record thirteen times, she found it no more moving than if she had been listening to the Paraguayan national anthem. Thanks to this training, she managed to stay dry-eyed throughout the funeral.

It is part of the definition of feeling that it is born in us without our will, often against our will. As soon as we *want* to feel (*decide* to feel, just as Don Quixote decided to love Dulcinea), feeling is no longer feeling but an imitation of feeling, a show of feeling. This is commonly called hysteria. That's why *homo sentimentalis* (a person who has raised feeling to a value) is in reality identical to *homo hystericus*.

This is not to say that a person who imitates feeling does not feel. An actor playing the role of old King Lear stands on the stage and faces the audience full of the real sadness of betrayal, but this sadness evaporates the moment the performance is over. That is why *homo sentimentalis* shames us with his great feelings only to amaze us a moment later with his inexplicable indifference.

9

Don Quixote was a virgin. Bettina first felt a man's hand on her breast at the age of twenty-five, when she was alone with Goethe in a Teplitz hotel room. If we can trust biographers, Goethe first experienced physical love during his trip to Italy, when he was almost forty years old. Soon after his return he met a twenty-three-year-old Weimar working-woman and turned her into his first lasting mistress. She was Christiane Vulpius, who in 1806, after many years of cohabitation, became his legal wife, and who knocked off Bettina's glasses in that memorable year of 1811. She was faithfully devoted to her husband (it is said that she protected him with her own body when he was threatened by drunken soldiers from Napoleon's army) and she was evidently also an excellent lover as we may judge from Goethe's joking reference to her as *mein Bettschatz*, my bed-treasure.

Nevertheless, in Goethean hagiography Christiane finds herself outside the bounds of love. The nineteenth century (but also our own time, which is still imprisoned by the past century), refuses to admit Christiane into the gallery of Goethe's loves, alongside Frederika, Lotte, Lily, Bettina and Ulrika. You may say that this is simply due to the fact that she was his wife and we have become accustomed to consider marriage automatically as something unpoetical. I believe, however, that the actual reason goes deeper: the public refuses to see Christiane as one of Goethe's loves simply because Goethe slept with her. For love-treasure and bed-treasure were mutually exclusive entities. Nineteenth-century writers often ended their novels with marriage. This was not because they wanted to save the love story from marital boredom. No, they wanted to save it from intercourse!

All the great European love stories take place in an extra-coital setting: the story of the Princess of Cleves, the story of Paul and Virginia, the story of Fromentin's Dominique who loves only one woman all his life without so much as kissing her, and of course the stories of Werther, of Hamsun's Viktoria, and Romain Rolland's story of Peter and Luce which once made women readers weep across Europe. In his novel *The Idiot*, Dostoevski let Nastasia Filipovna sleep with any merchant who came along, but when real passion was involved, namely when she found herself torn between Prince Myshkin and Rogozhin, their sexual organs dissolved in their three great hearts like lumps of sugar in three cups of tea. The love of Anna Karenina and Vronski ended with their first sexual encounter, after which it became nothing but a story of its own disintegration and we hardly know why: had they made love so poorly? or, on the contrary, had they made love so beautifully that the intensity of their pleasure released a sense of guilt? No matter how we answer, we always reach the same conclusion: there was no great love after pre-coital love, and there couldn't be.

This does not mean that extra-coital love was innocent, angelic, child-like, pure; on the contrary, it contained every bit of hell imaginable in the world. Nastasia Filipovna went safely to bed with a lot of vulgar rich men, but from the moment she met Prince Myshkin and Rogozhin, whose sex organs, as I said, dissolved in the great samovar of feeling, she found herself in the region of catastrophe and died. Or let me remind you of that beautiful scene in Fromentin's *Dominique*: the two lovers who yearned for each other for years without ever as much as touching, went out riding and the gentle, refined, reserved Madeleine proceeded to whip her horse into a mad gallop because she knew that Dominique, who followed her and was a bad rider, might get killed. Extra-coital love: a pot on the fire, in which feeling boils to a passion, and makes the lid shake and dance like a soul possessed.

The concept of European love has its roots in extra-coital soil. The twentieth century, which boasts that it liberated morals and likes to laugh at romantic feelings, was not capable of filling the concept of love with any new content (this is one of its débâcles), so that a young European who silently pronounces that great word to himself willy-nilly returns on the wings of enthusiasm to precisely the same point where Werther lived his great love for Lotte and where Dominique nearly fell off his horse.

10

Typically, just as Rilke admired Bettina, he also admired Russia, and for a certain period of time liked to think of it as his spiritual homeland. For Russia is the land of Christian sentimentality *par excellence*. It escaped both the rationalism of medieval scholastic philosophy and the Renaissance. The modern age, based on Cartesian critical thought, only penetrated there after a lag of some one or two hundred years. *Homo sentimentalis* thus failed to find there a sufficient counterweight, and became his own hyperbole commonly known as *the Slavic soul*.

Russia and France are the two poles of Europe that exercise eternal mutual attraction. France is an old, tired country where nothing remains of feelings but forms. A Frenchman may write at the end of a letter: 'Be so kind, dear sir, as to accept the assurance of my delicate feelings.' The first time I got such a letter, signed by a secretary of the publishing house Gallimard, I was still living in Prague. I jumped in the air for joy: in Paris there is a woman who loves me! She managed to slip a declaration of love into a business letter! She not only has feelings for me, but she expressly states that they are delicate! Never in my life had a Czech woman said anything of the kind to me!

Only years later was it explained to me in Paris that there exists a whole semantic repertory of closing formulas for letters; thanks to these formulas a Frenchman can determine with the precision of a chemist the most subtle degree of feelings that he wants to transmit to the addressee, without feeling them himself; on this scale, 'delicate feelings' expresses the lowest degree of official politeness bordering almost on contempt.

Oh France, you are the land of Form, just as Russia is the land of Feeling! That is why the Frenchman, eternally frustrated by not feeling any flame burning in his breast, gazes with envy and nostalgia towards the land of Dostoevski, where men offer their puckered lips to other men, and would cut the throats of anyone refusing their kiss. (Besides, if they did cut anyone's throat they would be forgiven immediately, for it was their injured love that made them do it and, as we know from Bettina, love makes people innocent. A love-sick murderer will find at least a hundred and twenty lawyers in Paris, ready to send a special train to Moscow to defend him. They will not be driven to do so by compassion – a feeling too exotic and seldom practised at home – but by abstract principles, their sole passion. The Russian murderer will fail to understand this, and once free will rush at his French defence lawyer to hug him and kiss him on the mouth. The Frenchman will back away in horror, the Russian will take offence, plunge a knife into his body and the whole story will repeat itself like the song about the dog and the crust of bread.)

11

Ah, the Russians . . .

While I was still living in Prague, the following anecdote went round about the Russian soul: a Czech man seduces a Russian woman with devastating speed. After intercourse, the Russian woman says to him with boundless contempt: 'You had my body. But you'll never have my soul!'

A splendid anecdote. Bettina wrote a total of forty-nine letters to Goethe. The word 'soul' appears fifty times, the word 'heart' one hundred and nineteen times. The word 'heart' is seldom used in a literal anatomic sense ('my heart pounded'), more often it is used as a synecdoche designating the breast ('I would like to press you to my heart'), but in the vast majority of cases it means the same as the word 'soul': *the feeling self*.

I think, therefore I am is the statement of an intellectual who underrates toothaches. *I feel, therefore I am* is a truth much more universally valid, and it applies to everything that's alive. My self does not differ substantially from yours in terms of its thought. Many people, few ideas: we all think more or less the same, and we exchange, borrow, steal thoughts from one another. However, when someone steps on my foot, only I feel the pain. The basis of the self is not thought but suffering, which is the most fundamental of all feelings. While it suffers, not even a cat can doubt its unique and uninterchangeable self. In intense suffering the world disappears and each of us is alone with his self. Suffering is the university of egocentrism.

'Do you feel contempt for me?' Hippolyte asked Prince Myshkin.

'Why? Should I feel contempt because you suffered and continue to suffer more than we?'

'No, because I am not worthy of my suffering.'

I am not worthy of my suffering. A great sentence. It suggests not only that suffering is the basis of the self, its sole indubitable ontological proof, but also that it is the one feeling most worthy of respect: the value of all values. That's why Myshkin admires all women who suffer. When he saw a photograph of Nastasia Filipovna for the first time, he said: 'That woman must have suffered a great deal.' Those words determined right from the start, even before we saw her on the stage of the novel, that Nastasia Filipovna stood far higher than all the others. 'I am nothing, but you, you have suffered,' said the bewitched Myshkin to Nastasia in the fifteenth chapter of the first part, and from that moment on he is lost.

I said that Myshkin admired all women who suffered, but I could also turn this statement round: from the moment some woman pleased him, he imagined her suffering. And because he was incapable of keeping his thoughts to himself, he immediately made this known to the woman. Besides it was an outstanding method of seduction (what a pity that Myshkin did not know how to make better use of it!), for if we say to any woman 'you have suffered a great deal' it is as if we celebrated her soul, stroked it, lifted it high. Any woman is ready to tell us at such a moment: 'Even though you still don't have my body, my soul already belongs to you!'

Under Myshkin's gaze the soul grows and grows, it resembles a giant mushroom as high as a five-storey building, it resembles a hot-air balloon about to rise into the sky with its crew. We have reached a phenomenon that I call: *hypertrophy of the soul*.

12

When Goethe received from Bettina the sketch for his monument, you may remember that he had a tear in his eye and he was certain that his inmost self was thereby letting him know the truth: Bettina truly loved him, and he had wronged her. He realized only later that the tear revealed no remarkable truth about Bettina's devotion but only the banal truth of his own vanity. He was ashamed for having once again given in to the demagogy of his own tears. Since turning fifty, he had had much experience with tears: every time somebody praised him or he was gratified by some beautiful or benevolent deed he had performed, his eyes grew moist. What is a tear? he asked himself, without ever finding the answer. But one thing was clear to him: a tear was suspiciously often provoked by the emotion brought on by Goethe's contemplation of Goethe.

About a week after the terrible death of Agnes, Laura visited a despondent Paul.

'Paul,' she said, 'we're alone in the world now.'

Paul's eyes grew moist, and he turned his head to hide his emotion from Laura.

But it was precisely this movement of the head that induced Laura to grasp him firmly by the arm: 'Don't cry, Paul!'

Paul looked at Laura through his tears and saw that her eyes, too, were moist. He smiled and said in a faltering voice: 'I'm not crying. You're crying.'

'If there is anything at all you need, Paul, you know that I am here, that you can count on me.'

And Paul answered: 'I know.'

The tear in Laura's eye was the tear of emotion Laura felt over

Laura's determination to sacrifice her whole life to stand by the side of her deceased sister's husband.

The tear in Paul's eye was a tear of emotion Paul felt over the faithfulness of Paul, who could never live with any other woman except the shadow of his dead wife, her likeness, her sister.

And so one day they lay down together on the broad bed and the tear (the mercy of the tear) made them feel no sense of betrayal towards the deceased.

The old art of erotic ambiguity came to their aid: they lay side by side not like husband and wife, but like siblings. Until now, Laura had been taboo for Paul; he probably had never connected her with any sexual imaginings, not even in some far corner of his mind. Now, he felt like her brother who had to replace her lost sister. At the start, that made it morally possible for him to go to bed with her, and later it filled him with a totally unknown excitement: they knew everything about each other (like brother and sister) and what separated them was not the strangeness but prohibition; this prohibition had lasted twenty years and with the passage of time was becoming more and more insurmountable. Nothing was closer than the other's body. Nothing was more prohibited than the other's body. And so with an incestual excitement (and with misty eyes) he began to make love to her, and he made love to her more wildly than he had ever done with anyone in his entire life.

13

There are civilizations that have had greater architecture than Europe, and Greek tragedy will for ever remain unsurpassed. However, no civilization has ever created such a miracle out of musical sounds as has European music, with its thousand-year-old history and its wealth of forms and styles! Europe: great music and *homo sentimentalis*. Twins nurtured side by side in the same cradle.

Music taught the European not only a richness of feeling, but also the worship of his feelings and his feeling self. After all, you are familiar with this situation: the violinist standing on the platform closes his eyes and plays the first two long notes. At that moment the listener also closes his eyes, feels his soul expanding in his breast, and says to himself: 'How beautiful!' And yet he hears only two notes, which in themselves could not possibly contain anything of the composer's ideas, any creativity, in other words any art or beauty. But those two notes have touched the listener's heart and silenced his reason and aesthetic judgement. Mere musical sound performs approximately the same effect upon us as Myshkin's gaze fixed upon a woman. Music: a pump for inflating the soul. Hypertrophic souls turned into huge balloons rise to the ceiling of the concert hall and jostle each other in unbelievable congestion.

Laura loved music sincerely and deeply; I recognize the precise significance of her love for Mahler: Mahler is the last great European composer who still appeals, naïvely and directly, to *homo sentimentalis*. After Mahler, feeling in music starts to become suspicious; Debussy wants to enchant us, not to move us, and Stravinsky is ashamed of emotion. Mahler is for Laura *the ultimate composer* and when she hears loud rock music coming from Brigitte's room, her wounded love for European music, vanishing in the din of electric guitars, drives her to fury. She gives Paul an ultimatum: either Mahler or rock; meaning: either me or Brigitte.

But how is one to choose between too equally unloved kinds of music? Rock is too loud for Paul (like Goethe, he has delicate ears), while Romantic music evokes in him feelings of anxiety. During the war, when everybody around him was disturbed by panicky reports, the tangos and waltzes usually played on the radio were replaced by minor-key chords of serious, solemn music; in the child's memory, these chords became for ever engraved as harbingers of catastrophe. Later, he realized that the pathos of Romantic music united all Europe: it can be heard every time some statesman is murdered or war is declared, every time it is necessary to stuff people's heads with glory to make them die more willingly. Nations which tried to annihilate each other were filled with the identical fraternal emotion when they heard the thunder of Chopin's *Funeral March* or Beethoven's 'Eroica'. Ah, if only it depended on Paul, the world could get along very well without rock and without Mahler. However, the two women did not permit him neutrality. They forced him to choose: between two kinds of music, between two women. And he didn't know what to do, because both women were equally dear to him.

Yet the two women hated each other. Brigitte looked with painful sorrow at the white piano, which had served no function for years except as a makeshift shelf; it reminded her of Agnes, who out of love for her sister had pleaded with Brigitte to learn to play it. As soon as Agnes died, the piano came to life and resounded every day. Brigitte hoped that furious rock would revenge her betrayed mother and chase the intruder from the house. When she realized that Laura was staying, she left herself. Rock was heard no more. Records revolved on the record-player, Mahler's trombones rang through the room and tore at Paul's heart, still pining for his daughter. Laura approached Paul, grasped his head with both hands and looked into his eyes. Then she said: 'I'd like to give you a child.' Both of them knew that doctors had already warned her a long time ago not to have any children. That's why she added: 'I am ready to do whatever is necessary.'

It was summertime. Laura closed her shop and the two of them left for a two-week seaside holiday. The waves dashed against the shore and their call filled Paul's breast. The music of this element was the only kind that he loved passionately. He discovered with happy surprise that Laura merged with this music; the only woman in his life whom he found to resemble the sea; who was the sea.

14

Romain Rolland, a witness for the prosecution at the eternal trial conducted against Goethe, had two outstanding characteristics: an adoring approach to women ('she was a woman and that's sufficient reason for loving her,' he wrote about Bettina), and an enthusiastic desire to ally himself with progress (by which he meant: Communist Russia and revolution). It is odd that this admirer of women at the same time praised Beethoven for his refusal to greet women. For this was what the episode in the Teplitz spa was all about, if we have understood it correctly: Beethoven, his hat pulled down over his forehead and his arms clasped behind his back, strode towards the Empress and her court, which was certainly made up of ladies as well as gentlemen. If he failed to greet them, he was an out and out boor! But this is hard to believe: Beethoven may have been a strange, morose character, but he was never boorish towards women! This whole story is obviously nonsense, and could have been accepted and retold only because people (including, shamefully, even a novelist!) have lost all sense of reality.

You will object that it is improper to probe into the authenticity of an anecdote that was obviously not intended as testimony but as allegory. Very well; let us then examine the allegory as allegory; let us ignore its origins (which we will never know exactly, anyway), let us ignore the tendentious implications that one person or another wanted to insinuate, and let us try to grasp, so to speak, its objective significance:

What does Beethoven's deeply pulled-down hat mean? That Beethoven rejected the power of the aristocracy as reactionary and unjust, while the hat in Goethe's humble hand pleaded for keeping the world as it is? Yes, that is the generally accepted explanation, but it is indefensible: just as Goethe had to create a *modus vivendi* for himself and his creativity, so did Beethoven in his own time; he therefore dedicated his sonatas to one prince or another and didn't even hesitate to compose a cantata in honour of the victors who gathered in Vienna after Napoleon's defeat, in which the choir sings out: 'May the world be again as it once used to be!'; he even went so far as to write a Polonaise for the Empress of Russia, as if symbolically laying poor Poland (a Poland that thirty years later Bettina would so bravely champion) at the feet of its invader.

Thus, if our allegorical picture shows Beethoven striding past a group of aristrocrats without taking off his hat, it cannot mean that aristocrats were contemptible reactionaries while he was an admirable revolutionary, but that those who *create* (statues, poems, symphonies) deserve more respect than those who *rule* (over servants, officials or whole nations); that creativity means more than power, art more than politics; that works of art, not wars or aristocratic costume-balls, are immortal.

(Actually, Goethe must have been thinking exactly the same thing, except that he didn't consider it useful to reveal this unpleasant truth to the masters of the world at the time, while they were still alive. He was certain that in eternity it would be they who would bow their heads first, and that was enough for him.)

The allegory is clear, and yet it is generally misinterpreted. Those who look at this allegorical picture and hasten to applaud Beethoven completely fail to understand his pride: they are for the most part people blinded by politics, who themselves give precedence to Lenin, Guevara, Kennedy or Mitterrand over Fellini or Picasso. Romain Rolland would surely have bowed much more deeply than Goethe, if he had encountered Stalin on a path in Teplitz.

15

This matter of Romain Rolland's respect for women was rather odd. Rolland, who admired Bettina simply because she was a woman ('she was a woman and that's sufficient reason for loving her'), had no admiration whatever for Christiane, who was without doubt a woman too! He considered Bettina 'mad and wise' (*folle et sage*), 'madly alive and madly cheerful' with a 'tender and mad' heart, and in numerous other passages he described her as mad. And we know that for *homo sentimentalis* the words madman, mad, madness (which in French sound even more poetic than in other languages: *fou, folle, folie*) designate an exaltation of feeling freed from censorship ('*les délires actifs de la passion*', Eluard might call it) and so are spoken with tender admiration. On the other hand, this admirer of womankind and the proletariat never mentions Christiane without linking her name, against all the rules of gallantry, with such adjectives as 'jealous', 'fat', 'ruddy and corpulent', 'importunate', and again and yet again: 'fat'.

It is strange that this friend of womankind and the proletariat, this herald of equality and brotherhood, did not find it the least bit moving that Christiane was a former working-woman and that Goethe exhibited quite extraordinary courage by living with her as a lover and then openly making her his wife. He had to face not only the gossip of Weimar salons but the disapproval of his intellectual friends, Herder and Schiller, who turned up their noses at her. I am not surprised that the Weimar aristocracy enjoyed Bettina calling her a fat sausage. But I am surprised that a friend of womankind and the working class enjoyed it. Why is it that a young patrician, maliciously showing off her cultural superiority over a simple woman, was so close to him? And why is it that Christiane, who liked to drink and to dance, who did not watch her figure and grew fat quite happily, never earned the right to that divine adjective 'mad' but was seen by the friend of the proletariat merely as 'importunate'?

Why did it never occur to the friend of the proletariat to elaborate the episode with the glasses into an allegory, in which a simple woman of the people rightly punished the arrogant young intellectual while Goethe, having taken his wife's part, strode proudly forward with head held high (and hatless!) against an army of aristocrats and their shameful prejudices?

Of course, such an allegory would be no less silly than the preceding one. But the question remains: why had the friend of the proletariat and womankind chosen one silly allegory and not the other? Why did he give preference to Bettina over Christiane?

This question gets to the heart of the matter.

The next chapter will answer it:

16

Goethe urged Bettina (in one of his undated letters) to 'step out of herself'. Nowadays we would say that he reproached her for being egocentric. But was he justified in doing so? Who fought for the rebelling Tyrolean mountaineers, for the posthumous fame of Petofi, for the life of Mieroslawski? Was it he, or she? Who was constantly thinking of others? Who was always ready for self-sacrifice?

Bettina. There is no doubt about it. Yet Goethe's reproach is not thereby refuted. For Bettina never stepped out of her self. No matter where she went, her self fluttered behind her like a flag. What inspired her to fight for Tyrolean mountaineers was not the mountaineers but the bewitching image of Bettina fighting for the mountaineers. What drove her to love Goethe was not Goethe but the seductive image of the child-Bettina in love with the old poet.

Let us remember her gesture, which I called the gesture of longing for immortality: first she placed her fingertips to a spot between her breasts, as if she wanted to point to the very centre of what is known as the self. Then she flung her arms forward, as if she wanted to transport that self somewhere far away, to the horizon, to infinity. The gesture of longing for immortality knows only two points in space: the self here, the horizon far in the distance; only two concepts: the absolute that is the self, and the absolute that is the world. That gesture has nothing in common with love, because the other, the fellow creature, the person between these two poles (the self and the world) is excluded in advance, ruled out of the game, invisible.

A twenty-year-old youth who joins the Communist Party or,

rifle in hand, goes off to the hills to fight for a band of guerrillas is fascinated by his own revolutionary image, which distinguishes him from others, and makes him become himself. It begins with a festering, unsatisfied love for his self, a self he wants to mark with expressive features and then send (by the gesture of longing for immortality I have already described) on to the great stage of history, under the gaze of thousands; and we know from the example of Myshkin and Nastasia Filipovna how such a keen gaze can make a soul grow, expand, get bigger and bigger until at last it rises to heaven like a beautiful, brightly lit airship.

What makes people raise their fists in the air, puts rifles in their hands, drives them to join struggles for just and unjust causes, is not reason but a hypertrophied soul. It is the fuel without which the motor of history would stop turning and Europe would lie down in the grass and placidly watch clouds sail across the sky.

Christiane did not suffer from the hypertrophy of the soul and did not yearn to exhibit herself on the great stage of history. I suspect that she preferred to lie on her back in the grass and watch the clouds float by. (I even suspect that she knew happiness at such times, something a person with a hypertrophied soul dislikes seeing because he is burning in the fire of his self and is never happy.) Romain Rolland, friend of progress and tears, thus did not hesitate for a moment when he had to choose between her and Bettina.

17

Strolling down a road in the other world, Hemingway saw a young man approaching him from a distance; he was elegantly dressed and held himself remarkably erect. As this dandy came closer, Hemingway could discern a slight, raffish smile on his face. When they were separated by just a few steps, the young man slowed his walk, as if he wanted to give Hemingway a last opportunity to recognize him.

'Johann!' Hemingway exclaimed in surprise.

Goethe smiled with satisfaction; he was proud that he had succeeded in producing such an excellent dramatic effect. Let's not forget that he had long been active as a theatrical director and had a sense of showmanship. He then took his friend by the arm (interestingly, even though he was now younger than Hemingway, he still behaved with the indulgence of the elderly), and took him on a leisurely walk.

'Johann,' said Hemingway, 'today you look like a god.' His friend's good looks caused him sincere joy, and he laughed happily: 'Where did you leave your slippers? And that green eyeshade?' And after he stopped laughing, he said: 'That's how you should come to eternal trial. To crush the judges not with arguments but with your beauty!'

'You know, I didn't say one single word at the eternal trial. Out of contempt. But I couldn't keep myself from going there and listening to the proceedings. Now I regret it.'

'What do you want? You were condemned to immortality for the sin of writing books. You explained it to me yourself.'

Goethe shrugged, and said with some pride: 'Perhaps our

books are immortal, in a certain sense. Perhaps.' He paused, and then added softly, with great emphasis: 'But we aren't.'

'Quite the contrary,' Hemingway protested bitterly. 'Our books will probably soon stop being read. All that will remain of your *Faust* will be that idiotic opera by Gounod. And maybe also that line about the eternal feminine pulling us somewhere or other . . .'

'*Das Ewigweibliche zieht uns hinan,*' recited Goethe.

'Right. But people will never stop prying into your life, down to the smallest details.'

'Haven't you realized yet, Ernest, that the figures they talk about have nothing to do with us?'

'Don't tell me, Johann, that you bear no relation to the Goethe about whom everybody writes and talks. I admit that the image that remained behind you is not entirely identical to you. I admit that it distorts you quite a bit. Still, you are present in it.'

'No, I'm not,' Goethe said very firmly. 'And I'll tell you something else. I am not even present in my books. He who doesn't exist cannot be present.'

'That's too philosophical for me.'

'Forget for a moment that you're an American and exercise your brain: he who doesn't exist cannot be present. Is that so complicated? The instant I died I vanished from everywhere, totally. I even vanished from my books. Those books exist in the world without me. Nobody will ever find me in them. Because you cannot find someone who does not exist.'

'I'd like to agree with you,' said Hemingway, 'but explain this to me: if the image you've left behind has nothing to do with you, why did you lavish so much care on it while you were still alive? Why did you invite Eckermann to join you? Why did you start writing *Poetry and Truth*?'

'Ernest, resign yourself to the idea that I was as foolish as you. That obsession with one's own image, that's man's fatal immaturity. It is so difficult to be indifferent to one's image. Such indifference is beyond human strength. One becomes capable of it only after death. And even then it doesn't happen at once, but only a long time after death. You still haven't reached that point. You're still not mature. And yet you've been dead . . . how long, actually?'

'Twenty-seven years,' said Hemingway.

'That's nothing. You'll have to wait at least another twenty or thirty years before you become fully aware that man is mortal, and be able to draw all the consequences from that realization. It won't happen any sooner. Just shortly before I died I declared that I felt such creative power within me, it was impossible for it to disappear without a trace. And of course I believed that I would live in the image I left behind me. Yes, I was just like you. Even after death it was hard for me to accept the idea that I no longer existed. You know, it's really very peculiar. To be mortal is the most basic human experience and yet man has never been able to accept it, grasp it, and behave accordingly. Man doesn't know how to be mortal. And when he dies, he doesn't even know how to be dead.'

'And do you know how to be dead, Johann?' asked Hemingway, in order to lighten the gravity of the moment. 'Do you really believe that the best way to be dead is to waste time chatting with me?'

'Don't make a fool of yourself, Ernest,' said Goethe. 'You know perfectly well that at this moment we are but the frivolous fantasy of a novelist who lets us say things we would probably never say on our own. But to conclude. Have you noticed my appearance today?'

'Didn't I tell you the moment I set eyes on you? You look like a god!'

'This is how I looked when all Germany considered me a pitiless seducer,' Goethe said with an almost grandiose air. Then, moved, he added: 'I wanted you to take me with you into your future years in precisely this way.'

Hemingway looked at Goethe with sudden, gentle indulgence: 'And you, Johann, how long have you lived since your death?'

'One hundred and fifty-six,' Goethe answered with some embarrassment.

'And you still haven't learned how to be dead?'

Goethe smiled: 'I know, Ernest. I've been behaving differently from what I've been telling you just a moment ago. But I permitted myself this childish vanity, because today we are seeing each other for the last time.' And then, slowly as one who would speak no more, he said these words: 'You see, I have come to the definite conclusion that the eternal trial is bullshit. I have decided to make use of my death at last and, if I can express it with such an imprecise term, to go to sleep. To enjoy the delights of total non-existence, which my great enemy Novalis used to say has a bluish colour.'

PART FIVE
Chance

1

After lunch she went back up to her room. It was Sunday, no new guests were expected and nobody rushed her to check out; the broad bed was still unmade, just as she had left it in the morning. The sight of it filled her with bliss: she had spent two nights alone in it, heard nothing but her own breathing and slept stretched out crosswise from one corner to the other, as if she wanted her body to embrace the whole of it, all that belonged only to her and to her sleep.

Everything was already packed into the suitcase lying open on the table; on top of her folded skirt lay a paperback edition of Rimbaud's poetry. She had taken it along because during the last few weeks she had been thinking a great deal about Paul. Before Brigitte was born she had often travelled with him all over France, sitting behind him astride the big motorcycle. Her memories of that time and of that motorcycle mingled with her memories of Rimbaud: he was their poet.

She glanced through those half-forgotten poems as if she were leafing through an old diary, curious whether its time-yellowed notes would now seem moving, ridiculous, fascinating or meaningless. The verses were as beautiful as ever, but something about it surprised her: they had no connection whatever with the motorcycle they used to ride. The world of Rimbaud's poems was far closer to a person of Goethe's century than to Brigitte. Rimbaud, who had commanded everyone to be absolutely modern, was a poet of nature, a wanderer, and his poetry contained words that modern man had forgotten or no longer knew how to savour: crickets, elms, watercress, hazel trees, lime trees, heather, oak, delightful ravens, warm droppings of ancient dove-cotes; and above all, roads, roads and paths: *In the blue summer evening I will go down the path, pricked by the corn, treading on the low grass . . . I will not speak, I will not think . . . And I will wander far, far like a gypsy, happy with nature as with a woman . . .*

She closed the small suitcase. Then she left the room, went briskly down the stairs to the hotel driveway, tossed the suitcase on the back seat of her car and sat down behind the wheel.

2

It was two-thirty and she should have been on her way, for she didn't like to drive at night. But she couldn't make herself turn the ignition key. Like a lover who has failed to say everything that is in his heart, the surrounding landscape stopped her from leaving. She got out of the car. There were mountains all around her; those on the left were clear and bright, and the whiteness of the glaciers shimmered above the green contours; the mountains on the right were wrapped in a yellowish haze that turned them into silhouettes. They were two different kinds of light; two different worlds. She kept turning her head from left to right and from right to left and then decided to take one last walk. She set out along a gentle path that led upwards through meadows towards a forest.

Some twenty-five years had already passed since she had come to the Alps with Paul on the big motorcycle. Paul loved the sea and mountains were foreign to him. She wanted to win him over to her world; she wanted him to be enchanted by the views of trees and meadows. They parked the motorcycle at the edge of the road, and Paul said:

'A meadow is nothing but a field of suffering. Every second some creature is dying in the gorgeous green expanse, ants eat wriggling earthworms, birds lurk in the sky to pounce on a weasel or a mouse. You see that black cat, standing motionless in the grass? She is only waiting for an opportunity to kill. I detest all that naïve respect for nature. Do you think that a doe in the jaws of a tiger feels less horror than you? People thought up the idea that animals don't have the same capability for suffering as humans, because otherwise they couldn't bear the knowledge that they are surrounded by a world of nature that is horror and nothing but horror.'

Paul was pleased that man was gradually covering the whole earth with concrete. It was as if he were watching a cruel murderess being walled up. Agnes understood him too well to resent his antipathy to nature, especially as it was motivated, if one can put it that way, by his humanity and sense of justice.

And yet, perhaps it was really just the ordinary attempt of a jealous husband trying to snatch his wife away from her father. For it was Agnes' father who had taught her to love nature. She used to walk miles and miles of paths with him, relishing the silence of the woods.

Once some friends drove her through the American countryside. It was an endless and impenetrable realm of trees intersected by long highways. The silence of those forests sounded as unfriendly and foreign to her as the noise of New York. In the kind of forest loved by Agnes, roads branch into smaller roads and still smaller paths; foresters walk those paths. Along the paths there are benches, from which you can enjoy a landscape full of grazing sheep and cows. This is Europe, this is the heart of Europe, this is the Alps.

3

Depuis huit jours, j'avais déchiré mes bottines
aux cailloux des chemins . . .

For eight days I had been scraping my shoes
on the stones of the roads . . .

writes Rimbaud.

Road: a strip of ground over which one walks. A route differs from a road not only because it is solely intended for vehicles, but also because it is merely a line that connects one point with another. A route has no meaning in itself; its meaning derives entirely from the two points that it connects. A road is a tribute to space. Every stretch of road has meaning in itself and invites us to stop. A route is the triumphant devaluation of space, which thanks to it has been reduced to a mere obstacle to human movement and a waste of time.

Before roads and paths disappeared from the landscape, they had disappeared from the human soul: man stopped wanting to walk, to walk on his own feet and to enjoy it. What's more, he no longer saw his own life as a road, but as a route: a line that led from one point to another, from the rank of captain to the rank of general, from the role of wife to the role of widow. Time became a mere obstacle to life, an obstacle that had to be overcome by ever greater speed.

Road and route; these are also two different conceptions of beauty. When Paul says that at a particular place the landscape is beautiful, that means: if you stopped the car at that place, you might see a beautiful fifteenth-century castle surrounded by a park; or a lake reaching far into the distance, with swans floating on its brilliant surface.

In the world of routes, a beautiful landscape means: an island of beauty connected by a long line with other islands of beauty.

In the world of roads and paths, beauty is continuous and constantly changing; it tells us at every step: 'Stop!'

The world of roads was the world of fathers. The world of routes was the world of husbands. And Agnes' story closes like a circle: from the world of roads to that of routes, and now back again. For Agnes is moving to Switzerland. That decision has already been made, and this is the reason why throughout the last two weeks she has been feeling so continuously and madly happy.

4

When she returned to the car it was already late afternoon. And at the very same moment that she was putting the key in the car door, Professor Avenarius, in swimming trunks, approached the jacuzzi where I was already expecting him, sitting in the warm water being bombarded by the violent currents under the surface.

That's how events are synchronized. Whenever something happens in place Z, something else is happening in places A, B, C, D and E. 'At the very moment that . . .' is a magic sentence in all novels, a sentence which enchants us when we read *The Three Musketeers*, the favourite novel of Professor Avenarius, to whom I said in lieu of a greeting: 'At the very moment that you stepped into the pool, the heroine of my novel finally turned the ignition key to begin her drive to Paris.'

'A wonderful coincidence,' said Professor Avenarius, visibly pleased, and he submerged himself.

'Of course, billions of such coincidences take place in the world every second. I dream of writing a big book: The Theory of Chance. The first part: the chance that governs coincidences. The classification of the various types of coincidences. For example: "At the very moment that Professor Avenarius stepped into the jacuzzi, and felt the warm stream of water on his back, in a public park in Chicago a yellow leaf fell off a chestnut tree." That is a coincidence, but without any significance. In my classification of coincidence I call it *mute coincidence*. But imagine me saying: "At the very moment *the first* yellow leaf fell in Chicago, Professor Avenarius entered the jacuzzi to massage his back." The sentence becomes melancholy, because we now see Professor Avenarius as a harbinger of autumn and the water in which he is submerged now seems to us salty with tears. Coincidence breathed unexpected significance into the event and therefore I call it *poetic coincidence*. But I could also say what I told you when I saw you just now: "Professor Avenarius submerged himself in the jacuzzi at the very moment that, in the Swiss Alps, Agnes started her car." That coincidence cannot be called poetic, because it gives no special significance to your entrance into the pool, and yet it is a very valuable kind of coincidence, which I call *contrapuntal*. It is like two melodies merging into one small composition. I know it from my childhood. One boy sang a song while another boy was singing a different one, and yet they went well together! But there is still one other type of coincidence: "Professor Avenarius entered the Montparnasse Metro at the very moment a beautiful woman was standing there with a red collection-box in her hand." That is the so-called *story-producing coincidence*, adored by novelists.'

I paused after these remarks because I wanted to provoke him into telling me some details about his encounter in the Metro, but he only kept twisting his back to let the pounding stream of water massage his lumbago and he looked as if my last example had nothing to do with him.

'I can't help feeling,' he said, 'that coincidence in man's life is not determined by the degree of probability. What I mean is that often a coincidence happens to us which is so unlikely that we cannot justify it mathematically. Recently I was walking down a totally insignificant street in a totally insignificant district of Paris when I met a woman from Hamburg whom I used to see almost daily twenty-five years ago, and then I completely lost touch with her. I took that street only because by mistake I got off the Metro one stop too soon. And she was in Paris on a three-day visit and was lost. The probability of our meeting was one in a billion.'

'What method do you use to calculate the probability of human meetings?'

'Do you happen to know of any method?'

'I don't. And I regret it,' I said. 'It's odd, but human life has never been subjected to mathematical research. Take time, for example. I long for an experiment that would examine, by means of electrodes attached to a human head, exactly how much of one's life a person devotes to the present, how much to memories and how much to the future. This would let us know who a man really is in relation to his time. What human time really is. And we could surely define three basic types of human being depending on which variety of time was dominant. But to come back to coincidence. What can we reliably say about coincidence in life, without mathematical research? Unfortunately, no existential mathematics exists as yet.'

'Existential mathematics. An outstanding idea,' Avenarius said thoughtfully. Then he added: 'In any event, whether it was a matter of one in a million or one in a billion, the meeting was absolutely improbable and it was precisely this lack of probability that gave it value. For existential mathematics, which does not exist, would probably propose this equation: the value of coincidence equals the degree of its improbability.'

'To meet unexpectedly in the middle of Paris a beautiful woman whom we hadn't seen in years . . .' I said dreamily.

'I don't know what made you assume that she was beautiful. She was the cloakroom attendant in a brasserie I frequented every day; she came with a party of old-age pensioners to spend three days in Paris. When we recognized each other, we looked at one another with embarrassment. Almost with desperation, in fact, of the kind felt by a legless boy who wins a bicycle in a lottery. As if we both knew that we were given the gift of an enormously valuable coincidence which will do us no good whatsoever. It seemed that someone was laughing at us, and we were ashamed in each other's eyes.'

'This type of coincidence could be called *morbid*,' I said. 'But I am trying in vain to figure out into which category to place the coincidence by which Bernard Bertrand was awarded the title of compleat ass.'

Avenarius replied in an authoritative tone: 'Bernard Bertrand was awarded the title of compleat ass because he is a compleat ass. No coincidence was involved. It was simple necessity. Not even the iron laws of history described by Marx involve greater necessity than this title.'

And as if my question had irritated him, he rose from the water in all his threatening majesty. I rose as well. We got out of the pool and went to sit down at the bar at the other end of the gym.

We each ordered a glass of wine, took the first sip and Avenarius said: 'Surely it must be clear to you that everything I do is a struggle against Diabolum.'

'Of course I know that,' I answered. 'That's precisely why I asked you what was the sense of attacking Bernard Bertrand.'

'You don't understand a thing,' said Avenarius, as if tired of my inability to grasp what he had already explained to me so many times. 'There is no effective or sensible way to fight Diabolum. Marx tried, all the revolutionaries tried, and in the end Diabolum always managed to appropriate every organization whose original goal was to destroy him. My whole revolutionary past ended in disappointment and now only one single question occupies me: what is a man to do when he realizes that no organized, effective and sensible fight against Diabolum is possible? He has only two choices: to resign and cease to be himself, or to keep on cultivating an inner need for revolt and from time to time give it expression. Not to change the world, as Marx once wanted, justly and in vain, but because he is urged to do so by an inner moral imperative. Recently I've been thinking about you. It's important for you, too, not to express your revolt merely through the writing of novels, which cannot bring you any true satisfaction, but through action. Today I am asking you to join me at long last!'

'All the same, it is still unclear to me,' I said, 'why an inner moral need drove you to attack a poor radio commentator. What objective reasons led you to do it? Why did you choose him and not someone else as a symbol of assininity?'

'I forbid you to use the stupid word "symbol",' Avenarius

raised his voice. 'That's how terrorist organizations think! That's how politicians think, who are nowadays nothing but symbol-jugglers! I have the same contempt for people who hang national flags from their windows as for people who burn them in public squares. Bernard is not a symbol for me. For me, nothing is more concrete than he is! I hear him talk every morning! His effeminate voice, his affectation and his idiotic jokes get on my nerves! I can't stand what he says! Objective reasons? I don't know what that means! I declared him a compleat ass on the basis of my most eccentric, most malicious, most capricious personal freedom!'

'That's what I wanted to hear,' I said. 'You did not act like a god of necessity, but like a god of chance.'

'Be it chance, or necessity, I am glad that you think of me again as a god,' said Professor Avenarius, his voice back to its normal, quiet tone. 'But I don't understand why you are so surprised at my choice. A person who jokes stupidly with his listeners and conducts campaigns against euthanasia is beyond all doubt a compleat ass and I cannot imagine a single objection that could be raised against that.'

When I heard Avenarius' last sentence, I was appalled: 'You are confusing Bernard Bertrand with Bertrand Bertrand!'

'I am talking of Bernard Bertrand who speaks on the radio and fights against suicides and beer!'

I clutched my head: 'Those are two different people! Father and son! How in the world could you have merged a radio commentator and a Member of Parliament into one person? Your mistake is a perfect example of what we classified a moment ago as a morbid coincidence.'

For a moment, Avenarius was at a loss. But he soon recovered and said: 'I am afraid that you aren't very knowledgeable about your own theory of coincidence. There is nothing morbid about my mistake. On the contrary, it clearly resembles what you called poetic coincidence. Father and son have turned into a single ass with two heads. Not even ancient Greek mythology came up with such a marvellous animal!'

We drank up our wine, went to the locker-room to get dressed, and then telephoned a restaurant to reserve a table.

6

At the very same moment that Professor Avenarius was putting on his socks, Agnes was remembering the following sentence: 'Every woman prefers her child to her husband.' Her mother said that to her, in a confidential tone (in circumstances now forgotten) when Agnes was about twelve or thirteen years old. The meaning of the sentence becomes clear only if we think about it for a while: to say that we prefer A to B is not a comparison of two degrees of love but means that B is not loved at all. For if we love someone, he cannot be compared. The beloved is incomparable. Even if we love both A and B, we cannot compare them because in making the comparison we are already ceasing to love one of them. And if we say publicly that we prefer one over the other, it is never a question of proclaiming our love for A (in that event, it would be sufficient to say merely: 'I love A!'), but of making it discreetly yet unmistakably clear that we don't care for B.

This analysis, of course, was not within the capabilities of little Agnes. And her mother surely counted on that; she needed to confide in someone yet at the same time did not want to be fully understood. But the child, even though she was not able to understand everything, sensed nevertheless that the sentence did not favour her father. And she loved him! She therefore did not feel flattered that she was given preference, but rather saddened that someone she loved was being wronged.

The sentence imprinted itself in her mind; she tried to imagine what it meant, in all concreteness, to love someone more and someone else less; before sleeping she lay in bed wrapped up in her blanket, and this scene floated before her eyes: there is her father, each of his hands holding a daughter. They are facing an execution squad that is only waiting for the order: aim! fire! Her mother goes to beg the enemy commander for mercy, and he gives her the right to save two of the condemned. And so just before the commander gives the order to fire, her mother runs up, tears her daughters out of her husband's hands and in terrified haste leads them away. Agnes is dragged by her mother and her head is turned back, towards her father; she turns her head so hard, with so much determination, that she feels a cramp in her neck; she sees her father gazing at them sadly, without the least protest: he is reconciled to her mother's choice because he knows that maternal love is greater than conjugal love and that it is his duty to give up his life.

Sometimes she imagined the enemy commander giving her mother the right to save only one of the condemned. She never doubted for an instant that her mother would save Laura. In her mind's eye she saw the two of them left behind, she and her father, face to face with the firing squad. They held hands. At that moment Agnes was not at all interested in what had happened to her mother and sister, she did not gaze after them, but she knew that they were rapidly moving away and that neither one had looked back! Agnes, on her little bed, lay wrapped up in a blanket, her eyes were full of hot tears and she felt inexpressibly happy to be holding her father's hand, to be with him and to die with him.

7

Perhaps Agnes would have forgotten the execution scene if the two sisters hadn't quarrelled one day when they surprised their father standing over a pile of torn photographs. Watching Laura shout at him, Agnes recalled that this was the same Laura who had left her alone with her father to face a firing squad and had left *without looking back*. She suddenly realized that their conflict went deeper than she had been aware, and for that reason she never mentioned the quarrel, as if afraid to give a name to something that should remain nameless, to wake something that should remain asleep.

And so when at that distant time her sister departed, angry and in tears, and she remained alone with her father, she felt for the first time a strange sensation of fatigue that came from the surprising discovery (it is always the most banal discoveries that surprise us the most) that she would always have the same sister for the rest of her life. She might be able to change friends, to change lovers, if she wished she would be able to divorce Paul, but she would never be able to exchange her sister. Laura was a constant in her life, which was all the more tiring for Agnes because from childhood on their relationship had been like a chase: Agnes ran in front, with her sister at her heels.

Sometimes she thought of herself as the princess of a fairy tale she remembered from childhood: the princess, on horseback, is fleeing an evil pursuer; she is holding a brush, a comb and a ribbon. She throws the brush behind her and a thick forest springs up between her and the pursuer. She gains some time this way, but soon the pursuer is again in sight; she throws the comb behind her and immediately it turns into sharp rocks. And when he is once more at her heels, she drops the ribbon which unwinds behind her into a broad river.

And then Agnes had only one thing left in her hand: dark glasses. She threw them to the ground and became separated from her pursuer by a field of broken glass.

But now her hand is empty, and she knows that Laura is the stronger one. She is stronger, because she has turned weakness into a weapon and into moral superiority: she is being wronged, deserted by her lover, she is suffering, attempting suicide, while the happily married Agnes throws her sister's glasses on the floor, humiliates her, forbids her to enter the house. Yes, for nine months, since the episode of the broken glasses, they haven't seen each other. And Agnes knows that Paul doesn't approve, even though he has never said so. He feels sorry for Laura. Her run is nearing an end. Agnes hears her sister's breath close at her back and she knows she is about to lose.

The sensation of fatigue is growing stronger. She no longer has the slightest desire to continue her run. She is not a racer. She never wanted to race. She didn't choose her sister. She wanted to be neither her model nor her rival. A sister is as much an accident in Agnes' life as the shape of her ears. She chose neither her sister nor the shape of her ears and yet she is chained to this nonsensical coincidence all her life.

When she was little, her father taught her to play chess. She was fascinated by one move, technically called castling: the player moves two chessmen in a single move: the castle and the king exchange their relative positions. She liked that move: the enemy concentrates all his effort on attacking the king and the king suddenly disappears before his eyes; he moves away. All her life she dreamed about that move, and the more exhausted she felt the more she dreamt it.

8

Ever since her father died and left her some money in a Swiss bank, Agnes had gone to the Alps two or three times each year, always to the same hotel, and she tried to imagine staying permanently in that part of the world: could she live without Paul and without Brigitte? How could she know? A solitude of three days, which is how long she generally stayed at the hotel, a 'trial solitude' of that kind taught her very little. She kept hearing the word 'Leave!' like the most wonderful temptation. But if she really left, wouldn't she soon come to regret it? It was true that she longed for solitude, yet she was quite fond of her husband and daughter and cared about them. She would need to have news about them, she would need to know that everything was all right with them. But how could she be alone, separated from them, and at the same time know all about them? Then, too, how was she to arrange her new life? Would she look for a new occupation? That would not be easy. Would she do nothing? Yes, that was appealing, but wouldn't she suddenly feel like an old-age pensioner? When she thought about it all, her plan to 'leave' seemed more and more artificial, forced, impractical, resembling one of those Utopian illusions of someone who knows in the depths of his heart that he is powerless and will do nothing.

Then suddenly one day the resolution to this problem came from outside, quite unexpectedly and at the same time in the most ordinary way. Her employer was starting a branch office in Bern and because it was common knowledge that her German was as good as her French, they asked her whether she would like to direct research there. They knew that she was married and therefore didn't count too much on a positive reply; she surprised them: she said 'yes' without an instant's hesitation; and she also surprised herself: that spontaneous 'yes' proved that her longing to leave was not a comedy she was playing for herself without really believing it, but something real and serious.

That desire eagerly seized the opportunity to be not merely a romantic daydream and to become a part of something completely prosaic: career advancement. When Agnes accepted the offer she acted like any ambitious woman, so that nobody could suspect the real reasons behind her decision. For her, everything suddenly became clear; it was no longer necessary to do tests and experiments and to try to imagine 'what it would be like, if only . . .' What she had been longing for was suddenly here and she was surprised that she was accepting it as an unambiguous and unblemished joy.

It was a joy so intense that it awakened a sense of shame and guilt in her. She couldn't find the courage to tell Paul about her decision. That's why she took that one last trip to her hotel in the Alps. (The next time she would already have her own apartment there: either in the Bern suburbs or in the nearby mountains.) In the course of those two days she wanted to think through how to break the news to Brigitte and Paul, so as to convince them that she was an ambitious, emancipated woman, absorbed by her professional career and success, even though she had never been such a person before.

9

Dusk had already fallen; her headlights on, Agnes crossed the Swiss border and found herself on a French route, which always made her nervous; disciplined Swiss drivers obeyed the rules, whereas the French, shaking their heads in short horizontal motions, expressed their indignation at those who would deprive people of their right to speed, and turned highway travel into an orgiastic celebration of human rights.

She started to feel hungry and scanned the route for a restaurant or motel where she could have a meal. Three huge motorcycles passed her on the left, making a terrible noise; in the glare of the headlights she could see the drivers, their outfits, like space suits, gave them the appearance of inhuman, extraterrestrial beings.

At that very moment a waiter was leaning over our table to remove the empty appetizer dishes, and I was just saying to Avenarius: 'The very morning that I started the third part of my novel, I heard a report on the radio I cannot possibly forget. A girl went out on the highway at night and sat down with her back to the oncoming cars. She sat there, her head resting on her knees, and waited for death. The driver of the first car swerved aside at the last moment, and died with his wife and two children. The second car, too, ended up in the ditch. And the third. Nothing happened to the girl. She got up, walked away and nobody ever found out who she was.'

Avenarius said: 'What reasons do you think could induce a girl to sit down on the highway at night and wish to be crushed by a car?'

'I don't know,' I said. 'But I would bet the reason was disproportionately small. Or to put it more precisely, seen from the outside it would seem small to us and quite foolish.'

'Why?' asked Avenarius.

I shrugged my shoulders. 'I cannot imagine any substantial reason for such a terrible suicide, as for example an incurable disease or the death of someone close. In such a case nobody would choose this terrible end, making other people die! Only a reason deprived of reason can lead to such an unreasonable horror. In all languages derived from Latin, the word "reason" (*ratio*, *raison*, *ragione*) has a double meaning: first, it designates the ability to think, and only second, the cause. Therefore reason in the sense of a cause is always understood as something rational. A reason the rationality of which is not transparent would seem to be incapable of causing an effect. But in German, a reason in the sense of a cause is called *Grund*, a word having nothing to do with the Latin *ratio* and originally meaning "soil" and later "basis". From the viewpoint of the Latin *ratio*, the girl's behaviour, sitting down on the highway, seems absurd, inappropriate, irrational, and yet it has its reason, its basis, its ground, *Grund*. Such a *Grund* is inscribed deep in all of us, it is the ever-present cause of our actions, it is the soil from which our fate grows. I am trying to grasp the *Grund* hidden at the bottom of each of my characters and I am convinced more and more that it has the nature of a metaphor.'

'Your idea escapes me,' said Avenarius.

'Too bad. It is the most important thought that ever occurred to me.'

At that point the waiter brought us our duck. It smelled delicious and made us forget the preceding conversation completely.

At last, Avenarius broke the silence: 'What are you writing about these days, anyway?'

'That's impossible to recount.'

'What a pity.'

'Not at all. An advantage. The present era grabs everything that was ever written in order to transform it into films, TV programmes; or cartoons. What is essential in a novel is precisely what can only be expressed in a novel, and so every adaptation contains nothing but the non-essential. If a person is still crazy enough to write novels nowadays and wants to protect them, he has to write them in such a way that they cannot be adapted, in other words, in such a way that they cannot be retold.'

He disagreed: 'I can retell the story of *The Three Musketeers* by Alexandre Dumas with the greatest of pleasure, any time you ask me, from beginning to end!'

'I feel the same way, and I love Alexandre Dumas,' I said. 'All the same, I regret that almost all novels ever written are much too obedient to the rules of unity of action. What I mean to say is that at their core is one single chain of causally related acts and events. These novels are like a narrow street along which someone drives his characters with a whip. Dramatic tension is the real curse of the novel, because it transforms everything, even the most beautiful pages, even the most surprising scenes and observations merely into steps leading to the final resolution, in which the meaning of everything that preceded it is concentrated. The novel is consumed in the fire of its own tension like a bale of straw.'

'When I hear you,' Professor Avenarius said uneasily, 'I just hope that your novel won't turn out to be a bore.'

'Do you think that everything that is not a mad chase after a final resolution is a bore? As you eat this wonderful duck, are you bored? Are you rushing towards a goal? On the contrary, you want the duck to enter into you as slowly as possible and you never want its taste to end. A novel shouldn't be like a bicycle race but a feast of many courses. I am really looking forward to Part Six. A completely new character will enter the novel. And at the end of that part he will disappear without a trace. He causes nothing and leaves no effects. That is precisely what I like about him. Part Six will be a novel within a novel, as well as the saddest erotic story I have ever written. It will make you sad, too.'

Avenarius lapsed into a perplexed silence. After a while, he asked me in a kindly voice: 'And what will your novel be called?'

'The Unbearable Lightness of Being.'

'I think somebody has already written that.'

'I did! But I was wrong about the title then. That title was supposed to belong to the novel I'm writing right now.'

We stopped talking, and concentrated on the taste of the wine and the duck.

In the midst of eating, Avenarius said: 'You work too hard. You should think of your health.'

I knew very well what Avenarius was trying to suggest, but I pretended not to notice, and silently tasted my wine.

After a lengthy pause, Avenarius repeated: 'It seems to me you work too hard. You should think of your health.'

I said: 'I do think of my health. I lift weights regularly.'

'That's dangerous. You might have a stroke.'

'That is precisely what I'm afraid of,' I said, thinking of Robert Musil.

'What you need is jogging. Night jogging. I'll show you something,' he said mysteriously, unbuttoning his jacket. Around his chest and his imposing belly I saw a peculiar system of belts, vaguely suggestive of a horse's harness. Attached on the lower right-hand side was a sheath containing a terrifyingly large kitchen knife.

I praised his equipment, but because I wanted to shift the conversation from a topic I knew all too well, I changed the subject; I wanted him to tell me about the only thing that was important to me and that I was eager to have explained: 'When you saw Laura in the Metro station, she recognized you and you recognized her.'

'Yes,' Avenarius said.

'I am interested in learning how you had come to know each other.'

'You are interested in trivia and serious things bore you,' he said with some disappointment, buttoning up his jacket. 'You're like an old concierge.'

I shrugged.

He continued: 'There is nothing interesting about it. Before I awarded the compleat ass his diploma, his picture appeared all over town. I waited in the lobby of the radio station to see him in person. As he got out of the elevator, a woman ran up to him and kissed him. After that, I followed them fairly often and several times my glance met hers, so that my face must have seemed familiar to her even though she didn't know who I was.'

'Did she appeal to you?'

Avenarius lowered his voice. 'I admit to you that if it hadn't been for her, I probably would never have carried out my plan with the diploma. I have thousands of such plans but for the most part they remain just dreams.'

'Yes, I know,' I agreed.

'But when a man is fascinated by a woman, he does everything to come in contact with her, even if only indirectly and in a round-about way, to touch her world, even from afar, and set it in motion.'

'So Bernard became a compleat ass because you liked Laura.'

'You may not be wrong,' Avenarius remarked thoughtfully, and added: 'There is something in that woman that preordains her to be a victim. That's just what attracted me to her. I was overjoyed when I saw her in the arms of two drunken, stinking *clochards*! An unforgettable moment!'

'Yes, I know your story up to that point. But I want to know what happened next.'

'She has quite an extraordinary behind,' continued Avenarius, ignoring my question. 'When she went to school, her friends must have wanted to pinch it. In my imagination I can hear her squeal each time, in a high soprano voice. That voice was a sweet promise of their future bliss.'

'Yes, let's talk about that. Tell me what happened next, after you led her out of the Metro as her providential saviour.'

Avenarius pretended not to have heard me. 'An aesthete might say,' he continued, 'that her behind is too bulky and a bit too low, which is all the more disturbing as her soul longs for the heights. But it is precisely in this contradiction that I find the crux of the human condition: our heads are full of dreams but our behinds drag us down like an anchor.'

God knows why, the last words of Avenarius sounded melancholy, perhaps because our plates were empty and every trace of duck had gone. The waiter leaned over us again to take away the dishes. Avenarius looked up at him: 'Do you have a piece of paper?'

The waiter handed him a blank bill, Avenarius pulled out his pen and made the following drawing:

Then he said: 'That's Laura: full of dreams, her head looks up at heaven, and her body is drawn to earth: her behind and her breasts, also rather heavy, look downward.'

'That's odd,' I said, and I made my own drawing next to his.

'Who is that?' Avenarius asked.

'Her sister Agnes: her body rises like a flame. And her head is always slightly bowed: a sceptical head looking at the ground.'

'I prefer Laura,' Avenarius replied firmly, adding: 'Above all, however, I prefer jogging at night. Do you like the church of Saint-Germain-des-Prés?'

I nodded.

'Yet you've never really seen it.'

'I don't understand,' I said.

'I was recently walking down the Rue de Rennes towards the boulevard and I counted how many times I was able to look at the church without being bumped into by a hurrying passer-by or nearly run over by a car. I counted seven very short glances, which cost me a bruised left arm because an impatient young man struck me with his elbow. I was allowed an eighth glance when I stopped in front of the church door and lifted my head. But I only saw the façade, in a highly distorted fish-eye perspective. From such fleeting and deformed views my mind had put together some sort of rough representation that has no more in common with that church than Laura does with my drawing of two arrows. The church of Saint-Germain-des-Prés has disappeared and all the churches in towns have disappeared in the same way, like the moon when it enters an eclipse. The cars that fill the streets have narrowed the pavements, which are crowded with pedestrians. If they want to look at each other, they see cars in the background, if they want to look at the building across the street they see cars in the foreground; there isn't a single angle of view from which cars will not be visible, from the back, in front, on both sides. Their omnipresent noise corrodes every moment of contemplation like an acid. Cars have made the former beauty of cities invisible. I am not like those stupid moralists who are incensed that ten thousand people are killed each year on the highways. At least there are that many fewer drivers. But I protest that cars have led to the eclipse of cathedrals.'

After a moment of silence, Professor Avenarius said: 'I feel like ordering some cheese.'

11

The cheeses gradually made me forget the church, and the wine called to my mind the sensuous image of one arrow on top of another: 'It's clear to me that you walked her home and she asked you up to her place. She confessed to you that she was the unhappiest woman in the world. At the same time her body was dissolving under your touch, it was defenceless, it was unable to hold back either tears or urine.'

'Tears or urine!' Avenarius exclaimed. 'A splendid image!'

'And then you made love to her and she kept looking at your face, shaking her head and repeating: "You're not the one I love! You're not the one I love!"'

'What you're saying is terribly exciting,' said Avenarius, 'but whom are you talking about?'

'About Laura!'

He interrupted me: 'It is absolutely essential that you exercise. Jogging at night is the only thing that can take your mind off your erotic fantasies.'

'I am not as well equipped as you,' I said, hinting at his harness. 'You know perfectly well that without a proper outfit you can't get involved in such an undertaking.'

'Don't worry. The outfit is not so important. At first I used to jog without it, too. This . . .' he touched his chest, 'is a refinement I developed only after a few years, and it wasn't so much a practical need that led me to it as a kind of purely aesthetic, almost impractical longing for perfection. For the time being you can manage perfectly well with a knife in your pocket. The only thing that's important is that you obey the following rule: first car, right front; second car, left front; third, right rear; fourth . . .'

'Left rear . . .'

'Wrong!' Avenarius laughed like a cruel teacher pleased by a pupil's incorrect answer: 'On the fourth car, all four!'

We laughed, and Avenarius continued: 'I know that lately you've been obsessed by mathematics, so you should appreciate this geometric regularity. I insist on it as an unconditional rule, which has a double significance: first of all, it throws the police off the track, because they see in the special arrangement of punctured tyres some kind of a meaning, a message, a code that they try in vain to solve; but more important, the maintenance of this geometric pattern introduces into our destructive act a principle of mathematical beauty that radically distinguishes us from vandals who scratch a car with nails or shit on its roof. I elaborated all the details of my method many years ago in Germany, when I still believed in the possibility of organized resistance against Diabolum. I attended meetings of the ecological group. Those people see the main evil of Diabolum in the destruction of nature. Why not? That's also one way of under-standing Diabolum. I sympathized with them. I worked out a plan for the organization of commandos who would puncture tyres at night. If the plan had been put into effect, I assure you that cars would cease to exist. Five commando units, three men each, would, in one month, have sufficed to make the use of cars in a city of average size impossible! I presented my plan to them in all its details, and they could have learned from me how to perform a perfect subversive act, effective and yet safe from discovery by the police. But those idiots considered me a provocat-eur! They booed me and threatened me with their fists! Two weeks later they took off on huge motorcycles and in tiny cars to a protest demonstration somewhere in the woods where a nuclear power plant was about to be built. They destroyed a lot of trees and they left behind them, in the course of four months, a terrible stench. Then I realized that they had long ago become a part of

273

Diabolum, and I decided this was my last attempt to change the world. Nowadays I am using my old revolutionary tactics only for my own, quite egotistical pleasure. Jogging through the streets at night and puncturing tyres is a great joy for the soul and excellent training for the body. Once again I urge you to do it. You'll sleep better. And you'll stop thinking about Laura.'

'Just tell me one thing. Does your wife really believe that you leave the house at night in order to puncture tyres? Doesn't she suspect that this is only a pretext to hide other kinds of nocturnal adventure?'

'One detail escapes you. I snore. That has earned me the right to sleep in the most remote room of the house. I am the complete master of my night.'

He smiled and I had a strong urge to accept his challenge and agree to go with him: for one thing, the undertaking seemed praiseworthy to me, and then too I was fond of my friend and wanted to please him. But before I was able to say anything, he called loudly to the waiter to bring us our bill, the thread of the conversation was broken and we became involved in other topics.

12

None of the highway restaurants appealed to Agnes; she kept passing one after another and her hunger and fatigue grew. It was already quite late when she stopped in front of a motel.

There was nobody in the dining room except a mother with a six-year-old boy who was one minute sitting down and the next boisterously running around the room.

She ordered a simple supper and examined the toy in the middle of the table. It was a small rubber statuette, advertising some sort of product. It had a huge body, short legs, and a monstrous green nose reaching all the way down to its navel. Quite amusing, she said to herself; she picked up the toy and looked at it more closely.

She imagined somebody bringing the figurine to life. Once it had a soul, it would probably feel intense pain if somebody tweaked its green rubber nose as Agnes was now doing. It would quickly learn to fear people, because everybody would want to play with its nose and its life would be nothing but constant fear and suffering.

Would the toy perhaps feel sacred respect for its Creator? Would it thank him for its life? Would it pray to him? One day someone might hold a mirror up to it, and from that time on it would yearn to hide its face from people by covering it with its hands, because it would be dreadfully ashamed. But it couldn't cover its face that way, because its Creator did not make the hands movable.

How odd, Agnes told herself, to think that the little man might feel shame. Is he responsible for his green nose? Wouldn't he be more likely just to shrug his shoulders? No, he wouldn't shrug his shoulders. He would be ashamed. When someone discovers his physical self for the first time, the first and most important feeling that comes over him is neither indifference nor anger, but shame: basic shame, which will accompany him all his life, sometimes intense and sometimes milder, dulled by time.

When Agnes was sixteen, she visited some friends of her parents; in the middle of the night she menstruated and bloodied the sheets. When she noticed it early next morning, she was seized by panic. She slipped stealthily into the bathroom, got a piece of soap and began to rub the sheet with a wet cloth; the spot not only grew bigger but soiled the mattress as well; she was mortally ashamed.

Why was she so ashamed? Don't all women suffer from monthly bleeding? Did she invent women's genitals? Was she responsible for them? No. But responsibility has nothing to do with shame. If she had spilled some ink, for example, and ruined her hosts' carpet and tablecloth, it would have been unpleasant and painful, but she wouldn't have felt shame. The basis of shame is not some personal mistake of ours, but the ignominy, the humiliation we feel that we must be what we are without any choice in the matter, and that this humiliation is seen by everyone.

No wonder that the toy with the long green nose was ashamed of its face. But what about Father? He was handsome, after all!

Yes, he was. But what is beauty, mathematically speaking? Beauty means that a particular specimen closely resembles the original prototype. Let us imagine that the maximum and minimum dimensions of all body parts were put into a computer: length of nose, three to seven centimetres; height of forehead, three to eight centimetres; and so on. An ugly person has a forehead eight centimetres high and a nose only three centimetres long. Ugliness: the poetic capriciousness of coincidence. In the case of a beautiful person, the play of coincidence happened to select an average of all the dimensions. Beauty: the un-

276

poetic average. Beauty, more than ugliness, reveals the non-individuality, the impersonality of a face. A beautiful person sees in his face the original blueprint drawn up by the designer of the prototype, and finds it difficult to believe that what he is seeing is an inimitable self. He is therefore as ashamed as a toy with a long green nose that is suddenly brought to life.

When Father was dying, she sat on the edge of his bed. Before he entered the last phase of his death agony, he said to her: 'Don't look at me any more,' and these were the last words she ever heard from his mouth, his last message.

She obeyed him; she bowed her head towards the floor, closed her eyes, and kept holding on to his hand; she let him leave slowly, unseen, for a world without faces.

13

She paid the bill and walked out to her car. The boy who had been so noisy in the restaurant came running towards her. He squatted down and stretched out his arms as if holding an automatic pistol. He imitated the sound of gunfire: 'Boom, boom, boom,' and riddled her with imaginary bullets.

She stopped, bent over him and said in a mild voice: 'Why are you behaving like an idiot?'

He stopped shooting and gazed at her with big childish eyes.

She repeated: 'Yes, you must be an idiot.'

The boy made a snivelling face: 'I'll tell my mum!'

'Go ahead! Go and tell tales!' said Agnes. She got into the car and promptly drove off.

She was glad not to have met the boy's mother. She imagined the woman shouting at her, shaking her head with short horizontal motions while lifting her shoulders and eyebrows, to defend her insulted child. Of course, the child's rights are above all other rights. Why did their mother give preference to Laura over Agnes, when the enemy commander allowed her to save just one out of the three members of the family? The answer was quite clear: she gave preference to Laura, because she was younger. In the hierarchy of age the baby has the highest rank, then the child, then the adolescent, and only then the adult. As for the old they are virtually at ground level, at the very bottom of this pyramid of values.

And the dead? They are under the ground. Even lower than the old. The old are still accorded human rights. The dead, however, lose all rights from the very first second of death. No law protects them any longer from slander, their privacy has ceased to be private; not even the letters written to them by their loved ones, not even the family album left to them by their mothers, nothing, nothing belongs to them any longer.

In the last years before he died, her father gradually destroyed all his belongings; no suits remained in the wardrobe, no manuscripts, no lecture notes, no letters. He erased all traces of himself without anyone being the wiser. Only in the case of the photographs did Agnes and Laura accidentally find him out. All the same, they were unable to prevent him from destroying them. Not a single one remained.

Laura protested. She fought for the rights of the living against the unjustified demands of the dead. The face that will disappear tomorrow under the earth or into the fire does not belong to the future dead but purely and entirely to the living, who are hungry and need to eat the dead, their letters, their money, their photographs, their old loves, their secrets.

But Father escaped them all, Agnes kept telling herself.

She thought of him and smiled. And suddenly it occurred to her that her father was her only love. Yes, it was quite clear: her father was her only love.

At that moment, huge motorcycles once again flew past her with great speed; in the glare of her headlights she could see the riders bent over the handlebars, filled with aggression that made the night tremble. That was precisely the world she wanted to escape, to escape for ever; so she decided to get off the highway at the first opportunity on to a quieter route.

14

We found ourselves in a Paris avenue full of noise and lights, and set out towards Avenarius' Mercedes, which was parked a few blocks away. We were still thinking about the girl squatting on a dark highway with her head in her hands, waiting for a car to run her over.

I said: 'I tried to explain to you that we all carry inscribed within us the reasons for our actions, what the Germans call *Grund*; a code determining the essence of our fate; that code, in my opinion, is in the nature of a metaphor. You cannot understand the girl we are talking about without a metaphoric image. For example: she goes through life as if it were a valley; she keeps meeting people all the time, and addressing them; but they look at her uncomprehendingly, and walk on because her voice is so quiet that no one hears it. That's how I imagine her and I am sure that she sees herself that way, too: as a woman walking through a valley among people who do not hear her. Or another image: she is at the dentist's, sitting in a crowded waiting room; a new patient enters, walks to the couch where she is seated and sits down on her lap; he didn't do it intentionally, he simply saw an empty seat on the couch; she protests and tries to push him away, shouting: "Sir! Can't you see? This seat is taken! I am sitting here!" but the man doesn't hear her, he sits comfortably on top of her and cheerfully chats with another waiting patient. These are two images, two metaphors that define her and enable me to understand her. Her longing for suicide was provoked not by something from outside her. It was planted in the very soil of her being, and it slowly grew and unfolded like a black flower.'

'I accept that,' said Avenarius. 'But you still have to explain why she chose to take her life on one particular day rather than another.'

'How do you explain why a flower unfolds on one particular day and not on another? Its time has come. The longing for self-destruction slowly grew until one day she was no longer capable of resisting it. I am guessing that the wrongs done to her were probably quite minor: people didn't respond to her greeting; nobody smiled at her; she was waiting in line at the post office, and some fat woman elbowed her way past; she had a job as a saleswoman in a department store and the manager accused her of not treating the customers with respect. Thousands of times she felt like protesting and shouting, but she never found the courage because she had a weak voice which faltered in moments of excitement. She was weaker than anyone else and was continually being insulted. When evil strikes a man, he shifts it on to others. That's called conflict, quarrel or revenge. But a weak man doesn't have the strength to shift the evil that strikes him, his own weakness insults and humiliates him and he is totally defenceless in the face of it. He has no other choice but to destroy his weakness along with his own self. And so the girl's dream of her own death was born.'

Avenarius looked around for his Mercedes and realized that we were in the wrong street. We turned and walked back.

I continued: 'The death she was longing for did not have the form of going away but of throwing away. Throwing away the self. She wasn't satisfied with a single day of her life, a single word she had ever said. She carried herself through life as something monstrous, something she hated and couldn't get rid of. That's why she longed so much to throw herself away, as one throws away a crumpled piece of paper or a rotten apple. She longed to throw herself away as if the one doing the throwing and the one being thrown away were two different people. She tried to imagine throwing herself out of a window. But that idea

281

was ridiculous, because she lived on the first floor and the store where she worked was on the mezzanine and had no windows. And she longed to die like a beetle, crushed by a sudden fist. It was almost a physical longing to be crushed, like the need to press one's palm against the part of our body that hurts.'

We reached Avenarius' flashy Mercedes and stopped.

Avenarius said: 'The way you describe her, one could almost feel affection for her . . .'

'I know what you're trying to say: if she hadn't decided to send other people to death as well. But that, too, is expressed in the two metaphors I used to introduce her to you. Whenever she spoke to anyone, nobody heard her. She was losing the world. When I say world, I mean the part of existence that answers our call (even if only by way of a barely audible echo), and whose call we ourselves hear. For her, the world was becoming mute and ceasing to be her world. She was completely locked into herself and her suffering. At least, could the sight of the suffering of others tear her out of her isolation? No. Because the suffering of others was taking place in a world she had lost, a world no longer hers. If the planet Mars were nothing but one huge ball of suffering, where every stone cried out in pain, it would not be able to move us to compassion because Mars does not belong to our world. A person who finds himself outside the world is not sensitive to the world's suffering. The only event that drew her away from her own suffering for a moment was the illness and death of her little dog. Her neighbour was indignant: she doesn't care about people, but weeps over a dog! She wept over a dog because the dog was a part of her world whereas the neighbour was not; the dog answered her voice, people did not.'

We fell silent, thinking about the poor girl, and then Avenarius opened the car door and nodded to me: 'Come on! I'll take you along! I'll lend you some running shoes and a knife!'

I knew that if I didn't go with him on his tyre-slashing expedition he would never find anyone else, and would remain isolated in his eccentricity as if in exile. I had an enormous desire to go with him, yet I felt lazy; drowsiness was creeping up on me, and chasing around dark streets after midnight seemed like an unimaginable sacrifice.

'I am going home. I'll walk,' I said and shook his hand.

He drove off. I gazed after his Mercedes with the guilty feeling of having betrayed a friend. Then I set out for home, and after a while my thoughts returned to the girl in whom the longing for self-destruction grew like a black flower.

I thought: one day, after work, she didn't go home but started walking out of the city. She wasn't aware of anything around her, she didn't know whether it was summer or winter, whether she was walking along a beach or along a factory wall; after all, for a long time now she had no longer been living in the world; her only world was her soul.

15

She wasn't aware of anything around her, she didn't know whether it was summer or winter, whether she was walking along a beach or a factory wall, she kept walking only because her soul, full of disquiet, required motion, and it was not able to rest in one place, for without movement it began to hurt terribly. Imagine an excruciating toothache: something forces you to pace the room from one end to the other; there is no sensible reason for it, because movement cannot diminish the pain, but without your knowing why, the aching tooth begs you to keep moving.

And so the girl kept walking and found herself on a highway with one car after another flashing by, she walked along the hard shoulder, passing one milestone after another, she wasn't conscious of anything, she merely stared into her soul in which she saw nothing but the same few images of humiliation. She couldn't tear her eyes away from them; only now and again when a motorcycle thundered past and the noise hurt her eardrums did she realize that an outer world existed; but that world was without meaning, it was empty space suitable only for walking and for shifting her painful soul from one place to another in the hope that it would hurt less.

She had long been thinking about letting herself be run over by a car. But cars speeding down a highway scared her, they were a thousand times more powerful than she; she couldn't imagine where she might find the courage to throw herself under their wheels. She would have to throw herself *upon* them, *against* them, and she lacked the strength for that, just as she lacked the strength to shout back at the manager when he reproached her unjustly.

She had left at dusk, and now night had fallen. Her feet hurt, and she knew she didn't have the strength to go much further. At that moment of exhaustion, she saw on a big illuminated sign the word *Dijon*.

At once, she forgot her exhaustion. The word seemed to remind her of something. She tried to recapture a fleeting memory: someone she knew came from Dijon, or else someone had told her something amusing that had happened there. Suddenly she came to believe that the town was pleasant and that the people there were different from the ones she had known before. It was as if dance music had suddenly broken out in the middle of a desert. It was as if a spring of silvery water had gushed up in a cemetery.

Yes, she would go to Dijon! She started to wave at cars. But the cars kept passing, blinding her with their lights, and didn't stop. The same situation, from which there was no escape, kept repeating itself over and over: she would turn to someone, address him, speak to him, call out, and he would not hear.

For half an hour she kept sticking out her arm in vain: the cars didn't stop. The city of lights, the happy city of Dijon, the dance orchestra in the midst of a desert, receded into the darkness. The world was withdrawing from her once again, and she was returning to her soul surrounded far and wide by nothing but emptiness.

Then she came to a place where a smaller route joined the highway. She stopped: no, the cars on the highway were useless: they would neither crush her nor take her to Dijon. She took the exit and found the quieter route.

16

How to live in a world with which you disagree? How to live with people, when you share neither their suffering nor their joys? When you know that you don't belong among them?

Agnes is driving down a quiet road in her car and she answers herself: love or the cloister. Love or the cloister: two ways you can reject the Creator's computer, and escape it.

Love: Agnes had long been imagining the following test: you would be asked whether after death you wished to be reawakened to life. If you truly loved someone, you would agree to come back to life only on the condition that you'd be reunited with your beloved. Life's value is conditional and justified only by the fact that it enables you to live your love. The one you love means more to you than God's creation, more than life itself. This is of course a derisive blasphemy towards the Creator's computer, which considers itself the apex of all things and the source of all meaning.

But the majority of mankind has never known love and of those people who believe they have known it, only a few would successfully pass the test conceived by Agnes; they would grasp at the promise of renewed life without asking for any condition; they would give preference to life over love and voluntarily fall back into the Creator's web.

If a person is not fated to live with the beloved and subordinate everything to love, there is a second method of eluding the Creator: to leave for a cloister. Agnes recalled a sentence from Stendhal's novel: '*Il se retira à la chartreuse de Parme.*' Fabrice left; he retired to the charterhouse of Parma. No charterhouse is mentioned anywhere else in the novel and yet that single sentence on the last page is so important that Stendhal used it for the title;

because the real goal of all of Fabrice's adventures was the charterhouse; a place secluded from people and the world.

In the old days, people who disagreed with the world and considered neither its sufferings nor its joys as their own withdrew to a cloister. But our century refuses to acknowledge anyone's right to disagree with the world, and therefore there are no longer cloisters to which a Fabrice might escape. There is no longer a place secluded from people and the world. All that remains of such a place is the memory, the ideal of a cloister, the dream of a cloister. Charterhouse. *Il se retira à la chartreuse de Parme.* The vision of a cloister. Agnes has been following this vision to Switzerland for seven years, following the vision of the charterhouse. The charterhouse of roads secluded from the world.

Agnes recalled the special moment she experienced on the day of her departure, when she took a final walk through the countryside. She reached the bank of a stream and lay down in the grass. She lay there for a long time and had the feeling that the stream was flowing into her, washing away all her pain and dirt: washing away her self. A special, unforgettable moment: she was forgetting her self, losing her self, she was without a self; and that was happiness.

In recalling this moment, an idea came to Agnes, vague and fleeting and yet so very important, perhaps supremely important, that she tried to capture it for herself in words:

What is unbearable in life is not *being* but *being one's self*. The Creator, with his computer, released into the world billions of selves as well as their lives. But apart from this quantity of lives it is possible to imagine some primordial being that was present even before the Creator began to create, a being which was – and still is – beyond his influence. When she lay on the ground that day and the monotonous song of the stream flowed into her, cleansing her of the self, the dirt of the self, she participated in that primordial being which manifested itself in the voice of fleeting time and the blue of the sky; she now knows there is nothing more beautiful.

The route she drove on to from the highway was quiet, and distant stars, infinitely distant stars, shone over it. Agnes drove on and thought:

Living, there is no happiness in that. Living: carrying one's painful self through the world.

But being, being is happiness. Being: becoming a fountain, a fountain on which the universe falls like warm rain.

17

The girl kept on walking for a long time, her feet hurt, she staggered, and then she sat down on the asphalt precisely in the middle of the righthand lane. She tucked her head between her shoulders, her nose touched her knees and her hunched back throbbed with the knowledge that it was exposed to chrome, steel, shock. Her chest was caved in, her poor weak chest burning with the bitter flame that let her think of nothing but her painful self. She longed for a shock that would crush her and put out that flame.

When she heard an oncoming car, she hunched down even more, the noise became unbearable, but instead of the expected shock she only felt a strong blast of air to her right that spun her half-way round. She heard the squeal of tyres, then an enormous crash; with her eyes closed and her face pressed to her knees, she saw nothing, and was amazed that she was still alive, sitting as before.

Once again, she heard the noise of an approaching car; this time the blast of air blew her to the ground, the noise of the crash sounded very near and immediately she heard screaming, indescribable screaming, terrible screaming that brought her sharply to her feet. She stood in the middle of an empty road; about two hundred yards away she saw flames, and from another spot, closer to her, that same indescribable, terrible screaming still rose from the ditch into the dark sky.

The screaming was so insistent, so terrible, that the world around her, the world she had lost, became real, coloured, blinding, noisy. She stood in the middle of the road, her arms outstretched, and suddenly felt big, powerful, strong; the world, that lost world that had refused to listen was now returning to her, screaming, and it was so beautiful and so terrible that she, too, felt like screaming, but she couldn't, her voice died in her throat and she was unable to revive it.

She found herself in the blinding headlights of a third car. She wanted to jump aside, but didn't know whether to go right or left; she heard the squealing of tyres, the car went past her and she heard a crash. At that point the scream that was in her throat finally came to life. From the ditch, still from the same place, the cry of pain did not cease, and now she answered it.

Then she turned and ran away. She ran screaming, amazed that her weak voice was capable of such a scream. At the point where the route crossed the highway there was a telephone on a pole. The girl picked it up: 'Hello! Hello!' Finally a voice answered at the other end. 'There's been an accident!' The voice asked her for the location, but she didn't know where she was, and so she hung up and started running back towards the town she had left that afternoon.

18

Just a few hours ago Professor Avenarius was lecturing me on the importance of slashing tyres following a strict sequence: first car, right front; second car, left front; third, right rear; fourth, all four wheels. But that was only a theory, with which he hoped to impress the audience of ecologists or his too trusting friend. In reality, he proceeded without any system whatsoever. He ran down the street and whenever he felt like it he pulled out his knife and stuck it in the nearest tyre.

In the restaurant, he explained to me that after each attack it was necessary to stick the knife back under one's jacket, to slip it into its sheath and then keep running with one's hands free. For one thing, it was easier to run that way, and then also there were reasons of safety: it isn't wise to risk somebody seeing you with a knife in your hand. The act of slashing must be short and sharp, never lasting more than a few seconds.

Unfortunately, dogmatic as Avenarius was in his theories, in practice he behaved quite carelessly, without method, and was dangerously inclined to take the easy way out. He had just slashed two tyres on a car in an empty street, then he straightened himself up and started to run, still holding the knife in his hand contrary to all his rules of safety. The next car he was aiming for was parked at the corner. He stretched out his arm while still four or five steps away (another rule broken: too soon!), and at that instant he heard a shout on his right. A woman was staring at him, petrified with horror. She must have turned the corner just as Avenarius' attention was concentrated on the intended target at the kerb. They stood stock still, facing one another, and because he, too, was frozen with fear, his arm remained rigidly raised. The woman couldn't take her eyes off the outstretched knife and again cried out. Only then did Avenarius come to his senses and slip the knife under his jacket. To calm the woman, he smiled at her and asked: 'What time is it?'

As if that question terrified the woman even more than the knife, she uttered a third piercing cry.

At that moment some late-night walkers were crossing the street and Avenarius made a fatal mistake. If he had taken out his knife once again and begun to wave it furiously, the woman would have recovered from her paralysis and fled, inducing any accidental passers-by to do the same. But he decided to act as if nothing had happened, and repeated in a friendly voice: 'Can you tell me the time?'

When she saw that people were approaching and that Avenarius meant her no harm, she uttered a fourth terrible cry and complained in a loud voice to everyone within earshot: 'He threatened me with a knife! He wanted to rape me!'

With a gesture of complete innocence, Avenarius opened his arms wide: 'All I wanted from her,' he said, 'was the right time.'

A short man in uniform, a policeman, stepped out from the small crowd that had formed around Avenarius. He asked what was going on. The woman repeated that Avenarius had wanted to rape her.

The short policeman timidly approached Avenarius, who pulled himself up to his full majestic height, raised his arm and said in a powerful voice: 'I am Professor Avenarius!'

Those words, and the dignified manner in which they were delivered, made a big impression upon the policeman; he seemed ready to ask the crowd to disperse and to let Avenarius go his way.

But the woman, now that she had lost her fear, became aggressive: 'You may be Professor Capillarius, for all I care!' she shouted. 'You still threatened me with a knife!'

A man emerged from the door of a house a few yards away. He walked in a peculiar manner, like a sleepwalker, and he stopped just as Avenarius was explaining in a firm voice: 'I've done nothing except ask that woman for the time.'

The woman, sensing that Avenarius was gaining the sympathy of the bystanders with his dignity, shouted at the policeman: 'He has a knife under his jacket! He hid it under his jacket! An enormous knife! Search him and you'll see!'

The policeman shrugged and said to Avenarius, in a manner that was almost apologetic: 'Would you kindly open your jacket?'

For a moment, Avenarius stood motionless. Then he realized that he had no choice but to obey. He slowly unbuttoned his jacket and then opened it wide, so that everyone could see the clever system of straps around his chest as well as the terrible kitchen knife that was attached to it.

The circle of people gasped in amazement, while the sleepwalker stepped up to Avenarius and said to him: 'I am a lawyer. If you need help, here is my card. I just want to tell you one thing. You are not required to answer any questions. You can demand the presence of a lawyer right from the start.'

Avenarius accepted the card and put it in his pocket. The policeman took him by the arm and turned to the bystanders: 'Go on! Move along!'

Avenarius did not resist. He realized that he was under arrest. After everyone saw the huge kitchen knife hanging at his belly he no longer found the slightest sympathy among the crowd. He turned towards the man who had introduced himself as a lawyer and given him his card. But that man was already leaving without looking back: he walked towards one of the parked cars and slipped the key into the door. Avenarius had time to glimpse the man stepping away from the car and then kneeling down by one of the wheels.

At that moment the policeman grabbed his arm and led him away.

The man by the parked car let out a great sigh: 'Oh my God!' and began to cry so hard that his body shook with tears.

19

Weeping, he ran upstairs to his apartment and immediately rushed to the phone. He tried to call for a taxi. He heard an unusually sweet voice saying into the receiver: 'Paris Taxi. Please be patient, someone will be with you shortly . . .' then he heard music, a chorus of female voices and heavy drumming; after a long interval the music was interrupted by the same sweet voice asking him to stay on the line. He felt like shouting that he had no patience because his wife was dying, but he knew there was no point in shouting because the voice speaking to him was taped and nobody would hear his protest. Then the music came back, the chorus of voices, the shouting and drumming, and after a while he heard a female voice that was real, as he could tell from the fact that this voice was not sweet but unpleasant and impatient. When he said that he needed a taxi to take him a few hundred miles from Paris, the voice immediately cut him off and when he continued to explain that he desperately needed the taxi, music once again sounded in his ear, drumming, the female chorus, and then after a long interval the taped voice asking him to be patient and stay on the line.

He hung up and dialled the number of his assistant. But instead of the assistant he heard at the other end the assistant's voice coming from an answering machine: a playful, teasing voice, distorted by a smile: 'I am glad that you finally remembered me. You have no idea how sorry I am that I cannot speak to you, but if you leave your number I will gladly call you as soon as I am able . . .'

'You idiot,' he said, and hung up.

Why on earth isn't Brigitte at home? She should have been

home long ago, he told himself for the hundredth time and went to look in her room, even though it was out of the question that she could have come in without his hearing her.

Who else could he turn to? Laura? She would certainly be happy to lend him her car, but she would insist on going along with him; and he couldn't possibly agree to that: Agnes had broken with her sister, and Paul didn't want to do anything against her wishes.

Then he thought of Bernard. The reasons he had stopped seeing him suddenly seemed ridiculously petty. He dialled his number. Bernard was in. Paul asked him to get his car out; Agnes had crashed into a ditch; the hospital had just called him.

'I'll be right over,' Bernard said and Paul felt a sudden surge of great love for his old friend. He longed to embrace him and to cry on his breast.

Now he was glad that Brigitte was not at home. Suddenly everything vanished, his sister-in-law, his daughter, the whole world, nothing remained but he and Agnes; he didn't want any third person to be with them. He was certain that Agnes was dying. If her condition were not critical, they wouldn't have called him in the middle of the night from a provincial hospital. Now he thought of nothing else except reaching her while she was still alive. To be able to kiss her one more time. He was possessed by the longing to kiss her. He was longing for a kiss, a last, final kiss with which he might catch her face, as in a skein, before it vanished and left him with merely a memory.

Now he had no choice but to wait. He started to tidy his messy writing table and was startled to realize that at a moment like this he was able to devote himself to such meaningless activity. What did he care whether the table was messy or not? And why had he handed out his card just now to a complete stranger? But he was not able to stop himself: he pushed all the books to one side of the table, crumpled up envelopes from old letters and threw them in the wastepaper basket. He realized that this is just the way a

296

person acts when disaster strikes: like a sleep-walker. The inertia of the everyday keeps him on the rails of life.

He glanced at his watch. Because of the slashed tyres he had already lost at least half an hour. Hurry, hurry, he was silently saying to Bernard, don't let Brigitte find me here, let me go to Agnes alone and let me arrive in time.

But luck was against him. Brigitte returned home shortly before Bernard arrived. The former friends embraced each other, Bernard went back home and Paul and Brigitte got into Brigitte's car. He took the wheel and drove as fast as he possibly could.

20

Agnes saw the upright figure of a girl in front of her, a figure sharply lit up by the car's headlights, her arms stretched out as if she were dancing, and it was as if a ballerina was pulling the curtain across at the end of a show, for after that there would be nothing and nothing would remain of the preceding performance, forgotten in an instant, nothing but that final image. Then there was only fatigue, a fatigue so deep that it resembled a deep well, so deep that the nurses and doctors thought she had lost consciousness, although she was still conscious and surprisingly aware that she was dying. She was even capable of a certain sense of surprise that she felt no sadness, no sorrow, no horror, none of those things she had until then connected with the idea of death.

Then she saw the nurse bend over her and heard her whisper: 'Your husband is on his way. He's coming to see you. Your husband.'

Agnes smiled. Why did she smile? Something occurred to her from the performance which she had forgotten: yes, she was married. And then the name emerged, too: Paul! Yes, Paul. Paul. Paul. It was the smile of a sudden encounter with a lost world. It was like being shown a teddy-bear you haven't seen for fifty years, and recognizing him.

Paul, she told herself silently, and smiled. And that smile remained on her lips, even though she again forgot the cause of it. She was tired, and everything tired her. Above all, she didn't have the strength to bear any kind of glance. Her eyes were closed so that she wouldn't see anyone or anything. Everything happening around her bothered and disturbed her and she yearned for nothing to happen.

Then she remembered once again: Paul. What was it the nurse had said to her? That he was coming? Her recollection of the forgotten performance that had been her life suddenly became clearer. Paul. Paul was coming! At that moment she wished intensely and passionately that he would not see her any more. She was tired, she didn't want anyone looking at her. She didn't want Paul looking at her. She didn't want him to see her dying. She had to hurry with her dying.

For the last time the basic pattern of her life was repeated: she was running and someone was chasing her. Paul was chasing her. And she had nothing in her hands; neither brush, nor comb, nor ribbon. She was disarmed. She was naked, dressed only in some sort of white hospital gown. She found herself on the last lap where nothing could help her any more, where she could only rely on the speed with which she ran. Who would be faster? Paul or she? Her dying or his arrival?

The fatigue grew deeper and she had the feeling that she was rapidly moving away, as if someone were pulling her bed backwards. She opened her eyes and saw the nurse in a white coat. What was her face like? She couldn't make it out. And then the words came to her: 'No, they don't have faces there.'

21

When he and Brigitte approached the bed, Paul saw the body covered with a sheet from head to toe. A woman in a white coat told them: 'She died fifteen minutes ago.'

The shortness of the time that separated him from the last moment in which she had still been alive exacerbated his despair. He had missed her by fifteen minutes. By fifteen minutes he had missed fulfilling his life, which had now suddenly been interrupted, senselessly severed. It seemed to him that during all those years they had lived together, she had never really been his, he had never really possessed her; and that for the completion, the culmination of their love's story he lacked a final kiss; a final kiss to capture her still living in his mouth, to hold her in his mouth.

The woman in the white coat pulled aside the sheet. He saw the intimately familiar face, pale, beautiful and yet completely different: her lips, though as gentle as ever, formed a line he had never known. Her face had an expression he didn't understand. He was incapable of bending over her and kissing her.

Next to him, Brigitte started crying, placed her head on his chest and shook with tears.

He looked once again at Agnes: that peculiar smile which he had never seen on her face, that unknown smile in a face with closed eyelids wasn't meant for him, it was meant for someone he did not know and it said something he did not understand.

The woman in the white coat caught Paul firmly by the arm; he was on the verge of fainting.

PART SIX
The dial

1

Soon after it's born, a baby starts to suck the mother's breast. After the mother weans it away from the breast, it sucks its thumb.

Rubens once asked a woman: why are you letting your boy suck his thumb? He must be at least ten years old! She became angry: 'You want to forbid him from doing it? It prolongs his contact with the maternal breast! Do you want to traumatize him?'

And so the child sucks his thumb until the age of thirteen, when he readily replaces it with a cigarette.

Later on, when Rubens made love to the mother who had defended her offspring's right to thumbsucking, he put his own thumb on her lips during intercourse; she began to lick it, turning her head left and right. Her eyes were closed and she dreamed that two men were making love to her.

That small incident was a significant moment for Rubens, for he had discovered a method for testing women: he put his thumb on their lips during intercourse and watched their reaction. Those who licked it were quite unmistakably drawn to collective pleasure. Those who remained indifferent to the thumb were hopelessly blind to perverse temptations.

One of the women in whom the 'thumb test' detected orgiastic tendencies was really fond of him. After love-making she took his thumb and clumsily kissed it, which meant: now I want your thumb to become a thumb again and I am happy that now, after all my fantasies, I am here with you, quite alone.

Metamorphoses of the thumb. Or: the movement of hands across the dial of life.

2

The hands on the dial of a clock turn in a circle. The zodiac, as drawn by an astrologer, also resembles a dial. A horoscope is a clock. Whether we believe in the predictions of astrology or not, a horoscope is a metaphor of life that conceals great wisdom.

How does an astrologer draw your horoscope? He makes a circle, an image of the heavenly sphere, and divides it into twelve parts representing the individual signs: the ram, the bull, twins, and so on. Into this zodiac-circle he then places symbols representing the sun, moon and seven planets exactly where these stars stood at the moment of your birth. It is as if he took a clock dial regularly divided into twelve hours, and added nine more numbers, irregularly distributed. Nine hands turn on the dial: they are the sun, moon and planets as they move through the universe in the course of your life. Each planet-hand is constantly forming ever-new relationships with the planet-numbers, the fixed signs of your horoscope.

The unrepeatable configuration of the stars at the moment of your birth forms the permanent theme of your life, its algebraic definition, the thumbprint of your personality; the stars immobilized on your horoscope form angles with respect to one another whose dimensions, expressed in degrees, have various meanings (negative, positive, neutral): imagine that your amorous Venus is in conflict with your aggressive Mars; that the Sun representing your social personality is strengthened by a conjunction with energetic, adventurous Uranus; that your sexuality symbolized by Luna is connected with dreamy Neptune, and so on. But in the course of their motion the hands of the moving stars will touch the fixed points of the horoscope and put into play (weaken, support, threaten) various elements of your life's theme. And that's life: it does not resemble a picaresque novel in which from one chapter to the next the hero is continually being surprised by new events that have no common denominator. It resembles a composition which musicians call: *a theme with variations*.

Uranus strides across the sky relatively slowly. It takes seven years for it to traverse a single sign. Let's assume that today it is in a dramatic relation to the immovable Sun of your horoscope (for example, at a 90-degree angle): you are experiencing a difficult period; in twenty-one years this situation will repeat itself (Uranus will then make an angle of 180 degrees with your Sun, which has an equally unfortunate significance), but the similarity will be deceptive because by the time your Sun is attacked by Uranus, Saturn will be in such a harmonious relationship with your Venus that the storm will merely tip-toe past you. It is as if you had a new bout of the same disease, except that now you would find yourself in a fabulous hospital where instead of impatient nurses you would be cared for by angels.

Supposedly, astrology teaches us fatalism: you won't escape your fate! But in my view, astrology (please understand, astrology as a metaphor of life) says something far more subtle: you won't escape your life's *theme*! From this it follows, for example, that it is sheer illusion to want to start all over again, to begin 'a new life' that does not resemble the preceding one, to begin, so to speak, from zero. Your life will always be built from the same materials, the same bricks, the same problems, and what will seem to you at first 'a new life' will soon turn out to be just a variation of your old existence.

A horoscope resembles a clock and a clock is a school of finality: as soon as a hand completes its circle and returns to its starting point, one phase is finished. Nine hands turn with varying speed on the horoscope dial and constantly some phase comes to an end and another begins. When someone is young, he is not capable of conceiving of time as a circle, but thinks of it as a road leading forward to ever-new horizons; he does not yet sense that his life contains just a single theme; he will come to realize it only when his life begins to enact its first variations.

Rubens was about fourteen years old when he was stopped in the street by a little girl roughly half his age, who asked him: 'Please, sir, can you tell me the time?' That was the first time a woman, a stranger, addressed him in a formal way and called him 'sir'. He was filled with bliss and it seemed to him that a new phase of his life was opening up. Afterwards he completely forgot the episode, and only recalled it when an attractive woman said to him: 'When you were young, did you think . . .' That was the first time someone had referred to his youth as a thing of the past. At that moment he evoked the image of the little girl who had once asked him what time it was, and he realized that those two female figures belonged together. They were figures quite insignificant in themselves, met by coincidence, and yet as soon as he established a connection between them they appeared to him as two significant events on his life's dial.

I will put it still another way: let us imagine that the dial of Rubens' life is placed on some great medieval clock, like the one in Old Town Square in Prague which I passed regularly for some twenty years. The clock strikes the hour and a little window above the dial opens: a marionette, a little girl of seven, comes out and asks Rubens what the time is. And then, many years later, when that same slow hand comes round to the next number, bells begin to sound, the window opens once again, a marionette, this time a young woman emerges and tells him: 'When you were young . . .'

306

3

When he was very young, he did not dare reveal his erotic
fantasies to any woman. He believed that every bit of his erotic
energy had to be converted into an astounding physical performance upon the woman's body. Besides, his youthful partners
were of the same opinion. He vaguely remembers one of them,
let us call her by the letter A, who in the midst of love-making
suddenly braced herself on her elbows and heels to arch her body
into a bridge, causing him to lurch and almost fall off the bed.
This sporting gesture was full of passionate meanings, for which
Rubens was grateful. He was living his first phase: *the period of
athletic muteness*.

Gradually, he lost that muteness; he felt very bold when for the
first time, while making love to a young woman, he dared to say
aloud the name of some sexual part of her body. But that boldness
was not as great as he thought, because the expression that he
chose was either a gentle diminutive or a poetic paraphrase. All
the same, he was enthused by his boldness (as well as surprised
that the girl didn't protest) and he began to think up highly
complicated metaphors in order to speak in a poetic, roundabout
way about the sexual act. That was the second phase: *the period of
metaphors*.

At that time he was seeing girl B. After the usual verbal overture
(full of metaphors), they made love. When she was approaching
her climax, she blurted out a sentence in which she designated
her sexual organ by an unambiguous, unmetaphoric expression.
That was the first time he had ever heard that word coming from
a woman's mouth (which, by the way, is also one of the famous
seconds on the dial). Surprised, dazzled, he realized that this

crude expression contained more charm and explosive power than all the metaphors that had ever been invented.

A short time later he was invited over by woman C. She was some fifteen years older than he. Beforehand, he recited to his friend M all the beautiful obscenities (no, no more metaphors!) which he intended to say to that woman during intercourse. But he failed in an odd way: before he dared to utter these expressions to her, she came out with them herself. And again he was astounded. Not only had she outstripped him in erotic daring, but most strange: she used exactly the same words that he had been preparing for several days. The coincidence fascinated him. He ascribed it to some sort of erotic telepathy or mysterious affinity of their souls. So he was slowly entering into the third phase: *the period of obscene truth*.

The fourth period was closely connected with his friend M: *the period of Chinese Whispers*. 'Chinese Whispers' was the name of a game he used to play when he was between five and seven years old: the children sat in a row and whispered a message to each other, the first to the second, the second to the third and so on, until the last one said it aloud and everybody laughed at the difference between the original sentence and its final version. As adults, Rubens and M played Chinese Whispers by saying cleverly formulated obscene phrases to their girlfriends, and the women, not realizing that they were involved in the game, would pass them on. And because Rubens and M had several lovers in common (or else they discreetly passed their lovers on to each other), they used them to send each other playful greetings. Once, during love-making, a woman used an expression that was so improbable, so oddly twisted, that he immediately recognized his friend's malicious creativity at work. Rubens was seized by an uncontrollable urge to laugh and because the woman took his repressed giggling as a sexual climax, encouraged, she repeated the sentence once more, and then for the third time she shouted it aloud, and in his mind's eye Rubens saw the ghost of his friend guffawing over his copulating body.

In that connection he remembered girl B, who at the end of the period of metaphors suddenly said an obscene word during love-making. Only now, after the lapse of time, did he pose himself the question: was that the first time she had ever said that word? He had never doubted it at the time. He thought she was in love with him, he suspected her of wanting to marry him, he was sure there was no one else in her life. Only now did he realize that somebody else must have taught her (or I might say, trained her) to say that word aloud before she'd been able to say it to Rubens. Yes, only many years later, thanks to the experience of Chinese Whispers, did he realize that at the time she was swearing her faithfulness to him, B undoubtedly had another lover.

The experience of Chinese Whispers changed him: he was losing the feeling (to which we are all subject) that the act of physical love is a moment of absolute intimacy, when the world around us changes into an endless desert in the middle of which two isolated bodies press against one another. Now he suddenly realized that the moment of love-making yields no intimate isolation. One is more intimately isolated walking down the crowded Champs-Elysées than in the arms of the most secretive of mistresses. For the period of Chinese Whispers is the social period of love: thanks to a few words, everyone takes part in embracing apparently isolated beings; society continually restocks the market of indecent fantasies and facilitates their distribution and circulation. Rubens coined this definition of a nation: a community of individuals, whose erotic life is united by the same Chinese Whispers.

But then he met girl D, who was the most verbal of all the women he'd ever known. During their second meeting she confided to him that she was a fanatical masturbator and that she achieved sexual climax by telling herself fairy tales. 'Fairy tales?

What fairy tales? Tell me!' he began to make love to her, while she narrated: bath-house, cabin, holes drilled in wooden walls, eyes fixed on her as she is undressing, a door that suddenly opens and four men enter, and so on and so on; the fairy tale was beautiful, it was banal and he was highly pleased with D.

But a peculiar thing began happening to him from then on: when he was with other women, he found in their fantasies fragments of the long stories told to him by D during their love-making. He often encountered the same word, the same verbal construction, even though the word or construction sounded quite uncommon. D's monologue was a mirror in which he recognized all the women he knew, it was an enormous encyclo-paedia, an eight-volume Larousse of erotic phrases and fantasies. At first he thought of her great monologue according to the principles of Chinese Whispers: via hundreds of lovers, an entire nation was gathering indecent fantasies in every corner of the country and putting them into her head, as into a beehive. But later he found out that this explanation was unlikely. He encountered fragments of D's monologue even in women he knew with certainty could not have had any indirect contact with D, for there was no common lover who could have played the role of messenger.

Then, he remembered his experience with C: he had prepared indecent sentences to say during intercourse, and she had beaten him to it. At the time he believed it was telepathy. But had she really been able to read sentences from inside his head? More likely, those sentences had already been present inside her own head long before she had met him. But how was it that they both had the same sentences in their heads? Clearly, there must have been some common source. And then it occurred to him that one and the same stream runs through all men and women, a single, common river of erotic fantasies. An individual does not receive a share of indecent fantasy from a lover by means of Chinese

Whispers, but by means of this impersonal (or super-personal or sub-personal) stream. To say that this river that runs through us is impersonal means that it does not belong to us but to him who created us and made it flow within us; in other words, that it belongs to God or even that it is God or one of his incarnations. When Rubens first formulated this idea for himself it seemed to him blasphemous, but then the sense of blasphemy receded and he immersed himself in the underground river with a certain religious humility: he knew that this stream unites us all, not as a nation but as God's children; every time he immersed himself in the stream he experienced the feeling of merging with God in a kind of mystic rite. Yes, the fifth phase was the *mystical period*.

4

But is the story of Rubens' life nothing but a story of physical love?

It is possible to think of it that way, and the moment when it revealed itself as such was also a significant event on the dial.

While still at school, Rubens spent many hours in museums looking at paintings, he painted hundreds of gouache pictures, and was famous among his schoolfriends for his caricatures of teachers. He drew them in pencil for a school newspaper, and between classes he drew them in chalk on the blackboard, to the great amusement of his fellow students. That period enabled him to feel what fame was all about: the whole school knew him and admired him, and everybody jokingly called him Rubens. As a souvenir of those beautiful years (his only years of fame), he kept that nickname all his life and insisted (with surprising naïvety) that all his friends call him by it.

This glory came to an end after school. He applied to the School of Fine Arts but failed to pass the examination. Was he worse than others? Or did he have bad luck? Oddly enough, I don't know how to answer this simple question.

With indifference he began to study law, and blamed the narrow-mindedness of his native Switzerland for his unsuccessful start. He hoped that he would fulfil his artistic vocation elsewhere, and tried his luck twice more: first, when he applied to the École des Beaux Arts in Paris and failed the exam and then when he offered his drawings to several journals. Why did they reject the drawings? Were they bad? Or were the people who judged them idiots? Or had drawings gone out of fashion? I must repeat once again that I have no answers to these questions.

Exhausted by his lack of success, he gave up further attempts. This meant of course (as he was fully aware), that his passion for drawing and painting was weaker than he had thought, and therefore that he was not destined for the artistic career he had assumed in his student days. At first he was disappointed by this realization, and then a stubborn defence of his own resignation began to resound inside him: why should he have a passion for painting? what is so praiseworthy about passion? isn't the cause of most bad paintings and bad novels simply the fact that artists consider their passion for art as something holy, as some sort of mission if not duty (duty to oneself, even to mankind)? Under the influence of his own resignation he began to see artists and writers as people possessed by ambition rather than gifted with creativity, and he avoided their company.

His greatest rival, N, who was his age, came from the same town and graduated from the same school, was not only accepted by the École des Beaux Arts but soon after gained remarkable success. During their school days everyone considered Rubens much more talented than N. Does that mean that they were all mistaken? Or that talent is something that can get lost along the way? As we can guess, there is no answer to these questions. Anyway, another circumstance arose: at a time when his failures induced him to give up painting once and for all (at the same time as N was celebrating his first success), Rubens was seeing a very beautiful young girl, whereas his rival had married a woman from a rich family, a woman so ugly that one look at her made Rubens speechless. It seemed to him that by means of this conjunction of circumstances, fate was trying to show him where his life's centre of gravity really lay: not in public life but in private, not in the pursuit of professional success but in success with women. And suddenly what only yesterday had seemed like a defeat now revealed itself as a surprising victory: yes, he would give up fame, the struggle for recognition (a vain and sad struggle), in order to devote himself to life itself. He didn't even bother to ask himself exactly why women represented 'life itself'. That seemed to him self-evident and clear beyond all doubt. He was certain that he had chosen a better way than his rival, wedded to a rich hag. In these circumstances his young beauty meant not only a promise of happiness, but above all a triumph and a source of pride. In order to consolidate his unexpected victory and to give it a seal of irrevocability he married the beautiful woman, convinced that the whole world would envy him.

5

Women meant 'life itself' to Rubens and yet he proceeded to marry a beautiful woman and thus give up women. He acted illogically, but quite normally. Rubens was twenty-four years old. He had thus just entered the period of obscene truth (in other words, it was shortly after he had met girl B and woman C), but his new experiences changed nothing about his certainty that there was something far higher than sex: love, great love, life's supreme value about which he had heard much, read much, sensed much and knew nothing. He had no doubt that love was the crown of life (of 'life itself', to which he gave preference over his career), and that therefore he had to welcome it with open arms and without any compromise.

As I mentioned, the hands on the sexual dial pointed to the hour of obscene truth, but as soon as he fell in love there occurred an immediate regression into the earlier phases: in bed he was either silent or spoke only gentle metaphors to his future bride, convinced that obscenity would expel both of them from the domain of love.

I'll say it in other words: his love for the beautiful woman brought him back to a state of virginity, because as I mentioned earlier, on pronouncing the word 'love' every European is transported on wings of enthusiasm into a pre-coital (or extra-coital) realm of thought and feeling, exactly where young Werther suffered and where Fromentin's Dominique almost fell off his horse. After meeting his beautiful woman, Rubens was therefore ready to put the hot pot of his feelings on the fire and wait for the boiling point at which feeling would turn into passion. There was one complication: he had at this time a mistress in another town (let's designate her by the letter E), three years older than he, whom he had been seeing long before he met his future bride, and for several months afterwards. He stopped seeing her only on the day he decided to get married. The separation was not due to a spontaneous cooling of affection for E (we will soon see that he was much too fond of her) but rather to the realization that he was entering a great and solemn period of life when it was necessary to sanctify great love through fidelity. However, a week before his wedding day (whose necessity he doubted in his heart of hearts) he was overtaken by an unbearable longing for E, whom he had abandoned without the least explanation. Because he had never called their relationship love, he was surprised that he yearned for her so much with his body, heart and soul. He was unable to control himself, and went off to see her. For a whole week he humbled himself before her, begged her to let him make love to her, besieged her with tenderness, sorrow, insistence, but she granted him nothing but the view of her griefstricken face; he was not permitted so much as to touch her body.

Dissatisfied and depressed, he returned home on the morning of the wedding day. He got drunk during the wedding feast and in the evening took his bride to their new apartment. Blinded by wine and sorrow, in the middle of love-making he called her by the name of his former lover. What a catastrophe! He would never forget the huge eyes that looked at him in terrible amazement! At that instant, when everything had collapsed, it occurred to him that his rejected lover was taking her revenge and that on the very day he entered into wedlock, her name for ever undermined his marriage. And perhaps in that brief moment he also realized the improbability of what had happened, the grotesque stupidity of his slip of the tongue, a stupidity that made the unavoidable collapse of his marriage even more unbearable. For three or four terrible seconds he didn't know what to do, and then he suddenly began to shout: 'Eva! Elizabeth! Heidi!' He couldn't think of any other girls' names at the moment, and so he repeated: 'Heidi! Elizabeth! Yes, you have become every woman for me! All the women in the whole world! Eva! Klara! Julie! You are all women! You are woman in the plural! Heidi, Gretchen, all the women in the whole world are in you, you possess all their names! . . .' and he made love to her with the speed and dexterity of a true sexual athlete; after a few seconds he saw that her staring eyes had regained their normal expression and her body which had turned to stone a moment ago was once again moving in a rhythm with a regularity that allowed him to regain his composure and assurance.

The manner with which he escaped from that hellish predicament bordered on the unbelievable and we have a right to wonder how the young bride could have taken seriously such a mad comedy. But let's not forget that both of them were captives of pre-coital thinking, which equates love with the absolute. What sort of criterion is there for love in the virginal phase? Only quantitative: love is a great, great, great feeling. False love is a small feeling, true love (*die wahre Liebe!*) is a great feeling. But isn't every love small when seen from the viewpoint of the absolute? Of course. That's why love, in order to prove itself true, wishes to escape the sensible, wishes to reject moderation, doesn't wish to seem probable, longs to change into the '*délires actifs de la passion*' (let's not forget Eluard!), in other words, wishes to be mad! Thus, the improbability of an exaggerated gesture can only be an advantage. To an outside observer, the way that Rubens got out of trouble seems neither elegant nor convincing, but in the situation it was his only means of avoiding catastrophe: acting like a madman, Rubens summoned the mad absolute of love, and it succeeded.

6

If Rubens, face to face with his youthful wife once again became love's lyrical athlete, this did not mean that he had given up his erotic vices once and for all, but only that he wished to enlist even vice in the service of love. He imagined that in monogamous ecstasy he would experience more with one woman than with a hundred others. There was just one question he had to solve: what tempo should sensuous adventure follow when going along the path of love? Because love's path was supposed to be long, as long as possible, perhaps even endless, he adopted a new principle: to slow down time, and not to hurry.

Suppose he imagined his sexual future with his beautiful bride as the ascent of a high mountain. If he were to reach the peak the very first day, what would he do then? He therefore had to plan his climb in such a way that it would fill his entire life. For this reason he made love to his young wife passionately and with physical zest, but using methods that were, so to speak, classical, free from the lasciviousness that attracted him (to her more than to any other woman) and which he postponed for future years.

And then suddenly something unexpected happened: they stopped understanding each other, they got on each other's nerves, they began to struggle over power in domestic affairs, she claimed she needed more elbow-room for her own life, he was upset that she refused to cook eggs for him, and faster than either of them realized they found themselves divorced. The great feeling on which he had wanted to build his entire life disappeared so quickly that he began to doubt whether he had ever felt it at all. This disappearance of feeling (sudden, quick, easy!) seemed

318

breathtaking, unbelievable! It fascinated him much more than his sudden infatuation had two years earlier.

Emotionally but also erotically, the net balance of his marriage came to nil. Because of the slow tempo which he had prescribed for himself, all he had experienced with the beautiful creature was naïve love-making without any great excitement. Not only had he failed to take her to the top of the mountain, he hadn't even arrived at the first look-out point. He therefore tried to see her a few more times after their divorce (she had no objection: once the domestic power-struggle ceased, she was happy to make love with him again), and he tried to slip in at least a few small perversions that he had been saving for future years. But he succeeded in doing almost nothing of the kind, for this time the tempo he had chosen was too fast and the beautiful divorcée understood his impatient sensuality (which had dragged her straight into the period of obscene truth) as cynicism and lack of love, so that their post-marital contact soon came to an end.

His short marriage was a mere parenthesis in his life, which tempts me to say that he returned precisely to the place he had been before he met his bride; but that wouldn't be true. The pumping up of amorous feeling and its incredibly undramatic and painless deflation came to him as a shocking discovery which announced that he had landed irrevocably *beyond the border of love*.

7

The great love that had dazzled him two years earlier made him forget painting. But when he closed the parenthesis of marriage and realized with melancholy disappointment that he had landed in a realm beyond the border of love his renunciation of painting suddenly appeared to him to be an unjustifiable capitulation.

In his notebook he again began to make sketches for pictures he longed to paint. But he came to realize that a return to art had become impossible. When he was a student, he imagined all the painters in the world moving along the same great road; it was the royal road leading from the Gothic painters to the great Italian masters of the Renaissance, and on to the Dutch painters and to Delacroix, from Delacroix to Manet, from Manet to Monet, from Bonnard (oh, how he loved Bonnard!) to Matisse, from Cézanne to Picasso. The painters did not march along this road like a group of soldiers, no, each went his own way, and yet what each of them discovered served as an inspiration to the others and they all knew that they were blazing a trail into the unknown, a common goal that united them all. And then suddenly the road disappeared. It was like waking up from a beautiful dream; for a while we look for the fading images until finally we realize that dreams cannot be called back. The road had disappeared, but it remained in the souls of painters in the form of an inextinguishable desire 'to go forward'. But where is 'forward' when there is no longer any road? In which direction is one to look for the lost 'forward'? And so the desire to go forward became the painters' neurosis; each set out in a different direction and yet their tracks criss-crossed each other like a crowd milling around in the same city square. They wanted to differentiate themselves one from the other while each of them kept discovering a different but already discovered discovery. Fortunately, people soon appeared (not artists but businessmen and organizers of exhibitions with their agents and publicists), who imposed order on this disorder and determined which discovery was to be rediscovered in any particular year. This re-establishment of order greatly increased the sales of contemporary paintings. They were bought by the same wealthy people who only ten years before had laughed at Picasso and Dalí, thereby earning Rubens' passionate hatred. Now the wealthy buyers decided that they would be modern and Rubens sighed with relief that he was not a painter.

He once visited New York's Museum of Modern Art. On the first floor he saw Matisse, Braque, Picasso, Miró, Dalí and Ernst, and he was happy. The brushstrokes on the canvas expressed wild relish. Reality was being magnificently violated like a woman raped by a faun, or it battled with the painter like a bull with a toreador. But on the next floor, reserved for contemporary paintings, he found himself in a desert: no trace of dashing brushstrokes on canvas; no trace of relish; both bull and toreador had disappeared; the paintings had expelled reality altogether, or else they imitated it with cynical, obtuse literalness. Between the two floors flowed the river Lethe, the river of death and forgetting. He told himself at that time that his renunciation of painting might have had a deeper significance than lack of talent or stubbornness: midnight had struck on the dial of European art.

If an alchemist of genius were transplanted into the nineteenth century, what would his occupation be? What would become of Christopher Columbus today, when there are a thousand shipping companies? What would Shakespeare write when theatre did not exist, or had ceased to exist?

These are not rhetorical questions. When a person has talent for an activity which has passed its midnight (or has not yet reached its first hour), what happens to his gift? Does it change?

Adapt? Would Christopher Columbus become director of a shipping line? Would Shakespeare write scripts for Hollywood? Would Picasso produce cartoon shows? Or would all these great talents step aside, retreat, so to speak, to the cloister of history, full of cosmic disappointment that they had been born at the wrong time, outside their own era, outside the dial, the time they'd been created for? Would they abandon their untimely talents as Rimbaud abandoned poetry at the age of nineteen?

Of course, there is no answer to these questions, neither for me, nor for you, nor for Rubens. Did the Rubens of my novel have the unrealized potential of a great painter? Or did he lack talent altogether? Did he abandon painting from a lack of strength or, on the contrary, from the strength that saw clearly the vanity of painting? Naturally, he often thought of Rimbaud and compared himself to him (even though hesitantly and with irony). Not only did Rimbaud renounce poetry radically and without regrets, but the activity to which he subsequently devoted himself was a mocking denial of poetry: it is said that in Africa he trafficked in weapons and even in slaves. The latter assertion is probably just a slanderous legend, yet as a hyperbole it is a good expression of the self-destructive violence, passion, fury, which separated Rimbaud from his own past as an artist. Rubens may have been increasingly attracted by the world of finance and the stock-market because that activity (rightly or wrongly) seemed to him the antithesis of his dreams of an artistic career. One day, when his schoolfriend N had become famous, Rubens sold a painting which N had once given him. Thanks to this sale he not only gained quite a bit of money, but he discovered a way to make a living in the future: he would sell to the rich (for whom he felt contempt) paintings by contemporary artists (whom he disdained).

There are surely many people in the world who make a living through the sale of paintings, and to whom it never occurs in their wildest dreams to feel ashamed of their occupation. After all, weren't Velasquez, Vermeer, Rembrandt also dealers in pictures? Rubens of course knew that. But though he was capable of comparing himself to Rimbaud, a slave-trader, he would never compare himself to the great painters who dealt in pictures. Not for an instant would he cease believing in his occupation's total uselessness. At first this made him sad and he blamed himself for his amorality. But then he told himself: what does it really mean to be useful? Today's world, just as it is, contains the sum of the utility of all people of all times. Which implies: the highest morality consists in being useless.

8

He had been divorced for some twelve years when F came to see him. She told him how a certain man had recently invited her to his house and then let her wait at least ten minutes in the living room, telling her that he had to finish an important telephone conversation in the adjoining room. Actually, he had probably only pretended to be talking on the phone, to give her time to look over the pornographic magazines lying on the coffee table. F concluded her story with this remark: 'If I had been younger, he would have succeeded. If I had been seventeen. That's the age of the craziest fantasies, when you can't resist anything . . .'

Rubens listened to F rather distractedly, until her last words jolted him out of his indifference. This would be his fate from now on: somebody would say something which would strike him as a reproach: it would remind him of something in his life that he had missed, allowed to slip by, irremediably wasted. When F talked of the time when she was seventeen, when she was unable to resist any kind of seduction, he recalled his wife who was also seventeen at the time he met her. He pictured the provincial hotel where they spent some time before their marriage. They made love while, in the next-door room, a friend of theirs was getting ready for bed. Rubens' young bride whispered to him several times: 'He will hear us!' Only now (facing F, who was telling him about the temptations of a seventeen-year-old) did he realize that at that time his bride had gasped more loudly than ever, that she had even shouted, and that she must have shouted on purpose so that their friend would hear. In the following days she kept referring to that night, asking: 'Do you really think he didn't hear us?' At the time, he interpreted her question as an expression of alarmed modesty and he reassured his bride (now, looking at F, the idea of his youthful stupidity made him blush up to his ears!) that their friend was known as a deep sleeper.

He looked at F and realized that he had no desire to make love to her in the presence of another woman or another man. But why is it that the memory of his wife, who fourteen years earlier had gasped loudly, even shouted, when she thought of a man on the other side of a thin wall, why is it that this memory made his heart beat faster?

An idea occurred to him: making love in a threesome, a foursome, can be exciting only in the presence of a beloved woman. Only if there is love can the sight of a woman's body in the arms of another man arouse amazement and exciting terror. The old moralizing truth that sex has no meaning without love was suddenly vindicated and gained new significance.

9

On the following day, he flew to Rome on a business trip. By four o'clock he was free. He was filled with ineradicable sadness: he thought of his wife, and not only of her; all the women he had ever known filed past his eyes and it seemed that he had missed them all, that he had experienced much less than he could have and should have. He wanted to shake this sadness, this dissatisfaction, and so he visited the picture gallery in the Barberini Palace (he went to picture galleries in every town he visited), then set out for the Spanish Steps and climbed the broad staircase to the park of the Villa Borghese. Long rows of marble busts of famous Italians, standing on pedestals, lined the avenues of trees. Their faces, frozen in terminal grimaces, were exposed like résumés of their lives. Rubens was always sensitive to the comical aspects of monuments. He smiled. He remembered a childhood fairy tale: a sorcerer casts a spell over guests at a feast: they all remain frozen in time, with open mouths, faces distorted with food, their hands clutching half-gnawed bones. Another memory: people fleeing from Sodom were forbidden to look back lest they turn into pillars of salt. That biblical story clearly indicates that there is no greater horror, no greater punishment than turning a second into eternity, tearing someone out of the flow of time, stopping him in the midst of his natural motion. Immersed in these thoughts (which he forgot a second later!), he suddenly saw her in front of him. No, it wasn't his wife (the one who kept gasping loudly because she knew that a friend was listening in the next room), it was someone else.

Everything was decided in a fraction of a second. He recognized her only at the moment when they were side by side and another step would part them irrevocably. He had to find within himself the decisiveness and speed to stop, turn (she immediately reacted to his movement) and address her.

He felt as if it was for her he'd been longing all these years, as if he'd been searching for her all over the world. Some hundred yards away there was a café, with tables under the trees and an incredibly blue sky. They sat down facing each other.

She was wearing dark glasses. He took them between his fingertips, carefully removed them from her face and laid them on the table. She did not resist.

He said: 'Because of those glasses I almost didn't recognize you.'

They sipped mineral water and couldn't take their eyes off one another. She was in Rome with her husband, and had only an hour to spare. He knew that if it had been possible they would have made love that very day, that very second.

What was her name? What was her first name? He had forgotten, and it was impossible to ask her. He told her (and meant it quite sincerely), that all the time they hadn't seen each other he had had the feeling that he was waiting for her. How could he admit at the same time that he didn't know her name?

He said: 'Do you know what we used to call you?'

'No, I don't.'

'The lute-player.'

'Lute-player?'

'Because you were as tender as a lute. It was I who thought up this nickname for you.'

Yes, he had thought it up. Not years ago, during their brief acquaintance, but now in the park of the Villa Borghese, because he needed to address her with a name; and because she seemed to him as elegant and tender as a lute.

327

10

What did he know about her? Not much. He vaguely recalled that he had known her by sight from the tennis courts (he must have been around twenty-seven, and she some ten years younger) and that he had once invited her to a night-club. In those days a certain dance was popular, in which the man and woman faced each other about a step apart, twisted their hips and alternately reached out one arm and then the other towards their partner. It was this motion of hers that imprinted her in his memory. What was so special about her? First of all, she never even looked at Rubens. Where was she looking? Into empty space. All the dancers had their arms bent at the elbow, and they pumped them alternately back and forth. She, too, made these motions, but just a little differently: as she moved her arms forward, her right forearm described a small circle to the left, while at the same time her left forearm described a circle to the right. It was as if these circular motions were meant to hide her face. As if she wanted to erase it. At the time, this dance was considered somewhat indecent, and it was as if the girl wished to dance indecently and yet at the same time to erase the indecency. Rubens was enchanted! As if until then he had never seen anything more tender, beautiful, more exciting. Then the music changed to a tango and the couples held each other tight. He couldn't resist a sudden impulse and put his hand on the girl's breast. He himself became frightened at this move. What would the girl do? She did nothing. She kept on dancing, with his hand on her breast, and looked straight ahead. He asked her, and his voice was almost trembling: 'Has anyone ever touched your breast?' And she answered in the same tremulous voice (truly, it sounded as if someone had lightly touched the strings of a lute): 'No.' And he kept his hand on her breast and the word 'no' sounded like the most beautiful word in the world; he was carried away; it seemed to him that he was seeing shame from close up; he saw shame as it *is*; it was possible to touch her shame (he was actually touching it, because her shame had gone to her breast, it dwelt in her breast, it had become her breast).

Why had he not seen her again? He didn't know, no matter how hard he thought about it. He no longer remembered.

11

Arthur Schnitzler, the turn-of-the-century Viennese writer, wrote a beautiful novella entitled *Miss Elsa*. The heroine is a pure young woman whose father is deep in debt and threatened by ruin. His creditor has promised to forgive the father's debt providing his daughter will show herself to him in the nude. After a lengthy inner struggle, Elsa agrees but is so ashamed by the exhibition of her nudity that she goes mad and dies. Don't misunderstand: this is not a moralistic tale intended to denounce the evil, depraved rich! No, it is an erotic novella that leaves you breathless: it lets you understand the power that nudity once had: it meant an enormous sum of money for the creditor and for the girl infinite shame leading to an excitement bordering on death.

Schnitzler's story marks a significant moment on Europe's dial: at the end of the puritanical nineteenth century erotic taboos were still powerful, but the loosening of morals awoke an equally powerful longing to overstep those taboos. Shame and shamelessness transected each other at the point when both had equal force. That was a moment of extraordinary erotic tension. Vienna encountered it at the turn of the century. That moment will never return.

Shame means that we resist what we desire, and feel ashamed that we desire what we resist. Rubens belonged to the last European generation that grew up knowing shame. That's why he was so excited when he placed his hand on the girl's breast and set in motion her shame. Once, while still at school, he had crept into a hallway from whose window he could observe his female schoolfriends stripped to the waist, waiting for chest X-rays. One of them saw him and started shouting. The others threw their coats over their shoulders, ran out shouting into the hallway and started to chase him. Rubens experienced a moment of fear; they suddenly ceased to be schoolfriends, colleagues, comrades willing to joke and flirt. Their faces were full of real anger, a collective anger determined to hound him. He escaped, but they continued in their chase and lodged a complaint with the headmaster. Rubens was reprimanded in front of the class. The headmaster, his voice expressing genuine contempt, called him a voyeur.

By the time he was forty, women would leave their brassières in the drawer and lounge on beaches showing their breasts to the entire world. He walked along the shore and his eyes tried to avoid their unexpected nakedness, because the old imperative was still firmly anchored inside him: not to violate feminine shame! When he met an acquaintance who was bare-breasted, such as the wife of a friend or a colleague, he was surprised to find that it was he who felt ashamed rather than she. He was embarrassed, and didn't know where to turn his eyes. He tried to avoid looking at the breasts, but that wasn't possible for bare breasts are visible even when a man looks at a woman's hands or into her eyes. And so he tried to look at breasts with the same naturalness as if he were looking at a woman's knees or forehead. But that wasn't easy, precisely because breasts are neither knees nor foreheads. No matter what he did, it seemed to him that those bare breasts accused him of not being in sufficient accord with their nakedness. And he had the strong feeling that the women he met at the beach were the same as those who twenty years earlier had denounced him to the headmaster for voyeurism: just as angry and united, demanding with the same aggression multiplied by their numbers that he recognize their right to show themselves in the nude.

In the end, he more or less came to terms with bare breasts, but he could not escape the impression that something serious had once again happened: on Europe's dial, another hour had struck: shame had disappeared. Not only had it disappeared, but it had disappeared so easily, almost overnight, that it seemed as if it had never existed. That it had only been an invention of men when they stood face to face with a woman. That shame had been their illusion. Their erotic dream.

12

When Rubens was divorced he found himself, as I said, once and for all 'beyond the border of love'. He liked that phrase. He often repeated it to himself (sometimes sadly, sometimes cheerfully): I will live my life 'beyond the border of love'.

But the realm that he called 'beyond the border of love' was not the shady, neglected courtyard of a great, beautiful palace (the palace of love), no, the realm was spacious, rich, beautiful, endlessly varied and perhaps much bigger and more beautiful than the palace of love itself. This realm was alive with all sorts of women; some of them left him indifferent, others amused him, but with some others he was in love. It is necessary to understand this apparent contradiction: beyond the border of love there is love.

For what pushed Rubens' amorous adventures 'beyond the border of love' was not a lack of feelings, but the desire to restrict them to the erotic sphere, and to deprive them of any influence whatever on the course of his life. No matter how we define love, the definition will always suggest that love is something substantial, that it turns life into fate: events that take place 'beyond the border of love', no matter how beautiful they may be, are therefore necessarily episodic.

But I repeat: even though they were expelled 'beyond the border of love' into the territory of the episodic, among Rubens' women there were some for whom he felt tenderness, whom he thought about obsessively, who caused him pain when they eluded him or jealousy when they preferred someone else. In other words, even beyond the border of love there existed loves

333

and since the word 'love' was forbidden, they were all secret loves and thus all the more attractive.

As he sat in the garden café of the park in the Villa Borghese facing the woman he called the 'lute-player', he immediately realized that she would become 'beloved beyond the border of love'. He knew that he would not be interested in her life, her marriage, her cares, he knew that they would see each other only rarely, but he also knew that he would feel an extraordinary tenderness towards her.

'I recall still another name which I gave you,' he said to her. 'I called you a Gothic maiden.'

'Me? A Gothic maiden?'

He had never called her that. These words had occurred to him a moment earlier, as they were walking down the avenue towards the café. Her walk made him think of the Gothic pictures he had been looking at that afternoon at the Barberini Palace.

He continued: 'Women in Gothic paintings walk with their bellies sticking out. And with their heads bowed towards the ground. Your walk is that of a Gothic maiden. A lute-player in an angelic orchestra. Your breasts are turned towards heaven, your belly is turned towards heaven, but your head, which realizes the vanity of everything, looks into the dust.'

They walked back down the same statue-lined avenue where they had met. The severed heads of the famous dead, resting on their pedestals, looked extremely proud.

At the park exit she said good-bye. They agreed that he would come to see her in Paris. She gave him her name (the name of her husband), telephone number, and told him the times when she was sure to be at home alone. Then she lifted her dark glasses with a smile: 'May I, now?'

'Yes,' said Rubens, and for a long while he watched her as she walked away.

334

All the painful longing that came over him at the thought of
having for ever missed his wife was transformed into an obsession
with the lute-player. For the next few days he thought of her
almost constantly. He again tried to recall everything that
remained of her in his memory, but he found only that one
evening in the night-club. For the hundredth time, the same
image came to his mind: they were among a crowd of dancing
couples, and she was just a step away from him. She looked past
him, into empty space. As if she didn't want to see anything of
the outside world but rather concentrated on herself. As if it
wasn't he who was a step away from her, but a huge mirror in
which she watched herself. She observed her hips alternately
twisting back and forth, she watched her arms describing circles
in front of her breasts and face as if she wanted to hide them, as
if she wanted to erase them. As if she kept erasing them and then
kept letting them appear again, while at the same time observing
herself in an imaginary mirror, excited by her shame. Her dance
was *a pantomine of shame*: a constant suggestion of concealed
nakedness.

A week after their meeting in Rome they met in the lobby of a
large Parisian hotel full of Japanese, whose presence gave them
a sense of pleasant anonymity and rootlessness. When he closed
the door of the hotel room behind them, he approached her and
put his hand on her breast: 'This is how I touched you when we
danced together,' he said. 'Do you remember?'

'Yes,' she said, sounding as if someone had lightly tapped the
body of a lute.

Was she ashamed as she had been fifteen years earlier? And

had she been ashamed fifteen years earlier? Was Bettina ashamed when Goethe touched her breast in the Teplitz spa? Or was Bettina's shame merely Goethe's dream? Was the lute-player's shame only Rubens' dream? No matter what the truth may have been, that shame, even if it was only an illusion of shame, even if it was only a memory of an illusion of shame, that shame was present, it was with them in the small hotel room, it intoxicated them with its magic and gave everything meaning. He undressed her and felt as if he had just brought her back from the night-club of their youth. They made love and he saw her dancing: she hid her face behind circling movements of her arms, while observing herself in an imaginary mirror.

Eagerly, they let themselves be carried away by that stream that flows through all women and all men, that mystic stream of obscene images where every woman resembles every other woman and yet a different face gives the same images and words a different power and enchantment. He listened to what the lute-player was saying, he listened to what he said himself, he gazed at the tender face of a Gothic maiden, at the tender lips pronouncing coarse words and he felt more and more intoxicated.

The grammatical tense of their obscene dreams was the future: next time you will do this or that, we will stage such and such a situation . . . This grammatical future converts dreaming into a constant promise (a promise that loses its validity at the moment of sobriety, but since it is never forgotten becomes a promise again and again). So it was bound to happen that one day he met her in the hotel with his friend M. The three of them went upstairs to the room, drank, chatted and then the men began to undress her. When they took off her brassière, she put her hands over her breasts, trying to cover them completely with her palms. Then they led her (she was dressed only in panties) to a mirror (a chipped mirror on the door of the dresser) and she just stood there between the two of them, left hand on left breast and right hand on right, gazing in fascination into the mirror. Rubens noticed quite clearly that while the two of them were looking at her (at her face and at her hands over her breasts), she did not see them. As if hypnotized, she observed only her self.

14

In Aristotle's *Poetics*, the episode is an important concept. Aristotle did not like episodes. According to him, an episode, from the point of view of poetry, is the worst possible type of event. It is not an unavoidable consequence of preceding action, nor the cause of what is to follow; it is outside the causal chain of events which is the story. It is merely a sterile accident which can be left out without making the story lose its intelligible continuity, and is incapable of making a permanent mark upon the life of the characters. You take the Metro to meet that woman in your life and a moment before you arrive at your station a girl you don't know and haven't noticed before (after all, you have a date with that woman in your life and are oblivious to everything else) suddenly feels faint and is about to collapse. Because you are standing right next to her, you catch her and hold her in your arms for a few moments until she opens her eyes. You help her sit down in a seat which someone has vacated for her and because at that point the train suddenly slows down, you free yourself from her with an almost impatient movement so that you can get off and rush after that woman in your life. At that instant, the girl whom you held in your arms just a moment earlier is completely forgotten. This event is a typical episode. Life is as stuffed with episodes as a mattress is with horsehair, but a poet (according to Aristotle) is not an upholsterer and must remove all stuffing from his story, even though real life consists of nothing but precisely such stuffing.

For Goethe, meeting Bettina was an insignificant episode; from a quantitative viewpoint, she took up only a tiny interval of his lifetime, and moreover Goethe tried as hard as he could to prevent her from ever playing a causal role in his life, assiduously keeping her outside his biography. But it is precisely here that we realize the relativity of the concept of the episode, a relativity Aristotle did not think through: for nobody can guarantee that some totally episodic event may not contain within itself a power that some day could unexpectedly turn it into a cause of further events. When I say some day, it can even be after death; this was precisely Bettina's triumph, for she became part of Goethe's life story when he was no longer alive.

We can thus complete Aristotle's definition of the episode and state: no episode is *a priori* condemned to remain an episode for ever, for every event, no matter how trivial, conceals within itself the possibility of sooner or later becoming the cause of other events and thus changing into a story or an adventure. Episodes are like landmines. The majority of them never explode, but the most unremarkable of them may some day turn into a story that will prove fateful to you. You may be walking down the street and from the opposite direction will come a woman who, while still far away, will look straight into your eyes with a gaze that will seem rather crazy to you. As she comes closer, she slows down, stops and says: 'Is that really you? I've been looking for you for such a long time!' and throws her arms round your neck. It is the same girl who fainted and fell into your arms as you were taking the Metro to see the woman in your life, who in the meantime has become your wife and given you a child. But the girl who encountered you unexpectedly in the street has decided to fall in love with her saviour and to regard your chance meeting as an intimation of fate. She will phone you five times a day, write you letters, visit your wife and keep explaining to her that she loves you and has a right to you until that woman in your life loses her patience, spitefully goes to bed with the refuse collector and then runs away from home, taking the child with her. And in order to escape from the lovesick girl who has in the meantime transferred all the contents of her cupboards into your apartment, you flee across the ocean where you die in hopelessness and misery. If our lives were endless like the lives of the gods of antiquity, the concept of episode would lose its meaning, for in infinity every event, no matter how trivial, would meet up with its consequence and unfold into a story.

The lute-player with whom he had danced when he was twenty-seven years old was for Rubens nothing but an episode, an arch-episode, an episode through and through, until the moment when he accidentally met her, fifteen years later, in a Roman park. Then the forgotten episode suddenly turned into a small story, but even that story remained completely episodic in relation to Rubens' life. It did not have the smallest chance of turning into a part of what we might call his biography.

Biography: sequence of events which we consider important to our life. However, what is important and what isn't? Because we ourselves don't know (and never even think of putting such a silly question to ourselves) we accept as important whatever is accepted by others, for example by our employer, whose questionnaire we fill out: date of birth, parents' occupation, schooling, changes of occupation, domicile, marriages, divorces, births of children, serious diseases. It is deplorable, but it is a fact: we have learned to see our own lives through the eyes of business or government questionnaires. To include in our biography a woman other than a legal wife already represents a small act of rebellion, and even this sort of exception can be allowed only if this woman played an especially dramatic role in our life, a statement which Rubens certainly could not make with regard to the lute-player. Besides, in her appearance and behaviour the lute-player fitted exactly the idea of the woman-episode: she was elegant yet not ostentatious, beautiful without being dazzling, ready for physical love and yet shy; she never bothered Rubens with confessions about her private life, and yet she never dramatized her discreet silence or tried to convert it into disquieting mystery. She was a real princess of episode.

The lute-player's encounter with two men in the Paris hotel was thrilling. Did the three of them make love to one another? Let's not forget that for Rubens, the lute-player had become 'beloved beyond the border of love'; the old imperative to slow down the course of events so that the sexual charge of love would not be too quickly exhausted, reawoke. Just before he led her naked to the bed, he motioned to his friend to leave the room quietly.

During love-making, their conversation in the grammatical future became once again a promise, which, however, was never to be fulfilled: soon after, friend M completely disappeared from Rubens' horizon and the thrilling encounter of two men and a woman became an episode without sequel. Rubens kept seeing the lute-player alone two or three times a year, when he had an opportunity to visit Paris. Then such opportunities stopped, and once again she almost vanished from his mind.

15

Years passed, and one day he was sitting with his friend at a café in the Swiss town where he lived, in the foothills of the Alps. At a nearby table he saw a girl watching him. She was attractive, with long sensuous lips (which he would have liked to compare to the mouth of a frog, if it were possible to consider frogs beautiful) and she seemed to be exactly the woman he had always longed for. Even at a distance of three or four yards he found her body pleasant to the touch and immediately accorded it preference over all other female bodies. She kept looking at him so intensely that, swallowed up by her gaze, he didn't know what his companion was saying and the only thing in his mind was the painful thought that in a few minutes he would leave the café and lose this woman for ever.

But he didn't lose her, because at the moment when he paid for the two coffees, she also got up and followed the two men to the building across the street where an art auction was about to take place. As they crossed the street she found herself so close to Rubens that it was impossible for him not to address her. She acted as if she'd been expecting it, and launched into a conversation, completely ignoring his friend, who accompanied him, silent and at a loss, into the auction hall. When the session ended, they returned to the same café. Having less than half an hour free for each other, they hurried to tell one another all there was to say. After a while, however, it became evident that they didn't have all that much to say, and the half hour lasted longer than he had anticipated. The girl was an Australian student, she was one quarter aboriginal (which was not apparent though she talked about it readily), she studied the semiotics of painting with a Zürich professor, and for a time she had made a living in Australia dancing topless in a night-club. All of this was interesting, yet at the same time it sounded quite strange to Rubens (why did she dance topless in Australia? why was she studying semiotics in Switzerland? And what was semiotics, anyway?) and instead of awakening his curiosity he was exhausted by the thought that he'd have to master all that information. He was therefore relieved when the half hour was over; at that point his initial enthusiasm returned (for he had not ceased liking her) and he arranged a date with her for the next day.

That day everything went wrong: he woke up with a headache, the postman delivered two unpleasant letters and during a phone conversation with a government office an impatient female voice refused to understand what he wanted. When the student appeared at the door, his gloomy outlook was confirmed: why was she dressed completely differently from yesterday? She wore enormous tennis shoes, above the shoes could be seen thick socks, above the socks grey linen trousers which oddly diminished her figure, above the trousers a windcheater. Only after he scanned the jacket could his eyes finally rest with satisfaction on her frog-like mouth, which was still as beautiful as before, providing he could mentally erase everything from the mouth down.

The unattractiveness of her outfit was not a serious matter (it couldn't take anything away from the fact that she was a pretty woman), what bothered him more was that he didn't understand her: why does a young woman coming to see a man with whom she expects to make love not dress to please him? was she perhaps trying to indicate to him that clothes were something external and unimportant? or did she consider her windcheater elegant and her enormous tennis shoes seductive? or did she simply have no consideration for the man she was seeing?

Probably because this way he had an excuse should their

meeting fail to meet his expectations, he immediately informed her that he was having a bad day, and trying to adopt a humorous tone, he recounted all the bad things that had happened to him since morning. She smiled with her beautiful, elongated lips: 'Love is a remedy for all bad omens.' He was intrigued by the word 'love', which he had lost the habit of using. He didn't know what she meant by it. Was she thinking of the physical act of making love? Or the feeling of love? While he was pondering, she quickly undressed in a corner of the room and slipped into bed, leaving her linen trousers on the chair and under the chair the huge tennis shoes with the thick socks which she had stuck into them, tennis shoes that paused for a while in Rubens' apartment on their long pilgrimage through Australian universities and European cities.

Their love-making was unbelievably calm and silent. I might say that Rubens at once returned to the phase of athletic muteness, but the word 'athletic' isn't quite appropriate because he had long ago lost his youthful ambition to prove his physical and sexual prowess; the activity to which they were devoting themselves seemed to have more of a symbolic character than an athletic one. However, Rubens didn't have the slightest idea what the motions they were performing were supposed to symbolize. Tenderness? love? health? joy of life? vice? friendship? faith in God? a plea for long life? (The girl was studying the semiotics of paintings. Shouldn't she rather tell him something about the semiotics of physical love?) He was performing vacuous motions and he realized for the first time that he didn't have any idea why he was doing it.

When they paused in their love-making (it occurred to Rubens that her semiotics professor undoubtedly also took a ten-minute pause in the middle of his two-hour seminar), the girl said (still in the same calm, even voice) a sentence in which the incomprehensible word 'love' once again appeared. Rubens had a fantasy: beautiful female specimens arrive on Earth from the depths of the universe. Their bodies look like those of terrestrial women, but they are quite perfect because on the planet they come from disease is unknown and their bodies are free from any malfunction or blemish. However, terrestrial men who meet them know nothing of their extra-terrestrial past and thus cannot understand them at all; they can never predict the women's reactions to their words and actions; they can never know what feelings are concealed behind their beautiful faces. It would be impossible to make love with such unknown women, Rubens thought. Then he corrected himself: perhaps our sexuality has indeed become so automatized that it would enable us to make love even with extra-terrestrial women, but it would be love-making without any excitement, an act of love turned into mere physical exercise devoid of feeling or vice.

The intermission was over, the second half of the amorous seminar was about to begin at any moment and he was eager to say something, something outrageous that would break her composure, but he knew he couldn't bring himself to do it. He felt like a foreigner involved in an argument, who must use a language over which he has poor command; he can't even shout an insult, for his opponent would ask him innocently: 'What did you mean by that, sir? I did not understand you!' And so he uttered nothing outrageous and made love to her once again in silent composure.

Then he saw her to the door (he didn't know whether she was satisfied or disappointed, though she looked rather satisfied), and was determined never to see her again; he knew that this would hurt her, because she would interpret his sudden loss of interest (surely she remembered how bewitched he'd been by her only yesterday!) as a defeat all the more painful since it was incomprehensible. He knew that he was to blame if her tennis shoes would now walk through the world with a step more melancholy than before. He said good-bye to her and as she disappeared round the corner of the street he was seized by a strong, tormenting nostalgia for the women of his past. It was as brutal and unexpected as a disease that breaks out, in one second, without warning.

He slowly began to realize what it was about. The hand on the dial had touched a new number. He heard the clock strike, saw the little window open and, thanks to the mysterious medieval mechanism, a woman in huge tennis shoes came out. Her appearance meant that his longing made a volte-face; he would no longer yearn for new women; he would only yearn for women he had already had; from now on, his longing would be an obsession with the past.

He saw beautiful women walking down the street and was startled that he paid no attention to them. I even believe that they noticed him, and he didn't know it. Before he had yearned only for new women. He had yearned for them to such a degree that with some of them he had made love only once and no more. As if he were now destined to atone for his obsession with the new, his indifference to everything lasting and stable, his foolish impatience that drove him forward, he now wished to turn himself round, to find the women of his past, to repeat their love-making, to carry it further, to make it yield all that had been left unexploited. He realized that from now on great excitements were to be found only behind him, and if he wanted to find new excitements he would have to turn to his past.

16

When he was very young, he was shy and wanted to make love in the dark. Yet he kept his eyes wide open in the dark, so that thanks to the weak rays that penetrated the drawn curtains he could see at least a little.

Then he not only got used to the light, but demanded it. When he found that his partner had her eyes shut, he urged her to open them.

And then one day he found to his surprise that he was making love in the light, but with his eyes shut. He was making love while remembering.

Darkness with eyes open.

Light with eyes open.

Light with eyes shut.

The dial of life.

17

He sat down with a sheet of paper and tried to make a list of the women in his life. Right from the start he met with defeat. In very few cases did he recall both names, and occasionally not even one. The women had become (quietly, imperceptibly) women without names. Perhaps if he had corresponded with them more often their names might have stuck in his memory because he would have had to write them on envelopes, but 'beyond the border of love' no amorous correspondence is carried out. Perhaps if he had been in the habit of calling them by their first names he would have remembered them, but ever since the unhappy incident on his wedding night he had decided to call all women only by tender, banal nicknames that any of them could at any time regard as her own.

He filled up half a page (the experiment did not require that the list be complete), replacing a number of the forgotten names by some characteristic feature ('freckled', or 'schoolteacher', and so on) and he tried to recall in each case the woman's curriculum vitae. This was a still worse defeat! He knew absolutely nothing about their lives! He therefore simplified his task and limited himself to just one question: who were their parents? With the exception of a single case (he had known the father before he met the daughter) he didn't have the slightest idea. And yet in the life of each of them parents must have played an enormous part! Surely they must have told him a lot about them! What value, then, did he place on the lives of his women friends, if he wasn't ready to remember even the most basic facts about them?

He admitted (not without some embarrassment) that women had meant nothing to him except as erotic experiences. He tried recalling these experiences at least. Randomly, he paused at the woman (nameless) he had designated as 'doctor'. What was their first love-making like? He pictured his apartment at the time. They entered and she immediately looked for the phone; in Rubens' presence she proceeded to tell someone at the other end that she unexpectedly had to take care of a certain obligation and could not come. They laughed at this, and then made love. Strangely enough, he could still hear this laugh but could recall nothing of the love-making. Where did it take place? on the carpet? in bed? on the couch? What was she like between the sheets? how many times had they met since then? Three times, or thirty times? Why did he stop seeing her? Did he remember a single fragment of their conversations, which must surely have filled a space of at least twenty hours, perhaps as many as a hundred? He vaguely recalled that she had often spoken to him of her fiancé (he had of course forgotten the gist of this information). A strange thing: what stuck in his memory was the fiancé and nothing else. The act of love was less important to him than the flattering and silly detail that on his account she had deceived someone else.

He thought enviously of Casanova. Not of his erotic achievements, which after all could be accomplished by most men, but of his incomparable memory. Some one hundred and thirty women saved from oblivion, with their names, their faces, their gestures, their statements! Casanova: utopia of memory. In comparison, how poor were Rubens' achievements! At one time, at the beginning of adulthood when he had renounced painting, Rubens had consoled himself with the thought that learning about life was more important to him than the struggle for power. The life of his colleagues chasing after success seemed to him not only aggressive but monotonous and empty. He believed that erotic adventures would lead him straight to the heart of life, a full, real, rich and mysterious life, the bewitching and concrete life he longed to embrace. And now suddenly he saw that he had been mistaken: in spite of all his amorous adventures, his knowledge of people was exactly the same as it had been at the age of fifteen. All this time he had been coddling himself with the certainty that he had a rich life behind him; but the words 'a rich life' were merely an abstract formula; when he tried to discover what this richness actually contained, he found nothing but a windswept desert.

The hand on the dial let him know that from now on he would be obsessed only with the past. But how is one to be obsessed with the past when one sees in it only a desert over which the wind blows a few fragments of memories? Does that mean he would become obsessed with those few fragments? Yes. One can be obsessed even with a few fragments. Anyhow, let's not exaggerate: even though he couldn't remember anything substantial about the young doctor, other women emerged in his mind with urgent intensity.

When I say they emerged in his mind, how do I imagine this emergence? Rubens discovered a peculiar thing: memory does not make films, it makes photographs. What he recalled from any of the women were at most a few mental photographs. He didn't recall their coherent motions, he visualized even their short gestures not in all their fluent fullness, but only in the rigidity of a single second. His erotic memory provided him with a small album of pornographic pictures but no pornographic film. And when I say an album of pictures that is an exaggeration, for all he had was some seven or eight photographs: these photos were beautiful, they fascinated him, but their number was after all depressingly limited: seven, eight fragments of less than a second each, that's what remained in his memory of his entire erotic life to which he had once decided to devote all his strength and talent.

I see Rubens sitting at a table with his head supported on the palm of his hand, looking like Rodin's Thinker. What is he thinking about? If he has made peace with the idea that his life has narrowed down to sexual experiences and these again to only seven still pictures, seven photographs, he would at least like to hope that in some corner of his memory there may be concealed some eighth, ninth or tenth photograph. That's why he is sitting with his head leaning on the palm of his hand. He is once again trying to evoke individual women and find some forgotten photograph for each one of them.

This leads him to another interesting observation: some of his lovers were especially adventurous in their erotic initiative and also quite striking in appearance; and yet they made hardly any mark on his soul, and left no exciting photographs. He was much more intrigued by his memory of women whose erotic initiative was muffled and whose appearance was unremarkable; those whom he tended to underrate. As if memory (as well as forgetting) brought about a radical revaluation of all values; whatever was willed, intentional, ostentatious, planned in his erotic life lost value, while adventures which happened unexpectedly, which did not announce themselves as something extraordinary, became in memory invaluable.

He thought of the women raised in value by memory: one of them had surely passed the age when he would still wish to meet her; others lived in circumstances that would make a meeting highly difficult. But then there was the lute-player. He had not seen her for eight years. Three mental pictures came to his mind. In the first, she was standing a step away from him, her arm was fixed in front of her face in the middle of a motion by which she seemed to be erasing her features. The second photograph captured the moment when he asked her, with his hand on her breast, whether anyone had ever touched her this way before and she answered 'No!' in a quiet voice, her eyes looking straight ahead. And finally he saw her (that photograph was the most captivating of all) standing in front of the mirror flanked by two

351

men, with her palms covering her bare breasts. It was odd that on all three photographs her beautiful, motionless face had the same appearance; looking straight ahead, past Rubens.

He immediately looked up her phone number, which at one time he knew by heart. She spoke to him as if they had parted only yesterday. He flew to Paris to see her (this time he needed no special occasion, he came solely because of her) and met her in the same hotel where many years ago she had stood in front of the mirror flanked by two men, and covered her breasts with her hands.

18

The lute-player still had the same figure, the same charming motions, and her features had lost nothing of their nobility. Only one thing had changed: from close up, her skin no longer looked fresh. Rubens could not help noticing; oddly enough, however, the moments he became aware of it were uncommonly brief, lasting hardly a few seconds; the lute-player quickly turned back into her image, as drawn long ago in Rubens' memory: *she concealed herself behind her image*.

Image: Rubens has known for a long time what that means. Hiding behind the bodies of his schoolfriends on the bench in front of him, he secretly drew a caricature of the teacher. Then he lifted his eyes from his drawing; the teacher's features were in constant motion and did not resemble the picture. Nevertheless, whenever the teacher disappeared from his field of vision, Rubens was unable (then and now) to imagine him in any way other than in the form of his caricature. The teacher *disappeared for ever behind his image*.

At an exhibition of a famous photographer's work, he saw the picture of a man with a bloody face, slowly lifting himself off the pavement. An unforgettable, mysterious photograph! Who was that man? What had happened to him? Probably an insignificant street accident, Rubens told himself; a wrong step, a fall, a photographer unexpectedly present. Not sensing anything unusual the man got up, washed his face in a nearby café and went home to his wife. And at the same moment, intoxicated by its birth, his *image separated itself from him* and walked off in the opposite direction after its own adventure, its own destiny.

A person may conceal himself behind his image, he can disappear for ever behind his image, he can be completely separated from his image: a person can never be his image. It was only thanks to three mental photographs that Rubens telephoned the lute-player after not having seen her for eight years. But who is the lute-player in and of herself, outside her image? He doesn't know much about that, and has no desire to know more. I can see their meeting after eight years: they sit facing each other in the lobby of a big Parisian hotel. What do they talk about? About all sorts of things, except the life they are both leading. For if they knew each other too intimately, a barrier of useless information would pile up between them and estrange them from each other. They know only the barest minimum about one another and they are almost proud of having concealed their lives in the shadows so that their meetings will be lit up all the more brightly, divorced from time and circumstance.

Full of tenderness, he gazes at the lute-player, happy that though she has aged somewhat, she still closely resembles her image. With some affectionate cynicism he tells himself: the value of the physical presence of the lute-player consists in her ability to continue merging with her image.

And he looks forward to the quickly approaching moment when the lute-player would lend this image her live body.

19

They kept meeting again as in the old days, once, twice, three times a year. And again years passed. One day he called to tell her that he would arrive in Paris in two weeks. She told him she wouldn't have time.

'I can postpone my trip by a week,' said Rubens.

'I won't have time then either.'

'So when will it suit you?'

'Not now,' she said, obviously embarrassed, 'not for a long time . . .'

'Has something happened?'

'No, nothing's happened.'

Both were embarrassed. It seemed that the lute-player never wanted to see him again and found it difficult to tell him so outright. At the same time, however, this supposition was so improbable (their meetings were always beautiful, without the least shadow) that Rubens kept asking her more questions in order to understand the reason for her rejection. But since from the very beginning their relationship had been founded on absolute mutual non-aggressiveness that also ruled out any kind of insistence, he stopped himself from bothering her any further, even if only by way of questions.

So he ended the conversation and only added: 'But may I call you?'

'Naturally! Why not?'

He called her a month later: 'You still have no time to see me?'

'Don't be angry with me,' she said. 'It's nothing to do with you.'

355

He asked her the same question as last time: 'Has something happened?'

'No, nothing's happened,' she said.

He fell silent. He didn't know what to say. 'Too bad,' he said, smiling with melancholy into the receiver.

'It's not anything to do with you. It really isn't you. It only concerns me.'

He had the feeling that those words were opening some hope for him: 'But then it's all nonsense! In that case we must see each other!'

'No,' she refused.

'If I were certain that you don't want to see me any more, I wouldn't say a word. But you said that this only concerns you. What's going on? We must see each other! I must talk to you!'

But the moment he said it, he told himself: no, alas, it's just her considerateness that prevents her from telling him the real reason, all too simple: she no longer cares for him. She is at a loss, because she is too fine. That's why he mustn't try to win her over. She would find him unpleasant and he would break the unwritten agreement that they should never ask anything from one another that the other does not wish.

And so when she said once again, 'Please, no . . .' he no longer insisted.

He put down the receiver and suddenly recalled the Australian student with the huge tennis shoes. She, too, was rejected for reasons she couldn't understand. If she had given him the opportunity, he would have consoled her with the same words: 'It really isn't aimed against you. It has nothing to do with you. It only concerns me.' All at once, he grasped intuitively that the adventure with the lute-player was over and he would never understand why it had ended. Just as the Australian student would never understand why her story ended. His shoes would

now walk the world with somewhat greater melancholy than
before. Just like the huge tennis shoes of the young Australian.

The period of athletic muteness, the period of metaphors, the period of obscene truth, the period of Chinese Whispers, the mystical period, all this was far behind him. The hands on the dial had brought his sexual life full circle. He found himself outside the dial's time. To find oneself outside the dial's time does not mean the end nor does it mean death. On the dial of European painting midnight had struck, too, and yet painters continue to paint. To be outside the dial's time simply means that no longer will anything new or important happen. Rubens continued to see women, but they were of no importance to him. The one he saw most often was G, a young woman whose main characteristic was a propensity to use coarse words in conversation. Many women did that. It was trendy. They said shit, fuck, asshole, and made it clear in this way that they did not belong to the old generation and its conservative manners, that they were liberated, emancipated, modern. And yet as soon as he touched her, G fixed her eyes on the ceiling and changed into a silent saint. Making love to her was always long and almost endless because she only reached orgasm, for which she eagerly longed, after great effort. She lay on her back, closed her eyes and worked, perspiring all over. This is more or less how Rubens imagined the death agony: we burn with fever and long only for the end, which refuses to come. During their first two or three encounters he tried to bring the end closer by whispering some obscene word to her, but because she always reacted by turning away her face, as if in protest, he remained silent from then on. She, however, after some twenty or thirty minutes of love-making always said (and Rubens found her voice dissatisfied and impatient): 'Harder!

Harder! More! More!' and at that point he always discovered that he couldn't go on, that he had been making love too long and at too fast a tempo to be able to thrust any harder; he would therefore slide off her and resort to a method which he considered both a capitulation and a piece of technical virtuosity worthy of a patent: he stuck his hand inside her and moved his fingers powerfully upwards; a geyser erupted, everything was wet, she embraced him and showered him with tender words.

It was astonishing how unable they were to synchronize their intimate clocks: when he was capable of tenderness, she talked coarsely; when he longed to talk coarsely, she kept stubbornly silent; when he felt like keeping still and going to sleep, she suddenly became talkatively tender.

She was pretty and so much younger than he! Rubens assumed (modestly) that it was merely his manual dexterity that enticed G to come to him whenever he called her. He was grateful to her for allowing him, during those long intervals of silence and perspiration spent on top of her body, to dream with his eyes shut.

Rubens came upon an old collection of photographs of President John Kennedy: the photos were in colour, there were at least fifty of them, and on all of them (all, without exception!) the president was laughing. Not smiling, laughing! His mouth was open, his teeth bared. There was nothing remarkable about it, that's what contemporary photos are like, but the fact that Kennedy laughed in *all* of them, that not a single one showed him with his lips closed, gave Rubens pause. A few days later he found himself in Florence. He stood in front of Michelangelo's David and tried to imagine that marble face laughing like Kennedy. David, that paradigm of male beauty, suddenly looked like an imbecile! Since then, he had often tried in his imagination to retouch figures in famous paintings to give them a laughing mouth; it was an interesting experiment: the grimace of laughter could ruin every painting! Imagine Mona Lisa as her barely perceptible smile turns into a laugh that reveals her teeth and gums!

Even though he spent so much of his time in picture galleries, it took Kennedy's photographs to make Rubens realize this simple fact: the great painters and sculptors from classical days to Raphael and perhaps even to Ingres avoided portraying laughter, even smiles. Of course, the figures of Etruscan sculpture all have smiles, but this smile isn't a response to some particular, momentary situation but a permanent state of the face, expressing eternal bliss. For classical sculptors as well as for painters of later periods a beautiful face was imaginable only in its immobility.

Faces lost their immobility, mouths became open only when the painter wished to express evil. Either the evil of pain: the faces of women bent over the body of Jesus; the open mouth of the mother in Poussin's *Slaughter of the Innocents*. Or the evil of vice: Holbein's *Adam and Eve*. Eve has a bland face and a half-open mouth revealing teeth that have just bitten into the apple. Alongside, Adam is a man still before sin: he is beautiful, his face is calm and his mouth is closed. In Correggio's *Allegories of Sin* everyone is smiling! In order to express vice, the painter must move the innocent calm of the face, to spread the mouth, to deform the features with a smile. There is only one laughing figure in the picture: a child! But it is not a laugh of happiness, the way children are portrayed in advertisements for nappies or chocolate! The child is laughing because it's been corrupted!

Only with the Dutch painters does laughter become innocent: Hals' *Clown* or his *Gypsy*. That's because the Dutch genre painters are the first photographers. The faces they paint are beyond ugliness or beauty. As he walked through the Dutch gallery, Rubens thought of the lute-player: she was not a model for Hals; the lute-player was a model for painters who looked for beauty in the immovable surface of features. Then some visitors jostled him; all museums are filled with crowds of sightseers as zoos once used to be; tourists hungry for attractions stared at the pictures as if they were caged animals. Painting, thought Rubens, does not feel at home in this century, and neither does the lute-player; the lute-player belongs to a world vanished long ago, in which beauty did not laugh.

But how can we explain why great painters ruled laughter out of the realm of beauty? Rubens tells himself: undoubtedly, a face is beautiful because it reveals the presence of thought, whereas at the moment of laughter man does not think. But is that really true? Is not laughter a lightning thought that has just grasped the comical? No, thinks Rubens: in the instant that he grasps the comical, man does not laugh; laughter follows *afterwards* as a physical reaction, as a convulsion no longer containing any thought. Laughter is a convulsion of the face and a convulsed person does not rule himself, he is ruled by something that is neither will nor reason. And that is why the classical sculptor did not express laughter. A human being who does not rule himself (a human being beyond reason, beyond will) cannot be considered beautiful.

If our era, against the spirit of the great painters, has made laughter the privileged expression of the human face, it means that an absence of will and reason has become the ideal human state. The objection could be raised that the convulsion shown on photographic portraits is simulated, and therefore subject to reason and will: laughing into the camera lens, Kennedy is not reacting to a comic situation but quite consciously opening his mouth and showing his teeth. But this only proves that the convulsion of laughter (a state beyond reason and will) has been raised by contemporary people into an ideal image behind which they have decided to conceal themselves.

Rubens tells himself: laughter is the most democratic of all the facial expressions: we differ from one another by our immovable features, but in convulsion we are all the same.

A bust of a laughing Julius Caesar is unthinkable. But American presidents depart for eternity concealed behind the democratic convulsion of laughter.

22

He returned once again to Rome. He spent a long time in the hall of a gallery containing Gothic paintings. One of them made him stop, fascinated. It was a Crucifixion. What did he see? In place of Jesus he saw a woman who had just been crucified. Like Christ, she was wearing only a piece of white cloth wrapped around her hips. The soles of her feet were braced against a wooden plank, while executioners were tying her ankles to the beam with strong ropes. The cross was situated at the top of a hill and was visible from far and wide. It was surrounded by a crowd of soldiers, local people, onlookers, all of whom watched the woman exposed to their gaze. It was the lute-player. She felt their gaze and covered her breasts with her hands. On each side of her were two other crosses with a criminal tied to each. The first leaned over towards her, took her hand, pulled it away from her breast and extended her arm in such a way that the back of her hand touched the horizontal beam of the cross. The other malefactor grasped her other hand and pulled it the same way, so that both of the lute-player's arms were extended. Her face continued to remain immobile. Her eyes stared into the distance. But Rubens knew that she wasn't looking into the distance but into a huge imaginary mirror, placed before her between earth and sky. She saw her own image, the image of a woman on a cross with extended arms and bare breasts, she was exposed to the immense, shouting, bestial crowd, and along with the crowd she gazed, excited, at herself.

Rubens couldn't tear his eyes away from this spectacle. And when he did so at last, he told himself: this moment should be inscribed into the history of religion under the title: *Rubens' Vision in Rome*. This mystic moment continued to affect him until evening. He had not called the lute-player for four years, but that day he was unable to control himself. He dialled her number as soon as he returned to the hotel. At the other end he heard an unfamiliar feminine voice.

He said uncertainly: 'May I speak to Madame . . . ?' calling her by her husband's name.

'Yes, that's me,' said the voice at the other end.

He pronounced the lute-player's first name and the woman's voice answered that the lady he was calling was dead.

'Dead?' he gasped.

'Yes, Agnes died. Who is calling?'

'I am a friend of hers.'

'May I know your name?'

'No,' he said, and hung up.

23

When someone dies on the screen, elegiac music immediately comes on, but when someone dies whom we knew in real life, we don't hear any music. There are only a very few deaths capable of shaking us deeply, two or three in a lifetime, no more. The death of a woman who was only an episode surprised and saddened Rubens, but was not able to shake him, especially as she had already departed from his life four years ago and he had had to come to terms with it then.

Though she didn't become any more absent from his life than she had been before, her death changed everything. Every time he remembered her he was forced to imagine what had become of her body. Did they lower it into the ground in a coffin? Or did they have it burned? He visualized her immobile face observing her self in an imaginary mirror with her eyes wide open. He saw the lids of those eyes slowly closing, and suddenly the face went dead. Just because that face was so calm, the transition from life to non-life was fluent, harmonious, beautiful. But then he began to imagine what happened to the face afterwards. And that was terrible.

G came to see him. As usual, they launched into long, silent love-making and as usual during those interminable moments he pictured the lute-player in his mind: as always she was standing bare-breasted in front of a mirror, looking straight ahead with a fixed gaze. At that moment Rubens thought to himself that for all he knew she may have been dead some two or three years; that her hair had already dropped off her scalp and her eyes had vanished from their sockets. He wanted to get rid of this image quickly, because he knew that otherwise he would not be able to continue making love. He drove the thoughts of the lute-player from his mind and forced himself to concentrate on G, on her quickened breathing, but his mind was disobedient and spitefully fed him images he didn't want to see. And when at last his mind was ready to obey him and stop showing him the lute-player in her coffin, it showed her in flames, just as he had once heard it described: the burning body (through some physical force which he didn't understand) raised itself, so that the lute-player sat up in the furnace. And in the midst of this vision of a sitting, burning body he suddenly heard a dissatisfied, urging voice: 'Harder! Harder! More! More!' He had to stop the love-making. He excused himself to G saying that he was in bad shape.

Then he told himself: after everything I've lived through all I have left is a single photograph. It seems to contain whatever was most intimate and most deeply concealed in my erotic life, its very essence. Perhaps I only made love in recent years so as to make that photograph come to life in my mind. And now that photograph is in flames and the beautiful, immobile face is twisting, shrinking, turning black, and falling at last into ashes.

G was supposed to visit him again in a week and Rubens was afraid in advance of the images that would trouble him during love-making. Wanting to get the lute-player off his mind, he sat down at the table once again, his head resting on his palm, and searched his memory for other photographs remaining from his erotic life that might help him replace the image of the lute-player. He managed to find a few and was happily surprised that they were still so beautiful and exciting. But in the depths of his soul he was certain that once he started making love to G, his memory would refuse to show them to him and would substitute for them, in the way of a bad, macabre joke, the image of the lute-player sitting in the flames. He was not wrong. Once again, he had to excuse himself in the middle of love-making.

Then he told himself that there would be no harm in taking a brief pause in his relations with women. Until next time, as they say. But this pause kept getting longer week by week, month by month. One day he realized that there would be no 'next time'.

PART SEVEN

The celebration

1

In the health club, the movement of arms and legs has for many years been reflected by mirrors; six months ago, at the insistence of the imagologues, mirrors even invaded the swimming-pool; we became surrounded by mirrors on three sides, with the fourth side consisting of a single huge window looking out on the roofs of Paris. We sat in our swimming trunks at a table by the edge of the pool which was full of swimmers puffing and blowing up and down. A bottle of wine, which I had ordered to celebrate an anniversary, stood in the middle of the table.

Avenarius didn't even bother to ask me what I was celebrating, because he was struck by a new idea: 'Imagine that you are given the choice of two possibilities: to spend a night of love with a world-famous beauty, let's say Brigitte Bardot or Greta Garbo, but on condition that nobody must know about it. Or to stroll down the main avenue of the city with your arm wrapped intimately around her shoulder, but on condition that you must never sleep with her. I'd love to know exactly what percentage of people would choose the one or the other of these possibilities. That would require statistical analysis. I therefore approached several companies conducting public opinion polls, but all of them turned me down.'

'I can never quite understand to what extent one should take your projects seriously.'

'Everything I do should be taken absolutely seriously.'

I continued: 'For example, I try to imagine you lecturing ecologists about your plan to destroy cars. Surely you didn't expect them to approve it!'

I paused. Avenarius kept silent.

'Or did you by any chance think they would burst into applause?'

'No,' said Avenarius, 'I didn't.'

'Then why did you make the proposal? In order to unmask them? To prove to them that in spite of all their nonconformist gesticulations they are in reality a part of what you call Diabolum?'

'There is nothing more useless,' Avenarius said, 'than trying to prove something to idiots.'

'Then there is only one explanation: you wanted to have some fun. But even in that case your behaviour seems illogical to me. Surely you didn't expect that any of them would understand you and laugh!'

Avenarius shook his head and said rather sadly: 'No, I didn't expect that. Diabolum is characterized by the total lack of a sense of humour. The comical, even if it still exists, has become invisible. Joking no longer makes sense.' Then he added: 'This world takes everything seriously. Even me. And that's the limit.'

'I should rather think that nobody takes anything seriously! They all just want to amuse themselves!'

'That comes to the same thing. When that compleat ass is forced to announce on his news programme that an atomic war has broken out or that Paris has been devastated by an earthquake, he will certainly try to be amusing. Perhaps he is already preparing some witticisms for such occasions. But this has nothing to do with a sense of the comic. Because whoever is comical in such a case is someone looking for a witticism to announce an earthquake. And someone looking for a witticism to announce an earthquake takes his activity absolutely seriously and it would never occur to him that he is being comical. Humour can only exist when people are still capable of recognizing some border between the important and the unimportant. And nowadays this border has become unrecognizable.'

I know my friend well, and I often amuse myself by imitating his way of talking and by adopting his thoughts and ideas; and yet there is something about him that always eludes me. I like the way he acts, it attracts me, but I cannot say that I fully understand him. Some time ago I explained to him that the essence of an individual can only be expressed by means of metaphor. By the revealing lightning of metaphor. But as long as I've known him, I have never been able to find a metaphor that would explain Avenarius and let me understand him.

'Well, if it wasn't for the sake of fun, why did you submit that plan? Why?'

Before he could answer me, a surprised shout interrupted us: 'Professor Avenarius! Is it possible?'

An attractive man in swimming trunks, between fifty and sixty, was walking towards us from the entrance. Avenarius rose to his feet. Both men seemed moved and kept shaking hands for a long time.

Then Avenarius introduced us. I realized that I was standing face to face with Paul.

2

He joined us at the table and Avenarius made a broad gesture in my direction: 'You don't know his novels? *Life is Elsewhere*! You've got to read it! My wife claims it's outstanding!'

I realized with sudden clarity that Avenarius had never read my novel; when he urged me some time ago to bring him a copy, it was only because his insomniac wife needed to consume mountains of books in bed. It made me sad.

'I just came to sober up in the water,' said Paul. Then he saw the wine on the table and at once forgot about the water. 'What are you drinking?' He picked up the bottle and carefully examined the label. Then he added: 'Today I've been drinking since morning.'

Yes, it showed, and I was surprised. I had never imagined him as a drunk. I called to the waiter to bring us another glass.

We started to talk about all sorts of things. Avenarius referred a few more times to my novels, which he had not read, and so provoked Paul to make a remark whose rudeness astonished me: 'I don't read novels. Memoirs are much more amusing and instructive for me. Or biographies. Recently I've been reading books about Salinger, Rodin, and the loves of Franz Kafka. And a marvellous biography of Hemingway. What a fraud. What a liar. What a megalomaniac.' Paul laughed happily. 'What an impotent. What a sadist. What a macho. What an erotomaniac. What a misogynist.'

'If you're ready, as a lawyer, to defend even murderers, why don't you come to the defence of writers who have committed no wrong except for writing books?' I asked.

'Because they get on my nerves,' Paul retorted cheerfully and poured some wine into the glass the waiter had just placed before him.

'My wife adores Mahler,' he continued. 'She told me that two weeks before the première of his Seventh Symphony he locked himself up in a noisy hotel room and spent the whole night rewriting the orchestration.'

'Yes,' I agreed, 'it was in Prague, in 1906. The name of the hotel was The Blue Star.'

'I visualize him sitting in the hotel room, surrounded by manuscript paper,' Paul continued, refusing to let himself be interrupted. 'He was convinced that his whole work would be ruined if the melody were played by a clarinet instead of an oboe during the second movement.'

'That's precisely so,' I said, thinking of my novel.

Paul continued: 'I wish that some day this symphony could be played before an audience consisting of the best musical experts, first with the corrections made in those last two weeks, and then without the corrections. I guarantee that nobody would be able to tell one version from the other. Don't get me wrong: it is certainly remarkable that the motif played in the second movement by the violin is picked up in the last movement by the flute. Everything is worked through, thought through, felt through, nothing has been left to chance, but that enormous perfection overwhelms us, it surpasses the capacity of our memory, our ability to concentrate, so that even the most fanatically attentive listener will grasp no more than one-hundredth of the symphony, and certainly it will be this one-hundredth that Mahler cared about the least.'

His idea, so obviously correct, cheered him up, whereas I was becoming sadder and sadder: if a reader skips a single sentence of my novel he won't be able to understand it, and yet where in the world will you find a reader who never skips a line? Am I not myself the greatest skipper of lines and pages?

'I don't deny those symphonies their perfection,' continued Paul. 'I only deny the importance of that perfection. Those super-sublime symphonies are nothing but cathedrals of the useless. They are inaccessible to man. They are inhuman. We exaggerated their significance. They made us feel inferior. Europe reduced Europe to fifty works of genius which it never understood. Just think of this outrageous inequality: millions of Europeans signifying nothing, against fifty names signifying everything! Class inequality is but an insignificant shortcoming compared to this insulting metaphysical inequality, which turns some into grains of sand while endowing others with the meaning of being!'

The bottle was empty. I called the waiter to bring us another. This caused Paul to lose the thread.

'You spoke about biographies,' I prompted him.

'Ah . . . yes,' he recalled.

'You were happy that you can at last read the intimate correspondence of the dead.'

'I know, I know,' said Paul, as if he wanted to counter in advance any objections from the other side. 'I assure you that rifling through someone's intimate correspondence, interrogating his former mistresses, talking doctors into betraying professional confidences, that's rotten. Authors of biographies are riff-raff, and I would never sit at the same table with them as I do with you. Robespierre, too, would never have sat down with the riff-raff that had collective orgasms at the spectacle of public executions. But he knew that he couldn't do without them. The riff-raff is an instrument of just revolutionary hatred.'

'What is revolutionary about hatred for Hemingway?' I asked.

'I'm not talking about hatred for Hemingway! I'm talking about his *work*! I'm talking about *their* work! It was necessary to say out loud at last that reading *about* Hemingway is a thousand times more amusing and instructive than reading Hemingway. It was necessary to show that Hemingway's work is but a coded form of Hemingway's life and that this life was just as poor and meaningless as all our lives. It was necessary to cut Mahler's symphony into little pieces and use it as background music for toilet-paper ads. It was necessary at last to end the terror of the immortals. To overthrow the arrogant power of the Ninth Symphonies and the *Fausts*!'

Drunk on his own words he got up and raised his glass high: 'I drink to the end of the old days!'

3

In the mirrors that reflected one another, Paul was multiplied twenty-seven times and people at the next table watched his upraised arm and its glass with curiosity. Two fat men emerging from the jacuzzi also stopped and stared at Paul's twenty-seven arms fixed in the air. At first I thought that he had frozen in this gesture in order to add dramatic pathos to his words, but then I noticed a woman in a swimsuit who had just entered the room, a fortyish woman with a pretty face, well-formed though rather short legs and an expressive though rather hefty behind that pointed towards the ground like a thick arrow. That arrow made me recognize her immediately.

She didn't see us at first and walked straight towards the pool. But our eyes were fixed on her with such intensity that they at last attracted her gaze towards us. She blushed. It is a beautiful thing when a woman blushes; at that instant her body no longer belongs to her; she doesn't control it; she is at its mercy; oh, can there be anything more beautiful than the sight of a woman violated by her own body! I began to understand Avenarius' weakness for Laura. I turned my eyes towards him: his face remained perfectly immobile. This self-control seemed to betray him even more than Laura was betrayed by her blushing.

She collected herself, smiled sociably and approached our table. We rose and Paul introduced us to his wife. I kept on watching Avenarius. Was he aware that Laura was Paul's wife? I didn't think so. But I wasn't certain, and in fact I wasn't certain of anything. As he shook Laura's hand he bowed, as if seeing her for the first time in his life. Laura took her leave (a bit too quickly, I thought), and jumped into the pool.

All of Paul's euphoria suddenly left him. 'I'm glad that you've met her,' he said with melancholy. 'She is, as they say, the woman of my life. I should congratulate myself. Life is short and most people never find the woman of their life.'

The waiter brought another bottle, opened it in front of us and filled all the glasses, so that Paul again lost his thread.

'You were talking about the woman of your life,' I prompted after the waiter had gone.

'Yes,' he said. 'We have a little girl, three months old. I also have a daughter from my first marriage. A year ago she left home. Without saying good-bye. I was unhappy, because I am very fond of her. For a long time I had no news of her. Two days ago she came back because her boyfriend had dropped her, but not before he had given her a child, a little girl. My friends, I have a grandchild! I am now surrounded by four women!' The idea of four women seemed to fill him with energy: 'That's the reason why I've been drinking since morning! I drink to the reunion! I drink to the health of my daughter and my granddaughter!'

Below us in the pool Laura was splashing along with two other swimmers, and Paul smiled. It was a peculiar, tired smile, which made me feel sorry for him. It seemed to me that he had suddenly grown older. His mighty shock of grey hair had suddenly turned into the coiffure of an old lady. As if he wished to counter an attack of weakness by exerting his willpower, he rose once again, glass in hand.

In the meantime we could hear from below the sound of arms striking the water. Keeping her head above the water Laura swam the crawl, clumsily but all the more passionately and with a sort of anger.

It seemed to me that each stroke was falling on Paul's head like successive years: his face was visibly ageing before our eyes. Already he was seventy and a moment later eighty, and still he stood there holding his glass in front of him as if he wished to stop the avalanche of years hurtling towards him: 'I recall a famous phrase from my youth,' he said in a voice which suddenly lost all its resonance: '*woman is the future of man*. Who actually said that? I forget. Lenin? Kennedy? No, no. It was some poet.'

'Aragon,' I prompted.

Avenarius said crossly: 'What does that mean, woman is the future of man? That men will turn into women? I don't understand that stupid phrase!'

'It's not a stupid phrase! It's a poetic phrase!' Paul protested.

'Literature will die out, and stupid poetic phrases will remain to drift over the world,' I remarked.

Paul ignored me. He had just noticed his image, multiplied twenty-seven times in the mirrors, and couldn't tear his eyes away. He turned, back and forth, to each of his mirrored faces and spoke with the high, feeble voice of an old lady: 'Woman is the future of man. That means that the world which was once formed in man's image will now be transformed to the image of woman. The more technical and mechanical, cold and metallic it becomes, the more it will need the kind of warmth that only the woman can give it. If we want to save the world, we must adapt to the woman, let ourselves be led by the woman, let ourselves be penetrated by the *Ewigweibliche*, the eternally feminine!'

As if these prophetic words had completely exhausted him, Paul was suddenly older by another ten years, he was a weak, completely enfeebled old man, between one hundred and twenty and one hundred and fifty years old. He was not even able to hold his glass. He crumpled into his chair. Then he said, sincerely and sadly: 'She came back without a word. And she hates Laura. And Laura hates her. Maternity has made both of them more pugnacious. Once again, Mahler blares from one room and rock from the other. Once again they want me to take sides, once again they're giving me ultimatums. They have started to fight. And once women start to fight they don't stop.' Then, with a confidential air, he leaned towards us: 'Don't take me seriously, friends. What I am about to tell you is not true.' He lowered his voice, as if he was about to impart a great secret: 'It has been extremely lucky that up to now wars have been fought only by men. If they had been fought by women, they would have been so consistently cruel that today there wouldn't be a single human being left on the planet.' And as if he wanted us to forget immediately what he had just said, he pounded the table with his fist and raised his voice: 'Friends, I wish music would cease to exist. I wish Mahler's father had caught his son masturbating and given him such a blow on the ear that little Gustav became stone-deaf for life, unable to tell a drum from a violin. And I wish that the electric current could be shut off from guitars and instead connected to chairs to which I would personally tie all guitarists.' And then he added very quietly: 'Friends, I wish I was ten times more drunk than I am.'

4

He sat at the table, crestfallen, and it was so sad that we couldn't bear watching him any longer. We rose, clustered around him and patted him on the back. And as we were patting him, we suddenly noticed that his wife had climbed out of the water and strode right past us towards the exit. She pretended we didn't exist.

Was she so angry with Paul that she didn't even want to see his face? Or was she embarrassed by the unexpected meeting with Avenarius? Whatever the case may have been, her stride as she passed us had something so powerful and attractive about it that we stopped patting Paul and all three of us gazed after her.

When she reached the swing door leading to the locker-rooms something unexpected happened: she suddenly turned her head towards our table and lifted her arm in the air in a movement so light, so graceful, so fluent, that it seemed to us a golden ball had risen from her fingertips and remained poised above the doorway.

Suddenly there was a smile on Paul's face and he grasped Avenarius firmly by the hand: 'Did you see? Did you see that gesture?'

'Yes,' said Avenarius and stared as Paul and I did at the golden ball that shone below the ceiling as a souvenir of Laura.

It was quite clear to me that the gesture wasn't meant for her drunken husband. It was not an automatic gesture of everyday leave-taking, it was an exceptional gesture, full of significance. It could only have been meant for Avenarius.

Of course, Paul did not suspect a thing. As if by a miracle, the years kept dropping off him and he turned once again into an attractive fifty-year-old proud of his shock of grey hair. He kept on gazing towards the door where the golden ball was shining, and he repeated: 'Ah, Laura! That's just like her! Ah, that gesture! That's Laura!' And then he told us, his voice full of emotion: 'The first time she waved to me like that was when I took her to the maternity ward. She had gone through two operations earlier, hoping to have a baby. We were all scared when her time came. To save me worry she forbade me to go inside the hospital. I stood by the car and she walked alone to the entrance and when she was on the threshold she suddenly turned her head, just as she did a moment ago, and waved to me. When I returned home, I felt terribly sad, I missed her and to bring her closer I tried to imitate for myself that beautiful gesture that had so bewitched me. If anyone had seen me they would have had to laugh. I stood with my back to a mirror, lifted my arm in the air and smiled over my shoulder at myself in the mirror. I did that about thirty or forty times and thought of her. I was at one and the same time Laura greeting me and myself watching Laura greeting me. But one thing was peculiar: that gesture didn't fit me. I was hopelessly clumsy and ridiculous in that gesture.'

He rose and stood with his back to us. Then he lifted his arm in the air and looked at us over his shoulder. Yes, he was right: he was comical. We laughed. Our laughter encouraged him to repeat the gesture a few more times. It was more and more comical.

Then he said: 'You know, it's not a man's gesture, it's a woman's gesture. By this gesture a woman invites us: come, follow me, and you don't know where she is inviting you to go and she doesn't know either, but she invites you in the conviction that it's worth going where she is inviting you. That's why I tell you: either woman will become man's future or mankind will perish, because only woman is capable of nourishing within her an unsubstantiated hope and inviting us to a doubtful future, which we would have long ceased to believe in were it not for women.

All my life I've been willing to follow their voice, even though that voice is mad, and whatever else I may be I am not a madman. But nothing is more beautiful than when someone who isn't mad goes into the unknown, led by a mad voice!' And once again he solemnly repeated a German sentence: '*Das Ewigweibliche zieht uns hinan!* The eternal feminine draws us on!'

Goethe's verse, like a proud white goose, flapped its wings beneath the vault of the swimming-pool and Paul, reflected in the triple mirrors, walked to the swing doors where the brightly coloured ball was still shining. It was the first time I had ever seen him sincerely cheerful. He took a few steps, turned his head over his shoulder towards us and lifted his arm in the air. He laughed. He turned once more, and once again he waved. Then, for the last time, he performed for us that clumsy male imitation of a beautiful female gesture and disappeared through the doorway.

5

I said: 'He spoke very well about that gesture. But I think he was wrong. Laura was not luring anyone into the future, she wanted to let you know that she was here and that she was here for you.'

Avenarius was silent, his face blank.

I said reproachfully: 'Don't you feel sorry for him?'

'I do,' said Avenarius. 'I genuinely like him. He is intelligent. He is witty. He is complicated. He is sad. And especially: he helped me! Let's not forget that!' Then he leaned towards me, as if he didn't want to leave my tacit reproach unanswered: 'I told you about my proposal to offer the public a choice: who would like to sleep secretly with Rita Hayworth or Greta Garbo, and who would rather show himself with her in public. The results are quite clear in advance: everyone, including the worst no-hopers, would maintain that they would rather sleep with her. Because all of them would want to appear to themselves, to their wives and even to the bald official conducting the poll as hedonists. This, however, is a self-delusion. Their comedy act. Nowadays hedonists no longer exist.' He pronounced the last sentence with great emphasis and then added with a smile: 'Except for me.' And he went on: 'No matter what they say, if they had a real choice to make, all of them, I repeat, all of them would prefer to stroll with her down the avenue. Because all of them are eager for admiration and not for pleasure. For appearance and not for reality. Reality no longer means anything to anyone. To anyone. To my lawyer it means nothing at all.' Then he added with a sort of tenderness: 'And that's why I can solemnly promise you that he will not be hurt. The horns that he is wearing will remain invisible. In fine weather they will have a sky-blue colour, and they will be grey when it rains.' Then he added: 'Anyway, no man will suspect someone known to rape women at knife-point to be the lover of his wife. Those two images don't go together.'

'Wait a minute,' I said. 'He *really* thinks that you wanted to rape women?'

'I told you about that.'

'I thought you were joking.'

'Surely, I wouldn't reveal my secret!' And he added: 'Anyway, even if I had told him the truth he wouldn't have believed me. And even if he had believed me, he would immediately have lost interest in my case. I was valuable to him only as a rapist. He developed that incomprehensible love for me that great lawyers seem to feel towards great criminals.'

'So then how did you explain everything?'

'I didn't explain a thing. They let me go for lack of evidence.'

'What do you mean, lack of evidence! What about the knife?'

'I don't deny that it was tricky,' Avenarius said, and I realized that I wouldn't learn anything further from him.

I kept silent for a while, and then said: 'You wouldn't have admitted the business with the tyres under any circumstance?'

He shook his head.

I was strangely moved: 'You were ready to go to jail as a rapist, in order not to betray the game . . .'

And at that moment I understood him at last: if we cannot accept the importance of the world, which considers itself important, if in the midst of that world our laughter finds no echo, we have but one choice: to take the world as a whole and make it the object of our game; to turn it into a toy. Avenarius is playing a game and for him the game is the only thing of importance in a world without importance. But he knows that his game will not make anyone laugh. When he outlined his proposal to the ecologists,

386

he had no intention of amusing anyone. He only wished to amuse himself.

I said: 'You play with the world like a melancholy child who has no little brother.'

Yes, that's the right metaphor for Avenarius! I've been looking for it ever since I've known him. At last!

Avenarius smiled like a melancholy child. Then he said: 'I don't have a little brother, but I have you.'

He got up, I got up too, and it seemed that after Avenarius' last words we would have no choice but to embrace. But then we realized we were in swimming trunks and we were frightened by the idea of our bare bellies in intimate contact. We laughed it off and went to the locker-room. It resounded with a high-pitched female voice accompanied by guitars, so we lost the taste for more conversation. We got into the elevator. Avenarius was going to the basement, where he had parked his Mercedes, and I left him on the ground floor. Five different faces with similarly bared teeth laughed at me from five posters hanging in the lobby. I was afraid they might bite me and I quickly went out into the street.

The roadway was filled with cars honking incessantly. Motorcycles drove up on the pavement and snaked their way between pedestrians. I thought of Agnes. It was precisely two years ago that I had first imagined her, while reclining in a deck-chair upstairs in the health club, waiting for Avenarius. That was the reason why today I had ordered a bottle of wine. I had finished the novel and I wanted to celebrate it in the place where the first idea for it was born.

The cars were honking their horns and I heard the shouts of angry people. It was in such circumstances that Agnes longed to buy a forget-me-not, a single forget-me-not stem; she longed to hold it before her eyes as a last, scarcely visible trace of beauty.

Faber International Fiction

All these books are available at your bookshop or newsagent, or can be ordered direct from the publishers. Just tick the titles you want and fill in the form below or submit a separate order.

Faber & Faber Limited, Cash Sales Department, PO Box 11, Falmouth, Cornwall TR10 9EN. Fax Number: 0326 77240

UK customers including B.F.P.O.: please send a cheque or postal order (no currency) and allow £1.00 for postage and packing for the first book plus 50p for the second book plus 30p for each additional book up to a maximum charge of £3.00.
Overseas customers including Eire: please allow £2.00 for postage and packing for the first book, £1.00 for the second book and 50p for each additional book.

NAME (Block Letters) ....

SIGNATURE ....

ADDRESS ....

....

☐ I enclose my remittance for ....
☐ I wish to pay by Access/Visa Card –

Number ☐☐☐☐☐☐☐☐☐☐☐☐☐☐☐☐

Expiry date ....